ANXIETY

STEVEN M. COX

Anxiety

Copyright 2024 by Author Steven M. Cox

Published by: Struggle Books

Cover designed by Kee Covers

Editors: Tarius Morris and Michelle Moore-Cox

All rights reserved. No part of this book may be reproduced in any form or by any electronic or mechanical means including information storage and retrieval systems, without written permission from the author. The only exception is by a reviewer, who may quote short excerpts in a review.

This book is a work of fiction. Names, characters, places, and incidents either are products of the author's imagination or are used fictitiously. Any resemblance to actual persons, living or dead, events, or locales is entirely coincidental.

Follow me on Twitter @StevenMCox2

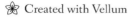 Created with Vellum

TABLE OF CONTENTS

Chapter 1: Anxiety
Chapter 2: Nightmares
Chapter 3: The Professionals
Chapter 4: All Hell Breaks Loose
Chapter 5: Turning Point
Chapter 6: Dystopia
Chapter 7: The Nightmare Box
Chapter 8: Journey's End
Epilogue

DEDICATIONS

There are a lot of people I would like to thank for helping me get to the point where this book has seen print, but I at first thought it would be a little too self-indulgent to name them all here. And then I changed my mind and went for it full-tilt.

    To my parents, Steve Cox Sr. and Lydia Cox (I never got used to her new married name of Jiggetts). You taught me strength of will and unwavering determination. I especially dedicate this to you, Mom, since you passed away before you got to see it reach print. I am so, so sorry for not having worked on it faster.

    To Max, Devon, Nadia, Todd and Valerie, for never backing down to injustice no matter how strong or ignorant the opposition.

    To my wife and kids for giving me a reason to keep fighting daily. Without you in my corner, not only would my books not exist, but sure I would not exist either. You represent the center of my universe, through which all great things flow.

    To Damian, Daniel, Chris, Dominick, Deborah, Cherisse, and Danielle. Your friendship means the world to me and has always meant the world to me. I shudder to think what I would have become without the influence you all have had on my life. The conversations, the laughs, the adventures shared shaped me into the person I am today...and I like that person very much.

To Debbie, Lori, Felicia, Jiselle, and Shanika for making my college experience as educational as anything on any syllabus. You all continue to teach me to this day.

Thank you all so much. This book is for you all. I hope you enjoy it.

ONE
ANXIETY

"Someday you will ache like I ache." -Hole

It's time to get up. Time to get up, shower, brush my teeth. I wanna eat breakfast before I have to go to work today. I never have time for breakfast. I know it's time to get up but I can't open my eyes. I can't open my eyes because I know it's there, right at the foot of my bed, waiting for me to get up. It won't attack me until I know it's there, until I open my eyes and *actually* see it.

So I lie here, in my dark bedroom, with my eyes shut tight. I'm terrified of my eyes slipping open and I see it there at the foot of my bed. I *know* if I see it, it'll rip me apart and leave nothing of me.

Most people would say there's nothing there at the foot of my bed, nothing in the dark, but they're wrong. I know it's there and it's waiting patiently for me to open my eyes. I know what it is too. It's not some formless shape in the dark. No, that would be easier in some ways. The thing lying in wait...hungrily sitting at the foot of my bed...is a shark.

This is the part where you accuse me of being crazy. You think it's impossible for there to be a shark there. How would it have gotten into my room? How could it breathe? How could it be so quiet as it waited for my eyes to open? There are too many reasons why there couldn't be a shark there. I know it's impossible without even a degree in marine biology. I *know* how crazy it sounds. But there is one thing I know beyond it all. There is a shark at the foot of my bed and if I dare to open my eyes, it's going to devour me.

Damn it! I need to pee. I need to pee and there's a fucking shark between me and my bathroom. Sometimes I wish I had a girlfriend. If she woke up first, she could confirm that I'm only tripping and there is no shark, there's *never* been a shark. But I don't have a girlfriend, I have a shark. It's hungry and it's waiting impatiently there in the dark.

But I need to pee. Really bad. I'm going to need to get up. Pee, shower, and get ready for work. Maybe still have time to get breakfast before I leave. My mind tells me there's nothing there to fear at the same time it's making me imagine the smell of...salt water?

I lie there, eyes squeezed shut, as I consider just wetting the bed. I live alone. I can just wash my sheets afterwards. One more reason to be grateful I don't have a girlfriend...though I'd rather have that than a shark. The need to pee grows worse and worse. I need to get up and go to the bathroom, shark be damned.

In my mind I imagine the shark eating me from the feet up, like Robert Show in "Jaws." *#JusticeForQuint*. I won't say I don't know a worse way to die because I know several. I know them *all*. But this is definitely one of the worst. I feel the sharp teeth as they sink into my legs. The pain is unspeakable as this creature violently rips into me. It's not like the movies though; this thing isn't slow animatronics but a monstrous creature from the murky depths of Hell. It whips me back and forth like a ragdoll, my blood adorning my walls like a twisted Jackson Pollack painting. I don't wanna die like that. No one in their right mind would. Better I just lie here and die.

But I have to pee.

I summon all of my strength, take a deep breath, and...finally opened my eyes. I'm alone. Alone in my room without a marine monster to be seen. Damn my dark imagination. I leap out of bed and rush to the bathroom to finally empty my bladder. I should *never* have waited. Not only could I have done internal damage to myself, but there was no shark. There's *never* a shark, not for the last nineteen years.

But that doesn't mean it won't be there tomorrow morning.

IT TAKES me a rather long time to get ready for work this morning. I'm extra careful in the shower because I'm deathly afraid I'll slip and fall and injure myself in such a way that I'll be conscious but unable to cry out for help. Or I'll have a heart attack and no one will know to look for me. Or maybe acid will come out instead of water; I think I heard of that happening once, something about someone messing with the building's water supply.

Once bathed and dressed, I hit the kitchen. Definitely don't have time to cook breakfast, but I don't mess with the stove anyway. I'm terrified of accidental gas leaks. Either I'll pass out and never wake up again or I can die in a fiery explosion. Sometimes I really hate having choices.

I hate the way my mind works. I hate seeing all the myriad ways a situation can go fatally wrong. I hate that impossible things, like sharks at the foot of my bed or acid from my shower, all seem just as plausible as a stubbed toe or a train delay. It makes it nearly impossible to get through my days and have any semblance of a normal life.

I skip breakfast. Don't feel like convincing myself I won't get radiation poisoning from my microwave. I leave my apartment after checking I've locked my doors thrice. I head for the subway because I don't do buses. EVER! Buses are terrible for a number of reasons. For one, they have to stop at red lights plus their normal stops; that's just *asking* for delays. While my job is rather cool about lateness, I don't want to be the one who gets fired because the buses are terrible. It could happen.

My other gripe about the bus has everything to do with crowding. I cannot be on a crowded bus. I will throw up right before I die from lack of oxygen. It *will* happen. As the bus fills with people, my chest gets tighter. When I was younger, and my mom brought me places by bus, I used to deal with my anxiety by biting into my arm. Hard. The pain used to distract me from my crippling fears, but I am too old to be doing that sort of thing now.

So I use the subway. The trains get crowded too, but at least there's more space. And if the train is crowded, I let it go and wait for the next one. Sometimes I have to wait for the fifth train. I always give myself more than enough time. I've lived in New York City my whole life; I know to compensate for MTA shenanigans.

As I stand on the platform, I keep my head on a swivel. There are a lot of dangers when you descend into the bowels of this city. There are rats the size of cats here. I worry about them swarming me if I'm not careful. Sometimes I worry that the next train will be a giant, train-sized rat. Like that terrible movie, "Night of the Lepus", I watched with my dad when I was a kid. I know it's impossible, just like the shark, but I imagine it anyway. I know, I *know*, I am unprepared to fight a giant rat.

Sometimes I imagine giant insects and arachnids as well. I can't beat them either. Luckily, the rumbling that comes down that tunnel is not a colossal rat, roach, or spider but the train I need for work. I find a seat this time, which is a miracle in and of itself. I know I won't be in it long. As the train gets more and more crowded while venturing into Manhattan, I'll get increasingly more uncomfortable and will need to be standing near the exit.

As I sit there, my eyes are darting back and forth. There's no telling who around me is a threat to my life, so I watch them…but not so closely that my stare will provoke them to violence. I also monitor my thoughts just in case one of the passengers can read minds. I don't think I have ever run into a genuine mind reader but who knows? Maybe they don't want to tip their hand and reveal themselves to *me*.

I keep earbuds in for the entire trip, but there's no music playing. I can't afford for that distraction to make me unaware enough to get caught off guard. I keep the earbuds in, so I don't have to talk to anyone. I get frequently approached by religious zealots. I'm an atheist, but I suspect they know somehow. I imagine them trying to set me ablaze in the train, purifying me of my supposed sins.

I don't get burned as a heretic today. I reach my office and I'm greeted by my colleagues. They're all smiles, but it's fake. They all know I'm a fraud and I'm not good at my job. They know it. They're all just making fun of me behind my back until they finally fire me and blackball me across the industry. Once they let me go, I'll probably never work again. I'll lose my apartment and starve to death.

"Hey Saul! How was your weekend?"

It's Lita Ramirez, the woman who works at the desk next to mine. I think about how beautiful she is and then I banish the thought immediately. I can't help but think that she can read my thoughts. She'll hear my thoughts, the nasty ones, and turn me into HR. They'll eviscerate me and rake me over the coals. I don't know how they'll be able to hold me responsible for random thoughts, but they'll find a way. It could happen. It *will* happen.

Besides, I don't *want* her knowing *these* thoughts. Filthy...but she sure looks good in those heels. I wonder what she'd look like dressed like Powergirl. No! Stop thinking like that, stop thinking like that!

"It was...it was fine," I lied. "Um...how about yours?"

"Well, it was great," she said. "Nicole and I went to karaoke Friday night, then I spent Saturday cleaning my apartment and paying bills. Yesterday I was just lazy and spent all day in bed watching Netflix."

I nod as she speaks and force myself not to think about being in bed with her and enjoying a day of Netflix. After a few minutes of painful small talk, I'm able to get to my desk and start fumbling through my work. This day is shaping up to be like all the others before it, terrible and terrifying, but it won't be. Something's going to happen today that changes absolutely everything.

The day went smoothly, for the most part, and then it was time for lunch. Usually, I just pick up some halal food from the truck outside and eat it at my desk. On this day though, Lita and Emily approached me all smiles and bubbly. I was suspicious immediately, but I always am when people go out of their way to be nice to me.

"Do you want to go to lunch with us, Saul?" Lita asks as she sits on the edge of my desk. "There's this new seafood place a couple of blocks down. I hear that the food is to die for!"

"I like...seafood," I admit. "Um, where is it exactly?"

"Just two blocks away," Emily stated. "We can sit there and eat lunch before we have to come here."

"That sounds good," I say. "Sure."

We head to the restaurant and it's fine. The place looks fine and I try not to think about the cooks ejaculating all over our food. We could very well all get herpes from this place because of some disgruntled worker. The food being delicious helped distract me, but not as much as my conversation with Lita. On my gracious, she is nothing but a pure delight. I have never met a more charming, captivating woman. She kept me from thinking about the herpes-filled lunch I was eating.

She's an artist in her free time, drawing and painting. She wants to start dabbling in photography. I tell her I'd like to see her art and she invites me to her place that weekend to see some of it. I can't remember a time I was so happy. We went through the week as we usually did, absent-mindedly shuffling papers, until the weekend rolled around. I ate lunch with Lita everyday that week, sometimes with Emily and other times just the two of us. By the time I went to her place on Saturday, we had gotten to know each other pretty well. We had even exchanged numbers and spoke all night, every single night. I even got to the point where I stopped thinking she was setting me up.

"Your place looks great," I commented as I looked at the Alvin Ailey pictures adorning her walls. "Alvin Ailey fan, huh?"

"Oh, I love the dance troupe," she lit up. "I make sure to catch at least three performances a year. Do you like them?"

"My Dad and I go see a performance every year," I nodded. "It's been our thing since I was a child."

"Looks like we got a lot in common, Saul," she smiled. "I'm really glad you went to lunch with us the other afternoon. I'm glad that we got a chance to know each other."

I smiled and tried not to imagine this evening ending with me in a tub of ice with my kidneys removed. I couldn't imagine anyone being so nice without a sinister ulterior motive. I hoped that Lita was being genuine. There's nothing worse than realizing your worst fears are true.

We ordered in pizza and watched a documentary about the history of Barbados and its connection to the Carolinas here in the U.S. It was an interesting enough program, but I didn't think that would be the choice for the evening. Judging by the action figures adorning her desk at work, I figured we'd be watching "Dr. Who" or "Star Trek." Maybe even a little "Farscape" if I was really lucky.

"Are you liking the show?" she asked.

"Oh definitely," I answered. "PBS is my third favorite channel. Just behind Sci-Fi Channel and the BBC."

"Something else we have in common," she smiled before flipping an errant hair out of her face. "I'm having a great night with you, Saul."

"Me too," I nodded but I was still nervous. There were about a million ways for this to all go wrong. "I'm really glad you invited me over tonight."

"Would you...like a drink?" she asked. "I have some wine."

"That would be nice," I nodded. "I'm not driving so I should be okay."

"Well, if you're not driving, then maybe you'd like something stronger," she suggested, hopping off the couch and hurrying to the kitchen.

Soon we were drinking tequila and quickly emptying the bottle. It was hard to stay nervous once I started getting tipsy, but I should have been terrified. While drunk, it would have been easy for her to take advantage of me, but I was too intoxicated to defend myself or make good decisions. Before I even knew what was going on, she was straddling me on the living room sofa and we were making out like horny teenagers left alone on a Friday night.

I was in Heaven. It wasn't so much because Lita is a great kisser (which she definitely is), but because I didn't feel a *bit* anxious. It was probably the first time since I was an infant that I felt truly free of fear. I never wanted that feeling to end. We fooled around on the couch for a long time before she broke our connection.

"Let's go to my bedroom," she said, her voice taking a huskier tone. "I want you so bad, Saul."

Suffice it to say I didn't need to be told twice. I followed her to her bedroom, eyes glued to the way her rear end swayed from side to side with her every step. I could feel my heart beating out of my chest. That beating exactly matched the throbbing of my manhood as I followed her. We entered her room and she proceeded to turn off the lights.

"I want to see you," I found myself saying out of nowhere.

It was insane to say that, If I could see her, then she could see me too. She could see the paunch around my middle, my untoned arms, my undefined legs. She'd be able to see my "average" (but I fear perhaps *less* than average) penis. She could have taken one look at me, scrunched up her nose, and sent me home devastated. She could have laughed at me and totally humiliated me; she could have went to work on Monday and told Emily about my gross doughy body and little dick. All of that could have happened, but that fear was eclipsed by my desire to see her body.

She smiled at my response and then nodded as she began to turn the lights back up. She didn't turn them up to a harsh degree, but high enough for me to see her luscious body as she started to disrobe. She hadn't been wearing much clothing that evening: a pair of low rise overly distressed jeans and a white top that showed a bit of midriff. She remained barefoot throughout the entire evening; I don't think she knew the things that did to me. Maybe it was best she never knew.

I watched her take off her top in one deft movement followed by opening the front enclosure of her bra. I saw her hesitate before removing the bra, but I couldn't imagine why. Her breasts looked amazing, just as beautiful as the rest of her. It's hard to believe someone so beautiful could be self-conscious in the slightest.

"Wow," I uttered at the sight of her topless. "You are...gorgeous, Lita."

"Thank you," she blushed. "Hold on. Let me do something first."

I watched her grab a tiny black remote control from her nightstand and then point it at the stereo on her dresser. Soon the bedroom was filled with the crooning of Teddy Pendergrass. She was ready. Was Teddy Pendergrass always queued up in her bedroom...or was she expecting to take me to bed tonight and made preparations accordingly? I stopped thinking on it when she started to undo her jeans.

I knew I was going to need to start removing my clothing soon, but I couldn't stop looking at her. I managed to kick off my sneakers and swiftly pull my shirt off over my head. She didn't run off screaming at the sight of me with my shirt off, so that was a good sign. We quickly ditched our pants and underwear and then hopped into bed.

It was good. It was really good. It would not be an exaggeration for me to say it was the best sex that I ever had. I hope beyond hope that she enjoyed it just as much. You can't always tell. She could have been faking all the moaning and yelling; she could have faked the squirting too, I suppose. We made love in a couple of positions that night, went through several of her condoms.

"Oh my god!" she exclaimed afterwards. "That was so good!"

"I really liked it too," I said nervously. Now that I came, the old fears began to resurface.

What was I supposed to do now? Did she expect me to leave or was it okay for me to stay the night? We hadn't actually discussed it because we got right into the sex. I started to get antsy and fidget a bit until she leaned in and kissed me. That kiss certainly steadied me.

"Mmm, let's get some sleep," she said. "Unless…you're not tired. I mean, if you got another round in you…I certainly don't have anywhere to go tomorrow."

So, I could see she definitely intended for me to stay the night, which solved one of my issues, but I was still nervous about falling asleep in her apartment. I'd be vulnerable and then anything could happen. I'd definitely lose a kidney then. But I felt safe with her, so I quieted my fears and stayed the night…after one more round.

I don't think I've ever had a more restful sleep in my life. Not since my childhood at least. It was Heaven. I honestly didn't want it to ever end…but the dawn always comes. That next morning, I laid next to Lita and wondered if the shark had found its way to her apartment. I mean, why couldn't it? It swims its ferocious ass to my bedroom, so why not come here too? I didn't want to open my eyes and risk us both being devoured. She didn't deserve a vicious shark attack just because she spent the night with me.

Before I could agonize over whether that aquatic monster was waiting for me, Lita cuddled up against me and all my fears vanished in an instant. I...wished I could live like that, fearless, for the rest of my life. I wrapped my arms around her and gave her an affectionate squeeze.

"You're up," she whispered as a smile crept across my face.

"Sorry," I apologized. "I didn't mean to wake you."

"No, it's fine," she said. "We should probably get up and get the day started. I need coffee, waffles...and more time with you.

Time with me? So this wasn't a one-night stand, thank god! That would have been really awkward come Monday morning when we went back to work. It was like she went out of her way to put me at ease without even knowing it. Was she what I had been searching for my whole life? I opened my eyes and there was no shark at the foot of her bed. We got up, bathed, and cooked breakfast together.

"Do you want some coffee?"

I was sitting in her kitchen when she asked that. She looked sexy standing there in an oversized T-shirt with Deadpool on it, pouring some java into a mug. I could watch her all day and never get tired.

"No, I don't drink coffee," I answered.

"I don't think I've ever heard a more blasphemous sentence in my life," she smiled. "Coffee is a gift from a benevolent earth goddess who wants nothing more than to see us happy."

She walked around the counter and sat across from me. She hadn't put on pants, showing off her smooth legs and thighs. She looked like perfection. The moan she did from first sip of coffee reminded me of our time in bed...and made me wish we were back there.

"What are you thinking about right now, Saul?" she asked.

"That I love hearing you moan," I admitted.

"Oh really?" she smiled. "You'll hear more of that later. Or maybe sooner. Definitely sooner."

"Good to hear," I smiled too as I wondered if she exaggerated the moan when she drank her coffee just to entice me.

"I am so glad that things worked out this way," she said. "You always seemed so unapproachable in the office. I'm glad to see who you are outside of that place."

"Yeah, work is odd," I shrugged. "I'm always so focused on work and trying not to get fired that I barely notice anything else."

"Fired?" she asked with a laugh. "You're the best worker we've got. Everyone knows it. We all say so all the time. What makes you think you'll get fired? Hell, you should be asking for a raise."

"You think so?" I asked, genuinely surprised by what she was saying. I always suspected that I was the weak link at our office. "I'll definitely consider it."

"That's something to consider on Monday," she said. "Right now, I want *all* your attention on me."

When I felt her bare foot travel up my calf and rest on my crotch, my potential raise became the last thing on my mind. We spent all weekend eating, sleeping, talking and screwing until I went home Sunday night. I missed her as soon as I left her apartment; at least I'd see her Monday morning at work.

I was filled with a sense of dread as soon as I got to my front door. Why though? That nightmare shark only existed in my bedroom. Did I think I would open my door and there would be criminals in my apartment? Or would the door open and I'd be attacked by a giant tarantula? I stood at my door, keys in hand, for several moments as I tried to figure out what threat lay in wait on the other side. When I entered my apartment finally, I found nothing out of the ordinary...as usual.

"What am I doing?" I asked myself angrily.

I needed to do something about all these irrational fears crippling my life. I couldn't go on living like this. I had discussed some of my fears with my doctor once. Not everything though. I was scared he might have me committed if he knew the true extent of my anxieties. At any rate, he recommended I see a therapist named Dr. Debbie Robinson, but I never went. After my wonderful weekend with Lita, I made an appointment. Now that I knew what it was like to live anxiety-free, I couldn't go back.

I saw Lita every night after work and we got closer and closer. The night of my appointment three weeks later was the only evening we didn't spend together. Dr. Robinson's waiting room was like any other doctor's I suppose. It was well-lit, soothing, not too crowded. The magazines were old and not at all interesting, but that was to be expected.

"Mr. Copeland?" she asked upon exiting her office.

"That's me."

"Step right in please."

Soon enough I was on her couch trying to figure out just how much to share with her. The possibility of being institutionalized was still a very real thing in my mind. I wanted to be better, not put in a cage. Ultimately, she told me that it doesn't help me if I hold anything back, so I opened the floodgates on that first night. Her hands were a blur as she wrote down a copious amount of notes.

"Whoa!" she exclaimed near the end of our first session. "That is a lot to unpack, Mr. Copeland."

"Imagine living with it every moment of every day," I said. "That's why I'm here."

"You have the most severe and varied case of anxiety that I have ever seen in my career," she continued. "I'm frankly shocked you get out of bed every morning with these thoughts weighing down on you."

"Can you help me?" I asked.

"I want to start by putting you on some tranquilizers," she replied. "Some Xanax or Ativan."

"Do I really need drugs?" I asked. "I'm not really comfortable with that."

"Are you comfortable with thinking people can read your thoughts?" she asked.

I didn't care for the attitude behind the question, but I appreciated the sentiment. So I agreed to it. She wrote me a prescription for Xanax and cautioned me not to take too long to start taking it. She also gave me some pills that she had in her desk drawer, obviously feeling I needed the medication sooner rather than later. I didn't know how I felt about that. She scheduled an appointment for the following week to check up on me. I didn't pick up my prescription like I said I would, but I did put the pills she gave me in my medicine cabinet...just in case. I didn't take the pills though. Frankly, I was afraid of the medicine. I was scared that it would destroy me.

I held out for the next two weeks, much to Dr. Robinson's disappointment. It was fine. I was with Lita at work and most evenings, so my anxiety was pretty well-checked now. I didn't consider taking those damn pills until *she* saw me for who I truly was, a huge mass of fears and insecurities.

She convinced me to go to a gallery in Midtown to see the work of her friend, Alicia. I tend not to go out places. I don't go to movies, never been to a concert, don't frequent restaurants or museums. I don't like crowds. My resistance to going out places only increased after 9/11. So, her suggestion to go to the gallery was initially met with silence on my part, but when I saw the look of disappointment on her face, I quickly agreed to the outing.

All in all, it was a pretty grand event. She bought a piece for her apartment, and I did too. Things didn't go wrong until I needed to use the bathroom.

"Oh, the restroom is right through that door, down the stairs, and to the back," Alicia stated.

"We'll wait for you right here," Lita smiled.

I went through the door and down the stairs as instructed to the gallery's basement. It wasn't creepy like most basements and surprisingly well-lit, so I wasn't particularly on high alert. I even passed a jovial couple who were on their way back upstairs after, presumably, having sex in the restroom if their smiles, blushing, and disheveled clothing were any indication at all.

I went to the bathroom and did my business, but when I exited the restroom, I found that the basement was pitch black! I panicked immediately. Did the randy couple turn the lights off on me? Was it on purpose or a mistake? Was it a prank or something worse? Were all the patrons in on it? Did they all lock me down here on purpose to do unspeakable things to me? Are they a cult that lures people into art galleries to sacrifice them to some savage god?

"Calm down, Saul," I said to myself as I stood in the threshold of the restroom as the light poured out from behind me. "There's no cult, no grody god. They just accidentally turned off the lights. I can make it to the stairs."

Make it to the stairs? The light from the bathroom was not going to help me to the stairs, particularly when the door was gonna close and blanket me in complete darkness. There was no way I'd find my way. They'd get me before I set one foot on the stairs.

"Shit!" I cursed. "Why'd I leave my phone at work?"

I never leave things under normal circumstances, typically triple checking everything before I leave, but Lita was in a rush to get out of the office and I didn't want to keep her waiting. I ended up leaving my phone and charger right there on my desk. I figured I'd retrieve them the next morning, but I didn't realize how vital they would be that night. The flashlight on my phone would have been extremely helpful.

"I'll just wait here until someone else comes down to use the bathroom," I thought to myself. "They've been serving champagne. Someone else is bound to come down here."

The place was full of people sipping terrible champagne, so it wasn't unreasonable to believe someone would come along eventually. So, I waited a bit, but no one else appeared. I started getting nervous again. By the time what felt like a half hour passed, I was full-on terrified.

"Where the hell is everybody?" I wondered. "I've been down here a long time; why hasn't Lita come looking for me yet?"

That's when I'm ashamed to admit I started thinking she was in on it. She made me drop my guard over the last few weeks, so I'd be unaware and defenseless when her creepy cult buddies finally made their move. I was thinking about that show "Nowhere Man" with Bruce Greenwood and how he went to the bathroom in an art gallery as a happily married man and exited as someone whose wife claimed not to know him. Was Lita going to turn on me just as his wife had? If I lived through this, I was going to need to re-evaluate my whole life.

More time passed and I just knew I had to try to make it upstairs. I wedged some tissue under the bathroom door to keep it open and then proceeded to venture into the dark to where the stairs were. It didn't take me very long to go tripping over something and stumbling in the dark. As I was sprawled out on the floor, I wondered what had tripped me up. Was it a dead body, another victim of the cult upstairs? Was it the outstretched arms or tentacles of some great beast, some eldritch horror that these cultists had called to our plane of existence? It occurred to me that I really didn't want to know as I scrambled to my feet and tried to make it to the stairs.

The darkness seemed to pulse around me, like it was a living thing. I groped about and found nothing. I called for help. It was a barely audible whisper; while I would have welcomed a timely rescue, I didn't want to be discovered by…something else. I called again and again to no avail. Before long, my calls turned to cried for help and they got louder and louder. Just when I thought I was going to break down and lose it completely, the lights flipped on.

"Are you okay?"

Lita, Alicia, and some tall dude were on the stairs looking down on me…I mean, at me. I was in a full-on panic and must have looked crazy. My girlfriend's face was full of concern…and some fear.

"Somebody turned the lights off," I tried to explain. "I couldn't find my way back to the stairs."

"No problem," the tall man smiled. "I've tried to get them to install motion sensor lights down here, but they're too cheap."

I exited the basement sheepishly and hung out with Lita and Alicia. We were all silent and I could feel all eyes on me. I was the scaredy cat that had cried like a baby. I was beyond uncomfortable. If you could die from embarrassment, they would have had to bury me right there.

"Can we get out of here?" I whispered to Lita after I got tired of the pointing and staring.

"Sure," she said. "Lemme get my coat."

She got her coat, said goodbye to Alicia, and we left the gallery. We got an Uber and rode off in silence. I was embarrassed by my screaming fit in the gallery, and she was probably quietly trying to broach the topic. Realizing how uncomfortable it must have been for her, I spoke first.

"I couldn't find the stairs," I commented.

"No, I get that," she stated. "But you sounded terrified. Are you afraid of the dark or something?"

I hesitated to respond. Our relationship was going well, and I didn't want to risk it by revealing how much of a mess I am. But I didn't want to lie to her either. I took a deep breath and then resigned myself to telling the truth.

"I suffer from anxiety," I admitted. "It gets pretty bad sometimes. I thought everyone had forgotten me down there and I..."

"...had a panic attack," she finished my sentence. "That's no problem. They have medication for that, you know? My sister got prescribed Valium and she's doing just fine."

"Yeah, I'll look into it," I said, surprised by how nonchalant her response was. I had expected her to run for the hills once she learned the truth.

"Being abandoned in an art gallery kinda reminds me of 'Nowhere Man'," she commented. "Have you ever seen that show? I think Bruce Greenwood was in it? And that woman from 'Millennium' too, I think."

"You're perfect, you know that?" I smiled as she referenced the same obscure TV show I had...though it could have just been her ability to read minds.

"Yes, but I love hearing it every chance I get," she laughed.

We ended up making out in the back of that Uber all the way to her place where we made love all night. I vowed I would take the pills Dr. Robinson prescribed to me the very next morning. The next morning, I told Lita I needed to get something from my apartment, but I'd be right back. I went home, got my pills, and held them in my hands as I stared at myself in the medicine cabinet mirror.

"Am I gonna take these things?" I asked myself as I looked at my reflection. "I really, *really* don't like drugs."

"Then pour them down the drain."

My reflection smirked at me...but I wasn't smiling. I've always been anxious about reflections. I don't like looking at my reflection for too long because I always suspect it will start doing something different than what I'm doing. And on this day, my reflection had gone rogue.

"What is this?" I asked as though any answer would make sense.

"I'm here to help you, pal," Mirror Saul smiled. "I can see you're struggling."

"Who are you?" I asked.

"Don't act brand new, Saul," he rolled his eyes in disappointment. "You know me. You hear my voice in your head all the time."

"You're my fear," I said.

"I'm your common sense," he rolled his eyes as though offended. "I'm what's kept you alive all these years. I'd advise you not to take those pills."

"Why not?" I asked, peeking at the pill bottle briefly before looking back at my reflection. "What's wrong with them?"

"Best case scenario, it'll dull your senses to my warnings," he shrugged. "I'm guessing you'll pop one of those pills and be dead by dawn."

"And worst-case scenario?" I inquired though I really didn't want to know the answer.

"You *know* the worst-case scenario, buddy," he laughed. "All hell breaks loose. All your worst nightmares come true."

"That's ridiculous," I argued. "You're being an alarmist. None of what we're afraid of could ever possibly happen. I mean, come on! A shark in the bedroom? That's all types of impossible and we know it!"

"Nothing is impossible," he shook his head. "It may be highly unlikely or improbable, but don't ever fool yourself into believing anything is impossible. You take those pills, and I can't help you anymore."

"You're not helping me *now*!" I exclaimed. "What are you doing for me? All you do is make me too scared to live my damn life!"

"You think you can live without me?" he laughed. It was both offensive *and* creepy. "Oh please! Give me a break! Is this about the girl? You're trying to get rid of me to make her like you more? You hardly know her and you're willing to die for her?"

"I'm not going to die," I insisted.

"Oh, no?" he asked. "How about now?"

That was when my reflection did the worst thing a reflection *could* do: it reached out and grabbed me by the throat. Its hands were mine but much stronger. I struggled to breathe as it tried to strangle the life out of me. I grabbed at those arms and tried to free myself. I refused to die by an assailant wearing my face and using my hands.

"Let...me...go!" I shouted before pulling away and falling backwards against the bathroom wall.

By the time I got to my feet, my reflection was back to normal. I examined my throat for bruises and saw none. I frowned and then quickly took the pill. After the freak out, I considered popping two pills, but I refrained. I didn't want to overdose on peace of mind. After swallowing the pill, I looked at my reflection a moment and then left the bathroom. I went to my living room sofa and took a seat.

"How long before it takes effect?" I wondered. I didn't want to be walking around the city high on tranquility.

I sat on the sofa and waited for something to happen. I found myself getting more and more nervous. What if Mirror Saul was right? What if those pills were the worst thing in the world? What if I get loopy and get hit by a car? I sat there and waited to see how this would affect me. And that's when it hit me. Everything...dissipated. All the weights I've carried, fears I've harbored were no longer there.

No. That's not right. It was all still there, all still a part of me, but I couldn't bring myself to care. It's like having memories you can't quite access. So far away and almost ethereal to the point that those fears just didn't matter. I smiled. I laughed. I looked around my apartment with new eyes, like a veil of fear had been lifted from them. I went back to the bathroom and stared at my reflection as it did nothing but mimic my movements.

All I wanted to do was rush out and see Lita and show her the new man I had become. I walked through the streets of New York more carefree than I'd ever been. I skipped taking a taxi and took the subway instead. It was incredible. Before, all I could think of was the million ways I could die down there, but today I could see the wonder of it all.

Millions of people going to and fro every single day. I could finally see why my father used to take me to the Transit Museum every year.

When I finally got to my girlfriend's house, I knocked on the door enthusiastically. I needed to see her, needed to share this change that had come over me. I didn't even freak when she took longer than usual to open the door. She could have been napping, using the bathroom, or even went to the bodega to get an order of lamb over rice. Nothing to be concerned about. I waited for an answer. And waited. And waited some more.

"Hey babe, how long you been here?"

She walked up behind me. She wasn't in any danger. She had indeed gone to get halal food from the bodega down the block. I could tell from the bag that she had gotten some for me too.

"Just got here a little while ago," I admitted. "You look...beautiful."

"Oh, you are a sweet talker, huh?" she smirked.

"I mean it," I said. "You are so beautiful to me."

"Thank you, Saul," she smiled and blushed.

"You're even more beautiful when you blush," I smiled.

"Oh, somebody's getting laid tonight," she laughed. "Maybe right after we eat too."

We entered the apartment and ate our food. That was when I told her that I had taken the pills. She told me she was proud of me and asked me how it was, how I felt. I told her how I used to feel and how much better I was now. She was happy for me and so was I. We finished our meal and then made love. That sex was bananas!!! Sex without fear is absolutely incredible! For the first time I wasn't afraid of coming too fast or taking too long or not making her climax or hurting her or being too quiet or too loud. It was all about our pleasure; I was finally free to enjoy sex with a partner and enjoy it thoroughly.

"Wow!" she exclaimed when we finally came up for air that evening. "What was all that?"

"It was incredible," I laughed as I tried to catch my breath.

"Yeah, but it was never like that before," she said breathlessly. "It was great before, don't get me wrong, but this was different level sex."

"Maybe because I took my pill," I shrugged.

"You sure they gave you anti-anxiety medication and not Viagra?" she laughed.

"Pretty sure," I stated. "How about I order us some dinner?"

"Seeing how I can't move my legs, I think that's a great idea, sweetie," she laughed again.

We ended up ordering pizza, watching some "Doctor Who" on TV, and then going back to the bedroom for more amazing sex before we went to sleep. Oddly enough, despite being more at ease than any other time in my whole life, I had a nightmare that night.

I found myself in a large, white room confronted by...myself. My reflection approached me in a black suit that fit him as comfortably as his skin. The suit seemed to writhe to the point where it hurt my eyes just to look at it. I had no choice but to lock eyes with him.

"So, are you proud of yourself?" he asked me, crossing his arms over his chest. "You took the pill and now there's no going back."

"Yeah, I took the pill and nothing happened!" I rolled my eyes.

"You're a fool," he told me. "You can't even perceive the changes that have *already* occurred. But you will. The morning is going to show you a much different world."

"This is alarmist bullshit!" I snapped. "Nothing has happened and nothing is *going* to happen. I'm fine! I'm better than I've ever been! I'm not going to listen to you anymore. You've never done a thing for me but hold me back!"

"I've saved your life," he said, looking hurt that I diminished the role he'd played in my life. He clearly fancied himself some kind of savior.

"You didn't *save* my life!" I protested. "You stopped me from *having* a life! Can't you see that?"

"You need to listen to me, Saul," he said. "I'm trying to protect you."

"No, I'm not going to listen to you," I shook my head. "I'm going to be just fine without you."

"You're wrong, Saul," he said sullenly. "No one is going to be fine."

The white room I was in went completely dark, darker than the basement of that art gallery, and I was swallowed by it. I should have been frightened by the abrupt nature of it, but I wasn't. I was more annoyed by the theatrics than frightened by them. The lights suddenly turned back on and I was no longer face-to-face with my sinister reflection, but a large shark (maybe a megalodon) that quickly gobbled me up in one bite.

"Shit," I cursed as I woke up with a start.

"Are you all right?" Lita asked, cuddled up against me.

"Yeah, it's nothing," I answered. "You can go back to sleep."

She drifted back off to sleep and I did too. I didn't have any more nightmares after that. The next morning, I woke up to the smell of bacon. My girlfriend was making breakfast, so I made my way to the bathroom. I peed, showered, and then popped another pill. I heard a bunch of noise outside through the bathroom window. It was a crowd of people plus police sirens and firetrucks. When I left the bathroom, I found Lita leaning out her living room window to see what was going on outside. At that moment, I was more interested in her booty as she stood there in nothing but an oversized T-shirt and panties than what was going on outside.

I snuck up behind her and wrapped my arms around her waist, pressing myself to her. She got surprised by my sudden appearance. I pulled her back into the apartment and began kissing her neck and back.

"I like waking up to this, not gonna lie," she moaned. "I made breakfast. There's some sort of ruckus going on downstairs."

"Not my concern," I shook my head as she turned around to face me while I still held her in my arms. "All I care about this morning is bacon and booty."

"Mmm, bed and breakfast combo, huh?" she smiled. "I can get behind that."

"And I can get behind *you*," I smiled.

"Calm down, horndog," she rolled her eyes. "How about you fix the plates and I'll go put on some shorts."

"Why are you putting *on* clothes?" I asked.

"It's temporary," she assured me. "Just gonna run downstairs right quick and ask my neighbor what's going on."

While I fixed the plates she put on a tiny, sexy pair of purple jogging shorts and sandals before heading downstairs. I waited at the dining room table and didn't touch my food. I considered getting dressed too, but I decided not to. I didn't want too much clothing in the way when we finally went to bed. She came back about seven minutes later.

"What's up?" I asked as she sat with me at the kitchen table.

"My neighbor, Mr. Shaw, died," she explained with a confused look on her face.

"Sounds like a lot of confusion for one man's death," I said before eating some of my eggs.

"It's an impossible death, Saul," she said. "Apparently, there was a shark in his bedroom, and it ate him this morning."

"What?" I asked. "A shark in his room?"

"Yeah," she nodded. "It's the craziest thing. Can you imagine?"

I knew I should have been scared. My shark finding its way into someone else's bedroom after the dire warning I received from Mirror Saul? This could have been a disaster in the making. But I had taken my pill so there was only one response I could manage.

"That *is* weird." And then I ate some more eggs.

TWO

NIGHTMARES

I can't say I wasn't shaken up at all about Lita's neighbor being eaten by a shark in his bedroom. After all, this was something that had been tormenting me every morning before work for several years. I was intimately familiar with that death. But I couldn't bring myself to be too worried about it though, no matter how hard I tried.

Lita, by contrast, was very concerned about what was going on. She got even more worried when more and more incidents began happening all over the world. Every week was a new report of something truly bizarre going on somewhere. There were strange attacks by wild animals and disappearances that couldn't be explained. We even watched a news report of a woman who stabbed her boyfriend no less than 113 times; apparently, she developed the ability to read thoughts...and she didn't like what was on his mind.

"That's crazy," Lita commented. "She thought she was a telepath?"

"Maybe she was," I shrugged. "You don't stab a man that many times unless you absolutely can read his mind."

"You're really taking all this in stride, Saul," she said suspiciously. "How can you be so cool about all this? Our whole world is turning upside down and you're cool as a cucumber. What gives?"

"Maybe this is how the world's always been," I shrugged again. "Like when we found out that brooms can stand up on their own. Maybe we've been lying to ourselves by claiming we knew the rules. Maybe sharks have always killed men in their bedrooms and maybe women have always suddenly developed telepathy."

"That broom shit still freaks me out," she admitted.

"The point is that I can't be freaked out every time the world doesn't fit the mold I think it should," I stated. "It'll take me away from enjoying my time with you."

"I guess," she allowed herself a small smile even though she was still obviously suspicious. "So, what do you want to do today?"

"Anything you want," I smiled back. "Been a while since we've gone to the movies. And then we can go to dinner."

"What movies are out right now and where do you want to eat?" she asked.

"I think there's a new Jordan Peele film out," I suggested. "That might be fun. As for dinner, I'm kinda in the mood for Italian food."

"Not Olive Garden again, Saul!" she protested. "We've been dating for a little while and we've been to that restaurant like seven times already."

"When you're there, you're family," I smirked. "I don't have a lot of that."

"Me either," she nodded knowingly. "But if I have to eat there one more time, I'm gonna scream."

"We don't want that," I said. "I prefer when you scream in the bedroom, not family friendly restaurant chains."

"You're being naughty, Saul, while I'm trying to be serious," she smiled. "Keep it up and we'll end up staying home again."

"Look at you always threatening me with a good time," I laughed.

Despite the flirting and kissing that followed, Lita and I went to this little intimate restaurant in Brooklyn, the same one my dad took me to when I graduated from high school. I ate the roasted chicken with wild rice and string beans while she tried out their meatloaf and mashed potatoes with corn. It was delicious and my girl even convinced me to have a couple of glasses of wine that night too. When we left the restaurant, we opted to take the subway home.

"Wasn't that better than a certain restaurant that shall remain nameless?" she asked me.

"Yeah," I nodded, "and they certainly had a family-style vibe."

"See, I'm full of great ideas," she smiled. "You should really listen to me more often."

"I definitely will," I said.

That's when I noticed a man stumbling about the subway platform and my eyes narrowed at the sight of him. My pre-medicated self would have been on the highest of high alerts because that was my default setting back then. Could he have been the guy looking to set me on fire with a hidden pickle jar full of lighter fluid and some matches? Or was he looking to stab me and slice my face off to add to his collection? Or was he something even more exotic? Vampire looking to drain me? Or a demon to drink my soul? The old me would have been so preoccupied with this guy that I wouldn't have even been able to focus on what Lita was saying.

"I can't wait for us to get home," she commented, leaning in to kiss me. "I'm feeling kinda horny tonight."

"I love it when you're horny *any* night," I smiled.

"I bet you'd like it if I was horny *every* night," she laughed.

"Well, yeah," I laughed too. "That goes without saying."

That's when we heard rumbling coming down the tunnel, but it sounded weird to my ear, like it wasn't really a train at all. I looked around and saw the confused looks on everyone else's faces. The rumbling sounded like…a fucking stampede actually, not a train. Seeing everyone's faces let me know the sound wasn't just in my head.

"What the hell is that?" Lita asked. "What's wrong with that train?"

"We need to get out of here," I said. "Like right now."

"Why?" she asked nervously. "What's the matter?"

Before I could explain or even mount an escape, they emerged from the dark tunnels. Millions, perhaps billions, of rats streamed from the darkness. A brownish-black writhing ocean of pestilence covered everything. We all ran for the exits, but escape was impossible. The staggering man was the first to get caught, too drunk to run for an exit. The rats brought him down quickly and began to gnaw at his flesh. He screamed out in abject terror...until the rats forced their way down his throat to get at the organs inside him.

"Don't look back," I told Lita as we raced towards the steps leading out of the subway.

More and more people were overtaken and then consumed by the rats, but Lita and I were almost in the clear. She made it halfway up the stairs, but I ended up surrounded by the red-eyed vermin. She stopped on the stairs and looked back, unsure of what to do as the rats slowly approached me. Neither of us had time to realize how odd it was that they ceased their pursuit of her to surround me; it was even weirder that they were taking their time to creep up on me rather than just eat me like they did with everyone else. I think we both assumed this was the end for me, like it had been for everyone else on the platform. But they seemed to hesitate, like they didn't know what to make of me.

"Saul," she whispered down to me, trying not to be too loud lest they remember she was there.

"Take it easy, fellas," I said, holding up my hands in surrender. "I think you've eaten enough."

The rats got even closer. I've had this fear for a long time and it had nothing to do with watching "Willard." It was Stephen King's "Graveyard Shift" that did this to me. They got closer and my heart almost stopped. They smelled awful, obviously having made their way up here from the sewers. Lita then threw something, a bottle of hand sanitizer, into the mass of rats. They all turned to face her and hissed so loud it was like a blimp sprung a leak. I could tell they were gonna attack her, devour her like they had everyone else.

"No!" I shouted. "Leave her alone!"

And then the rats froze, as though they understood me. What's more, they now seemed like...they were afraid of *me*. I tried to use that to my advantage.

"Get outta here!" I yelled at the vermin and they turned their attention back to me again. "I said, get outta here!"

That's when I heard and felt the rumbling coming from behind me. I knew whatever was behind me couldn't be good, but I was assured of it when I saw the terrified look on Lita's face. I didn't want to see it, but felt compelled to turn around and look. I immediately regretted that decision. The rumbling was a rat that stood fifteen feet tall on its hind legs and it was lumbering towards me.

The little rats made room for their god to walk through. All I wanted was for Lita to race up those stairs and get to safety, but she refused to leave me. I loved her for it, but it also meant she'd die right after me. When the giant rat finally approached and towered over me, I knew I was fucked.

The rat god was so big that I could see the fleas running through its matted, black fur. They were damn near the size of the regular rats running around on the ground. I felt nauseous at the sight of it. Running wasn't an option and neither was fighting. If I could have willed myself to die before they started eating me, I would have done that.

"You and your little army better get the fuck outta my face and go back to the bottom of the food chain where you belong," I said, using the last bit of courage I had.

The rat god sniffed me and then licked the top of my head with its coarse, slimy tongue. Now would have been a good time to die. But they left after that. The rat god and its minions left the platform, went into the dark tunnels, and then were gone. Lita then rushed over to me and grabbed my hand.

"Saul?" I heard her call me. "Saul, are you all right? Can you hear me?"

"What was that?" I asked.

"I don't know," she answered, "but we gotta get out of here and get some help. People...people died down here."

I nodded, letting my eyes look at the corpses with the devoured flesh. We made it to the street safely and then Lita flagged down a police officer. The officer seemed annoyed to be stopped, like he didn't want to do his job.

"People are dead down there, Officer," she informed him. "Come on!"

We followed the officer downstairs and when he found the first corpse, he immediately called for backup. The officer looked at us as though he briefly thought we might be responsible for the corpses littering the platform. He was sure no one human could have done this though. He was right.

"What happened here?" he asked. "Who...what did this?"

"Rats," Lita answered. "A bunch came out of the tunnels, started attacking people. We...barely got out."

"Rats," the cop asked in confusion. "Just when you think you've seen everything in this city."

There were nine dead this time. These weird events were getting more lethal. A man killed by a shark in his home. One man killed by his newly telepathic wife. And now nine killed in one fell swoop by millions of rats and their god. More bodies and, even more frightening, it was starting to hit closer to home.

You only get three strikes before you have to accept the truth of things. All of this sprung from my head; they were all my anxieties and they were taking physical form. How could I tell anyone about this though? How could I tell people that my fears were killing people? And what could I do about it?

In less than two hours, Lita and I were in the police station with Detective Roxanne Reynolds. We were given delicious donuts and nasty coffee. There was a lot of hustle and bustle, but I was keenly aware of all the eyes on us that night. Detective Reynolds brought us to an interrogation room to learn what we knew.

"Are you two okay?" the detective asked. "Do you need anything?"

"I need an explanation for what's going on," was Lita's immediate response. "I've never seen anything like that before and I have lived in this city my entire life. I didn't think it was even possible."

"I've seen the footage from the subway cameras and I can't really believe it either," said Reynolds, shaking her head. "A rat that big, the size of two men standing on each other's shoulders, controlling millions of regular-sized rats? It shouldn't be possible. We're calling...someone to go into the sewers to look for it and kill it. We didn't even know who to direct such a call to and if it wasn't for the fact that we're law enforcement, they wouldn't have believed us in the first place."

"Did you close the subways?" I asked. "They can start attacking trains. Or they could attack every platform at once. Or...who knows what else?"

"The subways are being closed now," she said, obviously not pleased by someone else telling her how to do her job. "We're trying not to cause a panic."

"People *should* panic, Detective," I said pointedly. "Those little bastards could kill us all depending on how organized they actually are."

The truth of the matter is that just about any species of animals could destroy us all if they were organized and had the mind to do so. I figured that out a long time ago. Our battle against birds and bugs would be the worst...if it ever truly came to that.

"Do you think they're capable of *thinking*, Mr. Copeland?" she asked.

"There was a rat about twenty feet tall and it licked me," I said angrily. "We need to assume they're capable of anything at this point."

"We're doing all we can," she informed us. "As you'd imagine, no one was prepared for this. We're dealing with unprecedented and, frankly, impossible circumstances. No one knows what to do."

"I'm *telling* you what to do, Detective," I said firmly. "You need to evacuate the subways and seal them off as best you can. They *are* organized and have a very cunning leader. More attacks are imminent."

"You got all that when King Rat licked you?" she asked, equal parts suspicious and annoyed by my insistence.

"Say I know a lot about Rodentia, say I've seen a lot of movies, say whatever you want," I told her. "If you want to save lives, do what I am telling you."

"I'll be right back," she frowned before leaving Lita and I alone in the interrogation room.

"You're really pushing her, Saul," my girlfriend immediately pointed out once we were alone. "What's going on?"

"I've seen this before, Lita," I said, crossing my arms over my chest.

"Where could you have *possibly* seen this before?" she asked in bewilderment. The idea was quite mad after all. "Did you use to work for some top-secret lab that did these kinds of experiments, but you quit over the ethical dilemma of it all?"

I laughed at her response. It was so amazing to hear and it actually made me feel better about everything that was going on. I just wanted to take her into my arms and hug her, but she needed to hear the truth.

"The same place I saw a man being eaten by a shark in his bedroom and homicidal telepaths," I admitted. "They're my fears, my anxieties. I don't know how or why, but they're taking physical form. All my nightmares are coming to life...and none of us are safe right now."

"I know you suffered from anxiety, but I didn't know you worried... about stuff like this," she said. "I mean, twenty-foot rats? Do you think about that every time you go into the subway?"

"Each and every time," I nodded. "Or, at least, I did until I started taking my pills."

"I'm sorry you went through that," she said, reaching out and rubbing my arm. "I didn't know. I only experienced *one* of your nightmares and almost shit my pants, so I don't know how you survived all day everyday with them. But how can your fears be taking physical form?"

"I think...they might have escaped when I started taking the pills," I said. "Right after I took the first one, your neighbor got killed by the shark."

"Shit!" she cursed in realization. "I encouraged you to get the pills! Does that mean this is my fault?"

"No," I shook my head. "Not at all. Upwards of forty million adults suffer from anxiety here. Many take medication for it. Nothing like this has ever happened before. No one could have possibly foreseen this."

"I still feel bad," she said sullenly. "I really liked my neighbor. Mr. Shaw used to go fishing and then he would give me his extras so I could cook up. I never did though; I don't know anything about cleaning and cooking fresh fish yanked right out of the ocean. I used to just give it to my Dad; he likes that kind of thing."

Right when I was starting to worry about her breaking up with me for being a colossal freak, Lita gave me the tightest hug I've ever been given in my life. Every moment I spent with this woman was another moment spent falling in love with her. I hugged her back and we kept that connection until Detective Reynolds returned. She looked like she had seen a ghost.

"You were right, Mr. Copeland," she said. "The rats attacked 42nd Street, Penn Station, and Grand Central Station. We don't know the exact number of casualties, but between the rats and the...tramplings it could be in the thousands."

"Oh my god!" Lita gasped, grasping my hand.

"We're evacuating every subway across the city and sealing them up," Reynolds continued. "There's talk of calling in the National Guard, possibly declaring a state of emergency. Our city is in real trouble."

"It's not just our city in danger," I said. "This is going to spread."

"Rats all over the country?" she asked.

"Possibly all over the world, but it won't just be the rats," I stated. "It'll be other things too. Worse things."

"What are you talking about exactly?" she asked suspiciously. "What do you know about this, Copeland?"

I hesitated to respond. If I told her the truth, I feared a psych eval would be in my future and I would never see the light of day ever again. But I possessed information that could save lives; I'd be a monster to keep it to myself. Whether anyone believed me or not was immaterial. So, I spilled my guts and told the detective everything. To her credit, she sat and listened to me without immediately running to get the butterfly net. As a black woman in America, I sensed she's used to not being believed and didn't want to do that to anyone else.

"What other anxieties do you have?" she asked after I was done telling my mad little story.

"That's...not the response I was expecting," I said. "This is usually the part of the movie where the people tell me I'm crazy and try to sideline me while things get worse. Then my girlfriend and I have to fix everything by ourselves."

"New York City was just attacked by millions of highly organized rats," she replied. "Either you're right or this is the weirdest terror attack in history. I'm willing to listen; make me believe."

I told her of some of the other monstrosities that stalked my other nightmares. Not the embarrassingly gruesome stuff, but enough to make her realize we were in serious danger. She nodded and then sighed deeply.

"Okay, we weren't prepared for the rats and I know Detective Alvarez is *still* going crazy trying to solve the shark case," said Reynolds. "There's no way we can handle the stuff you just described. How is this happening and how do we stop it?"

"Well, this started with me starting my anti-anxiety pills," I shrugged. "Maybe if I stop, everything else stops too."

"Then you should stop," the detective quickly said. "Problem solved."

"No, it isn't," said Lita. "Saul was really suffering before he started taking his medication. You can't ask him to do that. It's totally not fair."

"I don't doubt he was suffering, but it cannot compare to all the deaths that have happened or all the ones that are yet to come," Detective Reynolds frowned a little. "You can't *want* this, Mr. Copeland. You can't want that kind of death and destruction on your head."

"Don't do that to him!" Lita snapped angrily. "Don't you dare try to make him responsible for the world's problems! You need to find a way to stop these monsters without sacrificing my boyfriend!"

"I appreciate you being here to advocate for him, but we might not have another choice," said Reynolds softly, trying not to come off as combative. "I just wanted you to know that. Fighting these things might not be an option; we may be better served by…just making them go away back where they came from."

"I understand," I said before Lita could protest again. "I'll stop taking the pills. It won't be a problem."

"We'll have a few more questions for you and then I will drive you home personally," said Reynolds. "And, Mr. Copeland, thank you. Most of my colleagues, most people in general, would be skeptical of your story. But I want to thank you for this, for what you're going to do, for the sacrifice you're making."

"Don't thank me yet, Detective," I said. "This may not solve anything at all."

I didn't mean to sound pessimistic, but it was that kind of day. A bunch of people were dead because of my diseased brain. I wished I wasn't like this. I wished I'd never taken those damn pills. Sometimes I even wished I had never been born at all. I tried to remain upbeat despite it all, but it was getting harder to do that.

Detective Reynolds drove us back to Lita's place. We saw people all over the street wondering how they were going to get home without the use of the trains. People were on their phones, trying to reach loved ones to make sure they were safe since most people were unaware of precisely what was going on. I had never seen such widespread pandemonium in my city, not even on 9/11. I could barely watch. I tried not to feel guilty, but it was impossible. My brain kept telling me that this was all my fault.

"I've got to get back to the station," said Detective Reynolds when she dropped us off at the front door. "You two take care."

"Thanks," I said. "You have a good night."

She nodded before leaving. Lita and I went into the apartment and closed and securely locked the door. We didn't know what to say to each other, so we just went to bed after we took our separate showers. I needed to do more than bathe the filth of the day off; I also needed to scrub my head from when the giant rat licked me. The bedroom was as quiet as a crypt, but neither of us slept. We'd seen too much. I didn't know if we'd sleep again anytime soon.

I didn't take my pill that night or the next morning or for the next two weeks as our city tried to recover from the rat attack that had killed and injured so many. I slowly went back to my old self again right before Lita's very eyes. She pretended not to notice me changing, but she couldn't hide the disappointment in her eyes. Not any more than I could hide my sadness over seeing her disappointment.

Things were peaceful for about three and a half weeks until one night there came a terrible, violent pounding on the front door. It was actually a welcome change from the silence that had settled over our relationship. I went to the front door with my heart practically leaping out of my chest while Lita stood behind me with a knife. When I finally managed to gather the courage to open the door, there wasn't a crazed killer or drug-addicted thief there. No, it was Reynolds and she looked like Hell, like she'd been put through the literal wringer.

"Oh my god!" Lita exclaimed, rushing over to the injured cop to offer assistance. "Reynolds? What the hell happened to you?"

"Copeland!" the battered detective yelled out. "Your pills! Did you stop taking them?"

"Of course!" I exclaimed. "Why? What's wrong?"

"It didn't work," she said. "There was another incident."

She collapsed in our doorway, falling unconscious and bleeding out on our floor. I immediately picked up the detective and carried her to the living room couch while Lita closed and locked the door. Upon opening her coat, I saw the wound she was bleeding from and it looked bad. Bad and also really familiar too.

"Is she okay?" Lita asked.

"I need your first aid kit, babe," I said, trying to remain steady. "We need to patch her up quick."

We patched up the deep gashes as best we could with the limited supplies at our disposal and then simply watched over her as she slept. She slept for three hours straight while we looked at all the news channels for some clue as to what might have happened to her. We were befuddled because no one was reporting anything out of the ordinary. We wondered if we should be calling the police or an ambulance.

"Shouldn't we call somebody?" she asked nervously. "I think we should call somebody. I don't want a cop to bleed to death on my couch; how would we even explain something like that?"

"She skipped over hospitals to come straight here to us," I said. "I gotta imagine there's a reason for that. Hopefully she wakes up soon so she can tell us what's going on here."

"I'm up," Reynolds groaned. "Impossible to sleep with all your worrying and fretting. How long have I been out?"

"Three hours," I responded. "Why did you come here? What happened to you?"

"My station was attacked," she answered.

"By what?" Lita asked. "The rats again?"

"A...fucking...werewolf," the detective said pointedly. "A guy got himself arrested and was brought into the station. We tried to calm him down, but it wasn't working. Someone thought to tase him and then all hell broke loose. He didn't transform slowly like werewolf in London; his human form exploded and left there was a hulking hairy beast."

"Shit!" Lita whispered as the detective described what happened. "What happened then?"

"He proceeded to slaughter us all," she explained. "All of us. Cops, criminals, witnesses, secretaries. No one was safe. I think...I'm the only one who survived."

"It looks like you barely survived," Lita pointed out. "No offense."

"Do you have any silver, babe?" I asked.

"Like bullets?" the detective raised an eyebrow.

"Doesn't need to be a projectile," I answered. "If the guy who did this to you follows you here, I want to have a weapon on hand."

"If he follows me or if *I* transform?" Reynolds asked.

I gave her a look but didn't respond. I think we understood each other perfectly. This was bad. All the way bad. A werewolf was loose in New York, possibly more than one, and had killed people. Detective Reynolds had been slashed and was now likely set to become one herself. And worse still, refraining from taking my medication did not banish the monsters back to where they came from.

I really hoped I wouldn't have to kill Detective Reynolds before this was all over. She had been pretty good to me, all things considered.

"I got this silver cake knife," said Lita, walking up beside me. "Do you really think the werewolf will follow her here?"

"They have an incredible sense of smell," I replied. "He could probably trace her all the way to Staten Island if he wanted."

"No offense, but I kinda wish you had gone to Staten Island instead of coming here," my girlfriend said.

"No offense taken," the detective smiled. "I just figured you two should have a heads-up. The attacks may not be random. The shark killed your upstairs neighbor, the rats attacked the subway you were in first, and now a werewolf attacked the police station where you gave your statement before. I bet if we look hard enough, you'll have a connection to the woman who read her husband's mind and killed him too."

"Shit," I muttered.

"If fighting and running away from werewolves is on the agenda for today, I need to change my clothes," said Lita before rushing off to the bedroom.

"So, I guess these monsters aren't going anywhere," said Reynolds after Lita was gone. "You sure you haven't used your pills?"

"I swear, Detective, I stopped taking them after the subway attack," I replied. "I wouldn't lie about that."

"Do you think...this is how the world ends?" she asked, getting introspective because of the blood loss. "All throughout my church days, they talked about Armageddon. The Final Days. Is this it? The nightmares of a frightened man loose in the world?"

"I don't know about that," I said. "Church was always too fatalistic for me, building up to an end to everyone and everything. Made people look forward to it even. That makes it too easy for people to give up and stop fighting for what we have here. So, do I think this is the end of the world? Only if we stop fighting for it."

"Making speeches like that makes me feel bad about considering killing you to end this madness," she smirked. She probably thought I'd be shocked she wanted to put a bullet in my head. "Am I gonna turn into a werewolf?"

"Yes," I nodded, "but you should keep your mind even in wolf form."

"Wait, I'll still be me?" she asked. "So why did that dude attack us like that?"

"He was out of control even in human form," I explained. "And you guys tased him. That's probably why he went on the rampage. Or he might have just been a dick."

"So, if I'm still me, this will be like a super power then?" she asked.

"Enhanced strength, speed, agility," I nodded. "Your vision and sense of smell and hearing will improve. But you'll be hungry all the time…and we're all made of meat. And if you don't mind your emotions, particularly anger, the wolf will take over."

"And if the wolf takes over?" she asked.

"Then I stab you with this cake knife," I answered.

"I guess I should be grateful it wasn't a vampire," she said. "Anything else?"

"You seem to be healing pretty fast," I shrugged. "I'm gonna change my clothes too. I don't wanna fight in my pajamas either."

I went to the bedroom and found Lita in a T-shirt, jeans, and sneakers with her hair in a ponytail. This was her Flight or Fight outfit. She thought Flight was still an option. She smiled when she saw me, crossing the room to come hug and kiss me, before heading back to the living room. I looked at the silver cake knife in my hand and then changed into my workout clothes, gray shirt and sweatpants and my most comfortable sneakers. I knew already it was going to be a long night.

"Do you see anything out there, honey?" Lita asked as I sat at the window and stared down at the street.

"Your neighbor, Dana, just smoked a blunt and fucked some dude in her car," I answered nonchalantly.

"What?" she asked in shock, racing over to the window. "Dana with the big butt? Why didn't you call me, Saul? How did she fit all that booty *plus* a man in her car?"

"Where there's a will, there's a way," I said with a shrug.

"Focus," Reynolds grunted angrily, using the same tone as a grade schoolteacher trying to settle down a rowdy, distracted class. "You said he could find me here. We need to be on guard."

"Yeah, but that doesn't mean he *will* come here," I said. "He could be ruining someone else's night right now."

"Maybe you should call...someone," Lita suggested. "Alert someone what happened."

"I was thinking that," Reynolds said, sitting up to reveal her injuries were mostly healed. "I should get going. I have a job to do. I can't let the thing that killed my partner and all those other good men and women get away. And I definitely can't let it go hurt anyone else."

"Maybe we should go with you," said Lita. "You can't fight that thing alone."

"Thanks for the offer, but I can't bring you into this," the detective shook her head.

"Lita's right," I said. "You don't have a bit of silver on you, so you won't be able to harm this guy. Not in any meaningful way."

"Nice try, Copeland," she smirked, "but I can always use my new abilities to rip his head off. Werewolf or not, he's not coming back from a decapitation."

"You're not going out there without backup," Lita frowned. "So, deputize us if you have to, but we're going."

Reynolds smiled as she walked over to the front door. It was clear that she appreciated the offer, but she was adamant about not bringing us. She may have been afraid to face the werewolf alone, but she didn't want to see us get killed like her coworkers had already been killed. She was going to try to ditch us despite Lita's insistence. I could see it already.

"I'm not going to put you two into danger like that," she shook her head before she reached for the doorknob. "It was wrong of me to even come here like this."

Just as her hand touched the doorknob, three knocks came at the door. We all fell silent as we looked at the door. Who could it have been? We didn't need to wait too long before we figured it out. Three more knocks came at the door.

"Little pig, little pig, let me in," a deep growl came from the other side of the door.

"Shit!" Reynolds cursed, stepping back from the door as she pulled her gun from her holster. "It's him."

I gripped the cake knife tight in my hand. He had found his way here and now it was time for the fight. I glanced over at Lita and my heart dropped a bit. I realized that if things went poorly, I was going to lose my girlfriend thanks to the creatures in my head.

"Little pig, little pig, let me in!" the growl grew louder.

"Get behind me," said Reynolds as she aimed her firearm at the door.

"That gun won't stop him," said Lita. "You don't have any silver bullets."

"I'll blow out his kneecaps and then take out his eyes," she explained. "We can then use the knife after that."

"Mmm, someone's a strategist," Lita whispered.

The third knock on the door was followed by the door exploding in a splinter of wood and metal. The debris pelted us all before a six-foot tall white man with stringy, dirty hair entered the apartment with a devilish grin on his face. He had completely surrendered to his animalistic nature.

"You thought you got away from me, huh, girlie?" he smiled.

"Girlie?" Lita scrunched up her nose. "Please tell me he didn't really say that."

"I'll deal with you after I rip through her, girlie," he looked over at my girlfriend. "Just wait your turn."

"Eyes on me, asshole," said Reynolds, getting the werewolf's attention again. "We're not done with our dance yet."

He started walking towards her, seemingly unafraid of the gun pointed at him. I could tell from the look on his face that he was a talker. He was going to give some stupid, villainous monologue like some of the nightmares in my brain do. I hoped Reynolds would start shooting him before he had a chance to do that.

"I've been looking for you all night, sweetie," he smirked. "You and I are definitely going to pick up right where we left off. I've been following your trail of blood all over the place. Do you know how many people got in my way from there to here? A lot. Do you know how many of them I let live? None. I'd like to think that all that blood is on *both* our hands right now."

"How long have you been a werewolf?" I asked. I wanted to stop his posturing if nothing else. "Have you always been one or did you just wake up like this some time ago?"

"Do I...know you?" he asked me, looking me up and down. I couldn't tell if he was sizing me up to see if I was much of a fight or if I was going to be too many calories for him. "You kinda look familiar to me."

"I've been around," I nodded. "Now answer the question."

"No, I wasn't always like this," he said. "And I didn't get scratched by a beast out on the moors either. I just woke up a few days ago like this. I was freaked out at first. I mean, who wouldn't be? But I figured out the rules pretty quick and I have been making the most of it."

"Have you now?" I asked.

"Oh yeah, I have," he nodded. "Do you know how much people love that animal magnetism? I've been getting so much pussy that it's gotten kinda old. Been fucking with dudes too. Gotta say, from a guy who was as homophobic as they come, it's not bad. I can see why faggots love ass so much now."

"Congratulations on letting your dick lead you to enlightenment," said Lita, rolling her eyes. "Now get the hell out of my apartment!"

"Feisty," he laughed. "Is she yours, dude, or is that little chickie *your* significant other, Detective?"

"I don't belong to anyone," Lita protested.

"You will tonight," he smirked. "One scratch and I will be your sire and you will belong to me."

"That's vampires, you idiot," said Lita in disgust.

"So, you turned into a monster overnight and you didn't go see a doctor or anything," I said. "You've just been exploiting this curse to get laid and to hurt people?"

"If I'm honest with myself, I have always been a monster," he shrugged. "I just never had power before."

"Detective, would you say this is an unusual, unprecedented case?" I asked.

"Yes," she said without looking back at me.

"So, the old rules don't exactly apply, right?" I asked.

"What are you getting at, Copeland?" she demanded. "I'm kinda busy here."

"I don't think you need him to make a move before you take the shot," I informed her.

She got what I meant after that and squeezed off three shots at the intruder's knees. Two connected, taking out the right knee. That was when our new "friend's" eyes turned bloodshot red and he bared his teeth in a mixture of pain and anger. He was going to come for us; I could tell from the way his muscles flexed in his left leg. He was going to lunge for Reynolds and try to get her gun away from her. Somehow, I could tell precisely what this maniac was going to do as though I were reading his mind. And then it suddenly dawned on me why. He came from my head, which meant that I was the best person to stop him. I was the best person to put a stop to all of this nonsense.

Our "guest" was much faster than me though, so he lunged at Reynolds and hit her with a shoulder charge that threw the detective across the apartment. He hit her so hard that I think I heard some of her ribs crack. She was thrown into the kitchen and her body was slammed into the refrigerator. Reynolds was tough though; she didn't lose consciousness from that hit. In fact, I could tell from the look on her face that she was just made all the angrier from the attack.

Lita was behind me at this point, so I wasn't too terrified for her safety. This wolf was going to have to go through me to get to my girl and I wasn't going to let that happen. She kneeled over Reynolds and tried to help her up as I kept an eye on the wolf in our midst.

"Are you all right?" Lita asked.

"Peachy keen," Reynolds answered as she struggled to get to her feet. "You and Saul should get out of here."

"We're not leaving you," my girl said. "We're in this together."

"How cute," the intruder smiled. "It warms my heart to see your little group. I'm going to enjoy this though. It's kinda like eating lamb or something like that. They're sooooo cute that you just wanna cuddle them... but then you go right ahead and eat them anyway."

"Dude, were you always this fucking sick?" I asked. "Were you like this before the whole werewolf thing or what?"

I wanted to distract him and give Reynolds time to get her bearings so she could take another shot at him. I was hoping he would be more interested in me than the one who posed a threat to him. Turned out that I was right in a way. He cocked his head to the side and examined me. He silently took stock of me much in the same way as the rat god had in the subway. I didn't like it. I could feel a shudder of revulsion, but I didn't let it show.

"Do I...know you?" he asked me, giving me a suspicious look.

"Doubtful," I replied. "Nobody knows me."

"I've seen you before," he insisted. "Where have I seen you before?"

I considered telling him that he saw me on his mama last night, but I was just trying to be a distraction. I wasn't trying to get my throat ripped out in the process. I shrugged at him instead as Lita let Reynolds lean on her shoulder. He kept looking at me with those bloody red eyes as though he thought the answer was going to magically appear written all over my face. Suddenly, his eyes lit up with recognition as he figured out where he knew me.

"I saw you in my dreams," he smirked. "The night before I turned into this, you were in my dreams."

"Great, now you're flirting with me," I said.

"Your name is Saul," he said and now everyone fell silent. No one had said my name yet, but this creep somehow knew it. "That's it, isn't it?"

"Uh, baby?" Lita called out to me. "Are werewolves telepathic in your world?"

"No," I shook my head.

"Then how does he know your name, sweetie?" she asked through gnashed teeth.

She didn't like not knowing what was going on and neither did I. All I knew at this point was that I took some pills, they made me feel good and now all hell was breaking loose. I guess when you get dire warnings from the man in the mirror, you damn well better listen to him.

"Did you do this to me?" he asked. "Is that why you were in my dream that night? Is that why you're not at all fucking surprised that a werewolf just broke into your house? Wow! So, what are you, some sort of wizard or something? A genie? A demon? Did you peer into my heart and saw that all I wanted in the world was to finally give it to people like they've always given it to me?"

"I'm just a man," I assured him. "I had nothing to do with your transformation."

"You're lying," he laughed robustly. "I can...smell the fact that you're lying. It's in the sweat. You're the one who did this. But you smell human to me; nothing special about your scent whatsoever. So how did you do it?"

I felt myself grow hot in that moment, angry that he was blaming me for all of this even as I was secretly blaming myself. I didn't want to hear him say another word, so I swung the cake knife, aiming right for his neck. I was hoping that stabbing him in the neck would end this and set things right...at least for today.

I wasn't quick enough though. He caught my wrist when the blade was just a millimeter away from his throat. The werewolf's eyes narrowed as he stared at me. He was no longer gushing over me as he stared at me like I was just another steak to be devoured.

"You shouldn't have done that," he said angrily. "I was going to shake your hand for what you've done for me, but you're just another asshole trying to hold me down. But this is fine. If you gave me these powers, you could conceivably take them away. Unless you're dead."

"Don't do this," I said, trying not to let him know how much he was hurting my wrist as he squeezed it harder and harder.

"I got to," he shrugged. "You took a shot at me; I can't allow that shit. I wonder what a god tastes like?"

"I'm not a god, dude," I said. "I'm just a guy trying to live his life."

"Well, living your life won't be an issue much longer," he laughed.

"You talk too much."

Reynolds snuck over to us and put a bullet through the werewolf's temple. He released me as he was thrown to the floor. Lita ran over to me and wrapped her arms around me as Reynolds walked over to the intruder and put some more bullets into him, all in the head.

"Are you all right?" Lita asked. "Did he scratch you?"

"No, no scratches," I shook my head. "Are you all right?"

"Nothing can take me down," she answered.

"Good to hear you're both okay, lovebirds," said Reynolds, "but this isn't over. You're still telling me only silver will kill him, right? So, I'm gonna need that knife to end this."

"Right, here you go," I nodded before I started to cross over to her to give her the cake knife. It obviously needed to be wielded by someone much faster and more trained than me.

I only managed to take two steps in her direction before our uninvited guest reacted. He got to his feet, seized the detective, and began to fight with her. They struggled throughout the apartment while Lita and I watched. They tore through the living room and the kitchen like a tornado before he slammed Reynolds's head into the fridge. While she was dazed, he turned his attention back to me.

"I didn't forget about you, buddy," he smiled. "I plan to savor you."

"Gross," Lita commented as he approached us.

"I'm afraid you're going to be fasting today, asshole," said Reynolds, grabbing him by the arm and then throwing him out the kitchen window.

Lita and I watched on in horror as the werewolf grabbed Reynolds as he fell and pulled her from the window. Time seemed to freeze for a moment, but then we were able to react by rushing over to the window and looking out.

Lita lived on the third floor, so a fall from that height could have killed a regular human being. The intruder was a werewolf now, so he was certainly going to survive the fall. I didn't know how Reynolds was going to fare. She had been scratched and was healing at a remarkable rate, but there were still a lot of unknowns to be honest.

"They're alive," Lita said, watching as they both got to their feet and squared off again. "I don't know how, but they survived."

"We need to get down there," I said.

Before we moved towards the exit, the man who stormed the apartment made his terrifying transformation. Reynolds was right. It was not like werewolf in London at all; his human form exploded just like the detective said and left nothing but an eight-foot hairy beast.

"Holy shit!" Lita cursed at the sight of it. "What the fuck, Saul?!? That's the kinda things running around in your head?"

"Not anymore," I grumbled. "Now they're loose...like the absolute worst episode of '13 Ghosts of Scooby-Doo' or something."

"Can she beat him if she doesn't transform too?" Lita asked me.

"Not a chance," I shook my head as I headed for the exit with the cake knife firmly in my fist. "Let's go."

A part of me wanted Lita to stay up here in the apartment, but I thought it might be too dangerous. The last thing I needed was for this maniac to go after her, crawl up the side of the building, while I was down on the street. I would never be able to get to her in time.

We raced down the stairs and exited the building. When we got outside, we found Reynolds doing her best to try to avoid being slashed by the werewolf. She had accelerated healing now, but she didn't want to tax it to its limits. She looked tired, out of breath, and just about ready to succumb. I knew that if we didn't intervene, this was going to be the end for her.

"Hey asshole!" I yelled out to him just as he was about to finish Reynolds. "I'm not through with you yet!"

His attention was solely on me now as he passed Reynolds and started to saunter over to me. I hid the silver knife behind my back this time, thinking that would give me some sort of advantage. I could see all the lights turn on in the apartments as Lita's neighbors looked out to see what the hell was going on. I hoped that at least one of them was calling the police or the military and not just recording my eventual death on their cellphones.

"You're determined to die tonight, huh?" he growled as he approached me. "Your life's been that bad, huh?"

"Well, it certainly ain't been no crystal stair," I found myself saying out of nowhere as he got so close I could feel the heat emanating from his huge, hairy frame. "But I'm not the one who's going to die tonight... Travis."

"So, you *do* know me after all," he smiled, a terrifying wolfish grin spreading across his wide face. He was so amused it made his snout flare in suppressed laughter.

To be perfectly honest, his name just popped into my head out of nowhere. I have no idea why I called him Travis, but I was as surprised as anyone when he revealed it was his actual name. As I stood there with him towering over me, more and more details about him started to come to me.

"You...are a postal worker," I continued speaking as more and more facts filled my mind. "Constantly being written up because of your bad attitude. Your girlfriend broke up with you two months ago. You secretly think it's because you couldn't satisfy her sexually, but it's actually because you're always so negative all the time."

I shouldn't have said that part out loud, the part about him questioning his abilities as a lover. It was a fear most men had experienced at some point in their lives, but got irrationally angry if it ever got brought up. Travis's eyes seemed to get even redder than they were before to the point where they were glowing like Rudolph's nose at Christmas.

"Shut the fuck up, little mind-reader," he growled, backhanding me across the face and sending me sailing through the air. "You don't know what the fuck you're talking about."

I found myself lying on my back on the sidewalk outside of Lita's building. The strike had certainly loosened some teeth, but I was lucky to still be alive at all. He could have easily taken my head off with his newfound strength. Or he could have decapitated me with his claws if he had decided not to use the back of his hand for his assault. Darkness was creeping in from the corners of my vision and I knew it was only a matter of time before I lost consciousness. The only thing I had going for me at the moment was that I had managed to hold onto the silver cake knife despite being hurled backwards like a ragdoll.

"Oh, I know everything about you, Travis," I said as he slowly began to walk towards me while Lita raced over to Reynolds to try to help her.

"And I got news for you. You're right. She broke up with you because you're a miserable, negative loser...who ALSO has a small dick. And that's not just me reading your mind. Heather told me all about you while I was giving her the dick she really needed."

And that was when he had enough of me and started to gallop towards me on all fours like a stallion. I needed him to get in close. My plan was to stab him in the neck while he mauled me. I, most likely, wouldn't survive, but I could guarantee that Lita and Detective Reynolds would. And hopefully, with me dead, this werewolf would be the last of my nightmares that plagued the city.

He pounced on me and brought his mouth to my face, salivating over me as he prepared to make me his next meal. He opened his jaws and prepared to bite my face off, but he hesitated. It was like something just wouldn't let him do it. Was he scared? Scared that killing me would result in him no longer having this awesome new superpower and then he would have to answer for his crimes? No, that couldn't be it. His eyes told a different story. He looked confused, like even he didn't know what was keeping him from finishing me off.

No matter, I wasn't going to miss out on this golden opportunity. I swung for his neck again with the knife, hoping to end this for good, but he was faster than me again. He caught my wrist and then slammed it back down on the pavement, almost breaking it in the process. Now the confusion in his eyes was replaced by an entirely new level of rage as he opened his mouth to eat me.

Before he could finish me off, four black blades shot through his back and out through his chest. His jaw dropped as he looked down and saw that he had been run through. I looked over his shoulder to see where the four ninjas wielding black blades came from only to discover that there was another werewolf behind Travis and it had stabbed him in the back with his massive black claws.

"Leave him alone," the second werewolf growled and I could tell that it was Reynolds. She had figured out how to transform.

"You...bitch," Travis gurgled as his lungs began to fill with his blood.

Detective Reynolds didn't want to hear that. She had been through enough for one night. She opened her jaws and bit down into Travis's shoulder ferociously. She bit down so deep that most of his neck and shoulder were gone when she finally pulled away and let his blood spray everywhere.

Travis didn't know he was dead though. He pushed Reynolds away from him and started grasping at his wounds as though he were trying to stop the bleeding. He thought there was a chance. I am sure that the thought occurred to him to run off and find somewhere to hide, just long enough for his enhanced healing to fix him. I stole that hope from him when I plunged the cake knife into his chest, stabbing him deep in his heart.

He just stared at me with a look of shock on his face with the knife stuck in his chest. Piercing his heart with silver was the death of him. He could tell it was true as he slowly began to revert back to his human form right before our very eyes. He tried to pull the knife out, but he hadn't the strength to do so; he was getting weaker from the blood loss as he bled from the bite that Reynolds had given him.

He collapsed in the middle of the street right in front of Lita's building while all of the neighbors continued to watch from their windows. He died as a man in the street, no sign of the wolf he had once been. Lita then raced over to me while Reynolds proceeded to revert back to her human form. I didn't know if she was turning human because the werewolf who transformed her was dead or if it was just the emotional shock of having to kill someone, but after a few moments, she was standing naked over Travis's body. Apparently, when she exploded into her werewolf form, it destroyed all the clothing she had been wearing too.

"Are you all right, Saul?" Lita asked as she tried to help me to my feet.

"I've...been better," I admitted honestly.

I didn't really know what to say or think. It was all a bit too much to process, so I let my mind focus on the pain instead. That cleared my mind of everything else going on. The pain seemed to subside some when Lita hugged me tight though.

"What are we going to do, Saul?" she asked me eventually.

"We're gonna wait here until the police get here and then try to explain everything to them," I answered, trying not to wince from the slap Travis gave me earlier. "And then we're going to have to find some people who can help us prevent any more monsters from showing up. I gotta tell you, that was tough, but werewolves are the least of the things that we're going to have to fight."

"I don't think we're going to be able to explain any of this," said Reynolds, limping over to us. "The only thing working for us is that most of your looky-loo neighbors recorded this all on their cellphones."

"Yeah, they're pretty useless that way," Lita commented. "Why don't you both sit here on the curb while I call the police."

Reynolds and I sat on the curb while my girlfriend pulled out her cellphone. I could tell from the silence that the detective had something to say and didn't know how to say it. I wasn't really in the mood to answer any questions right then, but I knew she was eventually going to get around to saying something.

"What's on your mind, Detective?" I asked.

"Why don't I have clothes on?" she asked me.

"What?" I asked. This was not the kind of question that I was expecting after everything we had just gone through. "What are you talking about?"

"Don't werewolves keep their clothes when they go back to normal?" she asked. "Like The Hulk with his tattered pants?"

"Sorry to break it to you, but that doesn't make any sense," I shrugged. "With a transformation such as this, you would definitely lose your clothes. I mean, you exploded into your werewolf form; why would your clothes have survived when your skin didn't?"

"Saul Copeland, you're a weirdo," she told me.

"No one knows that better than me," I nodded. "I'm...gonna lie down now. Wake me up when this is all over."

I laid down right there on the pavement and closed my eyes, hoping that when I opened them again, all of our problems would be over. I wasn't going to get my wish.

THREE
THE PROFESSIONALS

About an hour after Travis the werewolf got killed in front of Lita's apartment building, I found myself in custody with Detective Reynolds and my girlfriend. We were kept in a cell by ourselves while occasionally cops walked by and peeked in at us. I was more tired than anything else at this point and I could tell Lita was too by the way she was leaning on me with her head on my shoulder. Reynolds, however, was more of a mystery; she was sitting down with her arms crossed as she studied the faces of every officer who passed the cell.

"Are you hungry, Detective?" Lita asked sleepily.

"I'm fine," she said, not even looking at Lita. Reynolds was probably upset that she had been asked this three times already. "Why do you keep asking me that?"

"Because I'm stuck in a cell with you and I don't want you to eat me," Lita said. "You know, considering your condition?"

"Don't worry, I'll start with your boyfriend if I get a little peckish," Reynolds afforded herself a little smile.

"I'm gonna let you get that one because I'm so fucking exhausted right now," my girlfriend grumbled before she returned her head to my shoulder and closed her eyes.

While Lita got some rest, Reynolds and I kept our eyes peeled to see what was going on. The station was quiet, more quiet than it had any right being under the circumstances and more quiet than you would expect for any police station in New York City. We had been in this cell for so long that I knew for a fact that the police had to have already looked through all the cellphone footage from the fight with Travis and knew what they were dealing with. I could only imagine that no one wanted to deal with it after the incidents with the rats.

We stayed in that cell for a good hour and a half until two detectives came to collect us and escort us to a quiet interrogation room. It was weird that we were all in the room together. It definitely ran contrary to what we had seen in TV shows.

"What is this all about?" Reynolds asked the detectives, but she didn't get a response. "Hey! You can talk to me! I'm a detective too!"

The two detectives quickly exited the room and then we sat there for about five minutes before a man in a black suit showed up. Reynolds sighed and rolled her eyes in exasperation as soon as she saw him, making Lita and I think they had some sort of history with one another.

"Here we go," said Reynolds. "The Feds are here. Right after local law enforcement has already done the heavy lifting."

"Good to see you too, Roxanne," the federal agent sighed as he took a seat at the rectangular table where we were all seated. "I'm...glad that you're okay."

Reynolds dropped her arms to her sides, clearly taken aback by the agent's soft tone. This was obviously not how they usually interacted. I could see that he was showing more concern for her than he ever had in the past.

"Of course, I'm okay, Trevor," she rolled her eyes, not wanting to be seen as vulnerable in front of me and Lita. "Nothing I can't handle."

"Well, you've always been tough, but I didn't know you were tough enough to fight a werewolf with your bare hands," he smirked at her.

"So...you know," she said. "You know that..."

"That Travis Tipton was a werewolf?" he asked. "Oh yeah, that cellphone footage was pretty damn conclusive. No one is going to be doubting the veracity of that, particularly not after everything that happened with the rats in the subway. People are slowly coming to the conclusion that this is a brave, frightening new world."

"So why are we here then?" Reynolds asked. "If you were already able to tell that this was a clean kill, then why do you have us locked up here?"

"You're not locked in here," he said. "We brought you here for your protection, in case anything else might be out there looking for you."

"I'm sorry, but who are you exactly?" Lita asked. "I know you've got a real Man in Black thing going for you right now, but a name would be appreciated."

"I'm Special Agent Trevor Grimes," the black man sitting before us said, flashing a flirty smile at my girlfriend that now made me roll *my* eyes. "FBI."

"So, you're like Mulder, the guy they send when the case is weird," she said.

"He's the guy they send when they want to annoy the hell out of me," Reynolds said. "What do you know, Trevor?"

"We know that New York's vermin problem got significantly worse when they fell under the leadership of some monster rat," he replied. "And we know that you now have fought a werewolf in the middle of the street...and that you are one too."

"Travis slashed me when he attacked my station," said Reynolds. "That's when I became...like him."

"Yeah, I know," he nodded. "I saw that Christina Ricci movie too. I am...sorry about all your fellow officers. They were all good people."

"Yes, they were," she frowned, clenching her jaw so that she wouldn't show any emotion over her loss. "At least I got the guy who did that to them. What else do you know?"

"We know that the woman who killed her husband because she was able to read his mind isn't crazy," he continued. "They've been running all types of tests on her and she is the genuine article. Apparently, before she killed him, she discovered that he didn't really love her and had been tolerating her for years. All types of dark thoughts that she simply couldn't handle. We also examined the shark that ate that man in his bedroom and it's very odd."

"Odd how?" I asked.

"It's very much a shark in all aspects except that intermingled in its shark DNA is a strand of human DNA," he stated.

"Human DNA?" Lita asked. "What does that mean?"

"It's my DNA, isn't it?" I asked. "It has a bit of my DNA in it because it came from me."

"We haven't tested your blood yet, Mr. Copeland, but we think that might be true," Trevor nodded.

"So, you know?" I asked sullenly. "You know how all this happened?"

"Oh no, not a clue," he smiled, "but we're reasonably sure it started with you somehow. It would be great if you could tell us anything you know about all this."

So, I told him everything and he surprisingly listened to me just as attentively as Detective Reynolds had when I first told her. He even took notes in a pad as I told him everything. I could feel Lita rubbing my back as I related everything that had brought us here. After I was done spilling my guts, he sat back in his chair and set his pad down on the table.

"So, what do you think we should do?" Lita asked finally.

"I think we're gonna start by going to collect Mr. Copeland's therapist and see what was in those pills that she gave him," he stated. "Maybe she wasn't a doctor. Maybe she was some kind of witch. Maybe it was a demon."

"A witch or demon?" Reynolds asked in confusion.

"Sure, why not?" he asked. "If werewolves are real and sharks can materialize out of nowhere, then who is to say that demons and witches aren't real too? I think we're going to have to consider every possibility. One thing is certain though; you three have been closer to this than anyone. You're all coming with me."

We didn't stay at the police station for too long as Agent Grimes brought us with him to his office. The man was true to his word. We were sitting right there when Dr. Robinson was brought in. They had obviously found my therapist out at dinner or something; I could tell from how she was dressed. Those were "night out on the town" clothes if I ever saw them.

"Mr. Copeland!" Dr. Robinson exclaimed as she rushed over to me. "What is going on here? I was waiting for dessert to arrive when these federal agents came in and said that they needed me. Are you all right? Did you do...I mean, did something happen with you?"

"They didn't drag me out of a clocktower with a rifle if that's what you're driving at," I frowned, "but something has happened. Did you see the video of the werewolf fight in the street?"

"I got an announcement on my phone while I was at dinner, but I didn't really pay too much attention," she responded. "It was probably some amateur film crew shooting a movie or something."

"It was real, Dr. Robinson," I shook my head. "I was there. Lita and I were attacked by a werewolf."

"So...you think you were attacked by a werewolf," she said, concern all over her face. "I see. This is...very distressing. Have you suffered from any other delusions?"

"These aren't delusions, lady!" Lita protested angrily. "You think they called you down to the offices of the FBI because one of your patients went off their meds?"

"And who are you?" Dr. Robinson asked.

"Lita Ramirez," she crossed her arms over her chest in defiance. "I'm Saul's girlfriend."

"Very nice to meet you," the therapist allowed herself a small smile. "Mr. Copeland speaks of you often. But to answer your question, the FBI could very well call me down depending on what my patient does when he is off his medication."

"Well, let me put your mind at ease, Doctor," said Special Agent Grimes. "Your patient is not having delusions. There was indeed a werewolf attack. The monster is dead, but the danger is far from over."

"Okay, I'm confused," said Robinson. "You're an FBI agent and you're insisting that werewolves are real."

"Werewolves didn't used to be real, Doctor, until you gave Copeland anti-anxiety pills," said Grimes. "So, I need to know what was in those pills and what were you hoping to accomplish when you prescribed them to him?"

"Why do I feel like I am being accused of something here?" the doctor asked defensively. "I gave Mr. Copeland the pills because he was suffering from extreme anxiety and the medication was meant to ease that suffering, The only thing I was 'trying to accomplish' as you put it was helping my patient. Now instead of being a hard-ass, why don't you talk to me like a person and tell me what's really going on here?"

I explained the situation all over again. I was really getting tired of having to do that time and time again. It was nice to have so many people willing to hear me out and believe my crazy story, but I was angry that I had to tell it again and again. I wish I could just get on television and let everyone know what happened. I wanted to tell the world that I had put them all in danger and that they needed to start watching out for themselves.

"I don't believe it," she said after I was done telling her absolutely everything that happened from the moment I took my first pill to the moment she arrived here at the office. "There's got to be some kind of rational explanation for what's going on. For instance, I heard that the rat attack in the subway was actually the result of some sort of unconventional terror attack."

It actually felt pretty good to have at least one person in the mix not believe me. Things were so damned crazy in my life, I had trouble believing everything that was going on. It only stood to reason it would be difficult for others to believe too.

"We don't have time for disbelief right now, Doctor," Grimes said angrily. "I am not in the habit of practical jokes and I expect to be believed when I tell you what we're facing here. Saul Copeland started taking the pills you gave to him and now all the things he was anxious about are running amok through the streets. Now I need to know if you had anything to do with this. Did you know this was going to happen when you had him take those pills?"

"Of course not!" she protested emphatically. "Anti-anxiety medicine has never had the effect that you're suggesting and I doubt it has had that effect now. There was no werewolf, just a deranged man who thought he was one. The vermin attack was probably cooked up by ISIS or something. The woman who killed her husband because she thought she was reading his mind was obviously just picking up subtle clues of his infidelity or something and *thought* it was telepathy. There are logical explanations for everything."

"And the shark that materialized in my neighbor's bedroom and ate him?" Lita asked. "You got an explanation for that one too?"

"I don't need to explain that one, young lady, because it clearly never happened," the therapist frowned. "It's impossible."

"It did happen," said Grimes. "I can take you downstairs to the lab right now and show you the shark's carcass. We've been trying to figure the damned thing out ever since it ate its victim."

"Can I have a seat and a glass of water?" she asked. "If you give me some time, I can probably explain the shark situation too."

"Look, Dr. Robinson, no one is trying to attack you here or anything," I interjected. "We just need to figure out how to fix things before they get any worse."

"And you somehow think I have something to do with this?" she asked.

"You're as likely a suspect as anyone right now," Grimes shrugged. "We honestly don't have a good grasp on where to start this investigation, but we know these creatures are real. We know they come from this young man's head. And we know it started when you gave him the medication. So talk to us."

"It was just regular medicine meant to relieve your anxiety," she explained calmly. "Approved by the FDA and everything. People use it and are just fine every single day."

"I believe her," said Reynolds. "I don't think she had anything to do with this. I think this is just going to go down in history as one of those unexplained mysteries of the universe."

"Luckily, I don't need an explanation," said Grimes. "I just need a solution. We know these are all manifestations of Copeland's anxiety and they have been given life."

"We thought that if he stopped taking the pills, those manifestations would go away, but they haven't," Reynolds picked up the ball and ran with it. "So far, we have been fighting these things as they appear and that seems to be working. The werewolf was a tough customer, but he died. The shark died eventually because it wasn't in the ocean. The telepath is locked up."

"I'd like to find a way to fight all of these creatures all at once, send them back where they came from, instead of battling them individually as they appear," Grimes continued. "We've already seen a number of fatalities and I don't think we've even reached the worst of this yet."

"Well, assuming that what you're all saying is absolutely true and not some elaborate hoax or prank, I think the next step is clear," said Dr. Robinson. "You should run some tests on Mr. Copeland's brain and see if there is anything unusual about it, something that would explain what's happening."

I knew that what she said made the most sense, but it also worried me. I knew that it meant a bunch of people in lab coats were going to start rooting around in my brain. I didn't like it when Robinson did it figuratively, so I knew I wasn't going to like when it became literal.

They quickly arranged for a series of tests. Dr. Robinson was there for each one, overseeing everything, while Lita was there to make sure that nothing happened to me. I think we were both very aware of the fact that someone was probably entertaining the thought of just killing me to stop all of these incidents. They had to think that killing me would prevent the next disaster somehow. I wasn't so sure about that though. If getting off my medication didn't put the toothpaste back in the tube, then most likely nothing would.

The testing lasted for a week and they ultimately uncovered nothing. I was disappointed that we weren't able to get any answers, but at least for the seven days where they were testing me, no other incidents happened. The only thing that got me through it was the fact that Lita was right there with me the whole time. Reynolds stayed with me too, taking on a big sister role to make sure that nothing happened to me while I was in the care of the federal government.

"Enough is enough," Lita said eventually. "You've been testing my man for a week now and I want to know what you figured out. Are you any closer to figuring out what's happening to Saul and how we can fix it?"

Ultimately, the doctors had to admit to finding nothing, which made Lita even angrier. She had hoped that the professionals were going to have an answer for us, but I never held out hope on that. I didn't think that science was going to solve this situation. This had all the markings of something mystical at play.

"So now what" she asked. "What's the next step?"

"I'm going to need your boyfriend to make a comprehensive list of all his anxieties and the best way to combat them all," Grimes answered. "I want to be able to identify and fight these things as soon as they appear... before they have a chance to harm anyone."

"That sounds like a good idea," I nodded. "Then we can have a task force dedicated to fighting these things."

"My thinking exactly," Grimes stated.

"*Our* thinking exactly," said Reynolds. "We came up with the plan last night."

"Last *night?*" Lita asked curiously. "You two spent the evening together?"

"Grow up," Reynolds rolled her eyes. "We were discussing the case."

"Yeah, that's what Saul and I were doing last night too...in case anyone heard anything through the door as they passed by our room," she smirked.

"So, this is what we're doing now?" I asked. "No more going to work every day? I work with the federal government to hunt down monsters spawned by my brain?"

"Hopefully it pays well," my girl shrugged. "It's going to take money to repair my apartment after what that werewolf did to it."

"This is all new, but I think we can arrange a leave of absence from your jobs and even get you a paycheck as government employees," said Grimes. "You are doing us a big favor with this. Saving the world should pay well."

"It would be better if we could keep getting our paychecks from work plus paychecks from this," said Lita. "Oooh, and not have to pay taxes until this is all over would be nice too. But I guess I won't be greedy."

Lita and I were now officially a part of this task force dedicated to fighting monsters. She was excited about it, but I had trepidations. I had been fighting my demons my whole life while they were solely in my head. I didn't know if I was ready to fight them in the physical world. Task force or no, I didn't truly believe these things could be defeated. I kept those thoughts to myself though; I didn't want to bring everyone down with my negativity.

We were making plans and contingencies, strategies to keep the world safe, but we hadn't even gotten halfway through my list of anxieties before the next attack happened. Luckily, it was something that we had prepared for already. Just because we knew what we were dealing with though didn't mean that we were going to have an easy time of it.

"So, this is the team?" I asked as we geared up that morning.

Lita and I had been relocated to a facility where we would always be on call. Reynolds had been moved there too even though she protested against it. Grimes insisted that time would be of the essence no matter what we were dealing with so he couldn't waste any by trying to collect us from different locations. I guessed that made sense, but I wonder how much of his decision hinged on the fact that he wanted to keep an eye on us? After all, Reynolds was a werewolf now and who knew what other shit was going to spring from my brain at any moment. Were we all under his watchful eye because we were assets or potential threats?

"I have a dozen agents already securing the scene and waiting for us to get there," Grimes responded. "I figure that should be enough for us to get the job done. Unless you think we're going to need more backup?"

"Not if it's the creature we identified," I answered.

"So far none of your anxieties have teamed up with each other so we don't really have any reason to believe they're doing so now," said Grimes. "But I am not opposed to calling in backup. After all, this is all uncharted waters for us right now."

"Then let's call in another dozen agents," I said. "Better to be safe than sorry."

"I agree with you," he nodded and then proceeded to call in another *two* dozen agents.

I had to admit that I really liked Agent Grimes. Over the last few weeks of putting things together, we had gotten to talk frequently. He seemed like a really good dude. He wasn't just interested in my anxieties and how to combat them, he wanted to know how I developed each one as well. He seemed to take a genuine interest in me.

An hour and a half later we were outside a small park in Staten Island. I counted myself lucky that I didn't have to take the ferry to get there. I don't do well on boats. I am deathly afraid of the water. Fish and shrimp are fine for eating, but I get shivers thinking about what other kinds of monsters reside in those murky depths. Our inability to breathe water should be all the evidence we need that we do not belong in the oceans.

"Now we've had sightings of it, but luckily no fatalities yet," said Grimes upon our arrival. "That's a very good thing. We should be able to wrangle it and take it down without getting anyone hurt."

"Are you planning to take it alive?" I asked.

"We were hoping to capture it and run experiments on it, hopefully find a way to put an end to all this," Grimes answered.

"I'd rather you kill the damn thing," I commented.

"And I would rather the people back at the lab have something to experiment on rather than you," he said. "Don't worry though. We're taking every precaution here."

I nodded as though I were in agreement, but I wasn't. I thought that none of these monsters should be allowed to live. I thought that they each represented a threat too great to our continued survival. And I wasn't entirely convinced that these things wouldn't start working together at some point. I had to stop thinking negative thoughts though; I couldn't afford to create more fears that we would have to fight later.

"Let's get this over with," I said eventually. "The longer we wait, the more chances that thing will have to harm someone."

"And you're sure that you evacuated the park of all civilians?" Lita asked.

"We did our best, but nothing is ever a hundred percent," he told us. "So, let's move."

We entered the park after that. Lita and I had weapons, but no guns. We weren't trained for that and no one wanted to give us that kind of firepower. But there are things in this world other than guns. I picked an aluminum baseball bat as my weapon of choice; it's the weapon I keep beside my bed at night when I sleep, so it was something I felt comfortable wielding.

Lita opted not to use a baseball bat, but she did take a stun gun with her plus a combat knife. She revealed that she had archery experience, so Grimes let her have a crossbow and a quiver full of arrows as well. If not for the crisis we were currently facing, how long would it have been before I realized I was dating a sexier version of Artemis?

I just hoped that these weapons were going to be enough to protect us if things went sideways. Common sense told me that we were probably going to be fine. We were surrounded by highly-trained men and women with weapons who were going to be the first line of defense if anything went wrong. Common sense said that Lita and I would probably not even get anywhere near this creature we were seeking. But I still felt a sense of dread. Somehow, I knew I was going to come face to face with another of my nightmares.

"How are you feeling, babe?" Lita asked me as we ventured through the quiet park.

"I've had better days," I admitted.

"Well, don't worry yourself," she said. "We're gonna finish this off and then head back home. We can order some pizza or something."

"That sounds good," I nodded. "Let's get this over with. I can't believe this is our lives now."

She was adjusting well to this new lifestyle, but I certainly wasn't yet. I was in a constant panic of Grimes coming to me to tell me of the new monstrosity we would need to go fight. Because none of my anxieties were small, harmless things; they were each something that had plagued me for years and I knew none of them would be overcome easily. If they were easy to overcome, wouldn't I have done that already?

Everything felt wrong that day. I mean, it could have been because we were in Staten Island and things never feel right when I'm there, but I doubted it. Everything felt like it was out to get me today, but honestly, it always felt like that to me. Everything was so quiet and still; there wasn't even a breeze blowing through the park.

"How are you doing, babe?" Lita asked me as we walked.

"Something doesn't feel right about this whole thing," I answered. "I just have a really bad feeling."

"No offense, babe, but don't you always have a bad feeling about things?" she asked, flashing me a smile that made me feel a little better about things.

"Very cute," I smirked.

"That's my specialty," she shrugged. "Cute all day and twice on Sundays. Look, we'll just catch or kill whatever little beastie is here in the park and then head back home. No fuss, no muss."

"Okay," I nodded. "No fuss, no muss."

Grimes and Reynolds were with me and Lita the whole time. No one expected us to really fight anything; we were more consultants than fighters. Grimes considered us part of his team, but he was very well aware of the fact that he needed to keep us alive. The thought process was that if I died, there was no one left to help them combat these manifestations. I am sure that some people had given thought to the possibility that my death was the solution we were all seeking in the first place, but Grimes didn't seem to subscribe to that theory. At least, not yet.

The creature we were hunting was a low-level concern, well, as low-level as any psychic manifestation of fear come to life possibly could be. I referred to it as The Possu, but I didn't know much about it. It was just a small brown creature, maybe a little bigger than a rabbit, with huge, huge eyes. My cousin's baby used to talk about this thing all the time and the family thought it was great. They were thrilled by the imagination on this little baby, but with each new story she came up with, all I could think about was where did these tales ACTUALLY come from? Was this something she had dreamt up, something she had seen, something from another world that only her little baby senses could detect? I was all at once fascinated and terrified by The Possu.

Eventually the baby grew up and didn't remember the stories of this fantastical creature, but I never forgot those tales. For me, The Possu existed right there in the corner of my eye, right where I couldn't see it or really perceive it, but it was there all the same. I imagined it to be a mischievous little imp, but I was not one for mischief of any kind.

It had been sighted here in this park, but it took a while for us to realize what we were dealing with. Most people who came across it thought it was just a weird little animal; New York had been seeing all types of little critters lately that weren't really indigenous to the city. The thing that finally tipped off our task force was all the people who reported that the thing walked on its hindlegs and laughed like...a human infant. After the events with the rats, this freaked people out enough to call someone. That call eventually came to us.

The perimeter of the park was closed so we knew it had to be in here somewhere. All we needed to do was track it down, put it in a cage, and bring it back to base. Some part of me couldn't wait for the moment, after we learned everything we could from the Possu, where we would kill it. I don't care how cute this thing may appear to be, I wanted to see it die screaming.

"Tell me again about this thing," Lita stated, breaking me from my thoughts. "What does it look like again?"

"Deceptively cute," I answered. "About two feet tall or so with black fur all over its body. It has the biggest, most expressive eyes you'll ever see. Like a puppy or a kitten or something like that."

"Sounds adorable," she said. "How can something like that be dangerous?"

"Anything can be dangerous," I replied. "In fact, the more innocent something looks, the more likely we are to lower our guard. That's when they get you."

"So should I have been extra cautious of you because of how cute you are?" she teased, trying to put my mind at ease about this whole thing.

"Women are constantly being killed by their lovers, so it wouldn't have hurt you to be a little more cautious," I answered. "It wouldn't hurt anyone to be a little more cautious about everything, truth be told."

She rolled her eyes and grunted her disapproval at my response. It wasn't what she wanted to hear. She wanted her words to change me, make me better, but that's not how it works. When you have anxiety, or any other mental disorder really, your loved ones just want you to get over it. They think they can just say a few words and your brain will simply...change for them. Maybe they just want you to stop suffering, but it *feels* like they just want to stop dealing with the fact that you're different. I ignored it and tried to give her a smile to put her at ease, but I'm not sure if it actually worked.

"I have a good feeling about today," she commented as we walked through that park, looking for our quarry so we could stop it before it could cause any trouble. "What could possibly go wrong on such a beautiful day?"

"I hope you're right, Lita," I said, trying really hard not to make a list of all the things that could go wrong on such a beautiful day.

For the longest time, the search turned up just about nothing. It was almost like it was a false alarm. I would have preferred it that way to be honest because then this would just be a pleasant walk through the park. Sure, a Staten Island park, but a park nonetheless. The thing though is that I don't really believe in false alarms; everything is something to be worried about in this world. I lived a life of constant vigilance because I always expected everything to go wrong at any given moment.

It took a while before we found anything and some of the soldiers started to get a little antsy. After the attack in the subway, everyone was on edge, including our armed forces. They signed up to defend us from serious threats and they were finally facing the greatest one the planet had ever seen...and now it was hiding somewhere. They wanted to be useful, particularly after the feeling of impotence we all felt when an attack happened.

"So is that the guy?" I heard one of the soldiers grumble, thinking he was out of earshot. "The big brain who knows all about this stuff?"

"Got to be," his buddy replied. "He's the weakest consultant I've ever seen, so he must be the analyst or something."

I didn't particularly care for how they were talking about me, but I let it go. Best not to antagonize people with guns, especially if the trouble they were going to be facing was all my fault. Eventually, Lita and I ventured into a shady area of the park with four of the soldiers by our side. When we got there, I thought I heard a sound and came to a stop.

"What's the matter?" Lita asked, noticing me looking around the area.

"We've got to keep going," one of the soldiers barked. "We've got a job to do."

"Something isn't right," I said, trying to tune out everyone so I could figure out what that sound was I was hearing.

"We gotta keep moving!"

"Hold on!" Lita exclaimed. "I think he heard something!"

I had definitely heard something, but with all the people yelling and going back and forth, I was having a hard time figuring out what it was. I craned my neck and strained my ears as I continued to listen and then it quickly became all too clear what it was. It sounded like wooden planks about to give way and buckle, like when you're standing on a floor about to collapse.

"Oh no," I whispered, but it was too late for me to say or do anything else.

The ground beneath our feet gave way and we fell into a giant, gaping maw. It felt like we would never stop falling, but eventually I hit the ground. A fall from such a height probably should have killed us, but we landed in thick liquid. It could have been mud, but my mind told me it was a pond of feces instead. I could tell from the grunts and groans around me that the others had survived the descent as well, but I couldn't see anybody. It was so dark down in that hole. The darkness seemed to be writhing around me like it was alive, like it was an entity unto itself that delighted in its newest meal.

"Lita!" I called out. "Lita, are you all right?"

"I've definitely been better, Saul, but I don't think anything's broken or anything," her response came out of the darkness. "Where are you?"

"Follow my voice," I instructed her as I reached for one of the three flashlights I always carried on me.

The first flashlight was busted, probably damaged from the fall, but the second one was fine. I turned it on and started to look around while continuing to talk to Lita. I was giving her a beacon to find her way towards. It was, I suppose, a beacon for any of the soldiers who had fallen into the pit with us as well. Eventually, everyone was huddled around me with their flashlights. The troops set up a perimeter around Lita and me quickly and set up giant searchlights around us. They had complained about having to carry so much equipment, but they quickly became grateful I had suggested the searchlights in the first place. We ultimately ended up wishing for the dark to return.

"Where the hell are we?" Lita asked. "This doesn't look like a subway or sewer. What the hell is this chamber doing underneath the park?"

"Doesn't look natural," one of the soldiers commented as he looked around. "Looks like someone just built this chamber and filled it with gunk."

"I don't think this is simple 'gunk'," I said, kneeling to get a closer look at the thick, crimson liquid sloshing around our ankles. "It looks and smells like blood. Old blood."

"How do you know what old blood smells like?" my girlfriend asked.

"He's right, ma'am," one of the troops stated. "I recognize the smell. Everyone keep your head on a swivel. I think we might have located the nest of the thing we've been hunting for."

"I have the sneaking suspicion that we didn't so much find this nest as we fell into the creature's trap," I commented as I looked up to see just how far we had fallen. "Call for help on your radio. We're going to need to get out of here as fast as possible."

They put out the call for assistance, but I kept looking around to see what was in the darkness with us. The blood was sloshing around our feet, but it could have been from us moving about. It said nothing of potential predators. I took my flashlight and looked around our feet and I saw nothing but the pool of blood. There was nothing there, nothing swimming around and waiting for its chance to pull us under. So where was the creature who set this trap?

"Are you okay, baby?" I heard Lita ask as she reached out and touched my arm. "You're being really quiet."

"We're in trouble," I responded. "Big trouble. Especially if we can't find out what built this trap. It's either here right now or it's going to come back."

"Shit," she cursed. "Maybe...maybe we can find a way to climb out of here or something?"

"Best just to stay put until someone responds to our distress call," said Private Cobb. "We don't want to venture off and get picked off one-by-one."

And then we heard the scurrying, soft and distant, but definitely there. We all got quiet and began looking around, but we could only see as far as our lights could illuminate and that wasn't very far enough for us to see the entirety of the chamber. The fear was palpable as we stood there looking for the source of the noises. It was only going to be a matter of time before these highly-trained, armed men would start firing into the darkness, wasting their ammunition before the real threat even revealed itself.

"Don't fire your weapons," I said firmly. "They're trying to scare you so that you use all your bullets for nothing. We just need to stay together and not take any shots until we actually see what we're up against."

It was sound advice, but I had no idea if anyone was going to listen to me or not. I didn't outrank anybody in that pit. I just hoped an actual authority figure would show up to give orders that would ultimately save us before it was too late. They listened for a while, even though they definitely didn't have to listen to a thing I had to say, but the longer we were down there, the more uneasy everyone got.

"Why won't they show themselves?" Private Bracken yelled. "Why are they fucking with us?"

"Keep your cool," I exhaled. "That's what they do. They want you to lose your shit so that they can take you easier. As long as we stand right here, keep our eyes open and watch each other's backs, we are going to be just fine."

"How do you know so much about these things?" Bracken asked me.

"I'm...a cryptozoologist," I lied.

"Like those guys who hunt Bigfoot and shit?" Cobb asked.

"Yeah," I nodded as Lita frowned at me. "Just like that. We're gonna be okay."

We might have been okay if the others arrived in a timely fashion to save us, but they didn't. It was becoming apparent that the radio signals from their walkies couldn't get out of the pit we had fallen into. It must have been like trying to make a phone call from your reinforced basement or something. If we were going to survive, we might have to start looking out for ourselves, but I wasn't ready to make that call yet. The park was full of our people; someone had to run across us eventually.

"How long are we going to stand out here?" Bracken asked eventually. "We can't just do nothing!"

They were going to freak out eventually and try to get out of there. I knew that they were going to need to feel like they were accomplishing something, taking their own fate into their hands. Their training taught them to believe in their own power and that left them with the desire to never feel powerless no matter what the situation. Some of us, though, felt powerless in the face of things all the time, so this was no different than a normal day.

"We can't just stay here hoping for a rescue," said Cobb coolly. "These creatures were spotted topside so there must be a way out of here. We're going to find it, get the others and firebomb the shit out of this whole area like we should have done right from the start."

"I cannot express in words how bad that particular idea is," I stated. "You're suggesting we venture into the darkness and hope we're heading in the right direction. You're also hoping that whatever opening they use to get to the surface is large enough for all of us to fit through. I don't know if those are assumptions I'm willing to bet my life on."

"Well, I'm the ranking officer here, so it's my decision to make," he said.

"I really think you should listen to him," Lita spoke up, fear creeping into her voice as she mulled over the idea of venturing out into the darkness. "I mean, what's the point of bringing along an expert with you if you're going to just ignore him and wing it?"

"I think we're going to be fine without the counsel of a cryptozoologist, ma'am," said Bracken dismissively. "We've trained for this and we're going to be fine."

I knew, without a doubt, that these soldiers were going to get themselves killed in a way too gruesome to even think about and I knew that I didn't want to be there to see it. In that moment, I knew something else too: I couldn't let their foolishness get Lita killed. That left me with only one option.

"I'm staying right here," I said, crossing my arms over my chest defiantly.

"Excuse me?" Cobb asked. "Are you defying orders?"

He was angry that I didn't just go along with what was decided. His was a life of following orders, listening to authority, or people would lose their lives. I saw things from a different perspective. I hadn't served in the military or law enforcement like my cousins, so I wasn't apt to run headlong into oblivion just because someone told me to. I wasn't keen on endangering myself *or* my girlfriend.

"I'm not in Uncle Sam's army and I didn't sign up to go through a meat grinder," I replied. "I'm going to stay right here where it's relatively safe."

"Meat grinder?" Private Poole spoke up nervously. "That sounds bad. Maybe we should listen to him, Cobb."

"Listen to him?" Cobb smirked. "The man's spent his whole life chasing after the Loch Ness monster and the damned Chupacabra and shit! He's of no use to anybody! Just another damned coward."

"Coward or not, our mission is to protect him and his girlfriend," said Poole. "We can't just leave him here."

"Fine, Poole," said Cobb dismissively. "You stay here with...the consultants. We'll be back with help shortly."

Lita and I stood there with Poole as Cobb, Bracken, and Matthews walked off into the darkness. I thought we would never see them again, all things considered. We watched the lights from their flashlights travel further and further away until they were completely consumed by the darkness. I shook my head as they disappeared from sight.

"What now, Saul?" Lita asked, touching my arm tenderly. "There's only three of us now. That makes us much more of a target than before."

"We're okay for now," I answered. "We're here with a light source. There's liquid all around so if they come for us, we will definitely hear them."

"And when they do come for us, do you think we can fight them off?" Poole asked.

I didn't have an answer for him right away. Could we fight them off? I didn't know. Lita and I weren't trained combatants and didn't have any firearms on us. Poole was the only soldier left and I had no clue how many clips he had for his assault rifle, but judging by the size of the trap we fell into, I had to believe we had several enemies we would need to fight off. So, no, I didn't have much faith in us fighting them off, but I didn't want to tell him that. I didn't want to share that info with Lita either; I scarcely wanted to acknowledge it myself.

"We need to stop asking questions and just keep our eyes peeled," Lita interjected. "There's no telling how long we'll have to wait before someone comes for us."

She had my back and I was grateful. It made me believe I was actually making the right decisions here. I really needed that because I was in no way confident in my choices. I knew what we were dealing with, of course, since it was a product of my own mind, but it was still a mysterious creature that could change its tactics on a whim if it wanted to. I hoped that I would be able to live up to the faith that she had in me.

We were only down there for another twenty minutes or so before people showed up above us. It was Grimes, Reynolds, and a few other soldiers with them. They assessed our situation immediately and started getting devices that could extract us from the pit. That was essentially when everything started to fall to shit. Our quarry (or were we *their* quarry?) must have seen that we were trying to escape their snare and they decided that it was time to strike.

"What's that sound?" Lita asked as they set up a crane and winch above us.

"Hopefully it's the sound of us getting out of here shortly, ma'am," Poole smiled as he stared upwards at the work being done above us.

"No, not that," she shook her head, frowning at the fact that she had once again been called 'ma'am' during this expedition. "It's coming from down here. Maybe the others are coming back?"

"Good," said Poole. "We can all get out of here together then."

Cobb soon came into view, just at the edge of the radius of light we had around us. He seemed hesitant to come any closer. He had a weird smile on his face as he stood there. Not sure what he was so pleased about since he was so upset when he left us. That smile on his face made me nervous right away. Nothing that followed made me feel any better.

"Hey Poole!" Cobb called out. "You should have come with us. You really missed out."

"Missed out on what?" our escort asked. "We're about to get out of here."

"You need to come over here and see this," he said. "It'll only take a minute."

I don't know what it was about Cobb in that moment that made me feel uneasy, but I knew we all should stay as far away from him as possible. Just as Poole was about to walk over there, I grabbed him by the arm. He looked over at me with questioning eyes and I just shook my head.

"Come on, Poole," Cobb called out. "What's keeping you?"

"Don't go over there," I said.

"Why not?" the soldier asked me.

"Something is wrong with him," I answered. "I don't know what it is, but something is different about him now."

"Poole, get over here and take a look at this!" Cobb yelled out angrily. "That's a direct order!"

Cobb sounded very mad when he gave that order, but the pleasant smile never left his face. His words, emotions, and facial expressions were not matching up like they should have. Poole and Lita spotted that too this time. Now all three of us were on the same page that something was wrong with Private Cobb.

"Why don't you come over here into the light?" I called out to him. "Let us get a good look at you."

"You're being weird, buddy," said Cobb. "I need you to come over here, Poole. It's really important."

"Don't do it, Poole," I warned him, slightly shaking my head. "I don't know what happened to him, but he didn't come back right."

Poole didn't want to believe me at first, but he cast a glance over at Cobb and felt the same kind discomfort I was feeling at the moment. Lita yelled for Reynolds to rescue us. They were attaching a platform to the crane that could be lowered down to lift us out of the pit. Like a barebones, makeshift elevator. It was taking some time to rig it up, but they assured us it would be ready in no time. I was under the impression we had less time than even that.

"What's over there, Cobb?" Poole called out, panic slipping into his voice. "Where's the others?"

"You need to come see," he replied. "You'll see the others too when you come over here. I can't explain it. You need to see it, Poole."

They were trying to lure us into the darkness and that couldn't be good for any of us. Poole kept talking to Cobb while Lita kept yelling for them to lower the basket to get us out of the pit. I needed my voice to be the only voice Poole listened to though. I wasn't trying to lose the only armed guard Lita and I had left.

"Come take a look at this, Poole, and bring the others with you," said Cobb, a little more insistently but with the same broad smile on his face. "You all need to see this."

"Listen to me, soldier," I said sternly, my tone changing so harshly that Poole turned to look at me. "If we go over there, we're going to die. I don't know what happened to them, but they've come back wrong. Or maybe the creatures are assuming their shape or something. I don't know. I just know that we're doomed if we walk over there into the darkness."

Poole's face tightened after that, like he forced his fears down to where most people keep their fears throughout the day, and then he aimed his rifle at Cobb. He ordered him to come into the light, demanded that he show himself. The basket started to lower towards us, but all I could focus on was the shrug that Cobb gave us and the creepy smile that stayed plastered on his face.

When Cobb finally stepped fully into the light, we all knew how much trouble we were in. Poole and I saw it first because we were looking in his direction while Lita only seemed concerned with the basket that was coming towards us. She looked over when she heard the silence though.

"What the fuck is that?" she asked, squinting in Cobb's direction. "What is that...*on* him?"

It was the Possu. When Cobb stepped into the light, we saw a small brown creature on his back, it's head visible over the soldier's shoulder. It looked like a monkey from a distance, but as Cobb got closer, we saw the differences. The Possu may have been the same size as a monkey, but its eyes were much larger, like the size of saucers. Its mouth was full of razor-sharp teeth that looked like they rip through bone with ease. Its fur was black and crimson.

The scariest thing about the creature didn't become apparent until Cobb shambled closer and closer. It was the monster's claws. It had driven them into Cobb's back and the back of his head. That's when I figured out precisely why it was trying to lure us all into the darkness.

"It's controlling him," I uttered. "It accessed his nervous system so it could drive him like its own personal car. That's why he was calling us over there; the monster had command over his vocal control."

"What?" Poole asked in disgust. "It can do that?"

"Apparently," I nodded.

"Is he dead?" Poole asked. "Did that monster kill Cobb or is he still alive like that?"

I told him I didn't know, but in all honesty, a part of me believed Cobb was still alive. His brain had to still be functioning for the Possu to be able to control him that well. I didn't think it was proper to let him know that though. Poole already seemed to be freaking out and I didn't need for him to have a full meltdown before we got out of the pit.

"Stop right there!" Poole yelled angrily as he aimed the rifle at Cobb as he continued to walk towards us. "Freeze or I will be forced to fire!"

He felt like he needed to give a warning, but I would have been okay with him opening fire right away. I didn't want that creature any closer to us than it already was to be quite honest. I didn't know what this thing was capable of beyond usurping a human's will. I had no intention of finding out what those claws and teeth were able to do. I looked up to see how close that basket was and it was still woefully far away.

"Shit!" I cursed before looking over at Poole. "Shoot it. You're gonna have to shoot it before it gets any closer."

"Are you crazy?" he asked. "I might hit Cobb."

"Cobb is already dead," I said fiercely. "That monster is just using his body like a puppet right now to try to kill the rest of us. You need to destroy it before it gets over here!"

"You said you didn't know if he was dead or not!" he protested.

He clearly didn't want to do it, not wanting to fire on his fellow soldier, but the longer he hesitated, the more danger the rest of us were all in. I pleaded with him to do what needed to be done before we all died. Thankfully he listened, even if it was at the very last minute. The burst of gunfire was so loud that it scared the shit outta Lita and me when it erupted from the rifle.

The bullets tore through Cobb and pushed him backwards, but he remarkably stayed on his feet. That was terrifying because nothing should have been able to stay upright after being struck that many times. There was a moment of silence then as shock overtook us. I guess we all kinda figured that the rifle would work. Poole tried again, sending bullets ripping through Cobb's flesh once more. The injured soldier stopped in his tracks this time, but he didn't fall down into the crimson muck around our feet.

"You need to lift us outta here right not!!!" Lita yelled up to the people operating the crane. "Come on!"

We watched as the creature on Cobb's back stared right at us angrily.

I spotted what happened before anyone else. One of the bullets had struck the Possu through the human shield it had been using. It was injured and I could see blood gushing from one of its four arms.

"An animal is at its most dangerous when it's injured," I commented, not really sure to whom, but needing to be heard all the same.

That's when the screaming started, the most blood-curdling cry to ever be heard by human ears and it was erupting both from the Possu and his mangled puppet, Cobb. The pitch kept getting higher and higher until our ears started to bleed like our eardrums were on the verge of bursting or something. We tried covering them with our hands, but it didn't help. The whole damned cavern seemed to be amplifying the sound and making it worse. The cavern shook around us so bad, it felt like the whole place was going to collapse on top of us.

"What the hell is it doing?" Poole asked, trying to be heard over the din made by the Possu. "Why is it doing that?"

I didn't have an answer for him. This creature may have come out of my head, but it was still as much a mystery to me as it was to anyone. Besides these monsters being dangerous and the fact they wanted to hurt us, I knew just as little as my military entourage. Ultimately, I just assumed it was hurt and that it was screeching in pain.

Before long, Cobb rushed towards us like an angry bull, but while his lower limbs moved with strength and determination, his upper body flopped about with no agency whatsoever. Poole fired off a few more shots, but it didn't matter because he was upon us before we could think. Cobb slapped Poole across the face and threw him down, smiling as the soldier fell into the liquid sloshing around our feet.

Cobb went for Lita next, but I instantly stood in the way. I reacted on instinct, not even realizing how afraid I was of the monster that had taken control of Cobb's body. I locked eyes with the soldier and I found myself facing an all-new fear. I could tell from how his wide eyes were quivering, that Cobb was still alive in there; The Possu hadn't killed him at all, just usurped his will and took over his body.

"Shit," I mumbled as I realized the truth. "I'm sorry."

Cobb dropped to his knees, his jaw hanging down like he was trying to catch his breath or something. His body had been pushed past the limits it should have been and I think he would have been happy to just finally keel over and die after it all was said and done. When he finally fell forward into the muck, I don't know which one of us was more relieved.

My relief was short-lived though because The Possu cast its giant eyes on Lita after it had already used up its previous host. It wanted her to be its next host and I couldn't allow that to happen. I didn't know what would happen when I got in the way though. Was the plan to fight it off, despite the fact that I knew that a handful of soldiers had already failed to do so? I was probably just going to get Lita and myself killed, but there was no way I was prepared to just do nothing.

At first, it was like tangling with a raccoon or something. It was like I had gone to take out the trash and a raccoon had jumped out of the can and was attacking me because I was invading its space. I grabbed it by the abdomen when it lurched at me and tried to hold it at a distance while it tried to claw at my face.

"Stop it!" I shouted as those huge, saucer-like eyes narrowed at the sight of me. "Leave me alone!"

Lita tried to come to my aid as the basket finally was lowered enough for us to be rescued, but I pleaded for her to keep her distance. I didn't want this creature to come anywhere near her, not after what I had seen it do to Cobb. I should have been equally concerned about myself though because it soon broke free of my grasp and started scurrying all over me. I couldn't believe anything was capable of moving that fast, but it was like it was touching every single part of my body all at once. I hated it. It immediately made me recall the time I took out the trash and a rat jumped out of it and ran across my body; to this day, I cannot forget the feeling of those little claws on my skin as it used me as a ladder to get itself down to the ground.

And then The Possu made it to my back and sunk its claws into my spine, taking control of my nervous system immediately, just as it had done to poor Cobb. Now I was trapped inside my own body, just as I imagine he must have been. I could see everything the Possu was doing with my body though, like I was a passenger and it was in the driver's seat.

"Oh no," I said, but the creature wouldn't let those words come out of my mouth. It had other plans for its new ride.

I watched as my hand reached out and grabbed Lita's wrist. It must have been a rough move based on the shocked, pained look on her face. I immediately tried to regain control, free my girlfriend before anything could happen to her, but that was easier said than done. It felt like I was trapped in a giant spiderweb and the more I struggled for control of my body, the more stuck I became. It was hard to breathe. The Possu kept things running in such a way that oxygen was still coming in, but I felt like I was suffocating.

The possessed (is that even the right way to describe it?) version of me was pulling Lita away from the basket and into the darkness, towards the same area where Cobb had returned from. I prayed that Poole would stop this before it was too late, that he would see I was not in control of myself and would do whatever was necessary to save her. I tried to smile when I saw Poole jump into action and try to stop Lita from being pulled off into the darkness. I don't know if the smile ever made it to my actual face, but I did try.

My elation was short-lived when I saw The Possu use my free hand to start strangling Poole. Was the monster capable of making me stronger or did I always possess this level of strength? Were all humans secretly this strong when you removed their apprehension and inhibitions? It was an interesting question, but I couldn't focus on that when the woman I had come to love was in so much danger. I cheered for Poole to win as I watched everything from my peculiar vantage point, but he had just as much trouble freeing himself as Lita. Hell, I wasn't doing so well freeing myself either.

It looked like we were all going to die down there in that pit, just a few steps away from the basket that would have hoisted us up and out to freedom. I figured that this mission was going to get me killed. I felt that as soon as Lita told me about her neighbor being killed by the shark in his bedroom, but I felt really bad about getting her involved in all of this. She didn't deserve to die just because she knew me and didn't run off screaming when she found out how much of a mess I really was.

"Let her go!" I yelled inside my own mind, hoping it would get The Possu's attention somehow.

I struggled against the metaphorical webs that were holding me in place and soon they became a lot less metaphorical. I found myself in an actual spiderweb suspended above the floor while hundreds, or maybe thousands, of those Possu stared up at me like I was their lunch. There was something about their large eyes that were scarier than the claws and teeth and their ability to control a man's body, for me at least.

"Hey, fellas," I stated as they looked up at me. "I don't suppose you'll help me get down from here and then give me back control of my body?"

They didn't answer, which was expected. I didn't think they were really capable of human speech anyway. They just watched as I hung there, a prisoner in a place that I should have had complete control over. The very thought of it was starting to make me angry until I felt the web start to move. I couldn't quite move as much as I wanted, but I was able to adjust my head to look above me and that's when I saw a large black shape moving around in the darkness above me.

"Shit," I cursed.

I'm not one of those people who suffer from arachnophobia or anything like that. Spiders and other creepy crawlies only really bother me under very specific circumstances. One of those circumstances is when they are large enough to make me their prey. Unless my eyes were completely deceiving me, the spider that was stealthily moving in the shadows was about the size of a family van.

"This isn't real," I commented, but I could not look away from those shadows. I needed to see what was coming for me. "This can't be real."

It was real enough to make the web I was stuck to shake more and more violently as the spider drew closer and closer. I tried struggling again, but I wasn't any closer to getting free. I gave up on that...until the spider finally revealed itself. A normal spider would have been terrible enough, but that was not what I was finally confronted with.

"Fuck!" I exclaimed just under my breath.

The spider wasn't normal. It had the eight long legs and the large bulbous body just like most of its kind, but this one had something more. Something that made me want to tear free from this web and start running off into the night forever. Instead of the usual face with the monstrous mouth and the eyes of a cold-blooded predator, it was my face there.

This was too much for me. I hate when body parts are in the wrong places or when there are more body parts than there should be. If I see people with eleven fingers instead of ten, I freak out and have to excuse myself immediately. A human face on the body of a spider, or any other freakish mismatch like this, is one of my greatest fears and it was now looking at me...with my own eyes.

"Hello Saul," the spider eventually spoke, right when I was convinced it was going to tear me apart. "Looks like you've got yourself into quite the predicament here."

I recognized the voice as mine, but I recognized the tone as someone else. It sounded like the me I saw in the mirror, the one that tried very hard to convince me not to take the anti-anxiety medication. He hadn't come here to eat me; he had come here to gloat over the fact that he was right. I couldn't tell which fate would have been worse.

"You look like you got yourself an upgrade of sorts," I commented. "Or is this how you always look when you're not in the mirror?"

"You're trying to be brave," he said. "That's good. Use that strength. I don't need you passing out before I tell you everything you're going to need to know."

Before long, I found myself being lowered to the floor where an army of The Possu were waiting for me. They didn't seem the slightest bit interested in ripping me apart though, so maybe I was safe for the time being. The giant spider seemed to be in charge of things here, so maybe I was given a reprieve until the arachnid was through monologuing. I don't know. It didn't take long for the spider to land right next to me.

"I understand you want to show me something, but can you...shift your form a bit?" I asked. "I'm liable to listen to you a little closer if you, you know, didn't look like a fucking nightmare."

"What form would you like me to take?" it asked. "Something like this?"

The Spider soon transformed in the blink of an eye into a perfect reproduction of Lita. I shivered at the sight of it because I could still feel the malevolence coming off it even though it now looked like my girlfriend. I simply shook my head and watched it go through a series of transformations like it was a television makeover montage. I hated it. It was making light of a horrific situation and I hated that it would do something like that. It eventually settled on being a porn actress named Vanessa Blue, one of my favorites, so that I would be even more unnerved by this whole situation. It was playing some sort of psychosexual game with me, and I didn't like it. It was trying to mix fear together with arousal for some reason and I was not down with that.

"Why aren't you looking at me, Saul?" it teased me. "You've never been afraid to look at these titties before."

"I'm sure titties is not what you wanted to show me when you released me from the web," I grimaced. "What do you want? What are those creatures in the pit? What is going on around here? Tell me and make it quick."

"You know, you used to be fun," it laughed.

"Now we both know you're lying," I smirked. "I have never been fun. I've been a neurotic mess my whole damned life."

"Yeah, you have been a hot mess your whole life, sure, but that's what I've liked about you," it told me as we walked through a sea of the Possu creatures towards a light off in the distance. "You've always been so closed off and buttoned-up, always so worried about the worst-case scenario coming to pass. And then you took those damned pills and now everything has just turned to absolute shit."

"Are you...are you going to help me fix all this somehow?" I asked, accidentally looking over at it and finding myself at eye-level to her enormous, ebony breasts. "Jeez, why do you look like that?"

"Is this form not pleasing to you either?" it laughed. "You're so picky today. I could make myself look like Avery Jane or Jade Jordan. Or maybe someone from one of those Pornhub categories you would never admit to visiting?"

"Shut the hell up," I said angrily. "Just make yourself...look like something else right now, please?"

"How about this, champ?" it suggested before turning into my father. "Is this better?"

"Well, you've finally picked someone I haven't masturbated to, so we're in business now," I sighed. "Let's do this please?"

My fake dad led me over to where the light was originating. It was a large rock wall with an old door in it. It was like the kind of rusty door you would find on an old ship that sunk a hundred years ago with a dirty porthole window you could barely see through. I had no idea why I was brought here.

"What is this?" I asked. I was somehow repulsed and drawn to the door at the same time. "What's behind this door?"

"The stuff nightmares are made of, kid," it said as it imitated an old actor who I had never seen before, but was still somehow sorta cognizant of. "Everything you've ever feared, from the fleeting thoughts to the ones that keep you awake all night, is behind this door. Or...at least they were. They've been escaping into the real world from this...portal in your brain."

"I'm aware," I frowned. "I currently have a little monster manipulating my nervous system like I'm some sort of marionette."

"Yes, The Possu is particularly nasty," it agreed with a solemn nod, "but if it hadn't trapped you in here, we wouldn't be able to talk directly like this. Now you took that medication, against my counsel, and it cracked open the door to this chamber. Your anxieties have been slipping out and causing havoc, like little farts at a board meeting."

"Disgusting," I shuddered.

"Focus," it continued. "They're slipping out one at a time right now, but I'm afraid that will no longer be the case."

"What do you mean?" I asked.

"The Possu is doing more than just using you as its own little sports car," it explained. "It's going to open up this chamber you see here, blow it wide open even, and then everything is going to escape. A veritable deluge of the worst horrors your rather prolific mind can conceive."

"What can I do?" I asked, starting to panic.

"You need to get back to the real world, gather your troops, and prepare for a fight, Saul," it answered. "The fight to end all fights. Because this is going to be the end of the world if you don't succeed."

"Shit," I cursed.

"Yeah, I really wish you had listened to me about those pills," it stated before we both looked at the chamber with the eerie light seeping out of it. "Some doors were never meant to be opened. And some doors can never be closed again."

"If I do everything you just said, do we stand a chance?" I asked.

"I honestly don't know," he answered. "I can tell you this though; without you, there is absolutely no way to save this planet."

"How do I free myself from...wherever the hell we are right now?" I asked.

"You're stuck here until that little monster on your back gets his claws out of you," he told me.

"What if that doesn't happen?" I asked. "What if it makes me drag Lita and Poole off into the darkness...and hurt them?"

"Then the world will fall soon after," he shrugged. "I'm not here to coddle you and make you feel better; I'm not really your dad. I'm the guy who tried really hard to convince you not to take those damn pills! So, if you manage to free yourself from this trap, you need to fight like hell to save the world from what you unleashed on it."

"I will, but I need to know something," I stated. "What are you really? Are you a part of me or are you something else entirely?"

He turned to face me and placed his hands on my shoulders at that point, trying to soothe me and calm my nerves possibly. He took a deep breath as our eyes met. He then let a slight smile curl the corners of his mouth.

"By the time this is all over, you will know precisely who I am and precisely who you are, Saul," he answered, "but you're going to need to be really brave and do the impossible."

"Being brave is impossible in light of what I'm up against," I muttered.

"Not for you," he shook his head. "You've witnessed every nightmare this universe has to offer and you're still standing. What's bravery if not that?"

I found myself smiling at the comment and then…the whole world seemed to shake. The reflection pretending to be my father vanished immediately and all The Possu swarmed me once again, surrounding me like their prey. Each one was chattering softly, but since there were so many of them the din of it all threatened to deafen me. I quickly covered my ears as I tried to keep the noise out, but it was to no avail, because they were noisier than anything I had ever heard before. Noisier than garbage trucks rumbling down your street when you're trying to sleep in. Noisier than the sun if sound could carry through space. Noisier than your girl's orgasms when she's fucking your best friend.

It didn't take long for a new sound to get added to the cacophony: me yelling for them to knock off their shit. It got louder to the point where it felt like the whole world was vibrating with their sound. The vibrations tore through me eventually and I felt this pain that felt like fire and electricity combined engulf my entire being.

Something about the pain was able to shift my vision. One moment I was in that dark void, a metaphysical representation of my mind, and the next I could see what was going on in the real world. In the real world, there was nothing but chaos as a bunch of doctors rushed all over the place. I was in a hospital? How much time had passed since I was in that pit?

Lita was there with me, talking to me, but I couldn't hear what she was saying. The Possu attached to my back hadn't given me back access to my auditory functions yet; hell, it was fighting me when it came to being able to peer into the real world. I kept shifting back and forth between my inner space and the outside world. As I shifted between realities, the pain was a constant. It kept ramping up as it set my very soul on fire.

My return to the real world was jarring as I got my sight and hearing and other senses back all at the same time. I was in a hospital and the lights were way too harsh for my eyes; it felt like I had been underground for days and now I was stepping into the sun for the first time. The noises that hit my ears were unsettling too, doctors and nurses running around and shouting orders in a panic, the beeps and whistles of various machines plus the sound of poor Lita crying somewhere in the sea of madness. The less said about the smells, the better.

I could see that the doctors had managed to dislodge The Possu from my back and it was now fighting them with all its strength. I watched as they finally managed to force the creature into a cage before turning their attention back to me. I could see the look of concern on their faces, especially Lita, and I could tell that it must have been touch-and-go for a while there.

"Saul, are you all right?" she asked, the first to speak to me when I finally woke up.

"What happened to me?" I asked.

While the professionals removed the monster and checked my vitals, Lita explained everything that had happened while I was unconscious. Apparently, The Possu took over my body and then tried to drag her into the darkness. It even made me fight Poole. It wasn't looking good for a while until they managed to overpower me and get me into the basket. We were lifted out of the pit and then they rushed me straight back to headquarters where they attempted to get that creature off my back.

According to Lita, I almost died several times as they made their attempts because the little monster was fighting them every single moment. Eventually, they removed it, shoved it into a cage, and I was free again.

"I have never been more scared in my entire life, Saul," she told me after she had told me the full story. "When that thing took over your body, you were a completely different person. You grabbed me and tried pulling me into the darkness."

"There are more of them in that pit," I commented. "It was probably trying to get one of them onto your back too."

"What...what was it like?" she asked me. "Could you see what it was doing or was it like you were asleep the whole time?"

"I saw brief glimpses, but not much," I answered. "I saw something else though."

"What?" she asked. "What did you see?"

"I saw that things are going to get a lot worse for us really fast, Lita," I said. "We need to tell everybody before it starts."

"I'm not getting it," she shook her head. "Before *what* starts?"

"Up until now we've been facing my fears one-by-one," I explained. "I think the little creature that attached itself to me did so on purpose. I think it was trying to speed up the process."

"That's terrifying," she said quietly as she thought about what I said. "We barely survived the cute little monkey creatures, Saul. I don't know if we can handle everything all at once."

"We're going to have to do just that," I said. "We need to tell everyone and make any preparations we can."

"All right," she said nervously. "I'll go get them so you can tell them what's going on. Are you going to be okay here by yourself? I promise that I will be right back."

I watched her hurry off while trying not to think about the bruises I saw on her arms from where I had grabbed her and on her cheeks from where she might have been struck in the face. I just had to hope that I wasn't the one who had smacked her around. Dear God, don't let it have been me that did that to her.

As I sat in the hospital room by myself, everyone racing around doing stuff of vast importance, I tried not to let my anxiety consume me. Perhaps if I stayed calm and didn't worry about anything, avoided all of my triggers, then we could avoid what my reflection had warned me about. It was worth a shot, so I sat there and tried to remain calm. I ignored the pain my body was in from The Possu's sharp intrusions into my nervous system. I didn't even think about what the long-term damage would be from what I went through, like some sort of paralysis or early dementia or maybe even some exotic cancer.

"No," I said through clenched teeth. "Stop it. Stop thinking about all that."

From there, I started imagining what my life would be like if I had been left with neurological damage from my encounter today. I could see myself in the doctor's office as he explains how even though I am barely in my fifties, I am going to start to lose my ability to walk very soon. He tries to explain there are many exercises and procedures we can try, tries to give me hope, and I thank him for it, but I already know what my fate is going to be.

I flash-forward to the day where I try to get up in the morning to go to the bathroom and my legs don't work and I fall to the floor of my bedroom. I see the look of surprise and fear on my face as I struggle to get my limbs to work, but it's no use. Another flash-forward and I am being rushed to the hospital. Another jump forward and I see myself in a wheelchair. Another jump forward and I am back in the office with a younger doctor this time. He's explaining that not only will I never walk again, but the trauma I experienced is now going to affect me cognitively. I am going to forget friends and family...lovers; I am going to forget myself in the end and it is going to happen quite rapidly.

"Please stop," I pleaded, my eyes shut tight but not enough to keep the tears from streaming down my cheeks. "I don't wanna think about this."

But my brain wouldn't listen to me as it showed me the miserable life that laid ahead of me since The Possu ruined my nervous system on a deep, fundamental level. It showed me all the terrible things I am going to experience and it showed me that I am going to be all alone for most of it. But it didn't just show it to me, oh no, because that would be too merciful. No, I felt every single bit of it: the loneliness, the pain, the fear, the hopelessness and despair. By the end of it, you couldn't convince me that I *hadn't* lived through it; that's how much a part of me it had become. I lived every single moment of that life!!!

After my brain showed me dying in a nursing home with no idea who I was, I was transported somewhere else. I found myself back at the rock wall my reflection had shown me, the one with the door with the circular porthole in it. I looked around quickly to see if my reflection was there with me, but I was all alone this time.

"Hello?" I called out into the darkness, but I got no response.

No, that's not true. I did get a response, but it wasn't an answer to my call. My call was met with screams of despair, the most torturous and pained cries for help erupted from behind the door that was before me. The door was shaking so violently that the rock wall it was situated in started to crack and crumble before my very eyes. The brightest light was pouring from the door, so bright that it hurt to even look at it, but I also couldn't bring myself to look away from it either.

"Is...is anyone there?" I called out again, despite every fiber of my being telling me to ignore that door and run as far away as possible. "Hello?"

The anguished yells continued and even got a little louder, but one voice rose above all that terrible noise and it sounded like me...only the voice was deeper and far more intimidating. That voice cut through all the noise and chaos and seemed to speak right to me.

"I'm here, Saul," it said in a way that seemed to reverberate in the deepest recesses of my troubled soul. "I'm always here...and I will *always* be here."

"Who are you?" I asked. "*What* are you?"

"Don't you know?" it asked, amusement tinting its deep, gravelly voice.

"Are you...my reflection again?" I asked. "Like from before?"

"In a way, but I am not the other guy you were talking to before," it responded. "I'm a...different reflection. A darker one, perhaps. More truthful."

"What...does that mean exactly?" I asked, holding up one of my hands as I tried to shield my eyes from the light coming from the chamber before me.

"Open the door and we can talk about it."

It wanted me to open the door, the same door my reflection had told me was the source of all these anxieties. I recoiled at the very thought of opening the door. I had already been warned: some doors were never meant to be opened and some doors can never be closed again. I took a step backwards and anguished cries got louder, making the very ground beneath my feet start to shake.

"Where are you going, Saul. You don't need to be afraid. Everything is going to work out precisely how it is supposed to. All you need to do...is reach out...and open the door."

"I'm not going to do that," I told it as I took another step backwards. "I'm never going to open that door."

"I thought you might say something like that," it laughed cruelly. "I guess I'll just have to do it myself."

I was immediately worried about that statement. The voice was coming from the other side of the door, but it made it seem like it had the power to open it. I knew one thing for sure: if that door opened, everything that was residing inside was going to spill out into reality and then we would all be doomed. No, worse than doomed. We would all be damned. Good and damned.

The laughter started to shake reality around us and make the rock wall crack and crumble even more. The bright light coming from the door was now coming from the cracks in the wall. The door bulged forward towards me like something huge was pushing on it from the other side. Something big and terrifying was trying to get out and find its way into the real world. I knew one thing for sure at that moment: I couldn't let that door open under any circumstance.

"Shit," I muttered as I rushed over to the door and started pushing on it to make sure it wouldn't open.

It was ridiculous really. There was no way that I could keep out all the evils that were hiding behind that door, but I threw my body in the way anyway. I tried to keep that door closed, but it was of no use. It was like keeping the power of the gods at bay. The wall started to fall to pieces while I pushed on the door with all my might. I knew it was stupid. Once the wall fell, they wouldn't need to go through the door at all. But as long as I was there, I wasn't going to let that door open.

"Give it up, Saul," the deep voice said from behind the door. "It's all over. You're not going to be able to stop this. We are getting out of here and we are going to swarm your world."

"Over my dead body," I said through gnashed teeth, anchoring my feet so that I would have the leverage to keep the door closed. "You're staying right where you are."

"I'm sorry, Saul, but you don't have what it takes to stop this," the voice bellowed from behind the door. "You've done your absolute best, but you are not the hero type. I think you should give up before you get hurt. No one will think less of you."

"You're trying to psych me out," I growled. "I'm not going to give up just because you try to convince me you're my friend."

"Is that what you think I'm doing?" it laughed before the door opened a bit to let a huge hand twice the size of my torso escape. Its talons were as long as four-by-fours and looked like they could tear through the hull of the Titanic. "No. We're not friends, Saul. Not even close. Now move… away…from…this door!!!"

That was when the door was flung open, and I was thrown back like an insignificant ragdoll. The door was open, and I was bathed in the eerie light coming from within. The rock wall crumbled to pieces, but the door still stood. And then the owner of the voice started to emerge from the chamber, but I couldn't bring myself to look. I didn't look but I knew it was coming towards me.

"You really should have run when you had the chance, Little Saul," I heard the voice as I closed my eyes and fought not to look at it. "I'm not going to show you any mercy. None of us are."

I snapped back to reality after that and found myself back in the hospital room, still waiting for Lita to come back with the people in charge of this whole operation. Instinctively, I knew I should get up and find the others, alert them to what was going on. I got to my feet to do just that and then after one step, I fell to my knees, threw my head back, and shouted to the heavens as loud as I could. It felt like everything, all the fear and anger and heartache I ever experienced, escaped through that yell.

That's when things got a hell of a lot worse for all of us. Watching that chamber burst open wasn't merely a metaphor; it was a herald of things to come.

FOUR
ALL HELL BREAKS LOOSE

Everything happened really fast after that. I went from an unknown species invading my body to watching an evil species claw its way out of the deepest recesses of my brain. Watching that old door fly open and the rock wall crumble to dust meant that everything had broken free. I knew we were going to start seeing the results of that sooner rather than later. I just didn't realize how soon it was going to be.

"Saul?" Lita asked as she rushed back into the hospital room. "Saul, are you all right? Why are you screaming? What happened?"

"Something happened," I told her, desperately trying to catch my breath.

"Something *else*?" she asked in shock. "So soon?"

"Yes," I nodded. "I think we're in trouble."

That was an understatement. Detective Reynolds and Special Agent Grimes soon ran into the room to see what was going on, but I should not have been their major concern at that moment. My anxieties were attacking the planet en masse and they started doing so as soon as that chamber in my head opened. I was starting to think that maybe all this wasn't so metaphorical at all. They were busy tending to me as the first of the monsters were loosed on our unsuspecting world.

While we had soldiers fire-bombing the hell out of the pit in Staten Island where the tribe of Possu were residing, the next disaster happened. Someone rushed up to Special Agent Grimes while he and Detective Reynolds were checking on me. He was sweating and out of breath and it was clear that he had news for us.

"Please tell me you have some good news for me, Foster," Trevor frowned when he looked at his subordinate.

"I'm afraid I don't, Sir," he shook his head. "We're getting reports of something...unusual."

"You need to be a lot more specific than that, Foster," Trevor allowed himself a wry smirk. "We're dealing with nothing but unusual around here."

"Yeah, but this...," he said and then he stopped as he carefully considered his words. "You need to see this for yourself."

Foster led us to a room where we could watch a news report, a place where we could see precisely what was going on in the world. For a team like ours, it was important that we were kept abreast of happenings all over the world as soon as they emerged. Everyone took a seat around the round table situated in front of the TV while I hobbled over to my chair and looked at it. My back was in terrible pain and I didn't know if I could sit without injuring myself.

"Are you all right, Saul?" Trevor asked, noticing my reluctance to sit.

"Yeah, just a little sore still from when...the creature was removed from my back," I answered. "I think I'll stand."

"Damn, you should be in a hospital bed right now, Saul," he softened. "You just got out of surgery. Lita, do you want to take him to the infirmary and we will give you the news after you've had a chance to recover a bit?"

"I promise I will go back and let the doctors check me out as soon as we see what's out there," I said, really not wanting to be a burden.

"Okay," he nodded. "Show us what's going on, Foster."

Foster turned on the television and all the news reports were focused on something going on in Florida. People were standing out on a beach looking out over the ocean and I knew that there was something terrible going on. I wasn't sure what at first though since so many of my fears spring from the fucking ocean, but the cameras soon made it apparent for us all to see.

"Oh no," I muttered when I finally saw it.

"What is that, Saul?" Trevor asked as he got to his feet and took a step closer to the television. "What am I seeing here?"

"It's a hurricane," I answered. "A hurricane the size of New Jersey and it's hanging off the coast of Florida. It has all the same things a normal storm does: thunder, lightning, wind."

"But...?" Detective Reynolds asked as she noticed me hesitate. "There's some sort of creepy catch, right? You're not just afraid of regular storms, right?"

"No," I shook my head. "This storm...is special."

"I don't suppose that means it's going to give us puppies and rainbows," Grimes frowned.

"Not even close," I shook my head. "You need to evacuate the area."

"The beach?" Lita asked.

"Florida," I stated. "You need to evacuate the whole damned state."

"The whole state?" he asked. "How am I supposed to do that?"

"Save as many of them as you can," I said. "Save them, Trevor. Don't let...them...die."

I think I passed out after that. It might have been from the stress or from the loss of blood. It might have been that the Possu had poisoned me with something on its claws. It could very well have been a combination of all those things. All I know is that one minute I was in the room watching that impossibly massive storm hovering off the coast of Florida and the next I was in a hospital bed with Lita by my side.

"What happened?" I asked. "How long have I been out?"

"You've been in and out of consciousness for the last week," she answered solemnly. "You got really sick, some sort of infection. It looked like we were gonna lose you there a few times. How do you feel?"

"Like shit actually," I answered truthfully as I tried to sit up. "How are you doing, Lita? I never meant to get you all wrapped up in all of this craziness."

"It really has been a lot of craziness, hasn't it?" she nodded as we sat in that quiet, dimly-lit hospital room. "Kinda non-stop almost from the time we first met. I mean, you were just the cute guy who worked with me in the office, and I had been going through a bit of a dry spell, so hooking up with you seemed like it was fun. But then you freaked out in the art museum and now I am sitting up here thinking this was a whole-ass bad idea. But I couldn't figure out how to end things because we work together, and it is definitely going to be awkward."

"No, I understand," I shook my head. "You didn't sign up for all this. I get it. If you want to go, Lita, it's fine. I would never think less of you for speaking your truth."

"Oh, thank God," she said, letting a smile come to her face. "I didn't know what to say or how to get out of this without sounding like a complete bitch. It's like those people who dump their significant others as soon as they hear they have cancer and shit. I just know that I am not cut out for all this, especially not after what happened in that damned pit in Staten Island."

"It's okay, Lita," I said as I felt my heart breaking inside my chest. "You don't have to explain anything to me. I wouldn't want to see you get hurt, so maybe it's best you get as far away from...all my craziness as you possibly can."

"You're the sweetest, Saul," she smiled wider before leaning over and giving me a kiss on my forehead. "I should never have been afraid to talk to you. Hit me up if you survive all this and we can get a coffee or something."

I watched her bound out of my hospital room so gleefully that she was basically skipping like we used to do in school. I was heart-broken, but I couldn't bring myself to cry over what had just happened. Everything she said made perfect sense. She hadn't signed up for all this. I couldn't expect her to stand by me through all this insanity when we had barely started dating a short while ago.

"Guess we're all alone on this one," I commented to no one in particular, a small smile of relief starting to grace my face. "It's probably better this way."

That was when I heard a disturbance in the corridor outside of my hospital room. It was minor at first and I assumed it was just some doctors and nurses running around helping injured people, but it got louder and louder. Eventually, I was able to hear a struggle and that turned into a full-on brawl. Before I could figure out what was going on, Lita was tossed back into my room and she landed sprawled out on the floor.

"What the hell?" I asked as I tried to get out of bed and go to her rescue.

Before I could go help her, a second Lita came into the room and stood over her angrily. She bent down, grabbed the injured version of her by the hair and dragged her over to my bed.

"I just spotted her coming out of your room," she seethed. "What the hell did she say to you?"

I was confused by what was happening, but I answered anyway. I explained how she had just broken up with me because she didn't want to deal with all this craziness. Angry Lita then turned to face Injured Lita and scowled at her.

"So that's it, huh?" she asked. "You thought you would come in here and shake my man's confidence by making him believe I wasn't on his side. Don't listen to this bitch, Saul, okay. She's not real. She's just one of these things that showed up to torment us."

"What are you talking about?" I asked, feeling more confused than I had ever been.

"Well, a storm appeared right off the coast of Florida and you were going to explain what it meant, but then you passed out," she explained. "We figured out what you were gonna say though when the weird shit started erupting from the storm."

"Weird shit like…?"

"Like this fake-ass lying bitch," she replied, showing me a completely different side of her. I really enjoyed seeing the fierce warrior woman who wouldn't let anyone take her man. "And then just two days ago I had to deal with a freaky old woman standing in the shadows of my bedroom and staring at me while I slept. That freaked me out."

"Are you saying other people's fears are taking shape?" I asked curiously.

"No, I think they're still yours," she answered, "but they are absolutely everywhere, like they were being spat out of that storm that was in Florida. Did you know that it would do that?"

"It did look like a portal to another world," I shrugged. "How have you been, Lita? You said I was unconscious for about a week?"

"I'll tell you all about it when I get rid of her," she said, referencing her double.

I didn't know what she planned to do with this nightmare version of herself, but I knew I was going to be glad to be rid of it. Lita gave her the once over, letting her eyes glide over the double's body with a look of disgust on her face. Moments later, she dragged the bruised woman out of the room where I heard her talking to some guards. After she handed off her prisoner, she returned to my room. She still had the scowl on her face though.

"I hope you didn't believe that shit she was saying even for a moment, Saul," she said angrily. "I would never dream of ditching you like that. I love you too much for that."

That was the first time she had said she loved me. I had told her a couple of times, but she wasn't quite ready to say it back to me then. Apparently, she was ready now…at the end of all things. A smile spread across my face, and she spotted it immediately. She crossed her arms over her chest and then rolled her eyes at the sight of the smile on my face.

"You love me, huh?" I asked.

"Yeah, yeah," she sighed. "Don't let it go to your head, Saul. I'm still mad at you."

"Mad at me for what?" I recoiled from the statement. "I've been unconscious for a week; what could I possibly have done to piss you off?"

"For one, I was scared to death the whole time you were unconscious," she answered honestly. "I didn't know if you were going to make it. We thought that little fuzzy creature had jacked up your body so much that you might not recover. I thought…I thought you were gonna die."

"Well, I'm still here," I smiled. "And you told me you loved me."

"Yeah, well, I'm mad at you for another reason," she frowned. "That bitch that I just had to toss out of here. Why didn't she have an ass? Is that how you see me, as some flat-bottomed chick?"

"Maybe one of my fears is that you might lose that butt at some point," I shrugged. "I don't know. I wouldn't take anything like that too seriously. My brain…is a weird place."

"Definitely true," she nodded before leaning in and giving me a kiss. "I'm so glad you're back."

"Me too," I smiled. "Now tell me everything that has been going on while I was sleeping."

"I will," she said after exhaling deeply. "But I can tell you now that you're not going to like any of it."

She laid down in my hospital bed and told me everything that had happened while I was asleep and none of it was good. Just as I had expected, seeing that chamber open was a metaphor of everything in my head that had suddenly gotten loose. She was holding back though, trying to spare me from the worst of it. That was fine. I knew that Grimes would tell me the truth when I saw him. It was nice to just lie next to Lita for a while…even if I was freaking out over the fact that I just saw a real-life doppelganger a few minutes ago.

"So…we're in trouble, Saul," she said as she cuddled up next to me in that surprisingly quiet hospital room.

"We're going to figure this out, baby," I said, holding her tight. "There's got to be a way to put things right. I just need to figure out what to do."

I got to spend a good twenty minutes with her before the sound of beeping and light conversation that permeates every hospital in the world was replaced with the sound of crisp shoes walking across clean linoleum and the barking of orders. I could see her roll her eyes and then sigh before she reluctantly climbed out of bed with me. Before I could ask her what was going on, the door to my hospital room burst open and a man with all the force and authority of a hurricane came blowing in.

"Well, so this is where you ended up," he rumbled angrily as he looked squarely at my girlfriend. "Back at your boyfriend's side."

"Yeah, and thank goodness I came to check on him," she crossed her arms over her chest defiantly. "Saul was being attacked by some doppelganger or something when I got here."

The man was dressed in a neat green military uniform covered in shining medals that looked like they were polished every hour on the hour. It looked like he had walked right out of an episode of G.I. Joe or something. I had never met the man before, but I certainly couldn't say that I didn't recognize him; he looked like the living embodiment of the military, the man featured in all the recruitment brochures. It still needed to be asked though.

"Um, who are you?" I asked in confusion.

"A doppelganger, huh?" he asked, seemingly not hearing a word I just said, before turning toward one of the soldiers who entered with him. "That's new. Add that to the list."

"Yes Sir," his subordinate responded before taking notes on a tablet. "Doppelganger. I hope...this thing has spell check or something."

"So where is the monster that attacked Copeland," the head soldier asked, looking around the room with an amused grin on his stone face. "Did you leave any of it that can be interrogated?"

"Interrogated or tortured, Major?" she asked.

"I'm sorry to interrupt," I said, a little more forcefully, "but *who* are you exactly?"

He let out a long, deep exhalation like he had less patience for me than he did any other living person on the planet. Not sure why he felt that way though since we had not been formally introduced yet. He walked over to the foot on my hospital bed and then fixed me with a hard stare.

"My name is Major Dorian Stone," he said. "I've been put in charge of cleaning up this mess you people made of this planet. Specifically, your mess, Mr. Copeland. I have no enmity towards Special Agent Grimes, but it is obvious that he was not the person for this particular assignment. He treated you like an asset, a friend even. That was a mistake. I'm going to treat you the way you deserve to be treated, like an enemy combatant that we turned to our side."

"Enemy combatant?" I blanched at the very thought. "I'm no one's enemy."

"Everyone is someone's enemy, Mr. Copeland," he stated, a slight smile curling the corners of his mouth. "We're at war with nightmare creatures. *Your* nightmare creatures to be specific. Now I can't be sure what side you're ultimately on, but until I know, you're not leaving my sight."

"This is bullshit, Stone," Lita spoke up. "Saul is not a bad person and I will not let you keep blaming him for…what's going on out there."

"Young lady, I am commander of this operation now," said Stone. "I do not have the luxury of coddling your boyfriend during this. Florida is gone, destroyed by that damned storm. California has been eaten by that giant, hungry maw off the west coast. There are werewolves, giant rats, and other shit all over the planet, taking lives indiscriminately. We have lost millions upon millions of people. I need to do whatever is necessary to save as many people as we can."

She hadn't told me about California. She hadn't told me…about how many people had died. I knew why she didn't, of course, but it still hurt me to my core to know how much pain and suffering I had caused around the world. Stone might have been right about me all along. Who can claim to have taken so many lives…and in just one week at that? I was starting to think I might be the worst thing to ever happen to this world.

"Where are Reynolds and Grimes?" I asked. "Were they fired or something? Did you throw them in the brig?"

"Reynolds is still with the team and so is Grimes," Lita answered.

"I'm still not so sure if the werewolf can be trusted," said Stone. "I don't like people around me that I cannot trust. A detective that can turn into a slobbering animal and rip my throat out is not my idea of a good teammate. But if you can't trust a police officer from the NYPD, then you're in worse shape than you think."

"Uh huh," I said, trying not to roll my eyes. "What are we going to do about these monsters? I'm ready to help."

"I'm glad to hear that, young man," said Stone. "Take a shower, get dressed and meet us out front. Don't dawdle. We've lost enough time already."

Major Stone and his assistant left the room after that, leaving Lita and I alone. I knew I should rush to follow his orders, but I had a question before I could get started with that.

"Is he real?" I asked.

"Yeah, he's for real," she nodded. "A real hard-ass. I think his face would shatter if he cracked a smile."

"No, no, no," I shook my head. "Is he real? I just saw a duplicate of you a little while ago and I'm wondering if this dude is real or not. I mean, he looks like the stereotypical Army guy you would see in any action movie. Hell, his name is 'Stone' for crying out loud. Did anyone check to see if he's...a real person?"

"I...assume so," she said as doubt crept into her voice. "I mean, they wouldn't just let him show up here without documentation to prove that he should be in charge, right? The country has to run better than that."

"What have you seen that makes you think the country runs smoothly, babe?" I asked, looking over at her.

"After your shower, we'll go make sure he is who he claims to be," she stated.

I jumped out of bed to find that my legs were wobbly. I guess it was because I had been unconscious for so long and not active. I don't know how long it takes for atrophy to set in, but I was definitely feeling weaker than I had been. I took note of it, but didn't let it stop me from going to the restroom to take my shower. As I entered the bathroom, I stood in front of the mirror and looked at my reflection. It looked so...normal. It didn't look menacing in the slightest, but I knew that most things didn't start off looking like they wanted to harm you. Most things tried to entice you so that you would be helpless when you fell into their trap.

That shower was the most stressful of my entire life. The bathroom was so small and tight and started to low-key trigger my claustrophobia. The upside of the room being so small was that it was almost impossible to slip and fall and break my neck in the shower; there was basically nowhere to actually fall. Unfortunately, since the room was so small, I couldn't get any real distance from the mirror in case my reflection decided it wanted to strike again.

My heart was beating out of my chest as I bathed that day because I knew that I wasn't prepared for what I was going to see when I finally stepped out into the world again. The few things that Major Stone had mentioned were enough to turn my stomach something fierce. I knew it was going to be terrible when I finally got to see the damage with my own eyes. I actually started to hyperventilate a few times. At first, I thought it was because of the steam from the shower, but eventually I figured out the real cause. I was having a fucking panic attack!

I thought I was going to pass out and, I don't know, fall against the wall or something. But then there was a knock on the bathroom door before it slowly creaked open. Lita came in and flashed that adorable smile and my anxiety faded. She entered and closed the door behind her.

"Do you want me to get your back?" she asked.

"Always," I smiled back.

I showered while she scrubbed my back for me, but we didn't do anything particularly naughty in there. I would have welcomed it, obviously, but she let me get out the shower, get dressed, and then we met the major in front of the hospital where I had been treated. I could already tell by the sheer number of soldiers moving around the area that things were as bad as they had told me…if not much, much worse.

The sky was black with crimson clouds dotting the skyline. Heavy metal barriers were surrounding the building and I could see tanks off in the distance driving down the streets. It looked like martial law had been declared while I was unconscious. My jaw dropped, terrified by just how bad things had gotten in a mere seven days. The smell of smoke and death wafted into my nostrils and the sting almost brought tears to my eyes.

"That's right, Mr. Copeland," said Major Stone as he approached with a frown on his face. "Look at the nightmare your diseased brain has wrought upon the earth."

"If you keep talking to my boyfriend like that, I am going to shove those medals where the sun doesn't shine, Stone," said Lita angrily. "This is some sort of astrological, cosmic bullshit and it landed right in Saul's backyard. He had no control over this, and I am going to need you to stop demeaning him for it. He's here helping us fight these monsters. You show him some respect or we're going to walk and let you solve this mess on your own. Got it?"

He had a smirk on his face as he studied us. His assistant stood there holding his breath, probably hoping Stone didn't just go off and shoot us both right there. He definitely didn't want to be a witness to something like that. Realistically, we weren't going to be able to leave unless he allowed it; he probably had every right to toss us into a cell until this was all resolved. He could have taken that stance, but he opted not to do that. I never understood why he chose a softer approach, but he smiled and then quickly apologized for his words.

"It's okay," I said. "I know we're all under a lot of pressure here. What do you need me to do, sir? Where do you want me to start?"

"I'm pleased to see you've finally accepted your new reality, Mr. Copeland, and I do believe that by working together, we can certainly make things right," he said before he extended his hand to me.

I could tell that Lita was annoyed when I shook Stone's hand. After the way he had spoken to me, she would have preferred for me to tell him to go fuck himself. I would be lying if a large part of me didn't want to do just that, but I knew that the mess the planet was in was my fault, even if Lita had trouble admitting that. I was willing to play ball for as long as I needed to if we could save the world and fix all of my mistakes.

I wasn't sure how much more bullshit my girlfriend was willing to put up with though. Hopefully, we were going to find a way to end this nightmare before I ever had to find out just how low her threshold for nonsense truly was. We boarded a jeep together, driven by Stone's assistant, and went back to the new headquarters where we were stationed.

"Gracie Mansion?" I asked when we arrived. "You ousted the mayor and took over his home for this operation?"

"The mayor is dead, Saul," Lita said sullenly.

"That army of rats you first encountered in the subway burst into his home and completely devoured him, his wife, and his children," Major Stone added coldly, not the least bit concerned that a family had been wiped out in such a gruesome manner.

"Try not to sound too broken up about it," I muttered under my breath, but the major turned around because he heard me anyway.

"I don't have time to break down and cry over one elected official and his family, Mr. Copeland, and neither do you," he barked. "They were just some of the millions of people who have died since this madness all started. I will mourn all of them after this is done, but for now our focus has to be on the ones we can still save. Do you understand?"

I nodded silently. I was out of line to assume that he was cold and uncaring in light of all this tragedy. Obviously, the work needed to come first. I had to keep reminding myself of that. Nothing was more important than getting the world back to normal. It looked as though he was willing to give his life for it.

Stone led us to a huge dining room and instructed us to take a seat at the large table before he left the room with the assistant whose name I still hadn't learned. I sat next to Lita and tried to quiet my mind, but it was difficult. All I kept seeing when I closed my eyes was the wreckage scattered all over New York as we drove from the hospital to Gracie Mansion. It was like the entire city was Ground Zero.

"Are you all right, babe," Lita said as she grasped my hand.

"Not really," I shook my head. "It's a lot to process. Even if we manage to stop all these monsters for good, how can we fix the damages?"

"I get how you're feeling," she stated. "I said the same thing when I watched **The Matrix** trilogy. That scene when they finally showed what the surface world looked like, I wondered what the people of Zion could possibly do to fix the world if they managed to overcome the machines. But the answer is simple: time. It will take time to get things back on track, but eventually the world will be like new again."

"That's...a lot of time," I said. "We could live to be a hundred years old and never see the planet fixed."

"That's okay," she smiled. "Living to be a hundred years old with you, raising our children and watching them raise our grandchildren in a world where we are all working towards the same common goal. I can't think of a better future than that."

"You don't have much of an imagination, do you?" I smirked.

"Oh, you're grumpy-grumpy, huh?" she laughed and made me feel so much better. "Don't think I didn't notice you ignored the entire idea of us having kids and grandkids together, Saul. We're definitely gonna talk about that."

I had nothing against starting a family with Lita. In fact, if I was ever going to be a husband and father, I could only imagine it being with her. At the moment, though, I couldn't imagine any future where we survived the horrific nightmares that I had loosed into the universe. I couldn't express that, not to the woman who held my hand with hope filling her eyes.

"If we make it through this, baby, we can start making our family right away," I said, looking deep into her eyes.

"I'll fight these monsters all by my lonesome if I have to, Saul," she told me. "We're going to make it through this. *Both* of us are going to make it through this."

She believed every word she said that day and it was just about enough to make me believe it too. That was before all the horrors that were to quickly follow. We had a few moments to ourselves before Grimes and Reynolds entered the room. They both smiled when they saw me sitting there.

"Good to have you back, Saul," Grimes spoke up first. "How are you feeling?"

"Like I really need to be productive right now," I answered. "I want to do whatever I have to in order to get things back to normal. It's time for this nightmare to end."

"I agree," said Stone, entering the room just as I finished speaking.

"Were you just waiting outside for the perfect moment to come in?" Lita asked.

"We just got a report of something happening and I need you to take a look at it right away, Copeland," said Stone, ignoring my girlfriend's comment. "There are a series of violent tremors happening in

Detroit right now and the place isn't exactly known for its earthquakes."

"So, this probably has something to do with my demons then," I said, crossing my arms over my chest.

Soon we were looking at a large, flatscreen television as the reports from Detroit started to come in from several reporters on the scene. As we all sat and watched, I had no clue what I was looking at. I couldn't tell what kind of monster we were dealing with. When I saw the storm appear off the coast of Florida, I knew what we were dealing with, but I didn't know what could be causing earthquakes in Detroit. It had to be something big though based on how violent the tremors were. The ground shook so much that it didn't look like one stone would stand upon another by the end of it.

"What the hell is going on?" Reynolds commented at the sight of the destruction.

"Looks like the worst earthquake to ever hit the planet," Grimes stated. "I've never seen anything like it. If it keeps up like this, it could crack the planet in half."

I didn't know if the science supported what he said, but it became a very real fear nestled deep in my brain with all the others. Hopefully, I would be able to hold onto this one and not let it get away. As we watched the devastation and the terrible loss of life unfold before our eyes, it became clear that this was no normal earthquake after all. There was something more, something far worse, going on here.

We were watching live footage from a news chopper when something enormous burst out of the ground, completely destroying downtown Detroit in one fell swoop. We all fell silent as we waited for the smoke to clear and give us a clear image of what we were up against now. When it finally showed up on camera, the room got even more silent than it had been before.

"What...is that?" Reynolds asked finally after a few moments.

"It kinda looks like...," Grimes started to speak before letting his voice trail off.

I recognized it immediately upon seeing it, but I didn't want to say it out loud. It was something so unexpected that I thought it would never show up in a million years. The smoke and debris cleared and there it was for all to see. Standing right there in the center of Detroit, right where the casino had been standing previously, was...

"It's a giant fucking dick!" Major Stone roared in a weird mixture of confusion and anger and humor. "What the hell is going on here, Copeland? Someone tried to diddle you in the restroom once and you've been scared ever since?"

Everyone looked to me for an answer, but I wasn't prepared to give them one. I opened my mouth to try to speak, but there were no words. I just shook my head, turned on my heels and then walked out of the room to find the nearest bathroom to lock myself in. I knew why there was a giant dick rampaging through Detroit, but there was no way I was in the slightest bit prepared to explain it to anyone else in the moment. I knew, however, that I wouldn't be left alone for very long, that someone was going to come looking for me eventually. I also knew it was going to be sooner rather than later.

I was in the bathroom for all of maybe seven minutes before a small, but assertive knock came at the door. I knew who it was right away, the only person who would want to come find and comfort me after seeing something like that. I didn't respond to the first knock and there quickly came a second.

"I'm not going anywhere until we talk, Saul."

Lita's voice was soft and soothing, but insistent. I believed her about her not leaving until we had a discussion about what had appeared on the TV. I had been sharing my anxieties with her ever since this nonsense had started, but I had never revealed anything like this. As far as she was concerned, it was time for me to come clean. Even though I really didn't want to talk about it, too many people had just died for me to keep it all to myself.

I opened the door and there she was with a concerned look on her face. She was alone, having left the others behind, but I knew they were expecting her to come back with some sort of explanation for what had just happened in Detroit. I stepped to the side silently and granted her access to the restroom. We were soon sitting criss-cross apple sauce on the floor as she waited for me to gather the courage to explain myself.

"When I was a kid, my parents both worked," I started speaking, staring down at the floor. I couldn't bring myself to look her in the eyes as I told her this story. "Most kids back then had both parents in the workplace. In my neighborhood, we all got babysat by the same elderly woman, a woman we all called Granny."

She sat there nodding slightly as she listened to my story. She didn't say anything, not wanting me to crawl back into my shell and not tell her what happened. I was still having a hard time meeting her gaze, but she was gracious enough not to make a big deal about the lack of eye contact.

"She watched like a dozen neighborhood kids at a time," I continued. "She also had a college-aged nephew who lived in the house with her named Nigel."

I think when I mentioned Nigel, Lita probably could tell where this story was going. I found it difficult to express it because it was something I hadn't talked to anybody about. I hadn't even had a chance to discuss this with my therapist yet. Lita sat there quietly as I told her how Nigel sexually assaulted all the children in Granny's care, making us all fellate him in turn. I was three at the time.

"It all stopped when I started going to kindergarten," I explained. "I went to school every day from that point and my grandmother used to pick me up from there and watch me until my parents got off work. You know, the worst part is that I didn't even realize that what he did was wrong until like third or fourth grade. They gave a presentation about good touches and bad touches, and only then did I realize I had been molested. Can you believe that? That I was so, so incredibly stupid that I needed to be told I was assaulted?"

"You weren't stupid then and you're not stupid now, Saul," she protested. "You were a kid. There are plenty of women, plenty of people, who don't realize they've been raped until sometime afterwards. It's something people have to process first sometimes. Olivia Benson talks about that *all* the time. So...what did you do after you learned in school that you were molested?"

"I went straight to the office in the school and called my mom," I answered. "I told her what I had just learned in school and I told her what had happened to me."

"What did she do?" she asked. "How did she react?"

"She didn't," I replied. "She just said 'okay' and that was the end of the conversation. I thought maybe we were going to talk about it later when she got home from school, but there was no further conversation. I started to think that maybe this was no big deal, maybe everyone just got sexually assaulted eventually. I mean, if it was something serious, my mother would have talked to me about this when she got home, right?"

"Maybe she didn't understand what you were saying to her, Saul," she offered with a shrug.

"Yeah, well, now I will never know why we didn't talk about it," I shrugged too. "My mother had a series of strokes and ended up in a nursing home, mostly unresponsive. She, um, died sometime after that."

"I'm sorry, Saul," she said.

"It's okay," I said, wiping a tear from the corner of my eye. "We've all been through shit."

"No, babe, don't do that," she said, reaching out and touching my chest while I looked away. "Don't diminish what happened. You went through something terrible, something nightmarish, and I am so sorry you had to go through that. And for what it's worth, I don't think your mother understood what you were telling her. There's no way she would have ignored the suffering of her sweet, little boy if she knew what you had gone through."

"I wish…I could hear her say that herself," I said, "but I never will."

"So…that's why that…kaiju cock is rampaging in Detroit," she said. "You've been traumatized because of what Nigel did to you."

"No, it's not that," I shook my head before looking over at her. "That wasn't…Nigel's penis on that screen. It was mine."

"Yours?" she asked.

"You didn't recognize it?" I asked.

"It was a little bit smaller the last time I saw it," she answered. "You gotta help me out here, Saul. I don't understand."

"The...abuse wasn't the worst of it, if you can imagine," I said after a deep breath. "The worst part was the research that followed after. As a male sexual assault victim, people like to insist that you're broken now, that you're going to turn into the same kind of monster that attacked you. They make it seem like it is inevitable."

She studied my face with quizzical eyes as I continued to tell her my story. It got harder and harder to talk about this. It's like walking through a snowstorm, your every step getting more and more labored until you just want to let the blizzard take you into its cold embrace. It would have been easy to just say "fuck it" and go join the others in the conference room. I kept going anyway.

"So, I've been scared for a good long time, Lita," I said. "Is it gradual? Will there be a series of subtle changes until I eventually wake up a monster or is it sudden? Is it like flipping a light switch? One moment, I'm me and then the next, I'm a danger to everyone I love? Will I see the signs? Will I see the signs in time to end myself before I...become like Nigel?"

The restroom fell silent for a long time as Lita looked at me. I tried hard not to meet her eyes as she looked at me with sorrowful eyes. She was pitying me, and I hated that. I didn't want anyone's pity, especially my girlfriend's.

"You're scared that your sexuality, represented by your...manhood, is going to be weaponized against other innocent people," she said. "That's not going to happen, Saul. You're a good man and you would never be like Nigel. Not in a million years."

"How can you know that?" I asked. "Look at what I've already done to this world. How can you possibly say for certain that I'm a good person?"

"Look, you might doubt yourself, babe, but I know you're a good person," she told me, clutching my hands in hers. "I'm an excellent judge of character."

"I guess we'll see," I said.

"Yeah, we will," she nodded before I forced a little smile. "I guess we should get back to the others now. We have some work to do. Yep, got to destroy that kaiju penis before it causes anymore damage."

"Oh God, is that what we're calling it now?" I rolled my eyes.

"Hey, I like the name," she shrugged. "But you're right, we need to go stop that thing. We both know how much it loves me, so we don't need it leaving Detroit and looking for me."

"You're a real piece of work," I smiled.

"What, am I lying?" she asked as we slowly got to our feet and headed for the restroom's exit.

When we returned to the makeshift war room that had been set up in Gracie Mansion, everyone stopped talking. They had been talking about me surely. Reynolds and Grimes looked at me with pity in their eyes, like they had me all figured out based on the monster they saw rampaging on the television. Stone, by stark contrast, looked at me with sheer annoyance plastered on his face.

"Wanna explain to me why I got a giant cock rampaging through Detroit?" he asked, his grizzled act starting to wear on even me.

"No, I don't think I will," I said pointedly. "We've got monsters on the loose and we need to put a stop to this right now. So, you're going to call up an airstrike or some shit and you're going to destroy that thing. We're going to destroy every fucking thing that shows up from now. We kill them and try to figure out how to stop them for good by studying their remains."

"Mmm, not sure what changed with you, Copeland, but I like it," said Stone. "I'm going to go order the strike. I'll be right back."

Stone rushed out of the room to do what he had obviously wanted to do right from the beginning. They have all these weapons at their disposal, so why not get some use out of them? As someone who collected action figures and never managed to keep them mint in box, I understood the sentiment. Reynolds and Grimes not-so-secretly exchanged a look before they slowly walked over to me.

"Are you okay, Saul?" Grimes asked as they approached.

"I'm fine," I convincingly lied. "We just need to put an end to this. I'll work with anyone who can do that, soldiers or shamans, warriors or witches."

"Do you think consulting spiritualists would help?" Reynolds asked. "The department consulted a psychic once to help locate a missing child."

"Did you end up finding the child?" Lita asked.

"Yes, but it was the dogs who found her, not the psychic," the detective stated grimly. "That one might not have been effective, but I am sure we can find one that is. That's if you think it would help."

"I am willing to entertain any possibility at this point," I answered honestly. "Does anyone know any good witches?"

"No, but if you need some bad ones, I can recommend some of my exes," Grimes stated, getting Reynolds to give him an involuntary side-eye.

The banter didn't continue for much longer, not that we were serious about consulting mystics anyway. I didn't think this had anything to do with magic. I didn't think the pills I took were really to blame either. This was all something else, something cosmic. I felt like I should know precisely what this all was, like it had the taste of familiarity about it, but it was all so nebulous. It just refused to take shape in my mind.

I don't know how much time took place before the television showed images of the bombing of Detroit. The Kaiju Penis roared like Godzilla, shattering any windows that hadn't already been broken, as it was bombarded with fiery death from above. It was the damnedest thing I had ever seen...in real life anyway. Never in a million years did I ever think I would see American fighter jets bombing the shit out of a giant cock before, my cock no less. The world had truly gone mad, just as mad as my worst nightmares.

"Is it weird that I don't know which side to root for in this particular fight?" Lita whispered into my ear. "I mean, a city has just been destroyed by a penis, but...it's *your* penis. It's gotta feel weird watching it get destroyed, right?"

"No," I lied with a solemn shake of my head. "Let it burn."

It was like an explosive action movie was playing out before our very eyes, something loud and nonsensical like the works of Michael Bay. You'd almost expect a buff, shirtless idiot to team up with a two-dimensional robot to combat the monstrosity that was laying waste to Detroit. I had to stifle laughter because the whole thing just seemed...so ridiculous somehow.

"How are we faring?" Stone asked as he returned to the room, ignoring us in favor of gluing his eyes to the television screen. "Did we kill the damned thing?"

"It doesn't look like the bombs are working," Grimes quickly answered.

"It's just getting mad," said Reynolds. "Are we even sure that conventional weapons are going to put something like that down?"

"You put enough bullets into something, it will definitely fall," Stone assured us, but how could anyone be sure of anything anymore? "We just haven't hit it enough yet."

We watched the melee for a bit, but it didn't seem like a definitive winner was going to be determined. The battle went on for another hour until the giant penis finally decided to slink down beneath the city through the very hole it had burst through. When the smoke cleared, downtown Detroit was nothing more than a charred ruin with a gaping crater right in the middle of it.

"It's over," said Stone.

"Not yet," I said. "Not until we figure out how to stop them all for good, send them all back where they came from. Where's my therapist, the one who prescribed the anti-anxiety pills to me? Is she...still alive? I mean, I know I missed a lot when I was unconscious."

"She's here," Stone grimaced, crossing his arms over his chest. "We... have been debriefing her."

I demanded to see Dr. Robinson and Stone acquiesced. He led me, Lita, Grimes and Reynolds past several soldiers until we were in the basement of Gracie Mansion. A sophisticated brig had been established down there and Dr. Robinson was in the very first cell. The therapist was sitting there in her cell and looked terrible, like she hadn't been able to do her hair or possibly even bathe in several days. I spun around and glared at Stone.

"What the hell is this?" I asked angrily. "Why the hell is she locked in that cage? What have you been doing to her? Have you...have you been torturing her or something?"

"I have been questioning her...aggressively...to find an answer to our dilemma," Stone stated. "She's been uncooperative."

"You're a bastard," I said, barely restraining my anger. "She tried to help me. *None* of this is her fault! You're going to let her out of there right now."

"Let's get one thing very clear, Mr. Copeland, I do not take orders from you," he said, barely restraining his own anger. He walked over to me and looked down at me, his 6'4 frame towering over my 5'5 body. "I take my orders, believe it or not, directly from the President during this... crisis that you and your therapist have created. I will do whatever I need to do, imprison and question whomever I see fit. I will even kill you and her if I get an inkling it would improve our chances here. That goes for your little girlfriend, the werewolf detective and the not-so-special agent who used to be in charge of this operation."

"Assholes don't survive situations like this, Stone," I said, trying not to be intimidated. "They're usually the last kill of the film."

"And they die the worst out of everyone," Lita added.

"We're not going to stop this horror show by becoming monsters," I said. "If you think that's the way to handle this, you may as well start handing this world over to the nightmares now. There won't be anything worth saving here."

"Oh, please grow up!" he protested immediately. "Do you think this is some sort of after-school special? Do you think we're going to hug your monsters until they decide to play nice? No, Copeland! This is war, something I am far more intimately familiar with than any of you. Now I know how to fight wars and, more importantly, I know how to *win* wars. If you do as I say, we might actually get to save the world and live long enough to tell the tale."

I found myself frowning because I really hated being scolded. What I hated even more in that moment was the nagging thought that he might actually have been right. I silently glanced over at Dr. Robinson and saw her looking exhausted and absolutely bereft of anything close to resembling hope.

"You're wrong, Stone," I said. "This isn't how you win a war. This is how you lose your soul. Now open that cell and let her out of there. Now. Please."

Stone's face tightened like he wanted to argue with me, but then he ultimately just motioned for Robinson's cell to be opened. She staggered out of that tiny little room and then gave me probably one of the most heartfelt hugs I had ever received.

"Thank you, Saul," she whispered.

"No thanks are necessary," I said. "You never should have been in there in the first place."

"And you…never should have been born!" she shouted before she pushed me into her cell and then rushed in with me after closing the door behind her. "You're a monster! A demon!"

The doctor was faster than anyone I had ever seen. In a flash, she had me on the cold concrete floor with her hands wrapped around my throat. You wouldn't have imagined she was as strong as she is by looking at her, but she was drawing from reservoirs of untold strength as she started strangling the life from me. Her sharp fingernails with the chipped red polish were piercing my skin, no doubt drawing blood, while Lita yelled for the cell to be reopened.

"Saul!" she shouted. "Get this door opened!"

I could hear my girlfriend, but it wasn't as loud as the doctor that was screaming in my face about how she needed to kill me because I was some sort of abomination. Her eyes were wide and bloodshot as she closed off my air passages. She was completely undone and she wanted to kill me more than anything else in the whole world.

Eventually, they managed to open the door to the cell and Grimes and Reynolds dragged Dr. Robinson off me while she screamed at the top of her lungs how I needed to be destroyed. Lita raced into the cell after

Robinson had been cleared and she knelt beside me, checking to see if I was all right.

"Still think I was wrong to keep her restrained, Mr. Copeland?" Stone asked with a smug smirk before he ordered his men to take Robinson away and sedate her.

I wanted to tell him how much of an asshole he was, but I couldn't think of what to say exactly. It felt like all the times I had argued with my father as a teenager, when he would make me so mad that my brain couldn't even formulate words. I could feel Lita rubbing my chest, trying to soothe me as she looked at the bruises on my neck.

"Saul, why didn't you fight back?" she whispered into my ear. "She tried to kill you and you didn't even try to defend yourself. I can't be the only one fighting for us, babe."

I slightly nodded at her without saying a word. I knew what she meant. She saw me almost get killed again and I didn't even fight for my survival. I...don't know why I didn't fight in that moment. I honestly don't know what came over me and therefore I had no explanation to give her about my actions.

An hour later, Dr. Robinson had been cleaned up, put into an orange jumpsuit, and then placed in a room with her wrists chained to the long table set before her. Once, we were sure she wasn't a danger to anyone, I was allowed into the room with her. The disdain evident on her face when I entered and sat across from her truly startled me. Every interaction I had with her before finding her in that cell was pleasant. I was left wondering what could have happened to change her like this.

"Are you okay, Dr. Robinson?" I asked. "You're looking much better."

"What do you want, Copeland?" she rolled her eyes at me dismissively. "Haven't you taken enough from us all already?"

"What have I taken from you?" I asked.

"Our lives are on the verge of ending, Copeland, and it is all because of you," she answered. "When you came into my office, I thought you were just a troubled young man suffering from anxiety. But that's not what you are at all. You are a monster who came to destroy the world with your horrific demons. My question is why did you need to come see me and drag me into this? The meds had nothing to do with this, so you could have unleashed these terrible things whenever you wanted. Why the hell did you involve me!"

I stopped and took a deep breath. I wanted to close my eyes for a second and clear my mind, but I couldn't trust that Robinson wouldn't attack me again while my eyes were closed. After I was done exhaling, I just shook my head and looked into her crazed eyes.

"I'm not responsible for this, Dr. Robinson, at least not consciously," I stated. "I took the medication that you gave me and then the next morning, a man was being eaten by a shark. I need you to focus and help me figure out what's going on. While I was unconscious, I saw some things. I was hoping you could help me interpret what I saw and find some clues that will help us stop these things."

"Really?" she sighed impatiently. "That's what I'm doing here? You could have just left me in my cell instead of putting us all through this charade. I don't believe for one moment that you don't already know what's going on here and how to put an end to it."

"Listen, the first time I passed out was when that creature latched onto me and took control of my body," I pressed forward. "I found myself, or my consciousness rather, in a dark cavern and I was trapped in a giant spider web."

"A web," she repeated, trying not to sound interested, but I could tell she was intrigued.

"Yeah, and I was trapped in the middle," I nodded. "A giant creature was approaching me from the darkness, but I couldn't bear to watch. I mean, it obviously had to be a spider, but I didn't want to see the damned thing. But soon I was approached by my reflection and he freed me from the web."

"Your reflection?" she asked. "What does that mean?"

"Well, right before I took the pills you gave me, my reflection warned me that I shouldn't take them," I answered.

"What did your reflection say?" she asked me, leaning forward as my story seemingly got more interesting to her. "What did it warn you would happen if you took the pills?"

"The usual fear-mongering," I shrugged. "Nothing too specific."

"*Usual* fear-mongering?" she inquired. "Was this not the first time that your reflection spoke to you."

"I don't want to sound crazy like I talk to my reflection all the time or anything," I rolled my eyes. "I think it was just that little voice in my head that's always warning me of dangers, telling me not to do this and not to do that. I think the hallucination with my reflection was just a...manifestation of my own fears about taking the medication. He told me that if I took the pills something terrible would happen."

"Something terrible?" she asked. "Was there anything specific that your reflection told you?"

"He told me that all hell would break loose," I said, remembering back to when I first took the pills. "He said all my worst nightmares would come true."

"And that's precisely what started happening," she said. "Is it possible that your reflection is more than just the voice of your subconscious?"

"What else could it be, Doctor?" I asked. "That voice has always been with me, even when I was a small child. This was way before I met you and started taking medication. I started this life with my parents...and that voice."

"It's been there forever, huh?" she asked. "What else did you see while you were unconscious?"

"My reflection walked me past those little creatures and showed me this rock wall with an old door embedded into it," I replied. "It looked like the kind of door you would see in a submarine. Had a porthole in it and everything."

"What was on the other side of the door, Mr. Copeland?" she asked, sounding more like a therapist and less like the woman who tried to murder me earlier.

"There was bright light, the brightest that I have ever seen, and there were these terrible screams and howls," I said, remembering how it happened. "It was terrifying but also familiar. The walls started to crack as the light intensified. And then the door burst open...and then I woke up."

"Did you see your reflection at any other time during all this?" she asked, slightly nodding her head as she took in all the elements of my story.

I told her everything I knew at that point, and she listened to every word just like she had when I first went to her office and told her about my anxieties and fears. After I was done talking, she took a deep breath as she thought about everything.

"Sounds like your reflection was trying to protect you...from all this," she said eventually. "Assuming he is not a separate entity like the other creatures, somewhere deep in your brain you knew that these dangers were real. I failed to recognize how serious your condition was and I am sorry, Mr. Copeland. I convinced you that everything was going to be okay and now the world is in danger."

"No apologies necessary, Doctor," I shook my head. "No one would have believed me. What can we do now, going forward?"

"You need to find your guardian angel again and speak to him," she replied. "You need to ask him if there is a way to fix this. Ask him if there is a way to stick those creatures back into the chamber they all escaped from."

"How am I supposed to do that?" I asked with a shrug. "He abandoned me when the shit hit the fan."

"You abandoned him first, choosing not to listen to his warnings," she said. "Totally my fault, but still. If you...apologize and ask for his help, maybe he will come back?"

"This all sounds crazy, Dr. Robinson," I exhaled.

"Crazier than everything else that has happened so far?" she asked. "You, and your reflection, were keeping these horrors locked up behind that wall. They got out. I think only the two of you have any chance of sending them back where they came from."

"Yeah, back where they came from," I said. "Except that means sending them back into my head...where I will have to deal with them again for the rest of my life."

"I'm sorry, Saul," she sighed. "I know it's not ideal, but it's the only way."

"Maybe my reflection and I can do one better," I said. "Maybe we can destroy these creatures instead of locking them up. Maybe there's a way to be rid of them forever."

"That would be terrific, but if the only options are taking back your demons or letting them destroy the world, you know what you have to do," she said.

"Yeah, I guess I do," I said sullenly. "Let me go get reacquainted with myself. Thank you for your help."

I left the room after that and joined Lita and others in the corridor outside. They all had expectant looks on their faces, like they thought that Robinson had given me the keys to our success. Perhaps she had. Her plan only worked, however, if I could find my supposed guardian angel and convince him to help me. And even then, we were only assuming he had some advice to give; he might have just told us that it was too late to do anything.

"Well, what did she say?" Lita asked first, sounding so hopeful that it was almost too much for my heart to take.

"She gave us a way forward," I said before looking over at Stone. "That's why we shouldn't torture people; they might *actually* be useful."

"Oh, is that the reason we shouldn't torture people, because they might be of use to us?" he smirked. "Be careful, young man, you're starting to sound like me. Besides, who can say that the torture isn't what loosened her tongue in the first place?"

"I'm not getting into this with you, Stone," I said bitterly. "Dr. Robinson told me what I needed to do. We have apparently had an ally that we didn't even know about."

"An ally?" Stone asked. "Who would that be?"

"The same creature that warned me not to take the medication in the first place," I revealed. "My inner voice, my fear, my reflection. Whatever you want to call it. It warned me this would happen, so she suggested that it might be on our side."

"So, she doesn't just think it's a figment of your imagination?" Reynolds asked.

"Nothing else has been so far, so there's a good chance this isn't either," I stated. "I just need to make contact somehow."

"Any idea how to do that?" Grimes asked.

"I think I might have a better chance if I were unconscious," I admitted.

"So, you're proposing we let you take a nap?" Stone asked. "Didn't you just wake up from a little bit of a coma already?"

"I thought we were trying to stop the apocalypse, Major," I said. "Shouldn't we stop acting like rational moves are our way out of this? When are you going to realize that pragmatism and all the old rules have officially been tossed out the window?"

"He's not exactly the type to think outside the box, babe," said Lita. "That kinda creativity has been bred out of him. He's been given a bunch of hammers and told that the whole world consists of nothing but nails. Let's go find you somewhere you can meditate or something."

Lita and I started to walk off, but I worried that we might have hurt Stone's feelings. I don't know if I imagined it or if I actually heard what came next.

"Are you all right?" Grimes asked.

"I'm fine," Stone replied. "You think I've fought in wars, *won* wars, and I am going to start boo-hooing because I got my feelings hurt?"

Lita took me to a huge bedroom in the mansion and I was able to tell right away that this was where she had been stationed since Gracie Mansion had become our new headquarters. She had moved her things and mine in here.

"They really hooked you up with this room," I commented.

"They really hooked *us* up," she quickly corrected me. "We're staying here together. It'll be nice to get some sleep in this bed instead of in that uncomfortable chair in your hospital room."

"You were there at the hospital with me the entire time?" I asked.

"Of course, where else would I be?" she asked, almost sounding offended by the question. "You thought I would just leave you there while all this craziness was going on?"

"No, but what about visiting hours," I asked. "No one made a big deal about that?"

"You're adorable," she smiled. "You think people still care about little rules like that after the world has gone to hell? Besides, even if those rules were still being enforced, no one on this planet had the power to keep me from your bedside until you were better."

I stopped in my tracks and walked across the room to where she was standing and took her into my arms. I held her tight, but not so much it would make her feel uncomfortable. I looked into her eyes and she looked into mine for several moments until she started to feel uncomfortable with the silence of it all.

"What's this?" she giggled nervously.

"I just wanted to tell you how much I love you, Lita," I said. "No one has had my back like you have and that means a lot to a guy like me. It means everything. You make me stronger."

"No, I don't," she shook her head. "That strength has always been there, Saul. You just never realized it. You've been holding these monsters at bay your whole life. Creatures that can tear the world apart have been kept imprisoned by you for decades. You're probably the strongest person in the world...and that was all before you met me."

I kissed her after that. I simply couldn't resist. She was just...too perfect. Too perfect and it overwhelmed me in that moment. One passionate kiss turned into several and soon we were in bed. Instead of meditating, she found a different way to relax me and when I finally did fall asleep afterwards, my reflection was waiting for me in my dreams.

In the dream, I was in the subway, but I couldn't tell where I was going. It wasn't terribly crowded and everyone was able to get a seat. I looked around me and no one seemed to even notice that I was there, so I hoped this would be mundane and not the makings of some terrible nightmare. I had had quite enough of nightmares at this point.

"Looking for me?" my reflection asked, catching me by surprise by sitting down next to me and then opening up a comically large newspaper to start reading.

"Yes," I stammered. "I need your help."

"Here we go," he said, expelling an exaggerated sigh and exhalation, as though he was trying to blow down a pig's house of straw. "You made the biggest mistake of your life, so big that everyone is paying the price for it, and now you're here to beg me to help you. All I've ever done is help you, Saul, and then you spat in my face and acted like I've always been the problem."

He sounded genuinely hurt and that struck me as weird. If this was just a part of me, just the little voice designed to keep me safe, why would it be acting so dejected right now? Maybe he was a separate entity altogether, something *sent* to me to keep me safe.

"I'm...sorry," I apologized. "I really had no idea that any of this would happen."

"You should have listened to me, Saul," he pouted.

"I know," I said. "I made a huge mistake, but I wanna fix it."

"Fix it?" he asked, scrunching up his face.

"Yeah," I nodded. "What can we do to make everything better?"

"What makes you think that anything can be repaired in this situation?" he asked as the train stopped to pick up more people.

"Come on," I pleaded. "It can't end like this. I can't be responsible for the world coming to an end. I just can't. Tell me...something please."

He looked around the train and cast a suspicious glance on all of the people starting to crowd onboard. I could see his face tighten and his brow furrowing. He was worried about something, and it made me feel like I should have been worried too.

"We should get out of here," he said as he got to his feet. "Come with me."

I started to follow him through the crowded train, but it was difficult. Every time I tried to stick close, another person tried to block my path. It seemed accidental at first, but eventually I could tell it was intentional. The people blocking me kept looking dead into my eyes and smirking like they knew precisely what they were doing all along. Soon they were bumping and shouldering me so hard, it was knocking the breath out of me. I felt like I was going to be buried beneath these strangers until...

"Saul!" my reflection yelled out from a distance. "Don't let them push you around! They only have power over you if you believe they do!"

I don't know if I actually believed him, but I certainly felt something course through me when I heard those words. I leaped up and immediately scattered the people around me. They stared at me like they wanted to try me, but with one stomp of my foot, they parted like the red sea. I then rushed to catch up to my reflection.

"What's your name?" I asked when I finally caught up to him.

"What makes you think my name isn't Saul, like yours?" he asked, barely glancing back at me.

"You don't say my name with the awkwardness of someone who has the same name," I replied. "Besides, if Danny Torrance and Tony can have different names, then why not you and I?"

"What would you like to call me?" he smirked as we continued to walk through the train, from one car to the next. "And don't say Tony; we're not doing that."

I tried to give it some thought while I attempted to keep close. I wasn't going to pick Tony as a name, too bland. I thought about figures from TV, movies, books that I kinda liked. Tuvok. Dr. Miles Hawkins. People from comic books and sci-fi mostly, but nothing seemed to fit just right.

"Lex," I blurted out eventually. "Short for Lexington."

"You're a weird dude," he smiled as he continued walking. "Lex it is then. Let's go. We need to get somewhere safe so we can have a real conversation."

"Isn't this place safe?" I asked. "I mean, we're in my brain."

"Can you imagine a less safe place than the confines of your mind?" he asked me seriously. "There are corners in here that I don't even like thinking about. No, we need to go find your happy place...if it even still exists after all the damage you've caused."

"My 'happy place'?" I laughed derisively. "What is this, kindergarten?"

"Kindergarten would be great for most people, but your experience was terrible," he sighed. "You walked in on the first day and every kid looked at you like you were there to steal their parents from them. Not a friendly smile in the whole damned place. God, you are such a fucking mess, you know that, Saul?"

"So where are we going?" I asked, scarcely noticing as the subway cars we were walking through a moment ago turned into the hall of my old elementary school. Things were changing and shifting around me like a dream and all I could do was try to keep up with my guide. "Wait, where are we? Weren't we just in...?"

"Keep up, Saul," he said sternly. "I cannot stress enough how bad it would be for us to stay in any one place for too long. Stay close."

I tried to keep up with Lex, but he was so much faster than me. He knew this place like it was the back of his hand while I stumbled around like a tourist in a foreign world. I was a stranger in a strange land and that strange land was the landscape of my own mind. How trippy was that?

I heard my name being called out as we were talking, and I looked away for a moment. Just a moment and I lost sight of my guide. I forgot all about him when I saw that I was standing in front of the house where Nigel lived with his grandmother.

"Shit!" I whispered at the sight of the place.

This was definitely not my happy place, far from it. It was the setting for every nightmare I have ever had. I could somehow feel myself sweating and my breath catching in my throat as the place loomed large in front of me. It loomed too large in fact, like it was getting bigger and bigger the more I stood there in front of it. My heart was racing so much I thought I was going to have a heart attack.

As afraid as I was in that moment, something compelled me to go closer to the house, venture inside even though I already knew what was likely to be found there. My feet kept carrying me towards that nightmare house even though my brain screamed at me to stay away. Just as I was about to cross the threshold into the house, a hand grabbed me by the shoulder and yanked me backwards so hard, I almost lost my balance and fell on my ass.

No longer was I outside Nigel's house, but rather inside one of my favorite comic book stores instead with Lex standing over me angrily. He had clearly saved me again and he was getting tired of having to do so.

"Didn't I tell you to stay close?" he asked.

"I tried but you move too fast," I answered before he helped me to my feet. "Thanks. Is...is this my happy place? Are we safe here now?"

"Not quite," he shook his head. "This is precisely where they'll come looking for you."

"Who will come looking for me?" I asked, dusting myself off. "What are these things? Something I made up or...?"

"No, Saul," he said getting inches from my face. "These are not little phobias that your brain created from watching horror movies at too young an age or from misfiring fucking neurons. These things are very real and they are distinct entities not remotely a part of you."

"How...did they get inside my brain, Lex?" I asked.

"I'm not sure where they came from or how they got there, but I know you, Saul," he replied. "I know you very well. You give off a very distinct...glow. I can recognize it from anywhere. These others though... they have no glow, Saul. They're just...I don't know, dark. Darker than dark even. Almost like fucking voids, black holes that tear and rip at the fabric of reality. All I know for sure, Saul, is that they don't belong in your head and they belong even less in the real world."

"You're scaring me, Lex," I said, quickly glancing around at the few people in the comic shop around us, noticing that they kinda-sorta looked familiar. "You're making them sound more like aliens or demons. You're making it seem like I'm possessed or something."

"No, Saul, you used to be possessed," he informed me, "but now your demons are roaming free. It's the planet that's possessed now."

"And you're going to help me?" I asked, a little distracted by the other patrons in the shop. I knew that I knew them from somewhere, but I couldn't quite place from where.

"If there is a way to help you, Saul, I will do it," he stated, his eyes darting back and forth at the strangers thumbing through current issues of Spawn and Black Panther. "But we're gonna need to be quick because your demons are not all gone. Some of them are still here...right now."

I was still listening to Lex, but I recognized the man standing over by the Manga section. It was Barry Parker, a dude I knew from middle school. How I could tell this was him all grown up is anyone's guess, but I just knew it was him. He was a bully, three or four years older than me because he had been held back a few times, and he just seemed to love tormenting me.

Barry was short, shorter than all the other kids even though he was older than us. That was probably what made him so...cruel, so vicious. He managed to get henchmen for himself, two really tall dudes who also must have been held back a few times because they were as tall as any adult. Any time Barry caught me in the stairwell, he would get his thugs to hold me while he punched me in the stomach. The only thing that used to save me was his girlfriend telling him how turned off she was by seeing him acting like this. He would then leave me alone to go apologize to her.

"Barry?" I whispered.

"That's right, four-eyes," he said, dropping a copy of '**One Piece'** to the floor as he started to saunter over to me. "Surprised to see me?"

"What the hell are you doing here?" I asked.

"I've been looking for you," he smirked before his two henchmen from middle school came up behind me and grabbed me by the arms to hold me in place. "You and I are about to relive the good old days."

I knew what that meant. He was going to punch me in the stomach just like he used to. And since his girlfriend didn't seem to be in the shop, there was nothing to stop him. Well, almost nothing. I thought to ask Lex to handle these guys, but something came to me in that moment as Barry began to walk towards me. You can call it an epiphany or a bolt from the blue, but it felt like righteous anger.

"Get the fuck away from me, Barry!" I yelled before I straight-leg kicked him backwards and sent him scrambling him to the floor.

He was shocked that I had done that to him, almost as surprised as me. Once I did it, though, I felt the need to do so much more. I shrugged off the henchmen and threw them both to the floor angrily. While they were down there, I kicked one in the face and watched him slide across the floor and then I immediately followed it up by kicking the other henchman in the stomach and sending him sliding across the floor.

"I'm so tired of your bullshit!" I screamed. "Keep your damn hands off me!"

As I yelled, the entire comic shop shook like there was a fault line underneath the place and Barry and his gang all clawed at their ears as if my voice was causing physical pain. As I kept screaming at them, their bodies started to disintegrate right before my very eyes. I should have been horrified, but it was honestly rather thrilling to see. I stopped yelling after I had reduced the three of them to nothing but ash.

"What the hell was that?"

I looked over and saw a look of shock on Lex's face, like he didn't know what to make of what he had just seen. I thought he would be impressed by what I had done, but he looked horrified. My smile quickly faded away. What had gotten into him? What did I do that was so wrong? I stood there like a chastised child and waited for Lex to explain what was going on.

"You have access to their powers, Saul?" he asked eventually. "How long have you been able to do that?"

"What makes you think this is *their* power?" I asked in confusion. "All I did was kick a bully and then..."

"Scream until they were reduced to ash?" he finished my sentence. "You think that's normal?"

"Well, maybe not in the real world, but this is all inside my head," I shrugged. "I figured it was like lucid dreaming and Nancy taking back the power she gave to Freddy Krueger or whatever."

"Oh yeah?" he asked incredulously. "Have you ever done any shit like that before? Have you ever been able to face any of your demons so fearlessly, destroy them so effortlessly? I hate to break it to you, but you have never been the 'final girl' type. You're either the black guy who dies at the start of the movie or you're the brainy type who sticks around to handle all the computer stuff for the main character until you're no longer needed...and then the monster quickly dispatches you too."

"That's pretty harsh, Lex," I frowned, but I couldn't dispute what he was saying either. "I'm not useless...as you just saw for yourself."

He frowned too for a few moments before he let his face soften a bit. He clapped a hand on my shoulder, trying to reassure me. We locked eyes and then he gave me a half smile. It was a little disconcerting, but I could tell he was trying at least.

"Don't lose hope, Saul," he said. "That ability you just showed, that strength, is going to come in very handy. I didn't know if you had what it took to fight back the darkness that's been unleashed, but that little technique shows promise."

"Does it?" I asked. "It's great when we are here in the mindscape, I guess, but it won't mean anything out there in the real world."

"Maybe we can find a way to transfer the power outside of here," he shrugged. "Now let's go. We need to find your happy place before more of these things show up."

We continued to move from one area in my mind to another, staying ahead of all my apprehensions. We tried to move fast enough for me not to think about all the things hiding in the shadows. There was one thing I worried about throughout the entire run: was Lita okay while I was sleeping? I mean, that giant penis could make its way to New York and destroy the building we were all in. If that happened, then this would all be over before we even really had a chance to fight back. I could only hope that my continued trek through the recesses of my brain was proof that there was still a world there to save.

"So where *is* my...happy place?" I asked Lex because it was taking a long time to get there. "And why is it so far away?"

"It's far away because you buried it down deep," he grumbled angrily. "I don't know how we're ever going to access it. I've only seen the place once during my travels through your brain."

"Why would I have buried my happy place down so deep?" I inquired. "You would think I would need it somewhere within reach, like, all the time."

"If the place was easily reached, those monsters would have found it and destroyed it by now," he explained. "I...don't know what you would be if that happened. You'd probably be a shambling shell of yourself, like a fucking zombie dead to the world. Or..."

"Or what?" I asked.

He stopped in his tracks and turned to face me. He had a look on his face like he was thinking of a nice way to say what he was thinking, but the words were eluding him. Something passed over his face, like sympathy or perhaps even pity, and then he simply shook his head.

"Forget it," he said. "We got to get where we're going before it's too late."

I wanted to press him for answers, but seeing as he was the only ally I had in the mindscape, I didn't want to alienate him. We needed to find my happy place or the slim chance we had of stopping my demons was going to slip right through my grasp like sand through my fingers. I had more pressing issues to be honest. The more Lex and I spoke, the more I was starting to become convinced that he really wasn't a part of me. So, what was he? Where did he come from? And what did he want from me? I didn't think those questions were appropriate for right then either. Instead, I just looked around at all the areas of my brain that I was led through.

The trek got tighter and tighter as we continued through the increasingly darker recesses of my brain, and I was not handling it well. Small rooms and tight windows and corridors that looked like I could get stuck in forever. I kept thinking about the spelunker who crawled into a crevice so tight there was no way to save him; all they could do was make him comfortable as he slowly died. I thought about the boulders pressing down on him, his breathing getting more and more labored and ragged, until his body got crushed like a tin can. Why didn't they just shoot him, put him out of the misery that had enveloped him?

I couldn't bear the thought. The idea of having my limbs restrained, my movements restricted, like that was a pure nightmare. I could never let that happen to me. I would rather be dead. Death would be a comfort if something like that ever happened to me.

"What are you doing? We gotta keep moving."

He was standing at the window of my kindergarten class that I used to look through when I wanted to daydream. That window would have been nearly impossible for a small child to squirm out of, so there was little chance I was making it through it.

"I can't fit through that window, Lex," I shook my head. "I'm way too big."

"You're 5'5 and weigh practically nothing," he grimaced. "Get over here."

"I really can't do it," I told him. "I'll get stuck in there and then the space will get tighter and tighter until it crushes me. I don't want to die like that, Lex."

"Listen to me, Saul, you need to come with me," he said with more determination in his voice. "We're almost there. We can't linger here for long when those things are still looking for you."

"I will be crushed under the weight of that, Lex," I stated.

"You're not going to be crushed, Saul," he said, trying to be sympathetic. "You're going to be just fine. You're seeing the space as being too tight to get through because your mind is trying to keep you from getting to your happy place. It's trying to keep you in misery, make you a victim of your demons. I need you to have the faith to come with me right now before they succeed in destroying you and everything else. Can you do that, Saul?"

I was still scared to absolute death, but he sounded so sure of himself. I gave him a slight nod and he returned it with a warm smile. I then watched him disappear through the small window and into whatever space was located on the other side. It was my turn now. As I stood there, staring at the window, I could hear things scurrying around behind me. It was clearly my demons. They had found me and were going to try to rip me apart before I could escape. It was now or never.

"Ah shit," I grumbled before I started to crawl through the window as well.

It wasn't as easy as Lex had let on. In fact, as I squirmed my way through that tight passage, I started to suspect that he straight-up lied to me to get me to do what he needed me to do. I crawled and crawled and crawled with what felt like rats gnawing at my feet the whole damned time. The space just got smaller and smaller, tighter and tighter, darker and darker, but I couldn't give up. I needed to keep going because there was no way I could allow myself to die there in the dark.

"Shit, shit, shit!" I kept grumbling as I continued to wriggle through that window which somehow turned into a dark cavern as I ventured further.

My breath became more and more labored the further I moved, and I was terrified that there didn't seem to be a light at the end of this dreary tunnel. It occurred to me that Lex could very well have been just another one of my demons, secretly plotting against me rather than coming at me directly. Instead of leading me to freedom, he could have been luring me into the tomb where I would be forever buried.

My vision started to blur and I was getting really dizzy and I could just tell this was it for me. I was not going to fix what I had done to the planet. I was never going to see Lita again. I was going to die a failure, the failure who succeeded in breaking the world in a way that could never be repaired. I cursed myself for everything that I had done, for being a small foolish man who couldn't keep a handle on his fears and insecurities when the world needed me most.

"I should die here," I commented breathlessly. "That's what I deserve."

Just when I was going to give up and let the rats eat me alive from the feet up, a hand punched through the darkness and reached out to me, light erupting from behind it. I used the last of my strength and will to reach out and grab onto the hand in front of me. It then yanked me free of the cavern, free of the darkness, and brought me into a place where the light was so bright that I could hardly see.

"I told you that you could make it."

My eyes hadn't adjusted to the light yet, but I recognized Lex's voice. He had pulled me to safety right when I was about to give up for good. It took me a few moments for my eyes to get used to the light and for my breathing to regulate after the tunnel pressed down on me and compressed my lungs. When my vision cleared, I could see where I was and it was...beautiful.

"Oh my god!" I exclaimed at the sight of it. "This...*this* is my happy place?"

"I thought you would recognize it as soon as you saw it," he said, crossing his arms over his chest.

It was the first library that I had ever visited, the one I went to during my first school trip back in kindergarten. It figured that my happy place would be a place full of books. I've always been more comfortable with fictional people than real ones. Fake people can only hurt you but so much. I hadn't thought of the place in a long time, but now that I was there, I could remember every moment of my trip like it had happened only yesterday.

We walked as a class for six or seven blocks to get here across very dangerous roads and I was nervus we were going to get hit, but when we finally entered the library, I was perfectly at ease. The place was small with red bricks, a simple building, but the inside was where the magic was located. I couldn't imagine how one normal-looking building could hold so much wonder. It was like it was bigger on the inside.

Lex and I walked over to the kiddie corner, where my fellow classmates and I were directed to find books and to get started reading. I remember finding a "Star Wars: Return of the Jedi" pop-up book and then going to sit in a quiet corner to read my acquisition. None of the other kids bothered me because they were too busy with their own activities and books. I didn't have to worry about my family arguing at home or worrying about bills, didn't have to worry about the things I heard on the TV when my grandma watched the news. It was just me and my book, a simple story where the good guys won and the bad guys definitively lost.

"This is perfect," I commented with a smile as I walked around the old place.

"This place made you so happy once upon a time that you weren't even afraid to cross that big street on your way back to the school when you left," said Lex. "You were just so thrilled that such a place existed that you forgot about the dangers of this world for the next several hours. We need you to find that kind of inner peace again."

"Your plan is for me to find inner peace?" I asked. "You think I'm a cartoon panda or something? I don't think you get how bad it is out there, Lex."

"I think you better not bring that negativity in here," he frowned. "Your happy place is like a fragile bubble; it won't take much for it to go pop and then you'll be lost forever."

As soon as he said that the ground trembled a little bit. That was when a young black boy walked over and tapped me on the leg. I recognized him immediately. It was me, me from when I was five years old.

"You can't talk about stuff like that here," he informed us. "It makes the library mad."

"I'm sorry," I said. "We'll be careful. You can go back to reading your book. My friend and I won't be any bother."

Little Me nodded and then walked off to his quiet corner to continue reading. The library was bright like an animated movie, but it got a little darker when we brought negativity into the atmosphere. We were going to need to take it easy or I wouldn't have a happy place left to go to.

"You said that coming here was the first step to fighting back, Lex,' I said as we took a seat at a table while kids ran to and fro. "We're here. Tell me what you know."

"Your demons were in your head, held behind a wall, Saul," he began speaking, his eyes darting around as though he were uncomfortable about all the children running around the place. "I don't know who planted these things inside of you, but they're not a part of you."

"How do you know that?" I asked. "They seem like regular insecurities to me."

"To you, they would be," he exhaled. "You've lived with them for so long, you can't distinguish them from any other thought in your head, but I can see the truth. They are not you. Those creatures give off a crimson aura while you, my dear boy, are the purest, brightest blue light that I have ever seen in my whole life. Those things could not have come from you. Not in a million years. After everything you've been through, you've never changed. You took the worst the universe had to give and you didn't let it turn you into a monster."

I knew what he meant, the things that had happened to me. Lex knew of my...troubles. His compliments warmed my heart. I think being in my happy place allowed me to accept his words more readily than when Lita said something similar in reality.

"Well, if that's all true, then I guess it's up to me to stop these creatures," I nodded. "I was able to contain them in my head, so maybe that's the best place for them. We just need to rebuild that wall and then find a way to trap everything back inside again."

"Sounds great," he said. "How do we do that?"

I had no idea, but I didn't want to say that. I wanted to give the impression that I knew precisely what to do next. Before I could ruin the moment by revealing that I had nothing, Little Saul walked over with a new book in his hand and put it down on the desk in front of us.

"You're going to need to read through this," he said. "It will teach you everything you need to know for when you go back to fight those things."

"Thanks, buddy," I said with a smile as Lex sat there with his arms crossed over his chest.

He left without saying a word and then I turned towards Lex. He smirked at the smile on my face.

"Don't act like you planned that," he rolled his eyes. "You were lost until he brought that book over here."

I wondered how long it was going to take to read the book, particularly since there was no telling how much longer I would remain in this dream, but something surprising happened when the tome was opened. The pages lit up with a blue-ish hue that bathed us all in a comforting warmth. I was going to start reading the words written there, but there was no need. Somehow the words and their meanings poured off the page and straight into my brain and maybe even my soul. I could feel something inside of me...change as soon as the words imprinted on me.

"Are you okay?" Lex asked as he noticed some kind of change come over me. "You look different."

"That's because I *am* different," I smiled. "I think I figured out how to create a direct path right here to my happy place. A bridge."

"You just got that from that book you just...absorbed?" he asked.

"Oh yeah, that and a whole lot more," I nodded. "I need to get back to reality. It's time to..."

"Not yet," said Little Saul as he took a hold of my arm. "You can't read just the one book. You need to read every book in here. Only then will have any chance of saving everyone."

"How long do you think I am going to be here, buddy," I said as concern crept into my voice. "I took a nap to get here but it's only a matter of time before someone or something wakes me up."

"You need to read as much as you can before you leave," he insisted.

"Maybe the kid is right, Saul," Lex stated, almost nervously. "He does seem to know a hell of a lot more than we do."

"That was before I read that book," I commented.

"Yeah, the book *he* gave you," said Lex pointing at the kid. "All I'm saying is we're dealing with something huge here and we might only get one chance to fix everything. We don't want to jump the gun and fail."

"With this power, how can we possibly lose?" I asked as I raised my hand and showed that it was glowing with some kind of strange energy. "I'm going to go back to reality and cram those creatures back behind that wall and reinforce it so that it lasts another million years."

"Very impressive, but the kid and I are both in agreement that you need to take your time with this," said Lex. "You've read so many books and watched so many movies where the protagonist gets cocky and fights the villain without being fully prepared. It never turns out well."

"What are you saying?" I found myself asking, frowning a bit and making the library tremble as a result.

"I'm telling you not to be Vegeta," he said crossing his arms over his chest. "Play this smart; don't make me regret sticking my neck out to help you."

He was right, of course, and all it took was looking into his eyes and then the eyes of Little Saul to realize that I needed to listen instead of rushing headlong into conflict. I exhaled deeply before I nodded and agreed to start reading through all the books I could get. I absorbed the essence of each tome and made it part of me, feeling stronger with each book I cracked open. By the time I was done with all the books in the fiction section, I felt like I was the most powerful creature in the universe. So powerful that I felt like I was going to burst at the seams.

"How do you feel?" Lex asked, looking at me suspiciously as I stood there slightly vibrating, my body emitting a soft buzz while light erupted from my pores.

"Strong," I admitted. I couldn't help smiling. "How do I get back to reality?"

"You should put in those shortcuts before you leave here," Lex stated. "You don't want to have to go through that whole thing again. Those sentries are going to be ready for you if you come through there a second time. It's important to be able to get here as quickly as possible."

"I understand," I chuckled giddily. "You worry too much."

"*I* worry too much?" he scoffed at the very thought. "Are those books laced with CBD oil or something because you sound high."

"You're going to wake up soon," Little Saul commented with a frown on his face. "You need to work fast."

I nodded and then proceeded to mold a golden lantern just by shaping the air around me. Once the lantern was complete, I set it down on one of the tables.

"This lantern will light the way to this place, so I will be able to return quickly no matter what," I told the others.

Lex looked at the golden lantern with the warm blue light emitting from it and he even seemed impressed with my new set of skills. Perhaps, we all thought, everything was going to work out just fine. That couldn't have been any further from the truth. None of us could truly comprehend in that moment just how much worse everything was going to get for us across the planet, but it wasn't going to be long before we all found out.

FIVE
TURNING POINT

Once I was done doing everything I needed to do inside my head, I awoke back in the real world. I didn't know how long I had been asleep, but it had to have been long enough for Lita to get tired too because she was cuddled up next to me. She was doing that little snore she does, but claims she doesn't. It brought a smile to my face and I realized that I was still feeling residual joy from having visited my happy place, a realm that had been closed off for me for so very long.

I couldn't wait to go tell the others what I had learned about fighting back against the madness that was ravaging our world, but I didn't want to wake up Lita either. After everything she had been through, she deserved as much rest as she could get. When the fight to take back our home from these nightmare creatures started in earnest, who knew how long it would be before we actually got some sleep. No, it was better for her to get her rest now, so we could start the fight at full strength.

I looked around the room a bit without jostling her. I never thought the day would come I would be sleeping in one of the bedrooms of the mayor's mansion. It seemed like an impossibility since I never had even the slightest political aspirations, but here I was. And it was a really nice bedroom too. The walls were adorned with old paintings, but I noted that they must have been thick because I couldn't hear anyone milling around outside. A place like this had to have people walking around all the time. That had to have been true even before this place became the command center for our fight against the end of the world. I didn't hear even a whisper from outside though.

I did, however, see the shadows of feet moving back and forth past the bedroom door. It was the only proof I had that there were even other people out there besides Lita and myself. I eventually found myself distracted by how much movement was taking place outside my door. It was a big building, too big for everyone to be right outside my room. There had to be offices and other spaces for them all to be occupying right then. The longer it went on, the more it started to bother me.

I kept watching the feet go back and forth, back and forth, until they eventually stopped right in front of the door and just lingered there. Now I was more than just a little bothered. I was now really concerned. All at once, I felt uneasy, like something terrible was about to happen. My eyes narrowed as more and more feet came to a stop right outside my door. Clearly, they were all here for a reason and it was time for me to find out precisely what it was.

I slid out of Lita's arms and then started to head towards the door. There was something I was forgetting, something picking at the back of my brain, but it didn't make itself apparent right away. It was something important though, I knew that, but I figured it would come to me at some point. No point in beating myself up over what I had forgotten.

When I got to the door and extended my hand for the knob, I froze. I was afraid, as afraid as I had ever been in my whole life, and it wouldn't let me touch the doorknob to see who was hanging around outside my bedroom door. I stood stock-still as I tried to shake the apprehension that had swept over me. What did I think was on the other side of that door, what made me too afraid to actually open it? I decided against opening it and took a different route instead.

"Who is out there?" I called out.

I could hear some whispers through the door, but couldn't make out what was being said. So, I called out even louder, determined to make sure that they heard me this time because I had no intention of opening that door until I knew precisely what I would find on the other side. When I called out the second time, the whispers on the other side of the door seemed to get a little louder, but I still couldn't make out what was being said. That frustrated me and so I yelled out for an answer one more time. The response I got chilled me to the bone.

"You forgot about the shark."

My eyes widened in realization that I had woken up from my nap and didn't once think about the shark at the foot of my bed. I had feared that blasted thing for years, but this time I didn't even think about it. I took no precautions whatsoever. And all that could only mean one thing: the blasted thing was behind me right now!

"Shit," I grumbled to myself as I slowly turned around, knowing what I would find there.

It perhaps would have made more sense to just open the door and flee, but I had left Lita in bed and there was no way I was going to leave her to that deep-sea devil. When I finally turned around, there was no shark, just Lita sitting up in bed, no doubt woken up by my earlier shouting.

"What's going on?" she asked.

Before I could scrape together some semblance of a response, the bedroom door exploded behind me, sending me and wood debris hurtling across the room. I landed on the bed next to Lita and instantly turned around to see what had caused the explosion...as if I didn't already know what I would find. A great white shark of immense proportions had just burst through the door and destroyed part of the wall as it gained access to the bedroom. Without any water, it was now hopping towards me and my girlfriend, obviously hoping to rip us to shreds with those rows upon rows of shiny white teeth.

Lita immediately scrambled backwards to the headboard but there was nowhere to go. The monster lumbering towards us had our only exit blocked. I could hear her shrieks of terror as she screamed "no, no, no" at the sight of this thing coming towards us. I should have been just as terrified as she was, but I wasn't, not this time. No, this time I was angry. No, that would be an understatement; this time, I was absolutely mad as hell.

"Nuh uh," I said in barely a whisper, next to inaudible compared to Lita's yelling. "Not like this."

I could feel her behind me, grabbing and clawing at me, expecting me to do something in the face of that giant maw threatening to swallow us both whole. She wanted me to protect her, but she didn't have faith there was anything that could be done when confronted with a creature designed by evolution to hunt and kill. Usually, she would have been right about that. But things had been anything but "usual" for quite some time now.

The shark threw itself onto the foot of the bed and almost completely demolished it. The lowering of the bed pulled Lita and myself closer to those massive jaws as the smell of marine life filled our nostrils. The shark's eyes were black, sure, just like Quint said, but this creature seemed to have an amused look on its face. It knew what it was doing and relished it.

When it opened its mouth to take its first bite of me, I grabbed it on instinct and held it open while my hands started to emit the same blue aura that they did in my happy place. Apparently, I brought some of that strength into the real world. The amused look was gone from the shark's face as I dug my fingers into its rough skin like a child sticking its fingers in clay.

"I said...not like this," I said, but the voice didn't sound like me at all. It sounded angrier, deeper, and echoed with a strange power.

The shark seemed confused as to how I was able to stop it with just my bare hands, but it didn't stop trying to eat me even as I held its jaws open. That made me even angrier. I was so mad...that I ripped the beast in half with one violent motion, sending blood and guts splashing everywhere. The body slumped down and rolled over onto the floor while I held the head in my hands.

"You need to leave me the fuck alone," I whispered to it while staring into its black eyes.

The shark's eyes widened in realization before it all turned to ash and blew away. Even the blood and guts disappeared. The only thing that remained as proof of what had just happened was the gaping hole in the wall from the monster's entrance. I stood on what was left of the bed and tried desperately to catch my breath, feeling like I was drowning in my own rage, until a hand clasped my shoulder. I turned around to see Lita there, looking just as confused as the shark about my newfound strength.

"What was that?" she asked.

"I think that was probably the shark that ate your neighbor," I replied, my shoulders rising and falling as I tried to get my breathing under control.

"No, not that," she shook her head. "What was with your hands glowing? What was up with the voice? How did you rip a shark in half? And...why are your eyes like that?"

Now I was confused. "What's wrong with my eyes?"

"They're black," she explained, pulling out her phone to show me how I looked in that moment. "Just like...a shark's eyes."

I didn't like the sound of that. I closed my eyes and placed my arms down by my sides and tried to calm down, let the anger that had welled up inside of me drift away. When I felt at peace again, I opened my eyes and Lita's look of concern turned into a smile.

"How do I look now?" I asked.

"Better," she nodded. "What happened to you?"

"I went to sleep and I guess I started dreaming or whatever," I replied. "I found my happy place and that gave me power, power I must have brought into the real world."

"What else can you do?" she asked.

"We're about to find out," I said. "Because I think this is all coming to an end."

"What makes you think that?" she asked.

"The shark showing up here just now is not a coincidence, Lita," I stated. "It was an assassination attempt. They're coming for me."

"Are you sure?" she asked.

"Yeah," I nodded. "So that means we've got an answer to one question at least. Killing me won't stop these manifestations, not if even the manifestations want me dead too."

"We need to let Major Bummer know that then," she smiled uneasily. "I'm not convinced that he's not still thinking of killing you to put an end to all of this."

"He can try and then he will see me go all black-eyed," I responded. "Let's go find the others and let them know what's going on. Stick close to me though. If the attacks are becoming personal, then I'm going to be ground zero for a lot of craziness."

"More than usual?" she asked.

"A lot more," I said. "Let's go."

We left the room through the crater in the wall and made our way towards the meeting area on the first floor. A nagging thought kept eating away at me. A monstrous shark bursting through a wall should have alerted the troops, sent them scrambling to find out what happened. But as we walked down that long corridor that led to the stairs, we didn't run into a single soul. My stride slowed down a bit as I pondered the reason. I knew I needed to slow down, stop rushing. If I hadn't been in such a rush, I would have noticed the missing shark before it got the drop on me.

"Wait, where is everybody?" I asked as I stopped in my tracks. "All that commotion and no one came running in here? Why not?"

She stopped and started thinking about it as well. You could tell from the look on her face that she came to the same conclusion as me only much quicker. An oppressive feeling of dread seized upon us both as we realized that this had to be some sort of trap. She grabbed onto my arm and looked me in the eye.

"We cannot get separated here, Saul," she said, her voice barely above a whisper. "You don't lose me and I don't lose you. You got it?"

I nodded that I understood and then we slowly started walking through the mansion, looking for any friendly faces within the confines of this horror show. The further we ventured down the hallway, the more decayed the walls started to look, like we had stumbled into a decrepit haunted house or something. Clearly something had changed while I was sleeping, finding the weapons to fight against the evils that were tormenting us. Perhaps we were up against an intelligent foe and not just mindless chaos; maybe it knew that I had gotten stronger and was trying to stop me before I could stop it. I didn't really have time to consider all the possibilities.

"I don't like this, Lita," I whispered as we continued to walk. "Something is very wrong."

"Things have been very wrong for a while, Saul," she said. "Are you saying it's gotten worse somehow?"

"Yes, the air around us feels heavy," I continued. "Like something is wrong…with the atmosphere or something. The sooner we get out of here, the better."

We made it to the staircase to find it blanketed in complete darkness. It wasn't just the light fixtures being damaged either. It seemed like the deepest, most oppressive darkness had settled in right there on the stairs and made it its new home.

"We've got to get downstairs," I said.

"I'm not walking through that, Saul," she shook her head. "No way. This is a trap."

"We've got to get off this floor and find the others," I told her. "It's our only chance."

"There has to be another staircase on this floor, Saul," she shook her head. "We don't have to go through that."

"What makes you think the others won't be like this or worse?" I asked. "The creeping darkness in front of us is not the worst thing we could have been confronted with. Just hold my hand and I swear I will get you through this."

She looked at me and studied my face, trying to see if she could trust me to protect her. I gave her my first Poker face because I wasn't sure of anything in that moment save for the fact that we needed to keep moving. She scrunched her face like she could see that I wasn't as confident as I claimed to be. She still looked absolutely adorable, even then, with evil surrounding us and threatening to consume us fully. Her face relaxed and she smiled up at me. She was ready to take that leap of faith with me and that suddenly made me feel more confident.

"Well, if you swear, then let's do this," she nodded, slipping her hands into mine. "I love you, Saul."

"I love you too, Lita," I assured her before I tightened my grip on her hand and pulled her into the pulsing darkness with me.

The moment we stepped into the darkness, I instantly regretted the decision. It was colder than any winter I had ever felt in my life, and it began to gnaw at my skin. I couldn't see Lita anymore once we were inside that mass; I couldn't see anything once we were inside. I could still feel her hand in mine as I walked along, but then these funny thoughts began to creep into my head. Yeah, I was holding her hand, but what if that was all there was to her now? What if her hand was now all that existed in this world? What if the darkness had consumed her completely and was cruel enough to let just the hand I was holding survive?

I used to be able to comfort myself by telling myself how ridiculous the very concept was, but I couldn't do that anymore. The world had been broken in such a way that even this impossible nightmare was just as viable as anything else my twisted mind could conjure. At this point, the possibility of being swallowed by shadows was just as likely as the sun rising on a brand-new day and that new, terrible reality was all my fault.

I tried calling her, but the darkness snatched my words as soon as they left my mouth, froze them solid, and shattered them into a million pieces before they had any hope of reaching her ears. Assuming her ears even still existed, that is. Who could be sure anymore? So, if talking to her was no longer possible, all I could do was keep venturing forward, walking with her hand in mine until we finally made out way to the light. Dear God, let there still be light in this cruel world that I had created.

Who was I kidding? If God existed and saw what I had wrought, He would never answer my prayers. I am the abomination that destroyed His greatest creation. I am the serpent in His garden. It was clear now that I was the devil that had spoken about in so many cultures over so many centuries. I was evil incarnate, made flesh. It was unintentional, but that made no difference to the millions who were suffering, the billions who would meet their gruesome ends by the monsters that slept in my diseased brain.

I tried not think as I kept pushing against the darkness. It was like walking against the wind or against layers upon layers of cellophane against a doorframe. It was trying to keep me there, trap me there forever, holding the severed hand of my real first love. And that angered me. I didn't want to be trapped there, with my greatest failure. I needed to break out and be free.

I needed to find the light.

I needed to find the light.

I NEED THE LIGHT!!!

I pushed and pushed and pushed, walking through the darkness inch by inch. My brain was filled with so many thoughts. What if there was nothing left of Lita but her hand? What if I had lost her? What if there was no end to this darkness? What if this was where I was always meant to be? What if this was my destiny all along, to be trapped in the void forever? What if time passed differently in the dark and by the time I emerged with Lita's hand (and not the rest of her), apes were ruling the planet or some shit like that?

"Just keep going," a tiny voice said above the thunderous self-doubt and insecurities. "Just keep walking."

Was that Lex, still with me at the potential end of all things? Was he a magical stowaway in my brain, helping to keep the dark thoughts at bay? I needed something to get me through it, but all I had was a disembodied voice and a severed hand. I kept pushing against the dark while it continued to fight back. The further I traveled, the worse the pressure got. Eventually, it felt like it was going to rip the very skin from my bones. It was like I was at a concert and I ended up standing right in front of the speakers; in this case, the music playing was head-banging heavy metal. I could feel my teeth rattling in my skull and it felt like my eyes were... liquefying or something. I could almost feel the same thing happening to my organs too.

Clearly, Lita was right. We should have found a way around this darkness. Going through it was a huge mistake. It looked like it was going to be the last mistake I ever had the chance to make. I could have just sat there on the ground and let myself be destroyed, but something compelled me to keep moving. I don't know what it was that kept these legs moving, maybe some tiny spark of hope, but I simply refused to stop.

I felt moisture on my cheeks and couldn't tell if there were tears of despair or blood pouring from my eyes because my brain was hemorrhaging from the pressure. I ignored it and kept venturing forward, but soon I began to feel tired. I wasn't going to be able to walk anymore. I already felt like I had been walking for hours. Right when I was prepared to give up, I saw a light, like someone had poked a pinhole into the darkness that was covering reality.

"There's the way out. You can make it."

Lex confirmed what I had already figured out: there was a light at the end of the tunnel. I kept heading towards it, despite how far away it seemed. The closer I got, the harder the darkness tried to push me back. Every step I managed to take was like its own little war. It felt like my knees would buckle as though I were carrying bricks on my back. With each step, I just wanted to die so the pain would just finally be over. Not even Lex's encouragement in my head was enough to make this ordeal any easier to handle.

But I made it. The little pinhole of light grew larger and brighter until it felt like I was walking right into the sun. I went from not seeing anything because it was too dark to not being able to see anything because I was blinded by the intense light. After taking one more step, the hardest step I have ever taken in my entire life, I was vomited out of the void and back into reality and found myself on the ground floor of Gracie Mansion. I blinked rapidly as I tried to get my vision back.

I could feel Lita's hand in mine still, but it wasn't moving. Some part of me was hoping that I was wrong about the darkness consuming her, eating away at everything but her hand. Some part of me wanted to believe we were both going to be okay. Lita's hand being motionless just confirmed my worst fears.

As I attempted to get my eyes to adjust to the light, I could feel several hands grabbing at me and there was a bunch of voices all around me. I couldn't tell if they were friends or foes, but I struggled against them anyway. After what I had just endured, I wasn't in the mood to be grabbed by anyone or anything, even if they were trying to help me.

"Get off me!" I heard myself yell as I struggled to be free of the hands. "Get off!"

"Calm down, Saul, it's me."

I recognized the voice immediately as Detective Reynolds. As my vision cleared, I was able to see her kneeling beside me, trying to help me to my feet. She had a harried look on her face that let me know that things had gotten really bad while I was passing through the void. With my vision clear, I looked over to see what was left of Lita. To my surprise and delight, she was completely intact; her hand was motionless because she had lost consciousness at some point during our trip.

"Oh, thank God," I commented, pulling her closer to me and holding her in my arms.

"What happened to you two?" Reynolds asked soothingly despite all the crazed people running back and forth around us. "Were you attacked?"

"The shark showed up again and tried to eat us while we were in the room," I answered. "We escaped and made it to the stairs, but there was..."

"Yeah, the giant shadow," she nodded. "They are at every stairwell right now. You don't even want to know what's at all the exits right now. Is Lita all right?"

"She's just unconscious," I replied, having already checked her pulse. "She's...she's gonna be okay."

"None of are going to be okay, Copeland, if we don't find a way out of this building," Stone barked as he walked over.

I knew we were in bad shape as soon as I saw Stone. There was chaos all around us, but he was always put-together and never had a hair out of place. I had gotten to the point where I simply chalked it up to the discipline of his military background. He wasn't looking so good now; he looked like he had been put through the wringer in my time away from him. His uniform was ripped and covered in blood and soot while he limped over to us.

"What happened to you?" I asked, looking up at him while I cradled my girlfriend in my arms.

"Had a little run-in with those creatures we encountered in Staten Island," he answered. "I just lost seven good men to those things. We'll mourn our dead later, but for right now I need to know if your little excursion into the Twilight Zone or whatever was successful."

"Kinda," I said.

"What does 'kinda' mean?" he demanded.

"Well, when the shark attacked us upstairs, somehow I was granted the ability to rip it apart with my bare hands," I said.

"Excellent!" he exclaimed, eyes widening in shock and delight. "Finally getting some weapons on our side of this fight! With your new abilities, can you get us out of here?"

"I don't know how to access my abilities yet," I shook my head. "I was able to do it because we were in immediate danger, but that's it. I am going to need more time, Stone."

I expected him to shout at me. It was no secret that he considered me at best worthless and at worst, the cause of all his troubles. I thought he was going to rip into me for another failure on my part, but instead he simply took a deep breath and looked down at me with a face full of understanding and perhaps pity.

"Don't worry, Copeland," he said. "We'll buy you as much time as you need. Reynolds, where is Grimes?"

"He's fortifying a few of the rooms, so we can have a bunker to settle into," she stated. "They're gathering in the dining area."

"Where's Dr. Robinson?" I asked. "Lita needs help."

"She's with Grimes," she revealed. "Come with me."

Major Stone told us that he'd cover us, so I scooped Lita up into my arms and carried her as I followed Detective Reynolds. We passed a lot of corpses as we walked swiftly through those hallowed halls. I could see they all met gruesome ends. Some were turned inside out while others were dismembered. It took everything in me not to throw up every step of the way.

"What happened here?" I asked. "How long was I gone?"

"Not very long," said Reynolds, agitation rising in her voice. "We were overrun by a bunch of these monsters all at once, different ones. We weren't prepared for them. We weren't prepared for them to be working together. I hope that new power of yours can turn the tide because we are not doing well."

"I've been told that it can fix everything," I told her. "I might be able to put everything back to the way they were before. I just need more time to figure it all out."

"Hopefully, we still have enough time left for that," she said.

We soon reached the room that Grimes had fortified and he eagerly let us enter. He smiled when he saw Reynolds, but he smiled even broader when he saw me. I smiled a little too. Ever since we first met, Grimes had been extremely nice to me. He was more understanding about all this nonsense than anyone could ever hope for. As a government agent tasked with saving the world from an inexplicable disaster, it would have been easy for him to throw me into a deep dark pit or have geniuses dissect me and experiment on all my bits and pieces. But no, he recognized that I was just as much a victim in all this as anyone and he sought to work with me to find a way back to normality. The smile he gave me now was hopeful, like he was glad that I had survived and that I had another chance to make things right. The smile faded a little when he looked down and saw Lita in my arms.

"Is she all right?" he asked.

"We passed through some sort of black hole or something," I tried to explain. "It...did something to us. When we got through to the other side, she was unconscious."

"Don't worry, Saul," he said reassuringly. "Dr. Robinson is here and she can fix her right up. Take her over there and get yourselves straight."

I carried her over to the corner of the dining hall where he had pointed while he walked over and started talking to Reynolds about something, probably our current state. I approached Robinson and she quickly urged me to lay Lita down on a makeshift gurney. She silently went about her business of checking her out and then sighed in relief.

"She's going to be okay, Mr. Copeland," she said calmly. "How are you holding up?"

"Not well," I chuckled nervously. "Even if I fix this, all of this, I can't possibly resurrect the dead. I'll have to live with that."

"This isn't your fault, Mr. Copeland," she shook her head. "You didn't kill anyone. We're all going to have to heal from this and it is going to be tough, but no one is going to blame you for this."

"*You* blamed me for this," I frowned. "Why wouldn't everyone else? When all this is over, I am going to be locked up or killed. They're going to dissect me to find out how this happened so they can make sure it never happens again. Even if I manage to fix all this, put absolutely everything right, there is no life for me afterwards. Not everyone realizes that yet. I am sure Stone knows how this is going to play out, maybe even Grimes and Reynolds, but Lita still thinks there's a life for us on the other side of this."

"Have you stopped to consider that maybe you're wrong about this, Mr. Copeland?" she asked. "I'm sure you feel like you're being reasonable, pragmatic even, but your brain ignores all positive outcomes and only shows you the negative. Sure, sometimes the worst happens, but that doesn't mean it will this time and it doesn't mean that bad times will continue. I choose to believe that if you do your best to save this world, then you will most certainly have a place in it afterwards."

"You really think so?" I asked. "You honestly think there's redemption at the end of this? Even for someone as fucked-up as me?"

"What I believe is irrelevant," she stated warmly. "If *you* don't believe you're worthy of redemption, then no one else's opinion is going to matter much. Not even Ms. Ramirez's. You need to believe in your own self-worth, your ability to be loved and accepted. It's the only thing that will save you. *You* are the only one who can save you."

I had heard that kind of talk before, on TV shows with therapists with degrees and lots of letters behind their names, but it was always difficult for me to buy into it. It was even harder to buy into it now after everything I had done. After everything that had gone wrong. After all the people who had died because of me.

"I'll leave you here with Ms. Ramirez while I go check on some of the others," she said, placing a hand on my shoulder. "There are others who need me right now."

I held Lita's hand and watched all the chaos unfolding around me. There were injured people coming into the dining room, beaten and bloodied, some of them hovering on the verge of death. I saw a man screaming his head off because his eyes had been ripped out. I had to quickly avert my gaze because I couldn't stand to see the destruction that had been wrought.

"How can I possibly fix all this?" I whispered to myself.

"We'll fix this together."

I looked down and saw that Lita was regaining consciousness. She smiled as soon as she saw me and I smiled back. I needed her to believe everything was okay even as good people died all around us. I could feel my stomach sink as the walls seemed to be closing in on me.

"Breathe Saul," she said, grasping my hand tight. "It's not over yet."

I heard her words, but it could have been very well over. All that kaiju penis that destroyed Detroit needed to do was burst out of the ground under Gracie Mansion and this fight would be over, for us anyway. I honestly couldn't understand how people were able to cling to hope so desperately when it looked like the end of the world from where I was sitting. So, I smiled at my girlfriend and nodded, not wanting to rob her of the last thing she and the rest had left.

Before long, Stone joined us and sealed the doors behind us, looking more tattered and exhausted than the last time I saw him mere minutes ago. Everyone was tired and hurt and it didn't take long for them to look to me for what I could do to turn the tide. Stone took a deep breath and then marched over to me. He took it upon himself to get the answers to our dilemma. I was more than a little intimidated when I saw him approaching me.

"I think we're in the endgame now, Mr. Copeland," he said as he stood before me. "The barbarians are at the gates and they're going to get in soon. Do you have anything for me? Anything that will help us win this war? Please, can you give me anything right now?"

My jaw dropped as I searched for words to say, but nothing came immediately. My eyes darted around the room for a few moments, and I could see that everyone was looking in my direction, they all wanted answers. I was the only one with an answer, the only one who could keep their hope alive. I knew I should say something to inspire them all, but all I had was the truth.

"Look, I want you to know that there is still a chance to set all of this right," I started. "You can all get your old lives back. We might...even be able to bring back all the people we've lost. I, just upstairs, ripped a shark in half with my bare hands. I...have the power to fight these things. I just need...more time to figure out how it all works."

"Time?" Stone grimaced. "How much time are we talking about? Because these barricades are not going to hold forever. If you're talking more than just a few minutes, then we are going to need to abandon this place and find somewhere else to hole up."

"We...might need to leave here, Stone," I said softly. "I...don't know how long it's gonna take me to get a handle on this, but I promise you that I will do whatever I need to do to save us all. Whatever it takes."

"Whatever it takes?" he asked, crossing his arms over his chest and wincing slightly from the pain he was in.

"Whatever it takes, Stone," I nodded. "I promise."

He studied my face for a little bit, trying to see if I had the kind of resolve to do what needed to be done. When he was satisfied that I wasn't full of shit, he turned around to give the orders that needed to be followed. The most...heart-breaking orders. Orders I would never be able to utter if I lived a full million years.

"We can't stay here," Stone declared to everyone capable of listening. "The defenses are going to collapse any moment and we cannot stay here. We need to move the asset, Mr. Copeland, to another safe location and give him time to reverse everything that has happened to our planet. Mr. Copeland is the asset, the only part of the mission that matters. Those too injured to come with us and keep up must remain here to cover our exit."

"Wait, what?" I asked. "What are you talking about? We can't just leave these people here! That's...that's insane!"

"It's the job, Mr. Copeland," Stone turned angrily to me.

"It's cruel and barbaric and I won't allow it!" I snapped back, not willing to back down over this. "I'm not going to let people sacrifice themselves for me, Stone! I won't let any more people die for me!"

"Are you kidding me right now, Copeland?" Stone raged against me, blowing up so loudly that he scared me just as much as anything else I had seen. "People are dying all over the world right now every moment, in terribly gruesome ways. All of them, *all* of them, are dying because of you, Mr. Copeland. They are dying because you are a fucking mess! And now these good men and women are going to need to sacrifice themselves to give you the time you need to get yourself together in order to save the world. So, if you don't want more people to die, get your shit together!"

I wanted to protest what he said, but I couldn't. I knew that it was the truth, the truth that no one had the heart to tell me all this time. I fell silent as Stone continued to give orders to his soldiers and made them check to see how much ammunition they all had left. If they were going to stay behind to cover our exit, they needed as many bullets as they could get.

"Are you okay, baby?" Lita asked, placing a hand on my shoulder as she walked up behind me.

"Not in the slightest," I replied, though I was glad that she was on her feet. I would hate to think she was going to get left behind, another casualty to this war I started. "These people are going to die because of me."

"This isn't your fault, Saul," she said, her hand gripping my shoulder tighter.

"I love you, babe, but I really wish you would stop saying that," I shook my head solemnly. "I need to stop deluding myself and start kicking myself in the ass until I can fix what I broke. Everything that I broke."

Her grip on my shoulder loosened a little and I could tell that she was hurt. I regretted it, but I needed to say it. Eventually, everyone was prepared for the move we were going to make. All the survivors were prepared for the role they were going to play in my escape.

"Everyone knows the plan?" Stone asked when all the preparations had been made. "When we start this withdrawal, we can't afford any mistakes. We need to make sure that the package makes it to the next safe zone."

Everyone acknowledged that they understood their roles and then it was time. Detective Reynolds and Special Agent Grimes agreed to stick with me and Lita, make sure we were protected. They were as agreeable and reassuring as could be under the circumstances, but they could only do so much to hide the truth of our reality. We were in trouble and not all of us were going to survive what came next. As I stood there with all my allies, even with my crippling anxiety and dark imagination, there was no way for me to foresee the loss that was coming.

Stone's plan was simple: we were going to fling the doors open and charge towards the exit, get to the streets, and try to secure one of the vehicles outside. We knew that the mansion was completely overrun with nightmarish creatures, but perhaps the outside world was different. Maybe there was still some safe harbor to be found. The soldiers still on their feet were supposed to mow down anything that got in the way while we raced for the exit. Real simple.

"Are you ready?" Grimes asked.

"No," I said.

"This plan is going to work," he assured me.

"Everyone's got a plan until the shit hits the fan, Grimes," I said. "I'm sure I don't have to tell you that. But we've got to do something."

He wanted to say something that would make me feel confident about our chances, but nothing occurred to him. It was fine. I didn't need false hope about our chances. I simply took Lita's hand like I did when we were on the second floor and told her to stay with me. I assured her that I would keep her safe no matter what.

I meant it. At the time I meant it. I...never meant to lie to her.

The doors to the dining area were thrown open and we expected to have a flood of monsters wash over us, but that wasn't the case. The corridor outside the door was completely clear; there weren't even any bodies of those soldiers who had been killed trying to retreat to safety. We were shocked into silence for a moment.

"Where are they?" Lita whispered. "Didn't we hear them on the other side of this door before?"

"Maybe they quieted down to hear our plans and went off to set a trap for us," I answered.

"Quiet down, people," Stone commanded. "It doesn't matter where they are because it doesn't change what we have to do. Now let's move... cautiously. We got a job to do."

We swiftly moved through that corridor, flanked by soldiers, cops, and government agents. There was no noise but our steps in that empty hallway. It was somehow more unnerving than anything we had already encountered. We moved along until we were mere feet away from the exit. The front door was in sight, but that wasn't all that could been seen.

"What are they doing?"

Blocking the front door, our exit, were dozens of soldiers and they were all armed with guns and eerie smiles on their faces. It took some of the others a few moments to figure out what was going on, but not me. I was aware immediately. They had heard our plans already and created a trap. The Possu had attached themselves to the dead and were piloting them to prevent our escape.

"Shit," I grumbled at the sight of the barrier.

"Step aside!" Stone barked.

One of the men blocking us stumbled forward, his movements all jerky and uncoordinated. Everyone stood their ground, but you could feel everyone's unease at the sight. I'm honestly surprised none of Stone's men got twitchy and opened fire.

"I have a different idea," the corpse in front of us stated with his head lolling off to the right like it was too heavy for its neck. "You give us The Creator and we let you go free. No one will be harmed. We promise."

I didn't bother to look at my so-called compatriots as I am sure they all cast their eyes toward me. It was no secret that many among them considered me the root of all their ills and that if they could...just be rid of me, then all of this would stop. I am sure there were plenty of secret meetings where they discussed murdering me in my sleep or, possibly, while I was wide awake and could see the bullet coming. In truth, they could have been right. It could have been all so easy, a simple bullet to the back of the brain and all these nightmare creatures simply fade away to nothing. We were risking a lot on the belief that I still had some part to play in the endgame of all this madness. How many millions had already died? How many more were going to before they cut the cancer out at the root?

"You can't let them take you," I heard Lex's voice in my head. "I don't know if they can kill you, but if you're in their custody, you'll never have the time to learn what you need to stop them and put things right. You're gonna need to stand up to them."

"Why would they trust you?" I called out to the shambling corpse in front of me. "What's to keep you from slaughtering them once you have me? You're using their friends as grotesque puppets! They know you're just waiting to do that to the rest of them!"

"We are an honorable race, Creator," he replied. "They can trust us… more than they can trust you. Listen, humans. Restrain him and bring him to us and we will let you all go. We will let your world live in peace."

"And do you speak for the others?" Stone asked. "The other…creatures that have been attacking us, will they honor a deal we make with you?"

"We are all one."

"Are you crazy?" Lita shouted. "We're not turning him over to those things!"

"I'm in charge here, madam, and I will decide what is in the best interest of this nation," Stone stated gruffly without even bothering to glance at my girlfriend. "So, as you say, you're all one? You are in a sense all one army working together against us. You're not separate factions."

"We are all one."

"Thank you," Stone smiled. "I couldn't figure out if these were all randoms attacks perpetrated by separate groups of monsters or one coordinated effort. You've confirmed it's the latter. So, you have a leader, a general, calling the shots. Where are they located? I need to hear from them directly that this deal we're about to make will be honored."

Lita's grip on my hand tightened and I immediately glanced over at her to see her mouthing words to me silently. I'm not much of a lip-reader, but her message was clear. Stone was selling me out and I needed to get out of there as soon as possible. I agreed with her, but I didn't know how escape would be possible when I was surrounded by all of Stone's soldiers.

"Can you get us in contact with your boss, so we can set up some exchange?" Stone asked. "It's not really a peace treaty until the ink dries."

"Our...boss is not here," the corpse stated while the others behind started chittering like cicadas.

"Where is he?" Stone asked as Lita and I took a small step backwards and then another, trying not to catch the attention of anyone else in our entourage. "Maybe we can set up a Zoom call or something? Even destructive nightmare creatures get WiFi, right?"

"You are stalling," the leader of the corpses said as he shuffled forward towards us.

"Stalling?" Stone asked. "No. I would never do that. I am just trying to figure you out. So far, we've had no intelligence save for what Copeland has been able to give us...and he is the very definition of unreliable. But you...you're a regular little chatterbox, aren't you?"

"You have no intention of surrendering The Creator, do you?"

"I swore an oath to protect this nation and its people," Stone answered. "You don't do that by sacrificing everything important. So, in answer to your question, no, I will not be surrendering Mr. Copeland to you. We do not surrender in the face of tyranny."

"That's fine," the monster smiled broadly as the chittering behind him grew louder. "We were never going to let you go anyway."

And that was it. All the reanimated corpses began to rush us as Stone's men opened fire upon them. Apparently, The Possu were a remarkable species, but they hadn't quite figured out guns, choosing to charge us instead of shoot us. I knew that wouldn't last long though. It was only a matter of time before they discovered the combat skills located inside the brains they hijacked.

"We gotta go," said Lita, yanking on my arm so we would duck down a corridor to get away from the gunfire and chaos. "Come on."

We raced down the hall with Dr. Robinson right behind us. Reynolds and Grimes, both armed, stayed behind to exchange fire with the creatures blocking the doors. Ideally, another exit could be found, but I wasn't holding out much hope for that. If they knew to block one exit, they were probably smart enough to block them all. It would have made more sense to just take cover until the shooting stopped and hope it was our side that won.

"Okay, where are we going?" I asked as we stopped in a quiet corridor.

"To find another exit," Lita answered quickly.

"No, they would have covered all the exits," I shook my head. "We should head back, try to get past those monsters and out the front door. Once we make it to the street, we can make a run for it."

"You wanna go back to where all the shooting was happening?" she asked in shock. "Are you insane? There's got to be another way out of here, like a window or something."

"Look, I don't like it any more than you do, babe, but I really do think the front door is the way out of here," I said. "At least we know what we're up against if we go that route."

"I know that I don't want one of those creatures to get their claws in me," she protested. "I saw what it did to you, Saul, and I never want that to happen to me."

"I promise that I will never let that happen to you, Lita," I said. "As long as I am here, you're not going to have to worry about anything. Didn't I take care of that big-ass shark upstairs? I will take care of anything else that comes for you just like that."

She had witnessed what I had done to the shark, but she was still afraid. She was more afraid of The Possu than even those rats from the subway. I don't blame her. Having one's will supplanted is one of my greatest nightmares, right up there with being trapped within the confines of your own mind. I needed her to know that I would protect her from whatever was out there.

"Trust me, Lita."

"Trust can be difficult to come by during tough times," Dr. Robinson offered, letting herself be known. "Maybe it's best if you escape on your own, Mr. Copeland. Lure the dangers away from us all."

"What?" Lita asked. "What are you saying right now?"

"Your boyfriend just wants to keep us all safe, reduce the bloodshed," Robinson continued. "The best way to do that is for him to go off on his own, lure as many of them as he can, while we try to get to safety."

"And what if they catch him?" she asked. "What if they catch up to him while he's out there. How *safe* will we all be when these monsters get what they're after?"

"You heard what they said," the doctor stated warmly. "They only want him. And Mr. Copeland only wants to keep you safe. It seems pretty clear what needs to be done here."

"What *needs* to be done is for you to get out of my face with that bullshit!" she protested angrily. "I'm not going to let you or anyone else sacrifice Saul. Not for anything."

"Your love for him is commendable, but I cannot let you make a decision that can damn this entire world to oblivion," Dr. Robinson commented, slightly shaking her head. "It's too big for you. You'd let sentiment doom us all, because you're young and emotional. You're unable to see the bigger picture. You need to let the adults make the decisions."

"Adults?" she asked in bewilderment. "I'm twenty-five years old! I haven't been a child in a very long time."

"I'm more than twice your age, young lady, so you are still very much a child from where I am standing," the doctor said soothingly. "Now if you will not listen to reason, perhaps you will listen to this."

That was when she produced a small handgun and pointed it at us. Her hand wasn't trembling in the slightest. She was committed to this course of action. Lita's anger was replaced with fear upon seeing the gun. Some fears are universal and having a gun pointed at you by a maniac is a big one.

"Dr. Robinson has been replaced by one of your nightmares," Lita commented.

"No, she hasn't," I shook my head. "That's the genuine article. She's betraying us."

"The fact that you're calling this a betrayal proves just how immature you're both being about this," she shook her head in annoyance. "I'm just making the rational call. Now step away from him and let him...run off to do what he must."

"What makes you think I would let him go by himself?" she asked.

"Because he would insist that you stay," Robinson said, glancing over at me. "Isn't that right, Mr. Copeland? You wouldn't want someone you love following you on this dangerous trek you're about to undertake, would you?"

"No, I wouldn't," I admitted. "I wouldn't endanger anyone if I could help it."

"Good," the doctor nodded. "Now why don't you run along and leave Ms. Ramirez here where she'll be safe?"

"There's no way I'm staying here with you," she argued before turning to face me. "Are you really thinking of leaving me with a gun-wielding psychopath? Come on, Saul! You can't honestly believe this is right? You need someone to watch your back out there."

"I don't want you getting hurt, Lita," I said, looking deep into my girlfriend's eyes.

"You think leaving me with *her* is safe?" she asked. "Nuh uh. I'm going with you, Saul, and there's no two ways about it."

She meant it. There was no way I was pulling a Frodo and ditching everybody for their own safety; she was definitely going to be my Samwise no matter what. It felt good to know that. I've never been with a woman that would stand by me through something of this scale. Hell, I once had a girl break up with me for drinking her orange juice, so she definitely wouldn't have dealt with all this.

"Fine," I nodded. "I guess it's just you and me from here on out."

"As if there could be any doubt," she smiled. "Let's go."

"No, no, no, no, no," Robinson said, cocking her gun as she grew angrier. "You're not going with him. He needs to do this alone."

"What is your *problem*?" Lita demanded, spinning to face the persistent doctor. "Why don't you just butt out? We've already made our decision and you're not about to change our minds."

"I'm not letting you leave with him," Robinson insisted. "He needs to be far away from us, from all of us. Let him go...and just die out there. He did this to us, so he should go face whatever the hell is out there...on his own. And you don't have to die out there with him."

"You're a fucking doctor!" she shouted. "Aren't you supposed to help people? Didn't you take an oath to do no harm?"

"I took an oath to do no harm to people, young lady, but I am not required to save a cancer," she frowned. "Your boyfriend is a blight on this world and the sooner we're rid of him, the better off we will all be. Now come over here and let him go."

"If I come over there, I am going to kick your ass and shove that gun..."

I stopped her right there. In her own deranged way, Robinson was trying to save Lita. But you shouldn't agitate people with guns; that much power in any person's hands is bound to change them...into something else. Dr. Robinson had probably never taken a life before, but I would be damned if she was going to start with Lita.

"I'm leaving, Doctor," I assured her, putting up my hands to let her know that I posed no threat. "Don't do anything that you'll regret."

I began to back away, further down the corridor where Robinson had caught up with us. Lita glared at Robinson before following behind me. I saw the doctor shake her head, no doubt disappointed by Lita's choice, but she didn't try to stop her again. When we rounded a corner and was no longer in Robinson's sight, we were able to breathe a sigh of relief.

"Were you really gonna leave me behind?"

I knew she was gonna ask me that. I was trying to come up with an answer, but she found her words before I had a chance to find mine. I suspect that would always be the case...for however long we lived. I took a deep breath as we walked along and prepared my response.

"I'll do anything to keep you safe," I answered. "If you're safer away from me, then I would definitely leave you."

"Stop," she grabbed me by the shoulder. "Wait. No. You don't get to do that, Saul. You don't get to decide what's best for me any more than Dr. Robinson gets to decide for me. Before we take another step, I need you to understand that fully."

"Oh, I understand," I nodded as I looked her in the eyes. "Do you? Do you really know what we're up against? The nightmares we'll be facing on our own from here on out? I don't know if I can stop them. I don't know if I will get a handle on these powers before they have a chance to find me and kill me. And they will save me for last, Lita. They will brutalize you, but they will keep you alive as long as possible to prolong your suffering. I don't want that to happen to you."

"I don't want that happening to me either," she stated. "But I love you, Saul. Happened quickly, quicker than I thought possible, but it's true all the same. You don't want these monsters to destroy me, but I don't want to go through the destruction of letting you go and never seeing you again. We're together on this, babe. That's just how it's going to be."

"Okay," I nodded, allowing myself a little smile.

"But all things being equal, let's try not to die horrible deaths, all right?" she added.

"Okay," I repeated. "Let's go."

The mansion was mostly quiet now as we walked through the corridors, looking for another way out of the building. There were plenty of dead bodies littered all over the floor, but the silence was the eeriest part of all. I made sure to keep my eyes on each corpse to see if they moved in the slightest; I didn't need to be trapped in a windowless hallway with zombies or something worse. It didn't take long, however, for us to reach a dead end.

"Not this again," Lita commented. "I can't do this again."

As I stood outside of that black void, rippling as it filled the entire width of the corridor, I couldn't agree more with her sentiments. Out of all the terrible things we had already experienced, this...thing was the worst of it for me. I would rather face that giant rat thing again, to be honest. I could feel my girlfriend gripping my hand tighter as she nervously tried to back away from this thing that was starting to look more and more like some sort of organism.

"Let's go back," I said. "There's got to be some other way out of here."

"Yeah, I wouldn't mind going through that crazy doctor," Lita stated.

"Is that so?"

We turned around and saw her standing there. Dr. Robinson had followed us and had her gun drawn already. Apparently, she wasn't quite done with us yet. I didn't need to see Lita's face to know she was done with the "good" doctor; her annoyance was radiating off her in waves. If I wasn't holding her hand, I think she would have charged right through Robinson.

"Step aside," she said. "We need to find another way out."

"You and your boyfriend's 'way out' is right behind you," said Robinson. "Step into...whatever that *thing* is and be done with it."

Lita tried to pull free so she could clip this older woman in the jaw, but I held her hand tight. I didn't think that Robinson was playing around. I'm not sure what had happened to her but she different than when we first met. Maybe it had something to do with the horrors she had witnessed or maybe it was because of whatever tortures Stone put her through when he was "questioning" her. I suspected it wouldn't take much for her to snap and simply shoot us both where we stood despite the oath she took so many years ago.

"You wanted us gone, Doctor, and we're trying to go," I explained calmly. "Just let us pass and you'll never see us again."

"I think we've put up with your nonsense for quite long enough," she frowned. "Just step into that thing and let it eat you."

"No, you can't make us go through that again," Lita protested, slowly shaking her head. "Are you nuts? I won't do it."

The tone of her voice was enough to express just how horrible the experience in the void had been, but that only seemed to delight Robinson further. She was thrilled at the prospect of being rid of me and I guess Lita's demise was just an unfortunate side effect of her plans. When she released the safety on the gun, we both knew she meant business.

"You're gonna have to shoot me, bitch, because I am *not* going in there," Lita said defiantly. "Go ahead and break your oath and shoot me. Then you can drag my dead body through there yourself."

"My oath doesn't mean anything anymore, young lady," she shook her head. "Nothing does. But if your boyfriend dies and puts everything back, our lives can go back to normal. We can get everything back. We can get our lives back...as soon as we get rid of him."

"Get behind me," I said, stepping in front of her. "I'll handle this."

"You will handle *nothing*, Mr. Copeland!" she shouted as I started walking towards her. "This is all your fucking fault! All this devastation is your fault! I should shoot you right where you stand!"

"Then do it, Doctor," I said as I continued to walk towards her. "Shoot me if you think that will fix anything. It won't though and I think you know that. I think you know that I am not responsible for this and that my...death won't solve anything. Killing me will not stop this nightmare, Doctor; it will just make you a murderer. And if we survive this, all of this, how are you going to live with yourself knowing that you killed an innocent man?"

"What are you doing?" she recoiled as I got closer and closer. "Are you...trying to hypnotize me? Trying to convince me to spare you, to keep this nightmare going? Get out of my head, you devil!"

Her hands started to shake as she brandished the gun. She was of two minds over this this whole thing. She was a good person deep down and didn't want to hurt or kill anyone, but when she looked at me, she saw nothing but a monster. I was the suffering of the entire planet. I was the reason she had been held captive and tortured for information by the military. I was the source of all the evil that had been visited upon her. And in that moment, when I was just a couple of steps away from her, I realized something.

"Shit, she's going to shoot me," I thought to myself before the gun fired, a thunderous explosion of sound bouncing off every wall in the corridor.

The bullet tore through my right shoulder like a burning hot beam, with so much force that it spun me around until I was facing Lita. The look of shock on my girlfriend's face told me all I needed to know.

Reasoning with Dr. Robinson wasn't going to work; she was now officially too far gone. Unless...

"Stop," I said, turning back towards the doctor. "Just stop and think! You don't want to do this, Dr. Robinson! You don't!"

When I turned back around to see the doctor, I knew I was going to see one of two things. She was either going to look completely horrified by what she had done or there was going to be a look that showed she was fine with everything. If it was the former, I had a chance to survive this still. If it was the latter, then the end was coming soon. Just my luck, Robinson looked resigned to all this.

"This is about to end," she said, her voice as steady as the hand that was holding the gun. "We're all about to be free, Mr. Copeland. Even you."

"Please don't."

Another shot rang out and I could feel the bullet rip into my gut that time. Damn. Now I was really going to die. I'd say I had a good run, but I was a neurotic mess my whole life and then took a pill that ultimately led to the end of the world. This was as bad a run as you were likely to get out of life. I immediately grasped my stomach and tried to keep my blood in, but it was gushing through my fingers.

"Saul!"

Lita ran to me as I fell to my knees. She was crying as she tried to help me, pressing down on my wound because we had all heard that we needed to keep pressure on gunshot injuries. We were probably doing it wrong though because there was nothing stopping the blood from pouring out. Robinson took a step forward and aimed that fucking gun at us. I was getting woozy and my vision was starting to blur, but I could see something quite clear: a blood-thirsty look in the good doctor's eye.

"Good-bye, Mr. Copeland," she said before another gunshot rang out.

I didn't feel any pain this time. It only took a few moments for me to realize why. Robinson had not been the one who fired that shot. Lita and I looked up to see that the doctor had been shot. When she fell to her knees and dropped her weapon, we saw that Reynolds was standing behind her. She had a terrible grimace on her face.

"Perhaps we should have left her in that cell that Stone had her in," she remarked before she walked over to us and knelt down. "Damn it, Copeland! Look at what you've done to yourself. You were supposed to stick close."

"He didn't do this to himself," said Lita as Reynolds tried to tend to my injuries. "That crazy bitch did it! As for sticking close, when people started talking about giving him up to the monsters, it seemed like a good idea to get out of there."

"I would never have let them take you, Saul," Reynolds said, her voice softening. "Either of you. And neither would Grimes. I can't speak for Stone, but Grimes and I will always have your back."

I believed her and I got the impression that Lita did too. She examined my injuries. She claimed the shot to the shoulder wasn't much to worry about, but she grimaced at the sight of the gut shot. She didn't need to say anything for me to realize how grim my injury was. I needed a doctor, someone who could patch me up a bit and send me on my way, but the only doctor we had wanted me dead.

"We gotta get you back to the main lobby, see if any of the medics are still there," Reynolds commented. "Do you think you can stand?"

"No," I winced as I tried to get to my feet. "I'm hurt pretty bad."

"All right, all right," she said. "Lita, you stay with him and keep pressure on this wound. I'm going to go get the others so they can help us move him."

She dashed off, making sure to take Robinson's gun with her before she did. The doctor was still alive, propped up against a wall, clutching her own gunshot wound. Her eyes were on me the whole time as we laid there bleeding to death.

"I'm dying," the doctor commented as realization swept over her.

"It's what you deserve," Lita said bitterly. "You tried to kill Saul."

"I tried to save us all *from* him," the doctor said weakly. "And now I'm dying."

"Well, maybe there's a lesson in that for you," Lita cut her eyes at her while she continued to tend to my injuries.

"I'm sorry this happened to you, Doctor," I said, just as weakly. "I'm so sorry for everything that's happened to you."

"Go fuck yourself, Mr. Copeland," she said angrily. "I hope you die first so I get to watch you go before I do."

"You're one nasty bitch, aren't you?" Lita asked.

"It's not her fault," I stated. "She's been through so much. These nightmare creatures have broken her."

"You've lived with these creatures every single day of your life and you never let it turn you into a cruel, nasty person, Saul," she said. "Maybe she's just weak."

I didn't argue…mostly because I was feeling woozy from the blood loss. I knew that if Reynolds didn't come back soon with a skilled doctor, this was all going to be over soon. It was time for me to start making my peace and there was one person who deserved to hear words of comfort more than anyone else.

"I want you to know, Lita, that I love you very much," I began. "I've never loved a woman as much as I love you. No matter what happens next, I want you to know how much I appreciate you having my back through all this craziness. You are perfect."

"What are you doing?" she cut me off. "Why are you talking to me like this?"

"Well, I'm, you know…" I stammered.

"No, stop it," she frowned. "From the sound of it, it's like you're trying to say goodbye and I won't hear it. Not now while I'm holding your guts in with my bare hands. You don't get to do the big farewell while I'm holding you together."

I fell silent for a few moments. I didn't know what to say. I knew that I was slipping away but I also knew that Lita was doing everything in her power to keep me alive. One woman trying to hold back a flood.

"Thank you, Lita," I said, finally deciding on the right thing to say. "Thank you for this."

I was starting to feel really sleepy. I knew it was from the loss of blood. It was my time to go, but at least I got to leave this world looking at Lita's beautiful face. There's no way I would rather go than by looking at my beautiful girl. After a few moments, I was so far gone that I didn't even realize that something was touching me, something besides Lita's soft hands. Before I could drift off from this mortal world, something tugged me back to reality, both physically and metaphorically.

"What's going on?"

I don't know if I said it or she did, but I became fully conscious when something ripped me out of Lita's arms and started dragging me down the hall. Something had wrapped around my left wrist and was pulling me away. As I focused my vision, I saw that the thing that had grabbed me was a tentacle that had emerged from the pulsating void. It had become a hungry maw looking to swallow me whole again.

"No," I protested feebly as I looked for something to grab onto, something that would save me from that hungry chasm. "Please no."

Before long, another tentacle caught my right wrist and dragged me even faster. Lita grabbed my ankles, desperately trying to save me from my fate. Just my luck. If I didn't die from blood loss, I could still be consumed by whatever was in the void.

"You can't have him!"

She fought hard to keep me here, but it was more than she could manage on her own. As I got dragged closer and closer to the void, she struggled even harder. Right when I was near the event horizon of the chasm, Reynolds returned with Grimes and a nervous young man with a medical kit in his hands. Now there were four people trying to keep the void from claiming its next victim, claiming me. My vision was blurred, but I could see they were doing their best, like they were trying to wrest me from the hands of a powerful god. As I laid there, my blood pooling out of me and a monster trying to eat me, I realized that I was not as unlovable as I had always suspected. I, honestly, felt kind of at peace. I barely even felt the pressure at my abdomen, the tell-tale sign that I was about to be ripped in half.

There were screams and cries, but I could scarcely tell what was being said anymore. It was all an incomprehensible din at this point as I lay there dying, my functions shutting down one by one. I tried to get my eyes to focus so I could see Lita one final time, tried to concentrate so I could hear that melodic voice in my ears before I departed, but it was to no avail. I was already much too far gone.

"I'm sorry," I tried to whisper, but I'm unsure if anyone heard me over all the noise and confusion.

I then closed my eyes, presumably for the last time. In the dark, I saw Lex again. He looked disappointed. I could very well guess why. He had given me a fighting chance against my personal demons, but now I was dying before the battle could even really start. I would be disappointed too...if I had enough life in me to still care.

"Why so grumpy?" I asked, more coherent inside my head than I was outside of it. "You never really had faith I could survive all of this anyway. I guess you were right."

"Not exactly," he shook his head, barely able to hide the pity in his eyes. "I doubted you had what it took to fight the horrors of your mind...at first. But recently you've given me hope that perhaps I was wrong. The way you stood up to Stone when he locked up the doctor was commendable; your loyalty may have been misplaced, but the strength was commendable. And the power you showed when you blew that shark to pieces? I've been watching that on loop in your memories ever since it happened. Saul Copeland, if you weren't betrayed by your doctor, I believe you could have saved us all."

"What are the chances I still might?" I asked, bolstered by Lex's compliments.

"What do you mean?" he asked in confusion. "You've been mortally wounded and Cthulu Junior doesn't look like it's going to let you go anytime soon."

"I know it looks bad right now, but it's looked bad before," I stated. "Maybe I can pull out another win."

"Okay, don't get yourself a swelled head," he rolled his eyes dismissively, but with a hint of a smile. "You did good work, but rallying after getting shot in the gut is something else entirely."

"Thanks, but 'good work' is not good enough, Lex," I commented. "I need to do great work. I need to do more than I have ever done."

"I...like this side of you, Copeland," he nodded. "So, what's the plan?"

"I'm injured badly, but what if I use the same powers that I used against the shark?" I suggested. "What if I use it on whatever is in that dark portal?"

"Do you...know how to do that?" he asked.

"I killed the shark when I was scared and under stress," I explained. "I'm currently a hundred times more scared and stressed out than I was before. I think I got this."

"Then let's get you conscious enough to fight back," he smirked.

My eyes burst open as though I had gotten a massive hit of adrenaline straight to my heart. I should have been in pain, but I wasn't. I looked straight at the portal that I was being pulled towards, opened my hands so that my palms faced it, and released the same energy that I used to rip the shark apart upstairs. I could hear shocked expressions from Lita and the others. It was the first time Grimes and Reynolds had seen me use these powers and I suspect they were in awe.

Louder than their gasps of shock, however, was the blood-curdling cries issued forth from the void. The damn thing was alive, just like I suspected, and it could feel what I was doing to it. Somehow, it made me feel good to be inflicting pain on this thing. It felt good to be on the giving side of it for a change.

"Die fucker!" I thought to myself as I increased the power coming from my hands.

Soon I was on my feet, filling the void with a strange energy that I still didn't understand, with my team at my back. The tentacles uncoiled from around my wrists and began to flail about as the screams continued. I thought we were winning. We probably all thought we were winning. The feeling didn't last long though. Tentacles emerged and thrashed about until Reynolds, Grimes and Lita were on the floor, several feet from where they had been standing. I looked back at them to see if they were okay...and that was my final mistake.

In the split second that I had my back turned, a tentacle wrapped around my waist. I looked back at the void in time to see tentacles take hold of my wrists and ankles as well. Another then wrapped around my neck so tight, it stopped my breathing immediately. Soon I was hoisted into the air while Lita and the others stared at me in shocked silence.

"Saul?" she uttered softly with tears in her eyes and my blood staining her shirt.

The tentacles spun me around so that I was facing her, my back towards the dark chasm behind me. I knew what this was. It wanted me to see them one last time before I perished. Or maybe it was using me as an example; to show them that not even I was safe from this nightmare. I wanted to say goodbye, thank them for everything they had done for me, but the tentacle around my throat was so tight that I couldn't get any words out.

Crack!

The tentacle broke my right arm by folding it backwards behind me. My mouth fell open as I tried to scream but nothing came out. The blinding pain was so intense, it felt like fire was spreading through my body. The second crack was left leg, pulled behind me in ways that no legs should possibly bend. Tears streamed down my face as I experienced the worst pain of my life. My pain was compounded as I saw the looks on the faces of Lita and the others.

Crack!!!

There went my left arm followed by my right leg. The tentacles folded me into human origami. I should have died or went into shock at some point, lost consciousness, but this monster wouldn't allow it. I stayed conscious for each successive snapping of bones. I was twisted into the shape of a human ball, a mass of flesh and shattered bones, and left to look at my team. I hung there, looking at them for several interminable minutes, while the tentacles squeezed me tighter and tighter and tighter. I was under more pressure than I had ever been before while I struggled to breathe and escape. I saw Lita standing there with her mouth agape until my eyes popped right out of their sockets. I heard her gasp one final time before the tentacles yanked me into the void.

And that was all there was to it.

SIX
DYSTOPIA

It's been ten months. Ten months since I watched Saul Copeland, my boyfriend, twisted and broken and shattered, get pulled into a dark void of no return. Watching something like that will do terrible things to you, but seeing it done to the man you had come to love, is much worse. Every time I close my eyes, I see him getting crumpled up like paper and then he quickly disappeared from sight.

Saul died trying to save the world from an evil none of us had ever seen before. An evil he had apparently been keeping at bay his entire life. Something happened and all the monsters in his head started seeping out, turning our world into a nightmarish dystopia. We believed that he was our only hope, the only thing that could put things right. And then the nightmares consumed him, leaving me with nothing but memories of a good man, a tortured man, who tried to do what was right.

After the void swallowed Saul, the tentacles went wild and started to pull the entire building down. Reynolds gathered me up in her arms and rushed me out of the building with Grimes behind us. I was in shock I think, but I could still hear Dr. Robinson laughing her fucking ass off. She got to see him die in the end, something she had tried to hasten with the gun she had taken from a corpse. If I had had time to kill the bitch before we fled, I would have strangled her until *her* eyes popped out. Popped out like my boyfriend's eyes had before...he was taken.

We made it outside in time to see the whole mansion fall to pieces, burying several good people under tons of debris. We all got into military transports and sped off as fast as we could as more and more buildings started to fall down, no doubt from their own tentacles. We got to safety, barely, but I was not okay for several weeks. Grimes and Reynolds tried to help me cope, but there was really nothing they could say that helped. At least, they managed to keep me with the group; once Saul was gone, Stone didn't really see the point of having me around any longer.

In the last ten months, things have gotten significantly worse for the Earth. Florida has been completely destroyed and California had a series of earthquakes so powerful that the entire state dropped into the ocean. Tornados have ravaged the middle of America every single day since Saul died. The rest of the planet was experiencing similar phenomena on an increasingly regular basis. Our world had become a living nightmare with the screams of people dying being the new white noise for those of us who still lived. The stench of death filled the air to the point where there was absolutely no escape from it.

Stone returned to Washington with us by his side to tell the President what had happened since all communications worldwide ceased to function as soon as Gracie Mansion fell. When we entered the bunker where the President and his staff was supposed to hole up for their protection, we learned precisely how dire things had become. Opening the bunker was like opening a tomb where the bodies hadn't decomposed properly.

I threw up as soon as the door opened, but Reynolds and the others managed to keep their cool. I still don't know how they did it. It smelled worse than anything I'd ever smelled before, and I knew that we were not going to find anything alive down there. The lights flickered on and off as we walked through the corridors to get to where our politicians were supposed to be hiding.

Stone led the way, his gun drawn as he descended further into the depths of the unknown. Everyone but me was armed at this point. There were a dozen of us now. Me, Reynolds, Grimes, Stone, and eight soldiers with assault rifles. I could tell that everyone was scared as hell...except maybe Stone. It's really hard to read that guy sometimes. It was like he was a robot or something.

We had been walking for about ten minutes before we started finding the first bodies. The first one we found was a soldier Stone identified as Bolton. He looked like he had been torn apart by an animal, his throat ripped out as though it had been devoured. As we continued on, we found more soldiers and secretaries and politicians and other workers. Stone seemed to know the names of each person we found, except for the ones who had their faces mangled too much for him to be able to identify them.

"We're about to enter the inner chamber, where the high-profile residents were staying," Stone commented at some point. "With all communications down, I really don't know what we are going to find in there. Everyone be ready."

I wasn't ready for what we found when he opened that door and I doubt anyone else was either. The room had one flickering light fixture that was barely hanging from a thread as all the others had been destroyed. There was blood and muscle and sinew all over the walls. Whatever animal had killed all the others we found in the facility had made it into the inner chamber as well.

"Shit," Stone uttered, the only sign that he wasn't an actual robot.

We heard something move in the darkness, responding to Stone's voice no doubt. He called out to it, but his call was answered with scurrying in the dark. We peered into the blackness, hoping the swinging light fixture would illuminate something that would tell us what we were up against.

We soon saw a shape rise from the floor until it stood a little over six feet tall. I started backing up immediately because I knew that whatever it was, it wasn't going to be benign. Stone aimed his weapon and called out to it again until it stepped forward into the light and gave us all a good look.

"Mr. President?" Stone asked, his voice seeming to crack a little bit. "Are you...are you okay?"

President Lance Palmer stood there with eyes as black as coal and blood smeared across his face. His teeth were gone and replaced with lines and lines of frighteningly-sharp fangs. It was clear to me, if not the others yet, that *he* was the animal who had killed everyone else in the facility. I looked around and saw that everyone was too shocked to react how they should.

"Shoot him," I said.

"That's the president of the United States," said Stone.

"Not anymore," I shook my head. "He's something else now. Kill him before he has a chance to kill the rest of us."

Stone hesitated. Of course, he would. His loyalty was to the President of the United States. He saw the man who he took his orders from when he looked at Palmer, not the monster he had become. It was looking like the other soldiers were hesitant to put this...thing down as well. That hesitation cost us dearly.

"Are you okay, Sir?" Stone called out.

Palmer was silent, except for deep wheezing, as he started to stagger towards us. For every three steps forward he took, I made sure to take one step back. Reynolds seemed to be the only one ready to put this shambling creature down if it got too close, while the others seemed to be too concerned that he was the Commander-In-Chief. I honestly started to wish I had a gun too.

"Hungry."

When the thing started to speak, I knew we were in real trouble. I wished Saul was beside me right then, holding my hand, telling me that everything was going to be all right. It would have been nice for him to tell us what kind of creature this was before it had a chance to strike. None of our wishes came true that day.

President Palmer soon leaped into the air like a fucking ninja, right at Stone! Palmer took him down with ease and then opened his mouth to take a bite out of Stone's throat. Before he could succeed, two of the other soldiers rushed in and pulled them apart. That was when things got worse. Palmer bit off one soldier's cheek before swallowing it down and then turned his attention to the other one long enough to rip out his jugular with his fangs.

That was when everyone started to open fire, filling the room with so much noise that I quickly had to cover my ears. My eyes remained open though. That's what allowed me to see that none of those bullets were affecting Palmer. It was like he had one of those Possu creatures on his back, but we could clearly see that wasn't the case.

Palmer killed off five soldiers before Stone called for a tactical retreat. Reynolds and I raced out of the inner chamber first while the others continued to fire their weapons. I could feel my whole body trembling as I watched the carnage before me. Palmer bit into Stone's shoulder and caused the man to cry out in pain before Grimes went to his aid.

"Everyone outside!" Grimes yelled decisively. "We're gonna seal him back into this room!"

Two remaining soldiers helped Stone to his feet and started to escort him out of the chamber while Grimes and the last soldier laid down what they thought was suppressing fire to keep Palmer at bay. Soon Stone and his grunts were with me and Reynolds.

"Get outta there, so we can seal the room!" Reynolds yelled out to her man.

Grimes and his partner tried to leave the chamber, but Palmer refused to be denied his final meal. The president bit the soldier's arm and made him drop his rifle before he gnawed on his face and devoured it gruesomely. Grimes was right at the exit, almost home free, when Palmer leaped onto his back and bit into his shoulder so deep, it looked like the arm would come loose from the socket.

I could see the fear and pain in that man's eyes as he started to get eaten alive. Reynolds tried to come to his aid, but he told her to stay back. He told her to close the door and seal it. She didn't listen. She rushed into the room, turning into her werewolf form as she did, and she immediately confronted Palmer. She dug her claws into the politician and pried him off Grimes. We watched as Detective Reynolds ate every single part of

President Palmer until there was absolutely nothing left. Only after eating each morsel did she return to Grimes to see how he was doing.

"How are you?" she asked, quickly reverting back to her human form, having worked hard to get a better handle on the transformations.

"I'm great," he grunted. "Don't I look ready to go out dancing?"

"Don't talk," she said. "You're losing a lot of blood."

"Yeah, too much," he replied. "I'm not going to make it, Roxy."

"Lita, go find a medical kit so we can patch up Grimes and Stone," she ordered me and I ran off to do as she commanded.

I walked through those eerily silent halls by myself, stepping over bodies and trying not to get blood on my shoes or…human viscera in my hair. I was scared nearly to death that there was something else just as nasty as President Palmer in here somewhere, but I pushed those thoughts aside. I needed to find something that would keep Grimes and Stone alive. I had lost too many people already. I finally found something in a little office that was surprisingly undisturbed and then retraced my steps until I was back at the inner chamber.

"Give that here," Reynolds commented gruffly as she took the medical kit and started to patch up our injured. "Just hold on, Grimes. I'm gonna fix you right up and then you can get back to annoying the fuck outta me."

While she worked on Grimes, a shaken young man with the name Cole on his fatigues was busy patching up Stone. Our orders had been to come to this bunker to inform the President what had happened in New York and work on a gameplan for what to do now that Saul was gone. We hadn't figured on the nightmares having found their way into the most secure place in the country.

"What the hell happened to him?" Stone barked as Cole bandaged him as best he could. "What the hell kinda creature was that?"

"I don't know," I found myself answering. "Saul told me about a lot of the dark stuff in his head, but I didn't recognize that thing. Kinda looked like some sort of…vampire or something."

"Didn't look like any damn vampire I've ever seen, young lady," Stone grumbled angrily.

"Well, I'm sorry if Saul wasn't afraid of the Bela Lugosi version of the character," I rolled my eyes dismissively. "His nightmares tended to run a little darker."

"Oh, I know all about that," he said, cutting his eyes over at me. "I've been dealing with his fears ever since they started popping up. And now the President of the United States and every other politician is dead. I'm not sure what we're supposed to do now."

"You do what you were always going to need to do: stop these creatures and save as many lives as you can," I told him. "That's the job, right?"

He grumbled and then looked away. We had all been through too much, it was a hard road just getting here to the bunker, so it was bound to lead to arguments. I know my nerves were frayed and I could see the cracks forming in everyone else. Stone was swayed by my words that day. In seven days, he had gotten rid of the corpses and turned the bunker into his new base of operations. He managed to get soldiers to gather in D.C. to make sure that it was a safe haven where people could feel protected. People thought we were turning a corner and after five months, it was easy to think that. Soon we had enough troops to protect the entire city.

Monsters attacked the city constantly, but every attack got repelled. We all got real fucking comfortable. *Real fucking comfortable.* Not me though. After shaking off the funk of losing Saul, I decided it was time for me to learn how to fight monsters. For five months straight, I studied with Reynolds and Grimes. She taught me how to kick ass while he taught me how to investigate things. I was such a bad-ass eventually that I was allowed to go on missions scrounging for supplies. He never said anything, but I think even Stone was impressed with me.

That brings us to today...ten months after losing Saul. I walked into the war room that morning feeling pretty good. I hadn't even thought about Saul yet, which was good, because remembering him and how he died had been giving me terrible nightmares every night. Stone was already there as usual, standing at his dark black podium, ready to give out his pronouncements like he did every morning. Grimes was already seated, scratching at his shoulder; it had been bothering him ever since President Palmer bit him months ago.

I smiled as I took my seat, noticing that Reynolds wasn't with us yet. She and Trevor had been fucking. They didn't want anyone to know so they never came to the meetings at the same time. It was weird. The whole world turned to shit and they still felt it important to hide who they were sexing. She always showed up a little less than ten minutes after he did. I sometimes wondered how the conversation went, as they decided how they could best keep their big secret. No one said anything though; we all pretended like they were really good at hiding what they were doing.

"Now that we're all here, we can begin," Stone said when Roxanne took her seat that morning. "As you all know, things have been pretty secure here at Haven."

"Hence the name," I blurted out.

We had started calling D.C by the name "Haven" because it more accurately reflected our new reality. The old ways had quickly died and this is what we had now. Stone shot a disapproving look my way, but I didn't care. I just smiled at him and he shook his head. He had started treating me like I was a daughter to him and, as a result, couldn't stay mad at me for long. It was nice to have him watching over me because we had still not found my parents, who had been in New Jersey; they refused to leave the home they raised me in. We had tried to collect them during our trip from New York to D.C. following Saul's death, but they weren't there. I still don't know where they are.

"Yes, Ms. Ramirez, and I would like to keep it that way," Stone continued. "Our continued safety comes down to intelligence, keeping ahead of what is out there. So, we've been debriefing everyone who comes here."

"What have you heard?" Roxanne asked, a little gruffer than she probably meant to.

"There are rumblings of someone or something who controls these monsters," Stone answered. "That confirms what we learned at Gracie

Mansion. I think if we pinpoint this leader, we can eliminate it and maybe it will destroy all the others. Like killing the head vampire."

I smirked at the comment. It was always funny when he tried to use pop culture references because they were always so dated. I decided not to give him shit about it this time though because I was curious about this new piece of information he had. I could tell from how Roxanne sat forward in her chair, that she was just as interested.

"We're getting word of an encampment in South Carolina," he continued. "We're hearing we can get answers there. I want to send some people to infiltrate that group and bring back information about where we can find the enemy. I want to be able to locate their leader and firebomb him straight to Hell."

"Sounds like a plan," said Trevor. "Who are you thinking of sending in? Simpson has gotten really good with undercover work recently. And Williams is small and gives off an unimposing vibe, but she is absolutely lethal."

"They can definitely go, but I want you and Reynolds on the case too," Stone said.

Oh boy! Trevor had been avoiding fieldwork ever since the mission to rescue President Palmer had gone so wrong. He had managed to get away with it because Stone didn't want to push, but it looked like it wasn't going to work this time. He needed to get back on the horse.

"Are you sure you need me on this?" Trevor asked.

"You are the best strategist we have here, Grimes," Stone frowned. "There is no one I trust more to assess this situation than you. I need you on this more than anyone else. Hell, you could probably pull this mission off without backup whatsoever."

Stone was trying to speak to his ego, but Trevor wasn't one to be led by something so base. He was going to talk himself right out of this mission if that was the technique Stone chose to employ. You would think that Roxanne would be able to convince him to go on the mission, but she never pushed him like that. She knew more than anyone about how traumatized her man was, so she was willing for him to move at his own pace. No, as it turned out, I was the one who convinced him to go.

"I'll go," I commented.

The room fell silent as all eyes fell upon me. Look, I get it. I am much younger and less accomplished than everyone else in the room. I met Saul doing data entry at a job that I had just gotten not that long prior; it was actually my first grown-up job after graduating from college. I wasn't a major in the United States military. I wasn't a secret agent like Trevor. And for Roxanne to be a detective, she must have been kicking ass on the job for quite a while. All they wanted to do was protect me, just like all they wanted to do was protect Saul. But I'm an adult and I can protect myself.

"What's the problem?" I asked, feeling my anger starting to rise.

"I don't know if we could use you on this mission," Stone answered after a moment.

"Why not?" I asked.

"You might be a liability," said Stone. "You were really close to Saul and as a result, these nightmares know you personally. It's hard to be an undercover agent when all the bad guys know your face."

"How are any of you doing undercover work then?" I asked. "You think they won't recognize the rest of you too? We've been partners right from the start. As far as all these monsters are concerned, we're all as famous as The Temptations."

I thought using an old band would work better in light of who I was talking to. They were all about twice my age after all. Stone and Roxanne tried their best to talk me out of it, but I wouldn't allow it. Before it could blow up into a full argument, Trevor slammed his hand on his table and got to his feet.

"She's right," he said. "If she's ready to get back into the field with us, then so be it. Just make sure you stick close to me and Reynolds. Things can get hairy out there, particularly if we're just being fed info to lead us into a trap."

I hadn't thought about that, the fact there might be creatures smart enough to set traps for us. We had the meeting at eight in the morning and by noon we were being outfitted with gear and weapons to go out into the field. Everything had to be hidden since it was an undercover mission, but we were definitely not going to be defenseless out there.

"A knife?" I asked, examining the weapon I was given. "That's it?"

"You were expecting the kind of gear James Bond uses?" Roxanne smirked at me. "We're operating with scraps as it is."

"What if we run into something that this little knife can't handle?" I asked defiantly.

"Then we'll rely on our greatest weapon," said Trevor stoically.

"And what's that?" I asked.

"Reynolds," he replied. "Now that she has complete control over her lycanthropy, she is a force to be reckoned with. Even more than she used to be, which is really saying something. She'll be able to handle anything out there."

"You say the sweetest things," she said before turning her attention back to me. "You have nothing to worry about, Lita. This is a simple run to gather information. We'll be back to Haven before anyone even misses us."

"You're both really confident," I stated, thinking about how unsure things were in the beginning.

She said we would be back before anyone even missed us, but I had no one to miss me. My parents were gone, out there in the wind somewhere. Who knows what happened to friends and co-workers. And, of course, Saul was gone too. The man I loved was no longer by my side, but there were times when I still felt his presence. When I slept at night, I could swear I could hear his voice calling me in my dreams. I knew it was all just wishful thinking on my part; with all the supernatural stuff going on in this world, why not the idea that my boyfriend was a ghost who walked beside me and kept watch over me still?

But Saul wasn't a ghost. Saul was merely a man, a most remarkable man, who was destroyed by his demons in the most gruesome display of violence that I had ever witnessed. I still had difficulty forgetting the moment when Saul's eyes popped out of his head. I really, really wished he was still here with me. I missed him.

Soon, I was in an SUV with Trevor and Roxanne, leaving Haven while at our rear was a jeep with Simpson and Williams. We were instructed to pretend we were regular people, just survivors traveling through the countryside and looking for a safe place. Simpson, a 6'1 black dude with more muscles than The Rock, was supposed to be married to Williams, a 5'4 black woman who looked like she couldn't harm a fly. Trevor and Roxanne were "pretending" to be a couple too and they happened to just find me on the road while they were traveling. We had our backstories and full gas tanks, so all we needed to do now was find this one encampment of people with the information that we sought.

"Can we listen to some music?" I asked from the backseat of the vehicle when we were about two hours into our trip.

"We don't have any working radio stations," Trevor stated, even though he knew I already knew that. Such a dad. "You're just going to enjoy the scenery."

The scenery. Right. As you can imagine, there wasn't much to look out through the windows of our luxury SUV. Monsters had ravaged our world for a year or so. There were plenty of dead bodies and abandoned vehicles if you were into that sort of thing; sometimes you would reach stretches of road where you could see houses still on fire. Obviously, you had to keep your windows rolled up at all times or the stench of death would choke the life out of you. In the new America, you needed to wear a mask at all times or you would just die. That wasn't the saddest part of our new reality; the saddest part was how many dead children I had seen during the last ten months.

"I should have brought a CD player," I grumbled.

I wasn't trying to be a brat or anything. I didn't feel like myself. Ever since Saul died, I felt like I had been faking my upbeat nature. I always had a smile on my face and playfully ribbed everyone around me, but inside I felt like my soul had been ripped out. By the time I made it to my room every night, my face hurt from smiling. Why is it only the *fake* smiles that cause pain?

"You still have CDs?" Trevor chuckled. "How old are you?"

"What song would you listen to if we had a radio right now?" Roxanne asked.

They were trying to put me at ease, something they had been known to do frequently after we lost Saul. I could tell they missed him too, but they must have known how heartbroken I must have been. They did everything in their power to make me feel okay, to distract me from my thoughts and memories of him, but they could only do so much. Eventually, I would have to go to my room, turn off the lights, and face my thoughts...and hear his voice echoing in my dreams.

"Probably Pink," I replied eventually. "Something off the 'Try This' album. All of those songs are good."

"I honestly don't think she's capable of making a bad song," Trevor commented.

"Wait, are you a fan?" I asked, sitting forward in my seat. "Is the big bad secret agent, America's answer to James Bond, a fan of THE Alecia Beth Moore Hart? Damn, I learn something new about you all the time. Did you know that about him, Roxanne?"

"Well, it's not like I've gotten to see his music collection," she answered, "but I could imagine him belting out some tunes in the shower."

"Do you have to imagine, or have you witnessed it firsthand," I asked slyly.

"We should change the subject before we have to play the quiet game for the rest of the way," she groaned, and I couldn't help but laugh.

"You guys are so cute," I said. "I don't know why you don't want people to know you're a couple."

"Who said we were a couple?" she asked gruffly.

"Oh, please," I rolled my eyes. "I have eyes and so does everyone else. You're not fooling anyone."

"Maybe we're just fooling ourselves," said Trevor. "Anything wrong with that?"

I didn't have an answer for that honestly. In the end, it was their own business if they wanted the world to know about their relationship or not. And so we rode along until we reached a barrier blocking the road, a felled tree plus some abandoned cars. I could hear Trevor groan at the sight of it.

"Terrific," he grumbled.

"Are we going to need to back out and find another route?" I asked.

"Nah, this looks like a trap," Roxanne answered. "How well did we vet the people who brought us the intel?"

"About as well as we could under the circumstances," he answered. "We know they didn't have any of those furry creatures latched onto them."

"The Possu," I offered. "That's what Saul called them. But one of his greatest fears was the idea of something circumventing his will, taking over his mind. He was so afraid of that, I can imagine that there are still other things out there that can do it, not just those little furry things."

"We're just going to have to hope that Stone has a handle on things back home and keeps an eye on the new arrivals," he said, gripping the steering wheel tighter than he had been before.

Was this Saul's legacy? He had been forced to live in fear his whole life and now, following his death, we were all forced to live in fear every single moment? I'd be lying if I said I wasn't a little resentful of that. He got to die and be free of all this while we were, what, meant to endure and carry on in this endless nightmare? Sometimes, I found myself so angry with him and I couldn't tell if it was because of the mess he had left or because I was one of the things he left behind?

"I'll go tell the others that we're going to have to back out of here," said Roxanne, exchanging a look with her not-so-secret beau before she looked back at me. "Sit tight. We'll be on our way soon."

She tried to flash me a reassuring smile that was anything but and I think that's when I realized that all hell was going to break loose very soon. Just as she was reaching for the door handle, Simpson appeared and tapped on the driver's side window. Trevor rolled it down and started exchanging words with the mountain of a man.

"What do you think?" Simpson asked. "Think it's a trap?"

"Could be," Trevor replied. "Let's back out of here and see if all the alternate routes are blocked off too."

Simpson nodded silently before starting to head back for his vehicle. Before he was even three steps from us, people came rushing from the wooded area lining the road we were on. Lots of people. They were all in tattered clothes and looked absolutely filthy from what I could see. Clearly, wherever they had gathered was not as well-maintained as Haven. They were struggling to survive and that was probably why they felt like they needed to ambush us.

Simpson handled being bum rushed exactly how you would imagine a man of his military pedigree would. He decked the first person who charged at him and sent him flying backwards with so much force, he knocked down three of his compatriots. When he saw how outnumbered we were, he tried to get to his jeep and join Williams on the inside, but he was quickly swarmed.

"What are they?" I asked, trying to determine what kind of creatures we were up against.

"They're people," Trevor answered through clenched teeth as he pulled out his handgun. "Just regular, scared, desperate people."

"So what do we do?" I asked, starting to get really nervous when I saw just how many people were pouring out of the woods. "Do we talk to them? Try to reason with them?"

When Trevor and Roxanne began firing their weapons out the windows, I knew that reason was not in the cards. Suddenly, I very much just wanted to be back in Haven instead of being attacked by a huge band of marauders. After everything I had been through, I hated to think this would be how I went out: sitting in the backseat of this hot-ass car with nothing but a knife to defend myself from these murderous hordes.

From the window, I could see Simpson throwing people off him as he struggled to get back to his vehicle. It was impressive. Despite how many piled on top of him, stabbing him with their knives and other makeshift weapons, he still managed to move forward. Williams flung open his door for him and started shooting as many people as she could to try to clear a path for her partner to get to safety, but the woods just kept vomiting out more foes for them to deal with. I didn't verbalize it, but I knew it was only a matter of time before they all ran out of bullets and then we would truly be doomed.

"Shit," I muttered under my breath as I pulled out my knife and got ready for a fight, probably the last fight of my entire life. "Shit."

Soon Simpson got into the jeep and began backing up, running over whoever was back there, giving Trevor the chance to try to do the same. It was looking pretty good for a while, like we were going to be able to get to safety, but there were too many people blocking the path. Our vehicles were being rocked back and forth by the waves of people throwing themselves at us, our windows were being smashed by rocks and fists and whatever else they could get to do the job.

"We're not going to make it out of this," said Roxanne. "We're going to need to make a break for it."

"We're going to jump out and make a run for the trees," said Trevor, ever the strategist. "I'll cover you."

He was sacrificing himself so that we would be able to escape. It was noble, but foolish. We were all pretty well surrounded and there was no way any of us were going to make it to the trees without being overrun. This was it, our last stand. At least...I would be with Saul again soon.

"Let's go!" Trevor practically roared as he shoved the door open and leaped out of the SUV with his gun blazing.

He had such a fierce, determined look on his face as he kept getting headshot after headshot, mowing down all the people coming for him. Roxanne kicked her door open and followed suit. They were like real-life superheroes trying to go out in a blaze of glory, but I was just sitting there scared with a combat knife.

They seized us as soon as we got out of the vehicles. Once we were detained, they stopped rampaging. We were all lined up against the SUV as they stared at us silently, the only sound was their heavy breathing from all the running they had done. After a few moments, a skinny white woman walked up to us and proceeded to look us all up and down.

"Five terrific specimens," she stated. "Not bad. The Master will be pleased."

"What master?" Trevor demanded. "Who do you serve?"

"You'll see soon," she said, bringing her face close to his. "Keep your mouth shut until then. The Master doesn't necessarily need all five of you."

And so we were prisoners being led through the woods to someone so powerful and charismatic that they were able to mobilize at least a hundred people and turn them into murderous marauders. Perhaps calling them murderous was a misnomer though; they hadn't killed anyone yet. In fact, it looked like their mission was simply to capture us. Who knows what they intended to do with us after we saw The Master. I knew that my compatriots had no intention of finding out. We had come out here for intel; once we got that, they were going to do whatever they could to escape and bring the information back to Haven.

We walked for what felt like forever through the woods, hiking over terribly rough terrain. It felt like I was going to twist my ankles several times during the walk. I should have worn combat boots like the others, but we still hadn't found any in my size, so I chose some sneakers designed for joggers. I still don't understand how the others were able to remain so calm as we walked to what could have been our gruesome deaths. Maybe that's all chalked up to the training you get in the military and law enforcement, I don't know.

After all that walking, we reached a ramshackle village that looked like it was put together with glue and scotch tape. This was clearly where they had all gathered. It was very well hidden. I doubt a plane flying overhead would have been able to see through the canopy of trees to see their encampment. We were soon taken to the biggest hut in the camp and placed on our knees in front of what looked like a very sad throne. A wicker chair throne. Ugh.

"Stay icy, everyone," said Trevor.

I don't know how anyone could "stay icy" in our situation. It seemed pretty clear to me that we were going to die now. I just don't know why I was so calm about that particular fate. Was I already anticipating seeing Saul again? Had I become so weak that I was welcoming death after losing my man? The very thought of that made me so angry that I could have fought off all the people who ambushed us single-handedly. While I contemplated all that, some tall, shabby-looking white man entered the hut and took a seat on the makeshift throne in front of us.

"Always nice to have visitors," he began and I knew already that I was going to hate him. "Where are you fine folks from?"

"We're just regular folks passing through," Trevor lied somewhat convincingly.

"Lotta guns for regular folks who are just passing through," he said as he examined the weapons that had been confiscated by his followers. "And my people tell me that you're all really, really good at using them."

"Please don't hurt us," said Roxanne, much better at playing her role than Trevor. She seemed like she was really on the verge of tears. "We're just trying to get to somewhere safe. We were...we were in New York when the whole place just went to shit. We couldn't stay there. We got these cars and some guns and we ran. We've been running from those monsters ever since."

He paused upon hearing her sob story, no doubt trying to figure out if she was telling the truth. She gave such an amazing performance that I almost believed her. We soon discovered that he believed her also.

"If safety is what you seek, my dear, then you've come to the right place," he smirked. "I offer you safe harbor along with the rest of my people here."

"That's very generous of you," said Roxanne, flashing him a fake smile. "Thank you. This is a terrific place. Much better than anything else we've seen. Are you sure it's safe, safe from all those monsters out there?"

"This is the safest place on Earth," he replied. "I've discovered the key to stopping those fearsome creatures. You may all rise so I can show you around your new home."

We all exchanged looks between ourselves before we got to our feet. I think we could all feel that this was all a little too easy. They went from ambushing us and taking us prisoner to offering us their version of hospitality? No, this was a trap of some kind and I wasn't waiting for the other shoe to drop. I'm sure the others were also looking at possible exit strategies as well.

We followed the leader through the camp and saw that his people clearly idolized him. They weren't too friendly to the rest of us though, giving us nothing but terrible sneers while they gripped whatever weapons they could, be they rakes, knives, or even a pitchfork stained with blood. As we walked along, I half-expected to see Ewoks or something since the camp looked like a faithful recreation of Endor. I don't know where he was taking us, but we were all starting to feel uneasy.

"Can you tell us your name?" Roxanne asked as we walked along.

"I am called Abraham," he replied with a warm smile. "My apologies for my rudeness. What are your names?"

We offered the fake names we had been given before we left Haven. Except for me. I was so damned nervous that I forgot most of my cover story, including the phony name I was supposed to memorize. So…I told him I was Lita. Luckily, Trevor and the others didn't look at me harshly or anything. Abraham smiled at us all before he continued leading us through the camp. We were soon standing outside of a hut that was larger and more ornate than any of the others we had seen.

"What's in there?" Trevor asked.

Abraham frowned at his question. Apparently, he was willing to tell Roxanne anything she asked, but he wanted no parts of her "husband." We needed an answer to the question though because there was something about this structure. It felt like bad vibes were emanating from it. Something terrible was behind that door, something that made me feel the deepest despair. I was more afraid now, standing in front of this hut, than I had ever been in quite a while.

"Yeah," said Roxanne nervously, her voice clearly quivering as she spoke. "What's in there? I…I feel nauseous just standing here."

"Is it something radioactive or something?" Trevor asked.

"Radioactive?" Abraham laughed. "Nothing so…small and mundane. In this small, understated building is the key to our safety, to our very salvation. Do you want to gaze your eyes upon it?"

"No," I found myself whispering and shaking my head. "There's nothing good behind that door."

Abraham threw open the doors to the hut and led us into the dark structure. Going inside was enough to make Williams vomit immediately. There was something in here giving off waves of some terrible energy. It didn't take long for our eyes to adjust to the darkness and for us to see precisely what we were up against.

"No," I said, stumbling backwards when I finally saw it. "Not that."

It was the vortex, one of the black holes that killed Saul and swallowed his body. I hadn't seen any of these things since he had died. I had hoped to never see another one ever again. Trevor and Roxanne ran to my side and tried to help me back up to my feet while Simpson and Williams continued to stare into that swirling black maw.

"So, you've seen our god before," Abraham laughed as his followers stepped up to trap us where we were standing. "I'm so glad. There's nothing better than a happy reunion."

"That *thing* is no god!" I shouted angrily. "That thing killed my boyfriend! We need to get out of here! All of us need to get as far away from here as possible."

Abraham and his people weren't listening. They were too busy chanting and praying to the damned thing. Trevor got me to my feet, but I felt a weight so heavy that it threatened to make me collapse all over again.

"This is the god that has kept us safe all this time," Abraham tried to explain over the din of the prayers. "It keeps all the other monsters away."

Yeah, it probably did, in the same way larger predators kept smaller predators away. As far as all the nightmare creatures that were released go, this had to be the apex entity. Even the kaiju penis that destroyed Detroit wasn't as frightening as this thing was. All I wanted to do was get as far away from that void as humanly possible as quickly as I could, but Abraham's people were blocking any sort of escape.

Things got worse when large tentacles began to emerge from the void, the same tentacles that had taken hold of Saul right before he died. Simpson and Williams didn't know what this meant because they weren't there before, but Roxanne and Trevor did. Their jaws dropped at the sight of it for a moment before they started fighting against Abraham's cultists. It was like pushing against a wall of bodies and they weren't making much progress.

"All we need to do to continue receiving our god's protection is to sacrifice a few people to his eternal glory," Abraham said, his voice rising higher and higher as a terrible screech emanated from the vortex. "Five people have walked into our camp; I think with such an abundance, we can certainly spare to sacrifice two of you."

It was clear that he meant Trevor and Simpson. Cult leaders are all the same. They want a harem of nubile women to worship them and getting rid of all romantic rivals is always a smart play. If he thought our guys were going to walk into oblivion willingly, without giving so much as a fight, then he was going to be very sorely mistaken. I watched as my compatriots fought with everything they had, breaking the noses, jaws, and even kneecaps of as many rabid cultists they could lay their fists on.

It wasn't doing much to turn the tide of battle that day though. The tentacles grabbed whatever unconscious cultist they could and then pulled them into the dark. I thought I had come up with a bright idea: attack Abraham and maybe his followers wouldn't know what to do without him. I pulled out my knife, which the cultists had failed to find on me, and I rushed Abraham, putting my blade to his throat. With him at my mercy, best believe that the chanting and praying all stopped. The only sound now was from that damned vortex.

"All of you stop where you are!" I shouted. "If even one of you crazy fuckers take another step, I will slit his throat!"

I don't know how much I meant those words at the time. I'm not a killer after all. I was so terrified though that I could see myself slitting that creep's throat and not giving it a second thought if it meant that I could get away from that damned vortex.

"You do not know what you're doing, young lady," Abraham laughed.

"I'm pretty sure I do," I replied, pressing my blade against his throat harder than before, letting him know that not only did I mean business, but I didn't like his fucking tone of voice. It was dismissive...and I don't care for that kinda attitude. "Your people are going to clear a path and allow me and my friends to go free or they are going to need to pick a new messiah."

"But what good is a messiah that doesn't die for his people?" he chuckled wildly while his followers all looked towards us and smiled creepily. "Family, when I die, you know what to do. Send me into the void, let me join with our god!"

I didn't realize how crazy these people were. Obviously, threats of bodily harm weren't going to work on these people. Roxanne and Trevor could see that things were going left and tried to make their way to me, but it was no use. Abraham lurched forward so that the knife would cut into his throat. I tried to pull away, but he grasped my wrist and began sawing the knife against his neck like he wanted to cut his whole head off.

"No!" I shouted as I tried to free my hand from his grip. "Stop!"

I could feel his blood washing over my hands and the sound of his gurgling as the life drained out of him was deafening in its way. He soon became dead weight in my arms and slumped down at my feet. I just stood there, frozen, with my hands stained red with Abraham's blood. Trevor and Roxanne ran to my side, the former pulling me into his arms to protect me.

"We need to get out of here," he said, looking over at Roxanne. "Now!"

Somehow, one of the tentacles found Abraham's corpse and managed to yank it into the vortex. It became voracious after eating the cult leader. Its tentacles started whipping around wildly and the suction from within increased, making it an even more powerful whirlpool. The tentacles were grabbing people left and right and then pulling them inside to be eaten just like Abraham. The worst part for me was the look of absolute joy on the faces of the cultists as they were pulled to their deaths. They were all so happy to be joined with their...god.

"I'll carve us a path out of here," said Roxanne.

Before I could figure out what she meant by that, she started her transformation. I had seen her turn into a werewolf before. Hell, my apartment was destroyed by a werewolf fight at the start of all this nonsense. I'd be lying if it still wasn't the damnedest thing to witness.

First off, John Landis was absolutely right about the shifting and breaking and stretching of the bones. Roxanne didn't seem too hurt by it, but it was nightmarish to watch; you can never get over watching a friend reshape their bodies like that.

Soon this 5'7 police detective towered over us in her new 6'5 form, covered in fur and sporting dangerous claws and fangs. She began cutting through the cultists as she tried to make a path for our escape, but even she was kinda overwhelmed by how many people were standing in her way. We needed to avoid the tentacles as we escaped. It took some time, but eventually Trevor and I were able to follow Roxanne out of the hut and into the woods.

"Reynolds, stay here with Lita," said Trevor once we were in the clear. "I'm going back for Simpson and Williams."

"No," she said. "I'll go back for them. You stay here with Lita."

"I'm in command of this operation," he barked.

"And you can be in command from here," she growled as he leaned against a tree for support. "Don't try to pull rank on me, Trevor. I'm a fucking werewolf and your best asset right now. I can get them out of there and bring them right here. Just sit tight."

She practically galloped back towards the hut with the mad cultists while Trevor leaned against a tree to keep on his feet. He was injured and bleeding, but he didn't want me to know how hurt he was. I didn't know what to do. I still had my knife, but it wasn't a medical kit. If he lost too much blood, there wasn't going to be much I would be able to do. Hell, if any of the cultists ignored the void and came after us instead, I wouldn't be able to defend the two of us either. I really, really wished I hadn't volunteered for this mission.

"We're gonna be okay," I told him.

"Of course, we are," he said through bloody clenched teeth, trying to comfort me while I was trying to comfort him. "This is...this is going to be okay."

I nodded and then looked towards the direction where Roxanne had run. I could hear screams and howls coming from that direction. There was something terribly violent going on over there and all I could hope was that she was winning and that she would be able to rescue Williams and Simpson. And then I heard something else, something above all the noise and carnage, something that chilled me right down to the bone.

The vortex was speaking again, emitting a much louder shriek than it had been when we were in the hut with it. It was getting louder and shriller to the point where I thought it would make my eardrums burst. Trevor and I had to cover our ears to try to keep the sound out of our heads and then there was an explosion. I could see pieces of the hut explode upwards and send debris everywhere.

"What the fuck was that?" I found myself asking. "Stay here, Trev. I'm going to go check to see if everyone is all right."

"No, you should stay here and let me check it out," he grunted in pain.

"Stop it with the macho bullshit," I sighed. "You're hurt and can barely stand up. Stay here and I'll make sure everything is all right. I will be right back."

I ran off after that, not really wanting to hear any more of his protests. In truth, he wasn't being macho. He was being a dad. He and Roxanne had kind of adopted me as their own after Saul died. They had been doing everything in their power to keep me safe, to make sure that I didn't go the same way as my boyfriend. He was probably damning himself for even allowing me to go on this mission, but I couldn't worry about that. Something had happened to the hut and I needed to see if our people were all right.

The closer I got to the hut, the more I wished I hadn't volunteered to do so. There were plenty of dead cultists littering the ground. I could barely walk through without stepping on someone. What made it worse was that not all of the bodies were in one piece. The explosion had clearly dismembered some of the people here. Everything in me was screaming to turn around and get out of there. If I'm being honest, if it was just Simpson and Williams in there, I might have let my fear convince me to leave. But I was not going to leave Roxanne behind.

I almost lost all my nerve when something grabbed my ankle. I thought it might have been one of the tentacles and that it would try to pull me to my doom. It wasn't that though. I looked down, ready to strike with my knife, only to discover that it was Williams. I'm not a doctor, but even I could see she was dying. She was covered in blood; her legs were mangled and her abdomen had deep lacerations gushing blood. There was no way anyone was going to be able to save her.

"Get out of here," she said, her voice gurgling as her lungs filled with her own blood. "There's nothing...nothing..."

She died right then without finishing her sentence. I couldn't honor her dying wish, get myself to safety, because I had to know if Roxanne was okay. She was in her werewolf form when all of this happened, so there was a better chance that she made it out of there alive. I had to know. As I ventured deeper through the mass of dead bodies, I found Simpson as well. His head at least; I don't know where the rest of him ended up. I wasn't too keen to look either. I just needed to locate Roxanne and get her to safety. There was no way I was going to see her relationship with Trevor go the same way mine with Saul had.

I soon discovered the vortex, vibrating and shifting before my very eyes. It had nearly tripled in size and had blown the hut that was housing it to pieces. That must have been the source of the explosion from earlier. I looked around quickly, my eyes darting back and forth, as I surveyed the area for Roxanne. I did everything in my power not to look directly at the gaping maw as it pulsed with wickedness.

"Roxy!" I called out. "Where are you? Can you hear me?"

The void stopped making its eerie shrieking sound and just started doing a low humming instead. This might sound crazy, but I got the impression that the fucking thing was looking at me, like it was waiting to see what I was going to do. I know that it wanted me to get closer, close enough for it to grab me with those damned tentacles, but I made sure to keep my distance from it. Soon I heard some movement and I stopped in my tracks to try to locate what was making it.

"Roxy," I whispered when my eyes finally caught sight of her.

She had reverted back to her human form after the blast and was lying half-conscious on the ground. The problem was that she was close to the vortex. I knew what this was immediately. It was a trap. It wanted me to come to her rescue and then it would catch me. Did it honestly think I would fall for something so stupid? I looked around me to see if there was some way for me to get to Roxanne without endangering myself in the process.

"Where are those tentacles?" I muttered as I crept closer and closer to my friend.

I didn't see them and perhaps that lulled me into a false sense of security. I stepped over body after body until I was a few feet away from Roxanne. I called out to her in a whisper, not wanting to attract the attention of anything that wanted me dead. I gripped my knife in one hand and then searched the ground for a stick or anything long enough to poke Roxanne and wake her up, but there was nothing.

"Roxy!" I hissed as loud as I felt comfortable with at the time. "Wake up! We got to get out of here."

She stirred a little bit, and I could hear her groaning a little, so she was clearly alive, but she was not waking up. I sighed as I resolved myself to the fact that I was going to need to go over there and get her myself. I started to gingerly walk over to her, but it felt like something was watching me the whole time. I knew what it was. It was the vortex staring at me like a giant black eye, waiting for me to slip up in its presence. It was making my skin crawl, like at any moment it was going to wink knowingly.

Everything inside of me was telling me to run away and just tell Trevor that I couldn't find his girlfriend, but I wasn't that kind of person. No matter how bad things got, I was never going to be that kind of person. I took a deep breath and then walked over to Roxanne with all the bravery I could muster in the moment. I reached her, knelt down, and started to shake her. I didn't realize how much danger I was actually in until she rolled over onto her back. I was in danger because Roxanne didn't roll over under her own power; she was pushed onto her back by the tentacle that was lying in wait underneath her, waiting for me to get this close.

I barely had time to think before the tentacle quickly coiled around my throat and prevented me from yelling out for help. More tentacles emerged to wrap themselves around my arms and legs and hoist me off the ground...just like they had done to Saul before they killed him. They had such a tight grip on my arms that I was forced to drop my knife. I thought I was going to die, that this nightmare world was finally going to snuff me out, but then Roxanne leaped to her feet and started cutting at the tentacles with the knife I had dropped.

Before I could even think that maybe I had been spared, I saw that the knife wasn't doing anything to slice through the tentacles. They were much too thick for that. Roxy attempted to transform into her werewolf self, probably thinking her claws would stand a better chance against the appendages coming from the void, but she was soon ensnared and hoisted off the ground just like me. And so there we were, side by side, about to share the same fate as my boyfriend. Then something impossible happened.

"Impossible" is not a word I just throw around, not anymore, not after everything we have all experienced since Saul's nightmares came to life. What happened next was something I never expected in a million years. The vortex began to pulse and writhe as though it were sick, making the tentacles weaken and start to lose their grip on me and Roxanne. It started to make a loud, retching sound that made it seem like it was going to vomit. I tried not to think about what it was going to throw up because I knew that whatever it was, I didn't want it all over me.

The sound got louder and louder and louder until I was sure you could probably hear it several counties away from where we were. I instinctively turned my face, so that whatever came out wouldn't get into my eyes and mouth. Soon, it spewed a thick, viscous purple liquid all over me and Roxy. It then did it a second and third time. On the third time, a body flew from the portal and landed a few feet away from me. I thought it was one of the cultists who had sacrificed themselves until I saw the body moving. When they looked up, I recognized them immediately.

"Dr. Robinson?" I found myself asking in shock.

The last time I saw this woman was in New York when she had gone mad and had shot Saul. She was still in Gracie Mansion when the place started to collapse. I figured her crazy ass had died there. And good riddance to the bitch. She had been nothing but trouble right from the very start. When she lifted her head fully, I discovered something else.

"What the fuck," I heard Roxanne shout out, indicating she spotted the same thing that I had.

Dr. Robinson hadn't come back to us whole. She was missing her eyes! There was nothing but deep, empty craters that led that deep into her skull. I honestly couldn't figure out how I wasn't seeing her brain. She crawled around on the ground without saying a word; she had to know she was crawling on dead bodies, but it didn't seem to bother her. She seemed more concerned with getting as far from here as possible.

Before long, the portal got so sick that the tentacles dropped me and Roxanne before wildly flailing all about. Once I was on the ground, I quickly made my way over to Roxanne and checked to see if she was okay. She was injured and was barely able to stand, but she wasn't going to die on me anytime soon.

"What the hell is going on?" she asked, keeping her eyes on the portal. "Was that Dr. Robinson?"

"It was her," I nodded, answering through clenched teeth. "Something took her eyes."

"It was the void," she said. "It destroyed Saul's eyes right before it consumed him too. It must have done the same thing to her before Gracie Mansion collapsed on top of it."

I remembered seeing Saul's eyes pop out of his head like that before he was sucked into the portal. I'm sure Roxanne wasn't trying to bring back that terrible memory, so I didn't hold it against her in the moment, but it still hurt to remember it. I shook the thought from my head as the vortex continued to make retching noises.

"We need to get out of here," I commented. "Can you walk?"

"To get out of here, I'll crawl if I have to," she nodded. "We need to find the others first."

"Simpson and Williams are both dead," I said solemnly. "I left Trevor out there in the woods a few yards. He's hurt."

"Take me to him," she told me.

We started walking towards where I had left Grimes as the vortex continued to get louder and louder. I saw Robinson crawling around and some part of me considered helping her to escape as well, but fuck it. After what she did to my man, why would I ever go out of my way to help her? She should have been grateful that I didn't kick her on my way out.

We were close to escaping from the clearing when the vortex erupted blackish purple ooze that slammed into me and Roxy from behind so hard that it threw us both to the ground. We tried to get up but then more of the liquid gushed out over us, practically gluing us to the ground. If we didn't get out of there soon, we were going to get buried under the stuff. We struggled to get back to our feet, shaking off something that felt like three weighted blankets, and then turned to face the void again.

"Oh no!" I exclaimed.

I watched as seven tentacles rose into the air, preparing to strike us all down and reduce us to jelly. There was no way we were going to be able to run out of there in time. It was going to kill us and there was nothing we could do about it. Roxanne knew it too. She gripped my arm and told me to close my eyes, but I refused. I wanted to see my end coming. I called it courage at the time, but I don't know if that's it. I kinda felt like how Saul felt when he was locked in that cell with Dr. Robinson, when she tried to kill him for everything that had happened. I felt as resigned to my fate as he had to have been.

Before the tentacles could end us, the vortex vomited again...another person this time. A figure draped in a heavy black poncho with a hood landed between us and the vortex. I could only see him from the back, but he cocked his head to the side as he looked at the gaping aperture in front of us. He raised his hands to the sky and fired waves of pure energy at the void.

"What the...?" Roxy asked, but she couldn't finish her sentence.

The tentacles withered and then withdrew back into the void. Roxanne and I watched as the void shrank more and more, screaming in agony as it did. Before long, the damned thing just blinked out of existence. After it was gone, he released a huge sigh of relief and put his hands on his hips. He looked like he was exhausted. Roxy called out to him to see who he was, but I already knew. I had seen those abilities before, in Gracie Mansion when the giant shark was ripped to pieces.

"Who is that?" Roxanne asked.

"It's Saul," I whispered to her.

When he turned around, I saw it was him. Or something that wanted me to think it was him. He walked towards us all smiles, but his eyes were still gone. His eyes were gone and had been replaced with two swirling black pools. They sorta resembled the vortex that he had just destroyed.

"Lita," he said, a broad smile spreading across his face. "Well, aren't you a sight for sore eyes?"

And so...I punched him.

One Week Later

AFTER EVERYTHING we had been through, it was tough getting back to Haven, but we managed to do it. Stone wasn't as pleased to see us as you would think. His best assets looked like they had been completely run through. Trevor and Roxanne had been taken to the infirmary for their wounds, but it looked like they were going to survive. Simpson and Williams never made it back and Stone was troubled by that (I could tell despite how stoic that man is), but not as troubled as the two new additions we brought back with us: a blind Dr. Robinson who had yet to speak and a "Saul" who simply wouldn't shut up. They were immediately put into our makeshift brig under constant watch while Stone brought me to the war room to get my report.

"What the hell happened out there, Ramirez?" he roared as soon as we were alone in the war room together. "We've got two severely injured, two dead, and two who *should* be dead who have somehow been resurrected? You've been gone for a little over a week and you bring all of this here?"

"I don't know what to say to you," I said, not even able to bring myself to look him in the eyes. "It doesn't make sense. None of what happened out there makes any sense whatsoever."

He exhaled for a long time and fell silent. He knew that I wasn't a soldier and couldn't communicate with me the same way he could his troops. He reached across the table and took one of my hands into his. Only then was I able to make eye contact with him.

"It's okay, Lita," he said. "It's okay. Just tell me everything that happened right from the start. Don't leave anything out."

I told him everything, letting the words spill out so I wouldn't have to focus on what had actually happened. The more I talked, the more I was able to disconnect from it all. I felt like my brain was going to break in half after everything that had happened. I had managed to drive back to Haven with Roxanne and Trevor in the backseat with the non-verbal Robinson while Saul was unconscious in the passenger seat. It would have been great if he remained that way for the entire ride. When he woke up, he started talking and all I wanted to do was knock him out again.

"So do you think that the portal you saw was the same one from New York or are they all connected?"

His question snapped me back to reality and stopped me from droning on and on. I blinked a few times and stared at him, giving myself time to process what he had asked me. I honestly didn't want to consider the implications of what we discovered out there. I wasn't ready to consider that the thing that emerged from the void was my man come back to me. I had been living in Hell so long that I had forgotten there was a god out there who answered prayers. I had forgotten and wasn't prepared to accept it.

"I don't know, but you better keep Robinson and...the other one locked up until we can figure out what's really going on," I replied.

"So, you don't think that's really Saul," he said slowly.

"I saw Saul die," I told him. "Whatever that thing is in that cell, it's not him. Now I'm going to go check on my team, what's left of it, and you go see what information you can get from the prisoners."

I left before he could ask me any more questions I couldn't possibly answer. I walked swiftly through the corridors towards the infirmary, not wanting to stop long enough to speak to anyone. I really needed time to myself. I quickly ducked into my bedroom, shut the door, jumped in bed and started screaming into my pillow as loud as I could. I thought that would be enough to get all my frustrations out, but it wasn't. Not even close. I found myself screaming and cursing and throwing things all over the small suite that had become my makeshift apartment. By the time I felt even a smidge better, everything in my space had been completely destroyed except for the mirror above my bathroom sink.

"What are you looking at?" I asked my reflection, the angry bitch who was staring back at me. "Huh? You think you could handle this better than I am? Then why don't you crawl your ass outta there and switch places with me for a bit?"

It didn't respond or do anything other than what I was doing, but I kept an eye on it just to be sure. Saul had already told me what his reflection did on the day he took those damned pills. It occurred to me that in this nightmarish new world, my reflection might be capable of doing the same. But no. It didn't do anything to raise my suspicions at all. I still shattered the mirror with my hairbrush and let the shards rain down into the sink. Better to be safe than sorry.

After I wiped my eyes, I stepped outside to find that Stone was standing there. Apparently, my neighbors ratted me out over all the noise they heard through the walls. I sighed and rolled my eyes as soon as I saw him. I could see from the variation of the lines on his face that he was now officially in "Dad Mode."

"I'm redecorating," I grumbled, trying not to meet his gaze.

"Are you okay?" he asked.

"I'm perfect," I responded bitingly.

"Good," he said. "Because Saul said he won't tell us anything until he gets to see you."

"That thing is not Saul," I protested. "It's just a monster pretending to be him."

"Good, then you shouldn't mind manipulating it into giving us some useful intel," he crossed his arms over his chest.

I tried to think of a way to get out of having to do what he was asking me to do, but nothing came to mind. Stone wanted me to question the thing impersonating my dead boyfriend, find out information that would save other lives. I wanted to say no, but I knew I had to do it. Perhaps the key to saving the world was getting the creature talking until it told us everything we needed to know to win. I sighed while looking down at my feet and then looked back up at him before agreeing to talk to "Saul."

"Fine," I declared. "I guess I gotta do everything around here."

We walked towards the brig, the section in Haven where potential threats were housed, until I was sitting across from Faux Saul. As soon as I entered the room, I could tell that this was not the man I loved. Not only that, but it was a pretty cheap knock-off too; he wasn't acting the way my man usually did. Luckily for it, there was thick plastic between him and me...or I would have tried to rip his stupid face off.

"Lita, you're finally here," he exclaimed excitedly, lighting up like a little puppy to see me. "I told them that I needed to see you."

"And now you're seeing me," I said dismissively. "What do you want?"

He recoiled a little bit, like he was confused as to why I was being so harsh to him. The look on his face made my heart break a little, but then I had to remember that this was not him, not the real Saul. This was just another monster trying to manipulate me. It was no different than the fake version of me that tried to break up with Saul while he was in the hospital. It examined my cold, expressionless face for a bit before it started speaking again.

"I wanna know why you're acting like this," he said as I listened for differences in his speech patterns. "I wanna know why you punched me in the face when I saw you. I also kinda wanna know what I was doing out in the woods, but that's minor compared to the other two."

"What do you remember from the last time you saw me?" I asked, keenly aware that Stone was at my back.

"We were in Gracie Mansion, I got snatched up by those tentacles after Dr. Robinson shot me," he began. "I remember getting hurt, like my bones were breaking. And then...I was back in the void again."

"And then?" I asked.

"Well, you know what it's like in there," he rolled his eyes, somehow, and started to fidget. "It's like time stands still and you can barely move because there's like extra gravity in there or something. It took what felt like forever for me to pull myself back together after what those tentacles did to me. And for the longest time I was blind because...well, you know. But the darkness sorta poured itself into the empty spaces where my eyes used to be and gave me...a whole new type of sight. Then I started walking, hoping I would pop out back on the second floor or back to the first-floor hallway. Instead, I was dropped off in the woods. Then I saw you... and then you hit me. I guess I exited quite a distance from Gracie Mansion."

He studied my face while I just stared at him silently for a bit. I didn't know what to say. He looked deeply concerned. He looked from me to Stone and then back again.

"What happened?" he asked finally. "How long have I been gone?"

"A little over ten months," Stone answered. "Gracie Mansion collapsed and we marked you down as deceased."

"Deceased?" Saul repeated. "You thought I was dead?"

"You *were* dead!" I shouted angrily. "I mean, *Saul's* dead! The *real* Saul! You're just a wicked, evil thing wearing my boyfriend's face! But I've got news for you; we're going to stop you and all your monsters! You don't get to win this, not after everything you've taken from me!"

I was so mad, madder than I had ever been in my whole life. I just wanted to break through that plastic partition and destroy the creature in front of me. I didn't have a weapon on me, but I was so angry that I was reasonably sure I could do it with my bare hands. I felt Stone's hand clasp my shoulder and while it didn't calm me down any, it did keep me in my seat.

"I am *not* a monster," he said as calmly as possible even though his rage was practically bubbling over. "I *am* Saul Copeland, always have been even though most days I wish I could be just about anyone else. Now I don't understand what's going on here or how I was gone so long, but I know who and what I am."

"Then tell me something, Copeland," said Stone. "My people witnessed you destroy one of those black holes with new abilities. Tell me about that."

He was frowning like a petulant child now, staring right at me as though I had hurt his feelings or something. I simply crossed my arms over my chest and stared right back at him. I wasn't going to be made to feel bad about the emotions of some imposter.

"Well, time passes different in the void...like Lita already knows from personal experience," he began, "so after I was...made whole again, I used my time to not only try to get to the other side of the tunnel but to also work on mastering the abilities I needed to fight these things. I got pretty damned good at it."

"How good?" Stone asked.

"I think I can fix the world," he revealed. "If I can find the leader of these things, the one calling the shots, I think I can end this once and for all."

"That's what I want to hear," Stone nodded.

"Wait a minute!" I protested. "You can't honestly be thinking about trusting this thing, can you? It's a monster! It's clearly lying to us so we'll let it out of this cell."

"I told you I am not a monster," Faux Saul spoke up. "And I am not trapped in this cell either."

Before Stone and I could ponder what he meant by that, he raised one of his hands and made the plastic partition completely disintegrate, showing us that he could have left at any time. My breath caught in my throat, fear seizing me in the moment, while Stone quickly pulled his weapon. Fake Saul kept his eyes, his swirling black whirlpool eyes, focused on me the whole time.

"Now can we please stop playing games?" he asked. "I need to fix what I started."

Stone didn't bother to try to contain Faux Saul anymore after that. It was clear that this thing had more power than us and couldn't be held securely in any of the prisons we had at our disposal. The creature got debriefed and was given a set of fatigues to wear and soon everyone started treating him like he was part of the team, like he was actually Saul come back to life to help us win the war. Everyone but me. I wasn't buying this whole Gandalf the White act. This thing was not my boyfriend and I set out to prove it.

It was the little things that confirmed it for me. Saul had always been really buttoned-up and reserved, most likely because of his anxiety. This Saul was all smiles and extremely outgoing. He was so personable; he was making friends with a bunch of people all over Haven. My Saul always kept himself to himself…and to me. I couldn't shake the feeling that he was trying to ingratiate himself with all the people here so that we wouldn't expect his inevitable betrayal later. I tried to convince Roxanne, Trevor, and even Stone that this was not the real Saul, but they only humored me and told me that we would all just keep an eye on him for now.

It didn't take me very long to figure out that I was going to have to expose him for what he was all on my own. I was the only one who hadn't had the wool pulled over my eyes. So, after having him here with us in Haven for a full five weeks or so, I decided to pay a visit to Faux Saul in his suite. He had a huge smile on his face when he saw me standing at his front door that night.

"Lita, I am so glad you're here," he said. "You've been avoiding me and I was hoping we could talk."

"That's why I'm here," I nodded, offering a small smile. "I wanted to talk to you too. Can I come in?"

"Have I ever been able to deny you anything?" he asked before he stepped aside and allowed me access to his place.

Faux Saul led me to his living room and we both sat down on his sofa. I felt uncomfortable sitting so close to a monster, but if I needed to kill him, it would be easier to do so from up close. With his powers, I would only get one real shot at it. I had my knife hidden in my sleeve, ready to strike at a moment's notice.

"I just want to say that I understand why you've been cold to me," he said. "I can understand that…seeing me die must have been difficult. And maybe you had started to get used to it, gotten to the point where you could move on, and then I just pop back into your life again. I'm sorry for all of this craziness. But I'm back, Lita. Really and truly back. And once I find and destroy the cause of all this madness, we can get back to our lives."

He was saying all the right things, but I just couldn't accept what I was hearing. Everything inside me kept telling me that this was simply not my Saul. He was just too different and it kinda pissed me off that no one else seemed to notice.

"You say that, but you're so different from before," I stated.

"I *am* different," he smiled broadly. "I feel the way I did when I was taking the pills Dr. Robinson gave me, but it's natural now. Something about going through the vortex a second time changed me all the way through. It's like this is the person I would be if I never had anxiety in the first place."

"Is that right?" I asked. "You can see how that would make it difficult for people to accept that you are who you say you are. You came back here with an entirely different personality."

"I guess I understand," he nodded knowingly. "I can't help it though; I feel amazing, Lita. I can't tone it down for people who want to see me continue to be miserable for the rest of my life. I mean, who would want that for me? No one who considered themselves to be a true friend."

I felt some kind of way about that. Could that be me? Could I have been so wrapped up in wanting my Saul back that I couldn't even recognize that this was him, only free of the burdens he had always carried around? Was I a bitch for not being able to accept him like this, for making his life hell because a happy Saul was not what I was used to? The knife pressed to my arm felt like a mistake now, like a cold condemnation of all my actions after finding him. I thought this evening was going to end with me plunging my blade into this imposter's throat, but now I had my own doubts that this was actually a monster.

"But that's over," he said excitedly. "You're here now. What made you change your mind about me?"

I didn't know what to say to that. I had honestly come here to get him to incriminate himself so I could have the evidence I needed to murder him. I searched my mind for anything to tell him, to extricate myself from this situation. I gave him a nervous smile as he watched me, waiting for a response.

"Well, I was thinking about how you destroyed the void with your new abilities and I was wondering if you think you have a good enough handle on your powers to set everything back to the way they were," I said finally.

"Oh yes," he said, raising his hands and making them glow with energy. "When we find this leader of theirs, I can destroy him just like I did the portal. I just need Stone to find him and point me in his direction. This could all be over really soon."

"Do you think your eyes will go back to normal after you win?" I asked.

"Why?" he asked. "You don't think I look like a cool anime character like this?"

"It's weird up close," I admitted.

"I don't know if my eyes will ever go back to normal, but I guess I could be one of those dudes who wears sunglasses all the time," he shrugged.

"Even at night?" I asked.

"Hey, when you're cool the sun shines twenty-four hours a day," he smirked.

He was care-free, charming, and just as lovable as ever. He was really putting me at ease. There was one problem with the whole thing: I still wasn't completely sure that this was *my* Saul. His story about being rid of all his anxiety was certainly plausible enough, but it still could have been a lie meant to lull me into a false sense of security. There was something else bothering me about the whole thing. Was it okay to accept this new version of Saul and forget all about the old one. I kinda felt like that bitch Laura Winslow, happy with Steve Urkel being consigned to oblivion as long as she got her perfect Stefan Urquelle. I hated that bitch.

"Yeah, the shades might work," I nodded. "You know, if you don't get those perfect brown eyes back. I gotta ask though, with your eyes so vastly different now, does the world even look the same to you anymore?"

"Almost everything looks the same, but there are definitely some improvements with what I have now," he replied. "I used to see danger in absolutely everything, in every interaction and in every move I or anyone else made. It's not like that anymore. Now I see the world as just a normal place. It must be how you normal people have always seen the world."

"Sure, us normals," I laughed.

"No, I'm serious," he said taking my hands into his. "You don't know how much of a gift it is to see the world the way you do. Now that I see it the same way, I am thrilled every single day. A day of peace, a day without abject terror. I wish I could have grown up like that."

Hearing him express himself like this was kinda heart-breaking. We had been talking about his feelings and his fears ever since his nightmares started coming to life, but he had never been so candid as he was in this moment. I guess I still didn't know what it was like to be him. It's ironic. He didn't really feel free of his nightmares until we were *all* living with them.

"Anyway, would you like something to drink?" he asked. "I have water and...well, just water."

"No, I'm good," I shook my head.

"I'm really glad you came over," he said with a slight smile. "Under normal circumstances, I would turn on the TV and we could watch something, but Stone told me that there's been no TV, music, or internet since...I disappeared."

"Yeah, but it's not like it's been dull or anything," I said. "The constant monster attacks have been all the excitement any of us really need."

"I bet," he said. "Don't worry. I'll fix all this and then we'll all get to return to watching mindless nonsense on our phones all day."

"Well, at least it looks like you have all your priorities in order," I laughed louder than I had planned to.

I'm not gonna lie. It felt good to be talking to my boyfriend again, even if it was a different version than I had been used to. I just hoped that I wasn't betraying Saul by liking this new version of him. I would hate to think that after all these years, I was just as bad as Laura Winslow.

We sat there and talked for a good long time until it got late and then it was time for me to go back to my suite. I could tell from the look on his face that he wanted me to stay. He wanted to pick up where we left off, but I was in no way ready for that. Not when there were still lingering doubts that he was who he claimed to be. He didn't push though. He simply walked me towards the exit so we could say our goodbyes for the evening.

"Can I see you tomorrow?" he asked.

"That depends on whether those new eyes of yours go through another transformation while you sleep tonight," I smirked, trying to be cute (just in case this was really my man). "Well, good night."

Right when I was about to leave his place, the non-functional TV on his wall switched on. The first such device to turn on since all this mess started and it just happened to be in his room while I was there. That couldn't be a coincidence. And it turned out that it wasn't. Saul began walking towards it while it displayed static just like the televisions from the old days.

"I thought you said that none of these things worked anymore," he commented as he approached the device cautiously.

"They stopped working after what happened at Gracie Mansion," I replied. "Could it be working again because you're back?"

"I don't think so," he said, walking up to the TV with all the bravery of a white person in a cheesy horror movie. "This is something else."

After a few moments, the static was replaced with the image of a dark figure wearing a cloak. It didn't take long for us to see that it was a live video. We could see the person on the screen moving as he/she/it prepared to speak.

"Hello, people of Haven," the stranger began. "I know you're all busy living your new lives imprisoned in that disgusting little cul-de-sac you've decided to make your home, so I will be brief. You have something of mine and I want it. If you do not give it to me, then I am going to come down there and get it from you. Trust me. You don't want that. None of your stalwart protectors are going to be able to do much if I decide to huff and puff and blow down the walls of your little community."

"Saul...?" I asked, walking up behind him as we watched the message being delivered to us through this formerly dead television set. "What's going on?"

"Your little hamlet just got a new addition to its population, a man named Saul Copeland, who was up until very recently imprisoned in one of my voids," the figure went on. "I want him returned to me. Do that and you will get to live. Defy me and you will all die screaming...those of you who do not drown in your own blood, that is."

"He's transmitting this message to every device in the world," said Saul.

"How do you know that?" I asked.

"Just listen to how he's wording it," he replied. "He's trying to appeal to all the Dr. Robinsons in the world. People who won't hesitate to sell me out to save their own skins."

"To save yourselves, you need do only one thing for me: bring Saul Copeland to me," he continued. "Bring him to Nevada. I got a nice little place set up in the desert out there. You won't be able to miss it. It's the only new architecture out there and it totally screams evil warlord. You have three weeks to bring him to me or I will bury Haven like it's no different than Pompeii. Tick-tock."

The screen went blank after that and then there was nothing but dead silence. After a few moments, Saul turned around to face me and I honestly never saw him angrier than he was in that moment. I asked him if he was okay.

"He's calling me out, Lita," he answered. "If he wants a fight, then fine. It looks like this is all going to be over much sooner than we thought."

"So, we're going to Nevada?" I asked. "Who does this guy think he is, Randall Flagg?"

"Doesn't matter," he shook his head. "He's the cause of all of this. He's the man who killed me in New York. Tortured me my whole life. And I'm going to finally find him and kill him."

Hearing him like this was really unsettling. He'd never been so angry, not in front of me anyway. I didn't say anything though because I thought his rage was justified. He was finally going to be confronting the source of all his misery. In his shoes, I guess I would be pissed off too. No more than five minutes later, there was furious knocking on the front door. When Saul opened the door, Stone barged in and stood in the middle of the living room.

"I'm assuming you saw the same message I just did," he said. "Every television, phone, and computer was playing the same message. That was him, the leader of these creatures. We finally know where he is."

"And I don't suppose you have a bunch of missiles you can fire and just destroy all of Nevada all at once?" Saul asked, crossing his arms over his chest.

"There could be innocent people there, Saul," I said, causing both men to look towards me. "We can't...just destroy the place if innocent people are still there."

He looked at me with confusion on his face, like he couldn't understand what I meant. His anger was overriding his common sense, his common decency. After a few tense moments, his face shifted and the compassion I usually saw there finally returned.

"Of course," he nodded. "You're right. I don't know why I said that. Well, that means we're going to have to do this the hard way."

"Meaning?" Stone asked.

"I'm going to have to go to Nevada and face him head-on," said Saul. "I'll leave today."

"Are you crazy?" I blurted out, unable to contain my shock over what I was hearing. "For one, your sense of direction is terrible. You used to get lost in New York and the city is literally a grid. You'll never find your way to Nevada from here all by yourself. Secondly, this is so obviously a trap; he's luring you out there to kill you and then there will be no one left to stand in his way."

"What do you suggest?" Stone asked.

"I know you probably never saw 'The Lord of the Rings", but I am suggesting we put together a team and get Saul to Nevada to make sure he puts an end to this," I replied.

"I know all about fellowships, young lady, but what concerns me is how do we ensure I don't end like Boromir," he frowned, kinda surprising me with his geeky knowledge right then. "We're not exactly operating from a position of strength here. We're basically the last vestiges of American society cowering in this community while waiting for our turn to die. What exactly do you think we're capable of right now?"

"We don't have time for you to squabble," Saul interjected angrily. "All the people here who saw that message aren't going to give you time to think and strategize. They're going to get their knives and pitchforks and they are going to come right here to collect me. And I will *not* be collected, Stone. So whether it is with an army or completely solo, I'm going to head to Nevada and I'm going to finish this once and for all."

"I've gotta say, Mr. Copeland, that I am liking this take-charge version of you a lot more," said Stone. "You're going to have a fellowship all right. The finest damned fellowship a man could ask for...because they're all going to be red-blooded Americans. You two wait here; I'm going to assemble the team."

He left after that and then I was left alone with Saul while he paced back and forth. The anger was coming off him in waves. I had seen this before. I used to see my father pace around just like this when I was a kid, whenever my big brother did something stupid or whenever my dad got a call about something his own brother, my uncle, did and now needed someone to come and bail him out. That being the case, I should have known better than to try to talk to him while he was in that state, try to talk him off the ledge as it were, but I slipped into the same patterns as my mother.

"Are you okay, Saul?" I asked, softening my voice in the same way my mother used to when my dad became a raging storm. "What are you thinking about right now?"

"I'm thinking about what it's going to feel like to have that monster's throat in my hands," he revealed without meeting my gaze.

"I feel you," I nodded. "It's going to be great to finally be over all this. I just want to make sure you don't lose yourself to, you know, vengeance or whatever."

"Like Batman?" he asked, turning to face me at last with a confused look on his face.

"Like a villain that Batman is trying to reason with, more likely," I corrected him.

"I'll be fine, Lita," he tried to assure me. "I'm going to go kill this monster and get my life back. No, better than that. I am going to get the life I should have had right from the beginning."

"That...sounds great," I said. "I really, really want that for you. I'm just worried about you."

"Worried about what?" he asked.

"I don't want you to lose yourself, Saul," I told him. "I am with you every step of the way with this. Let's go save the world. But I don't want you sacrificing yourself in the process."

"I'm not going the martyr route, Lita," he said, walking over to me and taking me into his arms. "Not at all. I'm going to be fine after all this. Better than fine. It's going to be like an exorcism of sorts; I am going to be rid of all my demons forever."

I didn't know what else to say, so I simply nodded. Before the hour was through, Stone had us both in the War Room with Trevor and Roxanne. The citizens of Haven had already started to gather and demand that Saul be turned over to them. Saul grew more and more agitated as we sat there discussing the plan.

"We have an armored vehicle that survived our escape from New York," said Stone. "That's what we'll be using to get to Nevada. I would bring an entire army with us, if I could, but I cannot bring myself to leave this place undefended."

"Then let's keep this strike force small," Trevor suggested. "Just the people in this room."

"We all just play defense for Saul and make sure he makes it to the end zone," Roxanne stated. "He uses those newfound powers to kill this monster and then we come home conquering heroes."

"I'm not interested in being a hero," Saul shook his head. "All I want to do is fix everything I fucked up. I'll be happy with that."

"Me too," said Stone. "This is no stealth mission. Our enemy knows we're coming. We're going to load up with as many weapons as possible and march right up to his front door. Meet me in the motor pool in an hour. I've got some more last-minutes arrangements to take care of before we leave."

With that, we were dismissed while Stone attended to his arrangements. Trevor and Roxanne went off to prepare together while I made sure to stick close to Saul. I still wasn't entirely sure that this was really my Saul, but I was willing to step out on faith a bit and hope that whoever he was, he was still a good guy who was on our side. If nothing else, he considered himself to be the real Saul and was determined to do the right thing. That had to count for something.

"You should relax," I told him. "We're traveling cross-country across dangerous terrain. You're going to be doing a lot of fighting to get to Nevada; you should save your strength."

"I don't know if I can relax," he said. "I've never been closer to being free of all...this nonsense...than I am right now. Do you know what this means, Lita? I win one little fight and then all our lives get better immediately."

"Yeah, I understand," I nodded, "but you're going to need to *win* that fight. If you lose, then we're all in deeper shit than we were before. And you're not going to win this fight if you're exhausted before we even get there."

"So, what do you suggest?" he smirked. "I should take a nap or something?"

"A nap, meditation, yoga," I shrugged. "Whatever it takes to make sure you're at full-strength when we finally confront this bad guy."

He huffed in annoyance before finally agreeing with me, walking over to his sofa and laying down on his back as though he were going to tell his therapist everything he had been through. I could tell just by looking at him that he was nowhere near relaxed and after everything that happened with Dr. Robinson, he wasn't inclined to discuss the inner workings of his mind. I found myself taking the seat next to the sofa, the one where I imagine Robinson sat during their therapy sessions.

"It's hard to relax when there's a monster out there who wants you dead," he grumbled.

None of us had been able to relax since all this started, but I didn't want to tell him that. He had been feeling guilty for too long as it was. I didn't want to pour any salt in all his open wounds. I just wanted to keep him level-headed enough that he wouldn't go running off half-cocked. He needed a team with him because we were only going to get one shot at this, one chance to change the world back to what it was before.

"I am so mad, Lita," he said out of nowhere. "I have never been so mad in my whole life. This creature...it's not just responsible for everything going on right now. It's been at the heart of all my fears and anxiety since the day I was born. I don't know how I know it, but I do. I can feel it at the center of my being. He has made my life a living hell right from the day I was born. Do you know what it's like to be given the opportunity to confront the person responsible for every bad thing that has ever happened to you?"

I couldn't answer that. I've had bullies in my life, mean girls who used to give me shit, but I typically gave back just as well as I took. I've had some exes who I was much too nice to. But I wasn't like Saul. I didn't have a straight-up villain who took pleasure in tormenting me from Day 1. This man, who had never considered hurting anyone, was now on a quest to commit cold-blooded, rage-fueled murder. I know that I should only have been concerned about one thing, getting our planet back, but I was worried about him too.

"Are you going to be okay doing this, Saul?" I finally brought myself to ask.

"What do you mean?" he asked, craning his neck to look over at me. "Do you think...I might lose?"

"No, I'm not worried about that," I shook my head.

"Then what is it?" he asked, sitting upright. "Tell me what's on your mind."

"It's just that you've come back different, Saul," I explained after taking a deep breath. "It's clear that everything you went through in the void has changed you. I just worry that...if you change any more than you already have...you might lose yourself entirely. You're too good a person to let this destroy you."

"I'll be fine," he frowned. "I'm going to win this."

"There are ways to win and still lose," I told him. "I wouldn't want that to happen to you."

"I would be willing to sacrifice myself, everything about me, to stop this thing once and for all," he told me with steely determination. "He's a monster, Lita. A monster who plunged this whole planet into despair."

"Yeah, but *you're* not a monster," I told him. "If he turns you into one during this final battle, then he truly won. I need you to know that and remember it just in case…"

"Just in case what?" he asked.

I didn't want to say the next part. I didn't even want to think about it, but it was important to express it anyway. I couldn't bear to look at him as I said it though.

"Just in case, I don't make it to the end with you."

All the life and color seemed to drain right out of him after I said that. This new worry-free version of Saul hadn't even considered the fact that I and everyone else might die still before he had a chance to kill his tormentor. He still thought there was going to be a happy ending to all of this.

"Tomorrow isn't guaranteed to anyone, Saul, never has been," I continued. "That's more true now than it has ever been. I might not still be there when you finally confront your demons. And just in case I'm not there to remind you to keep true to yourself, I need you to know that's what I want for you."

"I need you to know that I am not going to let anything happen to you, Lita," he assured me. "That's just not going to happen. They'll have to kill me…again…first."

I nodded slightly, but didn't say anything. It was a nice sentiment and all, but there was no way he could guarantee my safety in a world that had gone so completely mad. He had a lot of faith in his new abilities, but I still wasn't sure he had what it took to save us all. I wasn't going to keep pressing the issue though; I had decided that I would just keep a very close eye on him and try to do something if he went off the rails.

Stone came to collect us no more than twenty minutes after he had left and we were introduced to the team that was supposed to get us to Nevada. Not counting Trevor and Roxanne, we were given just three troops because Stone insisted that the rest of the soldiers needed to stay behind to protect Haven. I was more than a little underwhelmed.

"What is this?" I asked. "Three people?"

"These are the best of the best," Stone grumbled with his arms crossed over his chest.

"I don't doubt it," I said, not wanting to give the impression that the three people standing there at attention weren't good enough. "That's not what I'm saying. But the monster has finally revealed itself and this is our chance to end all our suffering. Shouldn't we be sending a full army?"

"On the surface, that sounds like a terrific idea, but what if this message from our enemy is a trap?" Stone asked. "What if he's intentionally luring us away from here so that he can attack Haven and have a better chance of killing all the people in our care? I won't allow that. Protecting these people is my main mission, if nothing else."

"Your main concern should be eliminating this threat," Saul spoke up angrily. "That's the best way to keep all these people safe. I shouldn't have to tell you that. It wasn't too long ago that you were thinking of putting a bullet in my head to save this world. What changed? Why aren't you keeping that same energy now?"

"Calm down, Saul," I whispered over to him. "He's just doing what's best for everyone."

"Uh huh," he nodded before he started pacing back and forth. "We're wasting time. Whether it's a small battalion or a huge army, the mission is still the same. You have to get me to Nevada so I can finish this once and for all. So, let's stop talking and head out."

"You're being rude," I said.

"Not as rude as he was being when he threatened to end my life," he snapped. "All in the name of being pragmatic."

While Saul went to a corner to sulk, I took the time to meet the folks who were going to be accompanying us. They were putting their lives on the line, so the least I could do was learn their names, right? First off, was a white man in his forties named Barry and built like a grizzly bear; his face was covered in hair like one too. He revealed that he wasn't an active-duty soldier when the demons escaped from Saul's mind. He had already served two tours in Iraq years prior and was running a hardware store in Paramus, New Jersey when everything went to Hell. When he found out about Haven, he scooped up his ex-wife and the kids she had with the man she cheated on him with and led them to safety. Um, he even saved his ex's new husband, which I got the impression he really didn't want to have to do.

Secondly, we had a white, thin-framed man named Crispin wearing wire-frame glasses. He was looking kinda awkward while standing at attention. Honestly, I didn't think he had the upper-body strength to even carry a rifle, let alone to be considered one of Stone's "best of the best" but I was trying not to be openly judgmental. I was going to leave that to Saul. Crispin had made it all the way here from Cincinnati, part of a convoy of about seventeen. I could see the sadness in his eyes when he revealed that he was the only one who survived long enough to set foot in DC. I caught a hint of a gay vibe off him, but my gaydar has never been that great.

And the last part of our group was Jessica Garcia, another Latina like me, but her family hailed from Guatemala and mine came from Columbia. She had been stationed in Florida and then the hurricane descended. She tried to help as many people as she could, but the storm was relentless. To hear her tell it, it was a storm made up of hundreds of other equally fierce storms.

"When you're being whipped by gale force winds, it's almost impossible to hold onto anything important to you," she had said.

She had managed to make it to DC with a handful of survivors. Her ten-year-old daughter wasn't one of them. Saul may have been off in the corner with his arms crossed over his chest like a petulant child while these soldiers introduced themselves and told their stories, but I knew that he had heard them. These three people, along with Trevor, Roxanne, and myself were going to be there with him every step of the way for this journey. If there was anything left of the man I knew, the man I loved, in there then he was touched by their stories and would do anything he could to make sure that life would go back to normal...one way or another.

"So, it's up to the seven of us to save humanity," I said.

"Well, there's going to be eight going on this mission," Stone spoke up in response to my statement.

"You're going too?" I asked in shock. "After everything you said about keeping this place safe from danger, I thought you would be leading the efforts here."

"I *am* going to be staying here, to protect this place from harm, Ms. Ramirez," he stated, his face as immovable as his namesake. "You're going to be bringing someone else along with you."

Stone didn't reveal who it was or why they weren't in the room with us for this briefing. It wasn't like him to be cagey about a mission. It didn't take very long for me to find out why he was being so tight-lipped. We left the new additions in the War Room and Stone led us to the last person who would be joining us on our expedition.

"No fucking way!" I yelled, standing outside the cell of that duplicitous bitch Dr. Robinson. "There is no way we are bringing her with us!"

"I can see why you would be hesitant to trust me, Ms. Ramirez," she had the nerve to say.

"How the hell do you see anything without any eyes?" I asked.

"Kind of a low blow," Saul leaned over and whispered into my ear. "I kinda lost my eyes in there too, but I see better than fine."

"Clearly, I wasn't talking about you," I whispered back, "but I am sorry if it offended you."

"The loss of my eyes has greatly improved my hearing, so your...whispers are awkward," Robinson revealed. "I requested to come along on this mission. Stone was skeptical of me, but he was at least willing to hear me out. I hope the two of you will listen as well."

"Why the hell would I listen to anything you have to say?" I demanded. "You almost killed Saul! Your actions led to the fall of New

York, made us all have to run with our tails tucked between our legs. We would have to be crazy to take you along on the most dangerous, most *crucial*, mission of our lives."

"Tell them what you told me," Stone commanded.

Dr. Robinson sighed like *she* was annoyed with *us*. I swear I almost throttled her. I stopped myself only because I knew that someone would have grabbed me before I had a chance to land all the punches I wanted. Secretly, I wondered what she had to say that was so vital that Stone would consider her an asset for the most important mission of this war, the most important mission of our collective lives.

"I learned things while I was in the void with Mr. Copeland," she stated. "Why he was discovering the many uses of his new, miraculous powers, I was learning something far different, but no less valuable."

"Spit it out, Robinson," Trevor said impatiently. It was good to know that others hated her just as much as I did. "Tell us what you know."

"While Copeland went through his little training montage like some supernatural Rocky Balboa, I was listening to voices," she revealed.

"Oh, so you went full-on psycho then, huh?" I asked. "Why am I not surprised?"

"Let her finish," said Roxanne, gently placing a hand on my shoulder.

"I thought the voices were internal at first, that I had lost my mind," Robinson continued. "I discovered that they were coming from outside of myself though. It was the monsters, the nightmare creatures that Copeland had unleashed. They were whispering their dirty little motives and desires. As time went on, one voice started to stick out above all the others. I started listening to it the most...because I had time and it seemed to be the most interesting. It was the same voice you all heard on the TV earlier."

"Did you tell anyone what you had been hearing before today?" Saul demanded. "Did you volunteer any of this intel before you decided to go on walkabout?"

"Why would I tell you people anything after you threw me into a cell?" she asked.

"Um, for the good of all humanity, Dr. Robinson," Saul replied.

"That should have been a good enough reason for you to tell us what you knew. Did you know he was in Nevada this whole time?"

She claimed she didn't know, but I got the distinct feeling that she was lying to us. I didn't trust this bitch in the slightest. I really didn't know why anyone else around was bothering to give her the benefit of the doubt. They were discussing taking her along on this mission while I thought she should have just been dumped into the deepest hole we could find. I could feel in my bones that she was bad news and that she was going to betray us at the worst possible time, probably get a bunch of us killed in the process.

"I didn't know for sure," she shook her head. "There was no real reason for me to believe anything I was hearing. For the longest time, I thought I was simply going mad for being in the void for so long."

"I'm going to allow you to join us on this trip," said Trevor stiffly, "but the moment I get the slightest hint of betrayal, I'm going to put a bullet right between your eyes and let these nightmares feast on your corpse. Am I clear?"

"I would say I *see* your point, but you don't sound like you're in the mood for levity," she answered. "Look, you're not going to need to worry about me. I just want this all to come to an end, so I can finally get my life back and never see any of you ever again."

"You're not really *seeing* us right now, bitch, but fine," I said, still seething with anger. "But you better be helpful during this trip."

It was decided that Dr. Robinson would accompany us on this trip. No more than twenty minutes after the decision had been made, we were leaving Haven and heading towards Nevada. It was a quiet trek in the beginning. We had two vehicles between and barely a word was spoken amongst us. I was in the lead vehicle, sitting in the backseat with Saul, while Trevor drove and Roxanne acted as navigator. The others were in the second vehicle, traveling with Robinson; I refused to be in the same SUV with her.

"How do you feel?" I finally asked Saul, needing to break the uncomfortable silence.

He had been staring out the window for the entire trip so far, not really saying anything because none of us were. He turned to face me with a bored expression on his face, like he barely heard me at all. It reminded me of when we would be sitting on the couch watching TV and his mind would just wander off to places unknown. I don't know what he was thinking about as we drove along those abandoned roads, but I know his mind was a million miles away.

"Huh?" he asked, confirming that he hadn't really heard me at all. "What did you say?"

"I asked you how you were feeling," I repeated, offering a small smile.

"I'm fine," he smiled back. "I guess I'm just ready to be done with all of this. Get on with my life, with you, and finally be happy without all of this hanging over my head. I was just sitting here thinking about how great our lives are going to be together when I finally put a stop to all this. Being normal. Talking about marriage and kids without being completely terrified of all the things I am going to screw up as a husband and father."

"Have you ever considered the possibility that a bit of anxiety might be a good thing," Trevor spoke up, surprising us both because I could have sworn that he hadn't heard a word we were saying in the backseat. "Maybe worrying about what kind of man, husband, and father you're going to be is precisely what keeps you from screwing up. We definitely have to end this global nightmare, but perhaps you're going to want to keep some of that anxiety when this is all over."

"I'll take that under advisement," Saul commented before reaching over and taking my hand into his. "When this is over, I think you and I should...move in together."

"That's a big step, Saul," I said, shocked he even suggested something like that. "I've never co-habitated with anyone before."

"Me either," he laughed. "I should be terrified, but I'm living a life without fear right now."

"Why would you be terrified?" I asked. "I'm a delight to be around."

"I doubt that Robinson would agree with you," Roxanne added. "I feel like she's had enough of you."

"She pulled a gun on me and mine," I said angrily. "She's lucky I haven't killed her already."

"Do you think when this is all over, she will go back to normal?" Roxanne asked. "Mentally, I mean?"

"I don't know," Saul shrugged. "Maybe. I'm pretty sure I can fix the planet, but I'm not sure how much I will be able to fix the people who lived through all this. We're just going to have to figure that part out together."

As we all talked amongst ourselves, I looked out the back window of our SUV and looked at the vehicle driving behind us. I wondered if they were having stimulating conversations too. I think I kinda felt bad for them. We all had a bit of a personal connection to this quest we were embarking on, but the soldiers that were accompanying us did not. They were here just to put things right. They didn't get severely injured like Trevor or turned into a werewolf like Roxanne. They weren't in love with the tortured soul that inadvertently created this dystopia we were trapped in. They were just good men and women volunteering to save the world.

"Do you think they're doing all right in the other truck?" I asked, continuing to look back at them through the window.

"They have walkies over there and we are all on the same frequency," Trevor responded. "If anything was wrong, one of them would have reached out to us. Don't worry, Lita. They can definitely handle Dr. Robinson. She's not the one we're all going to need to worry about during this trip."

Our drive was mostly uneventful. That surprised me and scared me all at the same time. Ever since all this nonsense started, Saul's nightmares kept finding us and attacking us. They seemed to always be able to home in on us no matter where we were. They were probably able to sense him or something; you never forget your home, after all. Hell, the last time we all left Haven, we were attacked by a swarm of cultists who worshipped those damn portals like they were gods. But now, when the end was in sight, our enemy was sending no one to confront us. I couldn't help but think there was a reason for that.

Everything looked terrible. The further we traveled, the more corpses we encountered littering the streets. We were approaching Kansas when we ran into our first real bit of trouble. Looming several miles in front of us were a series of huge tornadoes, reaching high in the sky and creating a dust storm that blotted out all sunlight. Trevor stopped the SUV and we all got out to look at the barrier separating us from Nevada.

"Typical," said Grimes. "We were halfway there."

"I figured this would happen," Saul commented. "Those storms are right above Kansas and, well..."

"Wizard of Oz?" Roxanne asked. "I get it. Those flying monkeys scared the hell outta me and so did that fucking evil witch. I still don't know who thought it was a good idea to make a Broadway musical about her."

"If we go in there, we are bound to face all of that plus much worse," he explained.

"Then we're just going to have to try to go around," said Grimes decisively. "This monster asked us to come out here, summoned us. There's got to be a way through; we just need to find it."

Trevor had a plan for us to try out and left me and Saul alone with Robinson while he coordinated with the others. It was clear they thought of us as nothing more than civilians and they were right to do so. I looked Robinson up and down in disdain.

"Do you have something to say to me?" she asked eventually, surprising me a bit because I didn't know she could tell I was looking at her.

"Why are you coming along with us, Robinson?" I asked her. "What are you really trying to achieve with your sudden altruism?"

"My altruism is not sudden, young lady," she said in annoyance. "I'm a doctor. I dedicated myself to helping others a long time ago. If anything, my attack on Mr. Copeland was the sudden lapse of judgment. As for why I have decided to come along, I just wanted to make sure you guys don't screw this up."

"Excuse me?" I recoiled at the very notion.

"What do you mean, Doctor?" Saul asked. "How do you think we might screw this up?"

"You're both young and stupid," she explained. "I don't want you ruining our one shot at fixing this by making a purely emotional choice at an inopportune time. When it is time to take the shot that will save us all, I don't need the two of you making googly eyes at each other or trying to save each other when you should be focusing on the big picture."

I wanted to hit her, but her words kinda rang true in that moment. When we were back in Manhattan, I refused to let Saul go off on his own. I loved him too much for that. He was willing to leave me behind to make sure that I survived this. What if things shook out that he had to make a choice between saving me or saving the world? I couldn't be sure that he would make the right choice in that moment. I couldn't make sure that I would either.

"We would have to be in a lot of trouble if we let your moral compass decide everyone's fate," Saul commented dismissively.

"I don't think you've been paying attention, young man, but we are in more trouble now than we have ever been in our collective lives," she shot back. "Our continued existence is going to depend on the members of this caravan making all the right moves. No room for errors in judgment or simplistic sentimentality. I don't know how much of humanity is still alive out there, but they deserve champions who are going to do everything they can to save them. You think I'm a danger to this group, but I think the real liability to our mission is the two of you."

I could tell from the look on Saul's face that he was angry, but I couldn't help but wonder if the bad doctor was actually right about this one point. I kept quiet about that though. The last thing Robinson needed was for anyone to agree with her. She needed to know she was wrong for almost killing Saul back at Gracie Mansion. After a while, Trevor and the others came back to tell us what had been decided.

"We're going to split up and try to go around this mass of storms," he said. "My vehicle is going to travel north and try to go through Nebraska and the Dakotas while Garcia is going to take the others South and see if they can go through Texas."

"Looks like you got good grades in Geography," I commented, "but you didn't see a lot of horror movies. Splitting up is the worst thing we can do right now."

"Ordinarily, I would agree with you," he replied, but we don't have the time and resources to all go North and discover there's no way through and then all have to double back to get back down to Texas to try again. We all agreed that this is just how we're going to have to handle this."

"Well, you're the expert strategist," said Saul. "If this is what makes the most sense, then let's get started."

And so, it was decided. Garcia took her people South towards Texas while the rest traveled North towards Nebraska. The ride got quiet again, all of us uneasy over the fact that we had split up in the way that we had. We didn't hear anything from Garcia, so we all hoped it was good news.

"The storm is following us," Saul commented casually.

"What?" Roxanne asked.

"The tornado we saw in Kansas," he stated. "It looks like it's headed right for us. Kinda slowly, but it's definitely headed this way."

"He's right," I said leaning over so I could look through Saul's window. "It's definitely coming this way."

"Grab the radio and check with Garcia," said Trevor. "See if any of the storms have peeled off and started chasing them too."

"I thought my eyes were playing tricks on me, sir," she responded. "But we do have two huge, but slow-moving tornados trailing behind us. Should we change the plan?"

"Negative," Trevor answered. "We're going to keep on until we make it past Kansas and then regroup in Colorado or whatever state is clear."

"The storms are his early warning system," Robinson spoke up. "He set them up, so he'll know when we are getting close. He's officially watching us right now through these storms."

"Can he do anything else with the storms, Robinson?" Saul asked.

"I'm not besties with your nemesis, Mr. Copeland, but I think it's safe to assume that he can use anything at his disposal to destroy us if he wishes," she answered. "We're probably safe for right now. I got the distinct impression that he wanted to meet you."

"If he wants to meet me so bad, then what's with all the theatrics," he asked. "Why not come right to me?"

"I've never had him on the couch to analyze him, but I would imagine that he is just as afraid of you as you are of him," she explained.

"That's promising," I said. "If he's worried, then he knows that Saul can kick his ass. All we have to do is get there and finish this."

"I appreciate youthful enthusiasm as much as anyone else, truly, but his fear of Mr. Copeland could result in him just striking out against us all in a blind rage," Robinson said. "There's no way we will survive if he brings all his might down on us."

"None of that changes the mission," said Roxanne. "We're going to keep an eye on the storms just like they're apparently watching us, but we are not going to turn away."

We drove and drove for miles with tornadoes chasing us at a nice, respectful distance. We got updates from Garcia and her team, word that they were still being followed as well. Saul kept peering out the back window, staring into the storm. It was almost as though it had him hypnotized. I remember wondering what it was that he saw in the storm. It wasn't until he shuddered with revulsion that I ventured to ask him what was going on.

"There are eyes in there," he answered.

"What do you mean?" I asked, looking out the back window and seeing just a regular storm. "Eyes?"

"It's probably too far away for you to see it but there are a ton of eyes in the storm and they are all looking at us right now," he replied. "It's...disgusting. I don't know if I ever told you this, but one of my triggers is seeing people or things with more body parts than they are supposed to have or if they have body parts where they aren't supposed to be."

I thought about what he said for a few moments and it occurred to me that I had the same fear. Something about body parts where they shouldn't be just freaked me the hell out. Roxanne pulled out a pair of binoculars and crawled into the backseat to give the storm a closer look. After a few moments, she confirmed that Saul was right. She then handed me the binoculars and told me to take a look for myself. When I finally saw it for myself, I almost threw up in my mouth; it took considerable effort to swallow it back down.

"Is that something you used to think about, worry about?" I asked.

"It's one of my worst intrusive thoughts," Saul explained. "Every now and then, when I'm sitting quietly, monstrosities like that pop into my head. Sometimes when you see me sitting and I shiver, you think I'm just cold or I got a chill, but in truth I'm usually thinking about something like that. My shiver is really just me trying to shake those thoughts from my mind. I never realized that I would shake them out of my head and into reality."

"I'm so sorry, Saul," I said. "No one should ever have to live like this."

"When we're done with this mission, no one will have to live like this again," Saul said in determination. "You don't have to keep looking at it, Lita. I'll keep my eyes on it."

I gave the binoculars back to Roxanne and then sat back down in my seat, turning my back on that storm full of all those disgusting, blinking eyes. I remember thinking at the time that I couldn't wait to finally get this all over with. If I knew then what was still ahead of us, I would have wanted the trip to last a little longer.

About an hour later, Garcia called us over the radio. She sounded like there was trouble. It didn't take long for us to find out why. She informed us that the storm that was chasing them was picking up speed. According to her, it wouldn't be long before it overtook their vehicle and who knew what would happen after that.

"Hang in there," was Roxanne's response. "Your vehicle is heavily armored. You should be able to weather that storm for a while. Make sure you keep an eye on Robinson. We still don't know where her loyalties lie in all this."

"Roger," said Garcia. "Robinson is secured. We're going to try to outrace this thing."

The other vehicle sounded off after that while we waited to hear word about whether or not they could successfully outrun a magical tornado in a manmade vehicle. Before they could let us know what was going on, we got some bad news of our own. Saul confirmed that the tornado that was behind us was picking up speed as well. Ours was bearing down so fast, it looked like we were only going to have a few minutes before we were engulfed.

"I hope those new powers of yours can help against that thing, Saul," said Trevor, "because this vehicle is not as armored as the one Garcia and the others are in."

"Just try to outrun it," said Saul. "Let's see how far we can get before we have to deal with this thing."

Trevor gave that tornado a real run for its money, but you can't outrun a force of nature any more than you can outrun your own thoughts and fears. And this thing, well unfortunately, this thing was both. As it got closer and closer, the sky darkened and we could hear the roar of the winds. At least, we *thought* it was the high-velocity winds, but we couldn't have been more mistaken.

"Keep it on the road, Trev," Roxanne commented as the storm started to lift our vehicle off the ground. "If this big bastard flips over, then we're fucked."

"I'm trying," he growled, gripping the steering wheel tight as though it were fighting him. "We're not going to outrun it. How about you, Saul? Can you disperse it or something?"

"We're about to find out," Saul stated.

I watched him lift his hands as the portals where his eyes used to be began to swirl faster and faster. I don't know what he was doing exactly, but I could see that something started to happen to the storm. It looked like it was starting to fall apart, but it kept pulling itself back together. Saul's jaw tightened as he continued to use his powers on the storm. I could see his frustration whenever the storm came back together. Things got worse from there, just about to the point where I wished I had stayed in Haven instead of tagging along.

Somehow the disembodied eyeballs were propelled from the storm and began to attach themselves to the outside of the truck! It didn't take long for them to completely cover the windows and start blinking so loud that it was almost as deafening as the storm itself. It took everything I had not to throw up at the sight of it. Everything was just an explosion of sound: the rapid blinking of the disembodied eyes, the wind from the tornado that descended upon us, the roars that came from inside the tornado, and the screams of everyone in the car. I just closed my eyes and covered my ears and hoped that it would all be over soon.

And it was. The storm sheared the roof right off the truck and started to pull us all into it, despite the safety belts that were supposed to keep us secure. I opened my eyes then and looked up to see that the storm had an actual eye at the center of it. The portal that Saul had disappeared into and returned from was in the center of the storm and we were all floating towards it! I could see the tentacles extending from the void, whipping about in an attempt to catch us. I could barely see or breathe as I floated upwards, but I still clung to hope that Saul would save us somehow.

When I felt a tentacle wrap tightly around my waist, I felt my hope start to fade. I could kinda see the tentacles grab hold of the others too and I knew it wouldn't be long before we were all in the void together. I also knew that I wouldn't survive a second trip inside, even with Saul by my side like he was the first time. I was so focused on the hungry maw trying to devour us that I didn't even feel those disembodied eyes pelting my body; I guess I had bigger concerns.

I closed my eyes when I was mere inches away from the void, not wanting to see myself get devoured once again. The only thing that got me to open my eyes was when I heard Saul screaming so loud that it drowned out everything else. I searched the storm for him and eventually saw him with no less than three tentacles coiled around him. He was thrashing around so much, they could barely hold him, while black and purple hued lights erupted from his empty eye sockets. It was clear he didn't want to go back inside that portal any more than I did.

"Let me go!!!" I clearly heard him yell over the cacophony of noises. "Now!!!"

And all at once, a blinding light ripped from every pore of his body. The light disintegrated the tentacles, blew the storm apart, and made the void collapse in on itself. It looked like we had been saved, but that was not to be. The storm had lifted us into the air and without its winds, we were going to plummet right back down to the ground!

I was a bit of a tomboy growing up, so I was always getting into some kind of trouble, and I got the occasional cut and scrape. I've even broken a few bones, much to my mother's chagrin, who wanted a girly girl as a daughter. Falling out of a tree was one thing, but falling out of a tornado was quite another. I fell on the ground, landing on my left arm so hard, I just knew that it had shattered. While I was wincing from the pain, my eyes welling up from the tears that I was struggling to keep back, I could see that Roxanne had fallen on her back not too far from me and Saul dropped to his knees a few feet to my right. I didn't see where Trevor landed, but I hoped he was okay too.

"Shit!" I remember thinking as I tried to get to my feet, the shooting pain running through my arm almost knocking me on my ass. "That's .. that's definitely broken."

I only got a few moments before I heard a huge crash. I spun my head around and saw that the truck had been dropped by the storm too. It fell upside down mere feet away from me. I exhaled a sigh of relief as I realized it could have easily just fallen on top of me. I tried twice more to get up, but I failed, so I just sat there and tried to catch my breath.

"Are you all right?"

Roxanne was already on her feet and checking on me. I guess she was lucky enough not to be injured in the fall. It could have been because of her werewolf healing abilities, which we already knew worked even when she was firmly in her human form. I told her that I thought my arm was broken and she nodded solemnly after examining it for herself.

"You're gonna be okay," she said. "I'll find the first aid kit we had in the truck and come back. I've got to see if our guys are okay."

"Saul is over there," I pointed with my good arm, "but I didn't see Grimes."

She ran over to check on Saul while looking back and forth for her man. I could see her face sink as her eyes failed to spot him. I could see her try to tend to Saul, but he was seemingly inconsolable. She then went looking for Trevor. She started calling his name, but got no response. As she began to panic, I started to get worried too. What if Trevor had been pulled into the void before Saul had had a chance to save us? What if he was still in there and now there was no way to get him out?

Suddenly, she stopped calling out for him and began walking towards our damaged truck. Her walk got slower and slower until she dropped on her knees in despair. Trevor wasn't in the void, suffering like Saul and I had, or even like Dr. Robinson had. He was crushed beneath the truck when the storm dissipated and dropped it from the sky. I watched as Roxanne shifted into her werewolf form to get the strength necessary to lift the vehicle off her man.

"Oh no," I found myself commenting as I watched her standing over Trevor's broken body. "No, no, no."

I knew precisely how she was feeling. It wasn't too long ago that I was in her place, having lost the man that I loved as well. Mine came back to me...presumably. I didn't see how hers would. She threw her head back and howled to the heavens. I always thought those cries from wolves were calls to other wolves, like calling a meeting. But now, hearing it up close with my own ears, I could feel the sorrow in that lonely baying. I wanted to rush over to comfort her somehow, but the pain from my shattered arm kept me just about paralyzed.

"Saul," I whispered to myself, looking over to him to see if there was something he could do, but he was still over there on his knees.

I knew that look on his face. He was in shock. I needed to get to him. I needed to help him and Roxanne. They needed to process what was going on and I felt like I could help, but I was hurting too. I just...couldn't even get to my feet. So, we all sat where we were, alone, as we tried to pull ourselves back together. I don't know how long we were there, but eventually I felt a hand on my shoulder.

"We got to go," said Roxanne, looking down at me with a grim, defeated look on her face. "We...we can't stay here."

"But what about Trevor?" I asked, barely controlling the tears in my eyes.

"He's gone," she said, averting her eyes from mine.

"We need to bury him or...or something," I said.

"We don't have the time or the tools to do something like that," she said, her voice taking on a new gruffness.

"I don't care," I shook my head. "He's one of us. He's one of us and I am not going to leave him here for the animals."

"There's nothing we can do," she barked. "Now let me fix your arm so we can get out of here."

She thought she could raise her voice at me, and it would make me snap to attention, but I wasn't some soldier in her army. My eyes narrowed as the tears dried up and my face contorted into a frown. I slowly got to my feet without taking my eyes off her.

"You can fix my arm...*after* I bury my friend," I said fiercely before I began walking over to where Grimes was lying.

I found myself walking across hot desert sand for several feet until I reached Trevor. He was lying on his back with his eyes open and his mouth agape. Seeing him like that made me cry all over again. His body was pulverized from the heavy truck falling on him, but his face still looked the same. Except...he looked like his death had caught him by surprise, because there was a shocked look upon his face.

"Damn Trev," I shook my head at the sight of him. "I am so, so sorry. This should never have happened to you."

The saddest part of all this was that Grimes had been gun-shy about going on missions ever since our failed attempt to rescue the president of the United States. He had been severely injured during that mission and I could tell he didn't want to be out there anymore. He had faced his mortality in a way he never had before, and it shook him. And then, against his better judgement, he went on the mission that ultimately returned Saul to us and that almost killed him too. I guess this was his third strike.

I started digging in that hot sand with my one good arm, trying to ignore the pain from my other arm. I dug and dug and dug as best I could. I didn't care if it took me a million years, but I was going to make sure that Trevor Grimes got the decent burial that his heroism demanded. Luckily, I wasn't digging alone for very long. Before long, there were huge werewolf claws helping to dig the grave right next to my little hand. Roxanne and I dug a grave six feet deep and then I watched her deposit her boyfriend into it.

"Thank you," said Roxanne after she reverted back to her human form. "He...he deserved a proper burial."

We sat in the silence, saying private prayers over our dead friend. It wouldn't be long before we had to address the elephants in the room, but not right now. For the moment, we were just honoring our dead. We sat there for an hour without talking before Roxanne shattered the quiet.

"Do you think he's going to be okay?"

She meant Saul. Of course, she meant Saul. Trevor was beyond the worries of mortal men now. I knew what she meant, but I didn't have an answer for her. Hell, there was still a voice in my head, tinier now, telling me this man wasn't the real Saul Copeland. I asked her to patch up my arm and she created the tightest splint you've ever seen and then I steeled myself to go talk to Saul, who was still on his knees in the sand and hadn't moved a muscle at all.

I walked over to him and then took a seat right next to him. He just kept staring straight ahead like he didn't even notice me approaching him. He was definitely in shock. After all the nightmares we had faced together, I had never seen him go completely catatonic. It wasn't until I touched his shoulder and said his name that he reacted at all. It was like his consciousness had been pulled back to his physical body and he looked at me and silver tears started to stream down his face.

"Are you okay?" I asked.

"I don't know if I can beat him," he revealed as the tears continued to pour from his empty eye sockets. "I left Haven with every intention to put a stop to all of this, I swear I did, but...this was just his first volley, and I was just about useless to us!"

"You weren't useless, Saul," I shook my head. "You saved us! You destroyed that storm and that void that was going to eat us! You got us out of there."

"That wasn't skill, Lita," he argued. "That was a scared outburst! And it didn't do much for Trevor or you. You got a broken arm and he's... dead. It could have been you, Lita. You could be the one dead right now."

"We could all be dead right now, Saul," I snapped. "All of us. I left Haven knowing that plenty of people had been killed already and that more were probably going to have to before we put an end to this. I'm sorry if you left under some delusion that this was going to be some happy little journey to slay a dragon and then save the world without sacrifices along the way, but this is what it was always going to be."

"I need you and Reynolds to go back home," he said after giving it some thought. "I can handle this on my own."

"Are you crazy?" I asked, a little harsher than I had intended to. "I'm not going back to Haven until this is done. We have a job to do."

"No!" he protested. "*I* have a job to do! This is my mess, Lita, always has been. I'm not going to let anyone else get hurt to end it. I'm not going to let anyone else sacrifice themselves for this. You and Roxanne are going back to Haven and you're going to stay there until this is all done."

He was serious. He thought I was going to abandon our quest and simply go back home. I guess he expected me to walk back since our vehicle had gotten totaled. I had asked him if he was crazy, but now I had my answer. He must have been insane if he thought he was going to order me to do something and I was just going to accept that. He was also insane if he thought I was going to walk my injured ass all the way back to DC.

"I'm not doing that, Saul," I shook my head. "We're going to end this together. You and me facing down this thing together. It was us in the beginning of this and it will be us at the end too."

"I was cocky, Lita, way too overconfident," he shook his head. "I didn't consider the possibility that we would lose. Or that I would lose you. I was so swept up in my emotions, my anger in particular, that I rushed straight at this monster. Straight at a being that I know absolutely nothing about. I think I really fucked things up."

"I'm glad you're not going to be cocky from now on, Saul, but I don't need you depressed either," I said seriously. "You and those powers of yours are not only our *best* shot at getting this world back to normal and saving all humanity, but you're also the *only* shot we have. So, I need you to get up on your feet and get back to work."

I didn't want to be hard on him, not after everything he'd been through in his life, but he really was the only hope we had and after everything that had happened with the tornado, it was clear he was going to need to be focused on our success more than ever. It seemed that my pep talk had done the trick. He got to his feet, dusted off the sand that was covering him and then slowly walked over to where we had buried Trevor.

"I'm sorry, Agent Grimes," he said, kneeling at the grave while Roxanne looked on. "I'm sorry that this happened to you. I'm sorry about everything. I'm going to make sure to put things right though. I'm not going to let your death be in vain. One way or another, everything is going to be okay."

After paying his respects, he offered his apologies to Roxanne, but she simply shook her head. She had lost her man, but she wasn't about to blame Saul for that.

"I have not blamed you for anything that has happened, Copeland, and I am not going to start now," she said. "The only person to blame is that asshole out in Nevada. And we are all going to take our anger and grief out on him when we finally confront him. Now I am going to see if any of our weapons and supplies survived the attack and then we can get moving. We don't want to be out here when it gets dark."

We gathered up what we could, but it didn't amount to much. Roxanne had a shotgun with several shells to go with it, two pistols (one for her and one for me), a few flashlights, a big backpack of provisions, and a baton that Saul seemed to gravitate to despite his particular gifts. We even found a walkie-talkie, so Roxanne immediately tried to call Garcia and the others.

"Garcia, come in," she said after switching to the proper frequency. "Are you out there? Report!"

We heard nothing but static on the line for the longest time. She kept trying to reach out to them until they responded after a harrowing three minutes or so. It didn't take long for us to hear a growl coming through the walkie.

"We're here, ma'am," said Barry, "but just barely. The storm descended on us and started ripping at our vehicle. It was clear we weren't going to be able to take much more of that, so we looked for shelter. Garcia drove us into a huge estate here in Texas, literally. We've got shelter but the truck is totaled and we have these giant tentacles trying to find their way into the house to snag us. We've already lost Crispin to those things. How are things going with you?"

"We're not doing any better than you," Roxanne explained. "Our vehicle has been destroyed along with most of our supplies. And...and we lost Agent Grimes."

"I'm truly sorry, ma'am," he stated. "We'll see if we can kill off these tentacles and then try to meet you in Nevada still."

"Okay," she nodded. "But don't engage with our target until we are all together. Copeland is the only one who stands a chance against it. If he is not there, you do not engage. Is that understood?"

"Yes, ma'am," he replied.

"And make sure to keep an eye on Dr. Robinson," she said. "I want you to consider her to be just as dangerous as those tentacles. Just as dangerous as anything else you're likely to see out there. Do not let your guard down around her just because she's blind."

"Copy," he said. "I will give you updates to our progress as time goes on."

Roxanne signed off and then looked at me and Saul. I got the impression that she looked at us as children and that she was babysitting. We weren't cops or soldiers. We weren't trained in anything useful. We were just regular workers who stumbled into some cosmic weirdness. We were tag-alongs, like in all those cop movies where they needed to bring the uninitiated. *Ride Along* with Kevin Hart. *Cop and a Half* with Burt Reynolds. *Bulletproof* with Damon Wayans and Adam Sandler. Ugh, I hated the idea of being the Adam Sandler half of any pairing, but here we were. The point is that we were not fighters. We were barely more than liabilities and I hated that feeling.

"Let's go," she said. "We need to find a car and get to Nevada before anything else happens."

I just remember in that moment wondering how she was able to be so strong, to carry on right after she had lost the man she cared about so much. When I lost Saul in New York, I was a wreck. The team poured me in the back of a vehicle and drove off to safety. If they hadn't been looking out for me, I probably would have died right there too. I was not some symbol of strength and perseverance in those moments; I was an emotionally fragile young woman. But Detective Roxanne Reynolds, now in my shoes, was picking herself up and leading a mission straight into hell, essentially, to save the whole world. I remember thinking she had to be the toughest bad-ass on the planet. The next leg of our trek was going to show me what being a bad-ass really was because I had not seen anything yet.

We walked into the next town and easily found a vehicle for Roxanne to hotwire. It was a luxury mini-van with crumbs and toys in the back. We tried not to think about what had become of the people who once owned this van as we silently drove off towards our destination. It was a long somber drive and we saw some horrific stuff along the way. We saw the Rocky Mountains aflame, like they were made of fire instead of rock and snow. We went through a neighborhood where snakes and frogs were raining from the sky. Then there was the school with all the white-eyed children who were playing a game where they would pounce on whatever came close, human or animal, and then they would stab it death.

At first, I would be asking Saul questions about where each fear originated, but it didn't take long for the abominations to get so bad that I stopped asking. I found myself getting sick to my stomach with each new monster we drove past. Roxanne had a question eventually though.

"Why aren't they attacking us?" she asked. "We're basically surrounded by these monsters and they just sit and watch as we go by them. Why aren't they trying to destroy us like the tornado did?"

"He wants to finish us himself," Saul answered flatly, as nonchalant as if he was ordering a corn muffin for breakfast or something. "He tested us with the tornado and I came up lacking apparently. He's not afraid of me anymore. He wants us to walk right up to his front door so he can strike me down with his own power."

"You sound like you've given up, Copeland," she said. "Are you saying we should just pack it in? Because I signed on for this mission because I thought there was a chance of success. If all I'm doing is driving you to the spot where this thing is planning to kill you, we can head right back to Haven right now. So what's up? What are we doing?"

I looked at Saul and waited for his response. He seemed like he had lost something, the confidence that he would be able to set things right. The tornado incident and losing Grimes had done more than just shaken his faith. It was starting to look it had completely broken him. I thought seeing him wracked with self-doubt, anxiety, and guilt was the worst states I would see him, but seeing him like this was infinitely worse. He was completely broken. It was like when Dr. Robinson tried to kill him in her cell and he didn't even try to defend himself.

"Well...I guess I should keep going," he shrugged. "If there's even the slightest chance that I can win, then I have to try. I owe it to the world."

That was when Roxanne slammed on the brakes and stopped the van right in the middle of the street. She then turned around to glare in the backseat at Saul. I could tell from the look on her face how angry she was. Her reaction was enough to frighten me and I think he had the same reaction.

"We can't afford for you to half-ass this effort, Saul," she said, using his first name. "Not even a little. This is not just simple life-and-death. We're talking about a world-ending event. And from what I can gather, you're the only person with any hope of keeping all life on Earth from ending. We need you to be fully committed to this. And if you're not, then we can go home and just enjoy what little time we have left."

"Look, I'm not sure of anything right now," he said. "I'm not sure if I'm going to be able to beat this thing."

"I don't need you to be sure of that," she said. "No one ever knows what the outcome is going to be. That's not important. What is important is whether or not you know you're going to put your all into the fight and leave it all out on the field. Are you going to do that or are we just wasting our time here?"

Saul seemed to mull over what she had just said to him. He lowered his eyes as he thought, but I knew that was because he was always nervous about making eye contact with people. He thought people got freaked out when he looked them in the eyes. Even more so now...that he had no eyes. I know he was searching his heart for the right answer and I was hoping he would find it. No one else could give it to him.

"Let's go end this," he said fiercely.

She studied his face for a few moments before she turned around and started driving again. While she drove, I continued to study his face. She might have believed him, but I still had my doubts, and I could tell that he did too. I took his hand and he looked over at me with those swirling black pools that had replaced his eyes. We had a whole conversation without saying a single word. I didn't mind giving him all the encouragement in the world because he was the only one who could save our world.

"You're going to be fine, Saul," I told him. "I know it. I just need you to know it too."

We drove through the states, not really knowing where we were, but Roxanne was convinced that she knew where she was going. Every now and then we got updates from Garcia's team. It didn't take long for them to dispatch the tentacles, find another vehicle and get back on the road as well. All of us on a collision course with destiny...until we suddenly weren't.

"What the hell is that?"

I was sleeping on Saul's shoulder when Roxanne asked the question. I barely heard it. But when Saul leaned forward, as though to get a better look at something, leaving me to fall down on the seat, I was wide awake and trying to figure out why. When I looked in the same direction as everyone else, it became clear what was wrong.

"What *is* that?" I found myself wondering aloud.

It looked like we had reached some sort of barricade that stretched from side-to-side for as far as the eye could see. It kinda looked like the wall that puta Trump wanted to build only this one was a neon pink color for some reason and seemed to be pulsating with some sort of energy. Saul immediately stepped out of the van and began to approach the pink wall. I loved his confidence, but I didn't share it in that moment. I rolled down my window, peeked my head out and called out to him.

"What are you doing?" I asked. "What is that thing and why are you getting so close to it?"

"There's something about it," he replied without looking back at me. "I can't explain it."

"Yeah, you see, that sounds like the kinda thing you should definitely stay away from then," I declared. "Maybe you should get back in the van and we'll just try to find a way around it."

"I don't think there is a way around it," he answered. "I think we're right where we need to be."

"What is he talking about?" Roxanne asked suspiciously. "Why does he seem like he's mesmerized by that thing?"

"I don't know, but I'll go get him," I said, not wanting to trouble her any more than we already had.

I got out and walked over to him. He barely recognized I was even there. When he extended his hand like he was going to touch the barricade, that's when I felt like I needed to intervene. I placed a hand on his shoulder and then pulled him back a step so that his fingers wouldn't graze the wall. That's when he looked back at me.

"What are you doing?" I asked. "You don't even want to touch the railings in the subway, so why would you be trying to touch this thing? It's clearly a trap."

"You don't hear it calling to you, telling you that everything is going to be okay?" he asked, smiling broadly as though he were in some sort of euphoric state. "It's beautiful."

It sounded like he had been hypnotized and I honestly didn't like it. Our enemy had already tried to kill us using brute force with a runaway tornado. What if this was his second attempt: mesmerize Saul so that he wouldn't pose a threat any longer?

"Sounds like the call of the siren to me, Saul," I said. "We can't have you driven mad when we're so close to where we need to be. Let's just get back in the car and see if there is a way around this wall."

He listened to what I had to say and then turned away to continue looking at the wall. He told me that he was all right and that he was going to stay here for a little while longer. I simply looked back at the van and shrugged at Roxanne. I could see her roll her eyes impatiently before getting out of the vehicle and walking over to us.

"What's going on?" she asked, resting her hands on her skinny hips.

"Saul thinks we should wait here for a while instead of trying to go around this block," I informed her. "I think he's being hypnotized by some sort of siren or something."

"Do you have some clue what this thing is, Copeland?" she asked.

"I'm not sure, but I have this feeling that we're supposed to be right here, right now," he answered. "You know what I mean?"

"I gotta tell you, Copeland, that I am not getting that impression from this thing at all," she shook her head. "It's not the warm and fuzzies; it's the dark and foreboding. I think we should listen to your girlfriend and get out of here before things get out of hand very quickly."

"I want to stay," he said, his voice getting deeper and angrier.

"Well, you can't," she said forcefully, her eyes narrowing. "I'm in command of this operation, Copeland. And you're going to follow my orders or..."

"Or what?" he snapped, his empty sockets filling with what looked like a crimson red storm. "What are you going to do if I go off the reservation right now? Are you going to bench me or whatever cop/sport euphemism you can scrounge up? Or are you going to act like my mommy and turn this mission around and take us all back home?"

"Why are you acting like this, Saul?" I asked, just as taken aback as Roxanne by his sudden shift in personality.

"I think the two of you should head back to Haven and leave me here," was his response. "I'll take care of everything from here."

It was clear that there was something wrong with him and it had something to do with this barricade that was blocking us from proceeding. Roxanne and I exchanged a knowing look, but knowing what we were up against still didn't put us in a position where we knew what to do about it. Thinking about our next steps was probably what made us not notice what else was going on in the moment. With everything that had been going on since the start of all this madness, you could forgive a person for not noticing the slight tremors beneath their feet.

"That's not going to happen, Copeland," she said, crossing her arms over her chest. "You're either going to get back in that van so we can continue this mission or I'm going to force you back into that van. So, which is it?"

"Oh, is that so?" he asked haughtily as he turned to face Roxanne with a strange smile on his face. "You're going to force me to do something I don't wanna do? That might have worked on the old Saul Copeland, God knows it has before, but that's not going to fly with this new and improved model."

Things were getting tense between them and I wasn't loving the fact he was referring to himself in the third person, like he was disassociating from himself. I knew it would be best if I poured some cold water over the whole situation. As I worked to defuse things, we still didn't notice the ground starting to shake. We should have though. It would have made things a lot easier for us all in the long run. I stood between them as they quarreled and tried desperately to ignore the raging storm where Saul's eyes were supposed to be. They argued back and forth, making threats both veiled and obvious, until the ground shook so violently, it damn near knocked us all down.

"What the fuck was that?" I blurted out.

The quakes were so bad now that they were enough to shake Saul from the daze he had just been in. We all looked around for the source of the disturbance, but we couldn't see anything. There were no storms, no stampedes of rampaging monsters. Saul issued forth a stream of expletives and I knew that he had probably figured out what we were up against in the moment…and it scared him. If it scared him, it was probably enough to make the rest of us shit our pants.

"Tell me something, Copeland," Roxanne commanded as she pulled out her pistol and got ready to shoot whatever was approaching.

He only said one word in response, but it was enough to bring instant recognition for her and myself. It only took one word and then we were all on the same page…and all afraid for our lives.

"Detroit."

"Jeez," I said.

"Not that big dick that destroyed Michigan," Roxanne commented. "It's here? Now?"

"We're not going to be able to fight that thing with guns," I said. "Saul, do you think you'll be able to fight it or turn it away?"

"Not a chance," he shook his head as he looked off into the distance. "I got my ass kicked by that tornado."

"So, this is it," Roxanne sighed. "I guess this is what I get for wishing to be fucked to death by a big dick that one time in college."

"Eww, gross, but same I guess," I said, trying not to look at Saul. "I guess this is it."

It looked like we had come to the end of our mission, the end of everything, as the kaiju penis that had destroyed Detroit burst from the ground no more than a couple miles away from us and then stretched upwards into the sky. When it slammed itself down on us, we would be completely destroyed, but at least it would be a relatively quick death. I imagine it would be like when we step on a bug; they're dead before they even really know it.

Just when the kaiju penis was about to descend and crush us to pulp, Saul grabbed Roxanne and I by the shoulders and shoved us into the pink barricade we had stopped at. Once inside, I immediately wished he had just let the giant, city-wrecking penis destroy us instead; at least our deaths would have been quicker.

The barricade wasn't as sturdy as it appeared from the outside. It felt like a soft, spongey membrane, almost like we were passing through Jell-O or something. I could see Roxanne and Saul through the pink haze as we slowly walked through the area. It was slow going, like walking through one of those voids with the tentacles inside, only it didn't feel torturous like one of those experiences. In fact, it felt like the exact opposite of that, like the feeling you get when you see your warm bed after a rough day at work. No wonder Saul had been mesmerized by it when he first saw it. Since it came from his head, it probably spoke to him in a way that it didn't for Roxanne and me.

"Keep going," I heard his voice say as though from the end of a long tunnel. "Faster."

"Why?" I asked with a smile, almost as though I were feeling a state of euphoria. "This place is great!"

"We're being followed!" he yelled in response.

"Followed by what?" I asked, looking back at him.

And then I saw it. The giant penis had followed us in as well. I guess it was too much to hope that the thing would be too big to follow us inside. We started running, but it was like moving through molasses. Our only saving grace was that the kaiju dong seemed to be having as much trouble navigating its way through this realm as us. It should have been as simple as staying ahead of that thing, but we were wrong. Somehow it was forcing its way closer and closer to us at a much faster rate than we were able to flee.

As I was running for my life, something struck me. We were in a vagina. That's why it was pink and spongy, and that was also probably why it attracted this monstrous penis all the way from Michigan. Who wouldn't travel all the way from Detroit for pussy that felt this good? If I survived this, I had every intention of asking Saul what this was all about? He explained where the kaiju penis came from, but was there a reason why this vagina was just sitting out in the middle of the Bible Belt?

We kept pushing forward and forward and forward until we finally got through the spongy membrane...and fell a few feet into what looked like a swamp. It might have looked like marshlands, but I knew a metaphor when I fell into it. I got to my feet and immediately shook off the...liquid I was covered in and watched as Saul and Roxanne got to their feet too.

"Are we safe?" she asked.

Saul looked up into the sky to see where we had fallen from, but it was all pitch black. He assured us that we were safe and then asked us if we were okay. I told him I was fine, but Roxanne just crossed her arms over her chest and looked at him angrily.

"So tell me something, Copeland," she sighed. "Whose pussy did we fall into here?"

I was struck speechless because I thought I was the only one who had figured out where we were. I kept my mouth closed though, not wanting to say anything. Saul's jaw sorta dropped at the question and it quickly occurred to me that he didn't realize where we were.

"What are you talking about?" he asked.

"We're in a vagina, Copeland," she answered. "And we were chased in here by a giant penis. I'm not sure what kind of trauma you're working through, but I know a sexual assault metaphor when I see it. So, whose vagina is this, Copeland."

"How am I supposed to know?" he asked defensively. "I didn't realize we were in a...vagina."

"It doesn't matter," I interjected. "We seem to be safe right now. What we should be doing is trying to figure out how to continue our mission."

"Good point," Saul nodded. "Try the radio, Reynolds. See if the others are okay."

"Yeah," she grumbled pulling out her walkie-talkie. "Maybe they can stage a rescue. Can't wait to hear their response when they find out we fell into a giant coochie."

Saul simply exhaled hard and then walked away a few steps. I followed him, not wanting us to get separated in a place like this. I knew that he was still our best chance of surviving all this madness. I have to admit it was kinda cute seeing him all flustered like this. Imagine being all nervous and tongue-tied over a vagina.

"Are you okay?" I asked and he slowly turned to face me.

"I'm quite confused actually," he replied. "Everything else that sprang from my brain has been an absolute horror. Not this though."

"Not sure why your brain might have conjured a warm, wet pussy?" I giggled. "I can think of a few reasons."

I found the whole thing to be kinda funny, a little bit of the ridiculous nestled in amongst all the horror we had been experiencing since all of this had begun. Saul obviously didn't see the humor in all of this though. He was somehow more disturbed by this than most of the other things we had already seen, even those disembodied eyes that were living inside the tornado. Now he had me wondering if I should have been more worried about this place than I currently was.

"What's wrong?" I asked. "What is all this? Can you tell us why we would be in a giant vagina? Were you...abused by more than just one person? A woman? Maybe a friend of your mom's or...?"

I couldn't help but think about all the terrible things he had been through, but I made sure not to let an ounce of pity show on my face. That's the last thing he would have wanted in this moment. He looked at me for a few moments as he thought about what his next words to me were going to be.

"No, it's nothing like that," he assured me with a shake of his head. "I just don't know if this...place...was conjured by our enemy. It doesn't *feel* malevolent, does it? It feels..."

"Cozy?" I asked, trying not to smile.

"Yeah," he nodded. "Cozy, inviting, welcoming. Why would our enemy create something like this for us."

"I mean, couldn't it just be like a Venus flytrap or something?" I shrugged. "Lure us into a false sense of security all with the intention of trapping us inside?"

"I suppose," he nodded. "If this was all a trap though, why did the kaiju penis continue to follow us, try to kill us, even though we were already trapped inside? What would have been the point of doing that?"

"I don't know," I shrugged again. "What do you think is going on?"

"I don't think he created this," he revealed. "I think...I might have created it. Like a safe space for us because we were under attack. I think that's why I was so drawn to it; it felt like my happy place, the place I discovered in my head when I was training to use my new powers."

"Your happy place...is a vagina?" I asked, still fighting back the urge to laugh. "Well, I suppose that's true for most guys, right?"

"I don't think this place is just *a* vagina at all," he continued. "I think it might be...*your* vagina."

"Is that why the place looks so familiar?" I laughed.

"Come on, Lita, this is serious!" he exclaimed in frustrated exasperation.

"All right, all right," I rolled my eyes. "So, you're saying this place is all me. These are *my* lady parts. What makes you think that?"

"Because the feeling I get while I'm here, the same feeling I got when I was in my Happy Place and training, is identical to the feeling I get whenever we make love," he explained.

"Aww, that's sweet, Saul," I blushed.

"It's more than sweet," he said. "If I was able to manifest something like this in the real world, then I'm more powerful than even I realized."

"That's great," I said.

"No," he shook his head solemnly. "Because that means that *he* knows it now too."

Before I could wrap my head around how bad it was that the monster that we were hunting now had definitive proof of how powerful Saul had become, Roxanne rushed over to us. She had a smile on her face, so obviously she wasn't as upset with Saul as she had been previously. She had good news.

"I just got off the radio with Garcia and her team," she informed us. "They managed to escape from the void with the tentacles and get back on the road. They drove through Texas until they reached the same pink wall, so clearly old girl has a pussy bigger than the Grand Canyon."

"Hey!" I protested instinctively. "Not cool, Reynolds!"

"What?" she asked. "Was I too raunchy? When did you turn into a little princess?"

"Have they felt any rumbling?" Saul asked. "Like the ground shaking or anything?"

"No," she shook her head. "They are awaiting orders on what to do next."

"I think they should go inside and then try to meet up with us," he suggested. "It's time for us all to stick together for the last leg on this journey."

"You think this is the last leg?" I asked, sounding hopeful.

He nodded. Roxanne gave the other team the order to go inside and then try to find us so we could all regroup. I just kept looking at Saul while she spoke. He looked worried.

"Everything is going to be okay," I told him. "This is good news. You were able to manifest a safe space in the middle of the country. Who knows what else you'll be able to manifest when the time is right?"

We were lucky. It only took us about twenty minutes to reunite with Garcia's team as they fell from the sky just like we had and practically landed on top of us. It should have been impossible since we had been many miles away from each other, but I wasn't about to question it. It felt like a terrific sign. We were all together again and heading towards the enemy that had ruined our world. I think even Saul was feeling hopeful in those moments. Regrettably, the feeling didn't last too long. We had barely been able to greet each other properly before the sky opened up above our heads and we saw the head of the kaiju penis that has been pursuing us.

"You thought you could hide from me in here?" a voice bellowed from the tip of the penis. We all recognized the voice from the television announcement back in Haven. "There is no place in the universe where you can escape from me!"

Our enemy had found us. Saul was right when he said that this was going to be the last leg of our journey. When the penis opened up above us, maniacal laughter erupted from inside. And then it ejaculated dark purple "semen" all over us. That's when Saul's Happy Place turned into something else entirely.

SEVEN
THE NIGHTMARE BOX

We were safe or at least we thought we were. We were in Saul's Happy Place, a giant vagina, *my* vagina, in the middle of the country. It manifested right from his mind in an attempt to keep us safe from harm. It was actually pretty amazing that he had become so powerful. But before we could really enjoy this small victory, our enemy decided to show us that our accomplishments were nothing compared to the sheer power that he wielded.

The "semen" that erupted from the kaiju penis, if we can even refer to it as "semen", covered us and flooded the place. It was like being doused with pure evil and it did what evil always seems to do when you let it take root. It changed everything for the worse. It changed Saul's Happy Place into something else entirely.

"It's a Nightmare Box," Saul commented as he looked around him.

It wasn't bad as far as names go, but I would later come to think of it as something else entirely. Hell. Saul told us that we couldn't stay there anymore. We needed to pass through this realm and come out the other side. He told us that the longer we remained there, the more danger we would be in. He told us that we needed to hurry. No one disagreed with him, not even Dr. Robinson, who seemed unusually quiet about everything that was going on.

Saul took the lead, and we followed him. He seemed to know which way was out and he seemed desperate to get there. I was right behind him, as was Roxanne and Garcia. Barry was in the back making sure we were all okay while simultaneously keeping a close eye on Dr. Robinson. We stuck close to each other because the feel of the realm changed considerably. The kaiju penis had impregnated it with danger and death around every corner. We could feel that we were longer safe.

"Are you sure this is the right way, Copeland?" Roxanne asked eventually.

"Yes," he nodded. "The only way out is through and we need to make sure we do it quickly...before anything shows up."

"So, you think those creatures from the outside world have invaded this place too?" Garcia asked.

"I know it," he replied. "That's what all that gunk was that covered us. It was that monster filling this place with all my worst nightmares."

"Hence you calling it a nightmare box," Garcia nodded. "So we can expect to see the same things we've been seeing all over the country?"

"You can expect to see a lot worse," he stated. "The thing that has been bothering me about this phenomenon right from the start is that we have yet to see my worst fears. The worst of the worst haven't revealed themselves and I don't know why. My guess is that they're probably going to show up here somewhere."

We were walking through a dark, eerie swamp with bog water sloshing around up to our waists. I tried not to think about what kinds of things were swimming around my legs at any given moment. There were dark trees all around us, so thick and heavy that you could barely see anything at all. I tried to look forward and not at the forests that were surrounding us. Something told me that there were things in those trees that I definitely didn't want to see.

It felt like we were walking for several hours before we found an embankment that allowed us to crawl out of the muck and get on solid ground. I was glad for it. I was worried that something in that marsh was going to drag us under and drown us. It was nice to be free of it, but Saul's facial expression did change in the slightest. He was still worried. He only got more uneasy when we saw a town in the distance.

"Looks like we made it through to the other side," said Garcia with a smile. "That wasn't so bad."

"I don't think we're out," he said.

"What makes you say that?" she asked. "We walked for miles through that swamp and then got out. Not only is the marsh gone, but so is that evil forest. There's even a town up there."

"Yeah, but the sky hasn't returned," he stated. "Clearly, we're still enclosed in something."

"Maybe we're not out yet, but we could be at the outer edge," said Roxanne. "Maybe the wall we pushed through to get in here is right there and when we push through it again, we'll be in that town."

"Hopefully, you're right," I said. "I also hope that whatever town that is, it's located in Nevada so we can finally get all this over with."

"I know we're all eager to get our lives back, but let's not rush this," Barry finally spoke up after not speaking a word for our entire walk. "We're only going to get one chance at this. If Copeland says that we should tread carefully, then we should definitely do that."

We all agreed with his assessment and then began walking towards the town that we spotted in the distance. We reached the town without passing through a pink membrane, so Saul was proven right about us still being on the inside of the Nightmare Box. I'd really hoped he would be wrong about that, but I guess I was asking for too much to get lucky in this one instance.

"This looks like a good chance to try to restock," Garcia suggested. "We should try to raid that shop over there."

"You're not going to find anything usable in here," Saul shook his head. "This place is nothing more than a trap we need to escape from. We should keep going and try to stay as inconspicuous as possible."

"Look, I understand where you're coming from, but if we don't at least get some water, we're not going to make it much further," Garcia said softly. "And even with your abilities, you can't be expected to win while dehydrated."

He fell silent as he thought about her words for a few moments. He couldn't deny that she made sense. We were all running on empty. None of us had eaten, drank, or slept in a very long time. Even he had to agree that you didn't want to fight the final boss with a low health bar. He simply shrugged and then plans were made to raid the surrounding buildings and homes for anything useful, specifically water.

Barry was instructed to keep watch over the three civilians while Roxanne and Garcia went from building to building doing their search. Everything was going okay at first, much better than any of expected it to be going. Saul was still unnerved by this place, but things were okay. There were no monsters or unexplained deaths at the moment. Everything was just quiet and eerily still. It was Robinson that finally broke the silence.

"They should have listened to you, Copeland," she said out of the blue. "We should have never stopped here."

I spun on her, determined to get her to explain herself or to shut her up for good, but I never got the chance. Before I had a chance to say a word or throw a punch, Roxanne and Garcia were running at full speed out of a nearby grocery store, yelling at the top of their lungs to run. Saul raised his hands, ready to use his powers on whatever monstrosity they had run into, but when he finally saw it, he realized that flight was so much better than fight.

"Ah shit," I heard him grumble.

It was a black spider the size of a mini-van and it exploded out of the front of the building on long, hairy, spindly legs. It stumbled a bit, which was the only reason why Roxanne and Garcia got as far as they did. Barry took a step forward, pulling out his assault rifle and taking aim at the creature. He was a man of few words, but he was big on action. He fired off a burst and it ripped into the side of the spider, making it stumble again as Reynolds and Garcia quickly approached us.

"We have to run," Roxy said when she finally reached us. "Now!"

"There's a toy store to your right," Barry stated. "Get inside. I'll handle this thing."

"No, Barry, we gotta go," said Garcia, tears streaming down her face in abject terror. "You can't fight this thing."

"I said I'll handle this," he said, tightening his jaw without glancing over at her. "Now get the others into that toy store and don't look back."

We left him behind and raced to the toy store, but Saul lagged behind us, keeping an eye on the giant spider. The toy store was locked, but a simple gunshot removed the barrier and opened the way for us. Roxanne ushered me and Dr. Robinson in first before yelling for Saul to hurry inside. He joined us on the inside and joined me as I looked out the window to see what was going on outside.

"He needs to come inside," I said. "We'll be safe in here, right?"

"Not even a little," Saul shook his head. "We won't be safe until we get the hell out of here. We won't be safe until we put the leader of these monsters down for good, Lita."

"Your boyfriend is right," Robinson said, amusement in her voice. "We need to run and keep running."

Barry was out on the street, firing his weapon, and it seemed to be doing damage to the thing. Roxanne and Garcia were in the entrance to the toy store, calling for him to join them. He refused, confident in his belief that anything, even monsters, could be killed. He took out the legs of the beast, stopping its advance. He removed the clip from his rifle and put in a fresh one before proceeding cautiously towards his kill.

"He did it," Garcia laughed excitedly. "That crazy bastard did it!"

"Do *you* think he did it, Mr. Copeland?" Robinson whispered to us a taunting voice. "Do *you* think the big guy just saved us all?"

I could hear her mocking Saul and I knew something was wrong. I instinctively yelled out to Roxanne to tell Barry to get away from the monster, to come join us where it was relatively safe. She looked back at me and saw the terror on my face and must have known how serious this was. She called Barry, warned him to keep his distance, but it was too late.

The spider wasn't dead, far from it, and it started to shake violently.

Barry took two steps back, but that wouldn't be far enough to save him from what came next. The creature's abdomen split open with a loud squishing sound that could probably be heard for miles around. As soon as the abdomen opened, dozens of smaller spiders scurried out and immediately swarmed Barry!

"We gotta go," said Saul. "Now."

"We've gotta help him," said Garcia.

"Nothing can help him," he said. "We gotta go or we're all gonna end up just like him. Follow me."

Just like that, Saul didn't say another word, opting to quickly venture deeper into the dark toy store. Somehow Robinson followed right behind him even though she didn't have any eyes to know where she was going. I gave one last warning to Roxanne and Garcia before I followed after Saul. I could hear Reynolds trying to convince Garcia, I heard her saying that the spiders were heading this way, but I didn't stay. I was right on Saul's heels when we heard a blood-curdling scream coming from the front of the store.

"Looks like Garcia won't be joining us for the rest of this quest," Robinson commented after the screaming had stopped, almost amused. "That's too bad. I liked her."

"You think this is funny?" Roxanne roared, grabbing the doctor by the throat in a rage. "We just lost two good people!"

"It's only going to get worse from here," the doctor chuckled. "We're at the core of his worst nightmares now. The odds of any of us making it out of here alive are slim to none."

I could tell from Roxanne's eyes that she had every intention of strangling the life from Robinson right in front of us. I wouldn't have even tried to stop her. I was still nursing all types of negativity towards the not-so-good doctor. Saul, on the other hand, was a little more practical at the moment.

"Let her live," he said. "There's still some use for her."

"What use?" I asked. "She's obviously been keeping intel from us and only doling out useful tidbits after someone has been killed! From where I'm standing, her usefulness ran out the moment she pulled a gun on us."

"I agree with her, Copeland," Reynolds growled as though she were about to transition to her werewolf form. "You're gonna need to give me a reason to keep her alive."

"She's going to walk us right out of this place and into our enemy's throne room," he replied. "Isn't that right, Doctor?"

"You want me to take the lead?" she smirked despite Roxanne's hands squeezing her throat. "The blind leading the blind?"

"You may be blind in the traditional sense, but I suspect your time in the void allows you to see some things very clearly," he frowned. "Now I'm not asking. You're going to lead us safely through here, not one more lost life. One more betrayal on your part and you'll get an intimate look at the insides of a werewolf's digestive tract."

"Hmm, you really know how to sweet-talk a woman, huh?" she laughed. "Fine. Let's go. It's a short trip, but there are going to be a lot more dangers along the way."

Reynolds reluctantly released her throat and then we all started following her through the dark, creepy toy store. The place was huge, but I figured it was because all of reality had been altered around us. This wasn't the real world after all, just another realm made to look like the world we came from. The place made me feel so uneasy that I found myself running my mouth just to comfort myself.

"So you're afraid of spiders or...?" I asked.

"Well, on some basic level we're all afraid of spiders and other bugs," he responded. "My fear comes from their abnormalities. They have more eyes than they should. They have more limbs than they should. Their bodies are completely alien when compared to ours. I cannot stand when things have more body parts than they should or when they have body parts in places where they shouldn't naturally exist. Insects and arachnids represent all that."

I slightly nodded as I listened to his explanation. He was right of course. As he explained it to me, the thought of it came to my mind, and it made me shudder in revulsion. What made it worse, of course, was the knowledge that we could very much see something like that along this path we were walking. As we walked, we soon entered a section of the toy store that looked like it was entirely dedicated to puppets and marionettes.

"Are you afraid of puppets too, Saul?" I asked as we crept along.

"No," he shook his head. "Why would I be afraid of something I could toss across the room, alive or not?"

"No reason, I guess," I shrugged. "Except for all the really scary movies about living dolls bent on killing people."

"Well, if everything in here is based on one of my fears, then you don't need to worry about puppets," he assured me. "You'll wish that was what we were facing though."

He was being foreboding. I hated when he acted like that. I really didn't need some harbinger spreading doom and gloom all over the place. I'm not saying he needed to put on a happy face for me despite all his troubles, but I didn't need him to act like everything was hopeless either. He was giving me emotional whiplash from going back and forth like this. Before I could say something about it, I saw something from the corner of my eye. It seemed as though something was moving right at the edge of my vision.

"Huh?" I found myself asking as I thought about investigating.

"Let's keep moving," said Saul suddenly. "We don't want to get stuck here."

I kept walking and ignored the thing I thought I saw until I thought I saw it again. It was still just movement at the corner of my vision to be sure, but it seemed to be more prominent this time around. This time I stopped to peer into the darkness to see what was there. I found myself looking at a shelf full of puppets when Saul jumped in front me with a stern look on his face.

"What are you doing?" he asked aggressively, standing in front of me with his arms crossed over his chest. "We've got to get out of here, Lita."

"I understand that, Saul, but I thought I saw something," I tried to explain, more than a little put-off by how he was acting right now.

"We can go shopping later," he frowned. "Right now, escaping should be our only priority."

"Shopping?" I protested loudly. "Have you lost your mind?"

I don't care how much I might have loved Saul, I learned a long time ago that you couldn't allow any man to talk to you all crazy like that. It was a lesson that I took to heart.

"Who do you think you're talking to like that, Saul Copeland?" I demanded.

"Sorry for being...curt, but I really think it's better if we get out of here right now," he said apologetically. "We *really* got to go."

"You weren't being curt," I stated. "You were being an asshole and I'm not going to stand for it no matter how much stress you're under. Do you understand?"

"Are you two having a lover's tiff *now*?" Roxanne asked in exasperation. "You young people with your social media and reality TV! You honestly think you have time for relationship drama when the world is coming to an end? Let's get a move on before I shoot you both myself."

Saul and I locked eyes for a moment before we returned to our walk. I was still fuming, but I was able to bite my tongue for the moment. I didn't know what I was liable to say if he stepped out of line again though. We walked for maybe another ten minutes or so through this labyrinthine toy store until I spotted something in the corner of my eye again. This time I was *beyond* certain that I had seen what I saw!

"There it is again!" I exclaimed. "There's something here following us!"

I peeled off from the rest of the group and began examining a shelf full of toys. I could already hear Saul huffing in annoyance. His annoyance was already getting under my skin.

"There isn't anything there, Lita," he insisted. "Please, let's just go."

"What is up with you, Saul?" I asked, spinning on my heel to face him. "Why are you acting like this? Are you helping these things? I knew you couldn't have been the real Saul, crawling out of that portal right when we needed him! You're just some evil thing pretending to be the man I love? Aren't you?"

He was shocked into silence when I said all that. Roxanne and Robinson didn't have anything to say either. While they stood there dumbfounded, not sure what else to say, I turned back towards the shelf of toys and pointed an accusing finger.

"I see you!" I yelled triumphantly.

Have you ever been so sure of something, so certain that you were right, that you couldn't be told otherwise? You thought you could revel in the truth and it would feel amazing, right? Why is that never the case? Being right just brought me, and everyone else around me, tremendous pain. As soon as I pointed out the thing that was moving around, a ghastly demonic visage emerged from the shelf. As soon as it came into view, we were all immediately frozen in place while our bodies were wracked with the most intense pain imaginable.

It felt just like what I experienced in the void. It felt like I was being crushed by all the pressure of the Marianas Trench and more. I knew my eyes, nose, and ears were already starting to bleed. All four of us found ourselves being lifted into the air by the monster standing before us. It was thirteen feet tall with red spindly arms and legs adorned with sharp spikes and oozing pores. Its giant mouth was full of rows and rows of jagged, but razor-sharp teeth. It had sunken red eyes as it stared at us in pure delight.

"What...is...that?" I asked, somehow managing to force the words out of my mouth.

"It's a...demon," Saul answered.

"A what?" I shrieked.

Saul didn't respond. I looked at him from the corner of my eye and watched as he seemed to steel himself. It was clear that he was about to do something, hopefully something to free us. If he was going to save us, I hoped he did it soon because I had never felt this kind of pain in my life. It felt like this demon was pulling me apart molecule by molecule.

"Dear God, please protect me, my family and friends from anything that seeks to do us harm, be they human or otherwise," he said, forcing the words out of his mouth like they were bullets. "I ask this in your son Jesus Christ's name. Amen!"

That final word was like a bomb had been set off. We were all released from the demon's grip and we dropped to our needs. "Amen" was enough to banish the creature and free us. I found myself on my knees struggling to catch my breath as I felt all my molecules trying to go back to where they were supposed to be. It didn't take long before Saul was standing over me and shoving his hand towards me, presumably to help me up to my feet.

"Demons hide right outside the edges of your vision, scurrying around like rats," he explained angrily as I looked up at him. "They cannot harm you until you acknowledge them. Once you call them out, reveal that you see them, then they will catch you in that stasis field you just felt."

"It felt like he was ripping me apart," I said, tears streaming down my cheeks.

"Kinda," he frowned. "He was ripping our souls right out of bodies, Lita. That's what was happening. And it happened because you didn't just listen to me when I told you that you didn't see anything."

That was when my pain and sadness subsided and was replaced with anger. I didn't like how he was talking to me. He was going to hear about it too. I got to my feet, without his assistance, and then glared at him.

"Oh, you're trying to put all this on me?" I demanded. "I did see something and it was real. I wasn't going to let you tell me otherwise."

"Yeah, you really stuck to your guns," he smirked. "And how did that work out for us? It almost got our souls damned to Hell! Look, I'm not trying to be mean or anything, but you people need to start following my lead or you're all going to die. I cannot protect you if you keep doing whatever you want."

"Who do you think you are, talking to me like this?" I asked.

"I suppose I'm the *fake* Saul Copeland," he replied angrily. "Isn't that what you said? After everything we've been through, you're still sitting up here thinking I'm some inhuman thing?"

"Not to put too fine a point on things, but I was calling you an inhuman thing before it was cool," Robinson laughed.

Maybe she was trying to bring levity to a tense moment or maybe she was being a bitch as always, but her comment allowed me time to stop and think. He was hurting. He had been hurting ever since this all started. Hell, he had been in pain even before these creatures crawled out of his skull and started running amok.

"The point is, if you people don't trust me, if you think that I'm actually one of those monsters just impersonating the real Saul, then maybe you should all stay away from me until this is all over," he said, his voice softening just a little. "How about that?"

"I believe in you," said Roxanne. "We might all be in uncharted territory here, but the one thing I have always been able to trust are my instincts. You crawled out of that void different, sure, but there's never been a doubt in my mind that you are Saul Copeland."

"Oh, and I know it's really you too," Robinson added. "I can see right through you...despite my particular affliction."

"I guess that just leaves you, Lita," he said. "What do you believe?"

So, it was just me then, the only person with trust issues in the group. He was looking into my eyes like he was expecting an immediate answer. I didn't have one. He just shook his head and turned his back before continuing to lead our group through that dark, creepy toy store. We only made it a few steps before he spotted a large jack-in-the-box on the floor. Usually, he would have been cautious about something like that, but I think I might have broken something inside of him.

"You should leave that alone, Copeland," Roxanne stated. "Just step over the box and keep going."

He heard her, of course he did, but didn't make any moves. He just stood there, his shoulders rising and falling as he found himself breathing and thinking in the dark. I watched him crouch down and pick up the toy and then absent-mindedly start turning the handle. The entire store was soon filled with the familiar tune, only now it was discordant enough to rake our eardrums with its janky notes.

"Please don't do that, Saul," I pleaded after I noticed the smile on Dr. Robinson's face.

"Who is Saul?" he asked. "I thought the real Saul died and I'm just some evil clone."

"You're being dramatic," I said as he continued to turn the crank.

"Maybe *all* evil clones are dramatic," he shrugged. "Who can say?"

I frowned as I realized he was going to stay all in his feelings until something shook him out of it. I didn't move fast enough though. I placed my hand on his shoulder just as the music from the jack-in-the-box came to a screeching halt. Despite the box being normal size for such a toy, the hellish clown that sprung out was thirty feet tall and practically filled the whole room. It looked down at us with its fiery red eyes and pale white face; its smile was so wide that we were able to see every rotten, yellowed tooth in its head.

"Aw, shit," I grumbled.

The giant clown grabbed me and Saul in its huge white gloves, roared in laughter, and then pulled us both into his cramped little box. All at once I found myself falling, but I couldn't see the ground. I looked around and saw Saul was falling too, but there was no sign of the giant clownish asshole that did this to us.

"Saul!" I yelled over the roar of the wind, reaching out for him.

"Who?" he asked angrily.

We were plummeting to our deaths, but he still had the wherewithal to be petty. I couldn't tell if it was irritating or cute, but since we were going to die, I didn't have time to figure it out one way or another. I yelled out his name again and glared at him until he realized that I meant business.

"Look, I'm sorry for hurting your feelings, but we got bigger concerns right now," I said, locking eyes with him as we fell. "We need to do something!"

He frowned and pouted a little bit, but he knew that I was right. The real Saul Copeland was reasonable and would do whatever was necessary to preserve a life, especially mine. I guess I doubted this was really him in the beginning, but that changed over time. I think the only reason I held onto the idea that this Saul wasn't the real one was to keep my heart protected in case I lost him all over again. Having it happen once absolutely destroyed me and I didn't want to open myself up to that again.

"I'm sorry, Saul, but you don't have time to mope," I said. "Let's get somewhere safe and then we can talk about everything."

He closed his eyes for a moment before opening them and reaching out for my hand. Once our hands were clasped together, he pulled me to him and tucked me into his arms. It felt so good to be held in that moment, despite the fact that we were currently falling to our deaths, that it was impossible for me to deny that this man was anyone or anything other than Saul Copeland.

"Are we gonna die?" I whispered.

"No," he answered with a simple shake of his head. "I'll never let that happen to you."

Soon our descent was slowed down and I could see that Saul had learned to fly. He had become my very own Superman. After a few moments, we set down on the roof of a commercial warehouse in the middle of what looked like New York City. It had to be an illusion, of course, because there was no way we made it back home, but it definitely looked like our city.

"Home again," I commented, but I could see the frown on his face.

"This isn't your home, Lita," he shook his head. "This is my home, the inside of my mind. This is where the worst of my nightmares are. We need to find a way out of here quickly and get back to Reynolds. We won't be able to survive here for very long."

"So, let's get off this roof and try to make it to the streets," I suggested. "We need to find a vehicle."

We started walking towards the roof access door to get into the building when I heard a loud clicking sound. I turned around and looked behind me, but didn't see anything. My eyes narrowed though because I knew for a fact that I heard what I heard.

"What's that?" I asked, looking around us. "Is it another demon?"

"No," he replied. "We need to get inside fast. These things usually can't open doors."

We reached the door leading into the building right when the "things" Saul was talking about decided to reveal themselves. My eyes widened and my jaw dropped when I saw a giant cockroach crawl from the street and climb on top of the building across from us. It was much bigger than the spider we had seen earlier, the one that had killed Barry and Garcia. This thing was about the length of seven or eight subway cars!

Saul shoulder-charged the locked door in an attempt to get it open, but that just made the giant bug notice us. I didn't know anything about insects or what their facial features meant, but I could tell that this thing saw us as food as soon as it turned its disgusting head in our direction. Before long, there were even more of the nasty things, standing on top of every building and they were all looking in our direction.

"Open the door, Saul," I whispered, as the clicking noise filled the air. "Now."

"I'm trying," he said. "This door always gets stuck when I try to escape."

I pulled out my pistol and held it to my side, ready to shoot the first thing that scurried towards me, but that only seemed to antagonize them. I don't know how they were able to recognize my gun as a weapon, but they knew, and it just seemed to make them angrier about the whole situation. In the blink of an eye, we soon had two roaches towering over us. I felt my heart sink in my chest as I realized that danger had never been closer.

"Let's go," Saul said, finally getting the door open and pulling me into the building before slamming the door shut behind us. "That was close."

"Too close," I shuddered in revulsion. "Let's not cut it that close ever again."

"I can't promise you that," he shook his head as we stood at the top of the stairs. "We're locked into a sequence now. This is my worst nightmare, which is actually a pastiche of several nightmares threaded together. I get battered around like a mouse toyed with by a cat until I finally wake up. But that's not going to happen this time because we're not actually asleep, are we? We might just experience this over and over again on a loop."

"You're forgetting something," I commented. "You have two things going for you that you have never had before."

"What's that?" he asked.

"Two secret weapons," I smiled. "You've got me and you've got your new powers. Although, I don't know how much help I'm going to be if there are any more nasty bugs crawling around this place."

"The giant bugs are just the appetizer, Lita," he said seriously. "It's all going to get much, much worse from here. I wish...I wish you weren't here with me. I wish you were back there with Reynolds and Robinson. You'd have been much safer there."

He turned and started walking down the stairs and I followed him, trying to ignore the chill that tap-danced up and down my spine over what he had just said to me. When we reached the next floor, I recognized where we were. It actually brought an undue smile to my face.

"It's the office!" I exclaimed as we entered our workspace. "I never thought I would be glad to see this place!"

"Trust me, you won't be glad to see it for much longer," he grumbled. "Familiar places can hold horrors just as stark and terrifying as anything you'll find in the unknown."

"What does that mean?" I asked. "What...what are we going to find here, Saul?"

"Just be ready," he said. "Get your gun out."

"Will a gun work on whatever is here?" I asked cautiously.

"It might slow them down a little," he shrugged. "I don't know. I've never had a gun any of the other times I've been here."

I knew I needed to keep my wits about me in light of what he said and where we were, but it was hard not to feel at ease here. I instinctively walked over to my desk and it brought a smile to my face. It honestly felt like it had been a million years since I had been here last. I didn't even feel like the same woman who used to sit at this desk secretly playing Yahtzee on my phone whenever things got quiet and boring. I ran my finger across my desk and saw that there wasn't a bit of dust on it, like I had just been sitting here yesterday or something.

"You have excellent recall, Saul," I said as I picked up the River Song Funko Pop figure that I kept on my desk. "Everything looks like our office, right down to the smallest detail."

"Yeah, that's meant to lure us all into a false sense of security," he frowned. "Keep your guard up. Things are going to move fast when it gets started."

I didn't know what he meant and it kinda rubbed me the wrong way that he wouldn't just tell me what was going to happen. I mean, wouldn't I be in better shape if he told me precisely what I was dealing with? I took a seat at my desk and did a full spin in my chair. I wondered where everyone else was at. I mean, our co-workers had to be part of this nightmare too, right? As soon as I wondered about them, that's when I heard their voices. They were all chattering as they presumably all came back from lunch together.

I looked up to see the crew entering the office and then I realized what we were up against. I recognized the voices as soon as I heard them, but what I saw was something completely unfamiliar. What came through the door wasn't human, or at least, not completely. I recognized the bodies of my co-workers...and almost vomited at the sight of the giant insect heads attached to them!

It wasn't cute, like an anthropomorphic cartoon character. Nothing so palatable. This was nothing but pure nightmare fuel. I thought the creatures that had attacked us on the roof were disgusting enough with that huge size, but this was worse. No one should have to see insects this close up. I immediately got to my feet and gripped my gun while Saul gripped the baton that he had gotten from Roxanne earlier. Our "co-workers" froze in their tracks as soon as they saw us standing there.

"Steady," I heard him whisper as everything around went still, like time had stopped or something. "Steady now."

The moment seemed to linger forever, like the instant before those big fight scenes in anime, but it couldn't have lasted more than a few seconds. In a mere blink of an eye, the office was filled with the sound of clicking, like it was filled with enraged cicadas. And then they charged right at us, like they were intent on ripping us apart. I was shocked by the speed with which they moved, but I guess I shouldn't have been; we've all seen how quickly roaches scurry when you turn the lights on. None, however, were faster than the bullets I started firing from my gun.

The chatty girl from accounting was the first to go followed by the dude who keeps borrowing my stapler from me. Those were easy ones. I felt myself start to hesitate when it came to the coworkers I actually *liked*. Like the guy who always replaces the water jug in the kitchen area or the receptionist I sometimes ate lunch with. I knew everyone's names, of course, but it was hard to recall them when their heads had been replaced with Kafka-esque nightmares.

I soon noticed that no matter how many of them I blew away, they just kept coming. Waves and waves of monsters rushing towards me, and I knew I didn't have enough bullets to take them all out. I knew that amongst all the other clicks filling my office space, it wouldn't be long before I heard the horrifying one that indicated that my gun was now out of ammunition. And when that happened, I would be forced to either fight these things off with my bare hands or run like hell.

I could see from the corner of my eye that Saul had already made his choice, putting down these creatures with swings from his baton. He was wielding it like it was a baseball bat and was absolutely devastating our coworkers with it. He had lived this nightmare before. He had lived this nightmare several times before, it would seem, and he knew what he was doing. I was just a visitor here, doing whatever I could to survive.

Click. Click. Click.

Well, that was it. No more bullets and the hordes of monsters were still coming at me. I quickly looked around to see if there was anything I could quickly grab to defend myself, but there wasn't much around. I had a knife, of course, but I really didn't want these things getting anywhere near me, so close combat was not for me. Before long, I spotted something that could prove useful; I grabbed the fire extinguisher off the wall and started spraying it at the hybrid monstrosities who were approaching me. The creatures didn't like it and some retreated while others slipped and fell to the floor. It didn't help much though because the others just climbed over them in their attempt to get to me.

"Saul, I could really use some help here," I called out to him, having to take several steps back as the monsters got closer and closer with each lunge that they took.

He rushed over to me and stepped between me and the bug faces, but we were outnumbered, and it was only going to be a matter of time before we were overrun. When the fire extinguisher finally ran out, they leaped all over us. I could feel their weight on me as they dogpiled on top of me, their hands ripping and pulling at my body violently. The pain was nothing, though, compared to the terror I felt by having all those giant insect faces close to mine. Those mandibles were tearing at me until my screams were so loud that they were all you could hear. I was screaming louder than all that insectile clicking too.

Just when I felt like my brain was going to absolutely break into a million pieces, leaving me insane, all the coworkers were thrown off me and Saul. When I opened my tear-filled eyes, I saw Saul standing there, almost glowing with energy. Our coworkers all stepped back, unsure of what he was going to do. He gave them all a stern look before extending his hand to help me.

"Are you okay?" he asked.

"I've been better," I answered, still shaken as I took his hand and let him help me to my feet. "I really wish you had done that sooner. We've got to get out of here, Saul. I don't like it here."

It turned out we had nothing more to worry about from them though. Our boss, Carol, told everyone to get back to work and they all returned to their desks and started typing on their keyboards as though they hadn't just tried to kill us. They went back to work as though they didn't have giant insect heads growing out of their necks! Just like that, it seemed to be all over. My heart was still beating out of my chest, and I was finding it difficult to breathe, but at least we had a bit of a break from all the madness of this...Nightmare Box. But if things were truly under control, then why was Saul standing there like Batman with his hands balled into fists, his eyes darting around like he was expecting another attack at any moment?

"What's wrong?" I asked nervously, not really sure I wanted to know at this point.

"This isn't over, Lita," he answered. "This is basically just the halfway point of my worst nightmare."

The halfway point? We were only halfway through and I was already fighting to keep myself sane. I tried to shake off everything I had seen and experienced, but it was sticking with me. I wanted to be brave, needed to be brave after everything I had said back in Haven, but I felt myself losing my nerve. There was something about this place that seemed to be sapping every bit of courage out of me.

"So what's next?" I asked, faking the funk. "We can handle anything."

That's when the light that had been pouring through the windows darkened, like clouds had passed over the sun. When I looked, though, I could see that the source of the shadows was not clouds at all. I looked out those wall-length windows and saw a giant face right outside the building. It had the face of a cherub, like an actual cupid, but there was no way you couldn't feel the absolute malice living behind those huge, inquisitive eyes.

"What the hell is that?" I asked.

"It's a giant baby," he replied. "I think...it might represent my fear of becoming a father before I'm ready. I'm not sure. It isn't always so easy to make sense of all the things in my head."

I couldn't care less what the origin of this particular fear was. The only thing that concerned me was how were we supposed to fight against something so massive with no weapons to speak of? I still had my knife and Saul had his baton, but those would be nothing more than toothpicks to the monstrosity that was looking at us with those wide eyes.

"What do we do?" I asked. "Do we run? Try to get to a lower floor or something? What do you usually do when this happens in your nightmares?"

"No," he shook his head. "This is the part where it catches us."

All of our bug-faced colleagues started clicking louder and louder as the giant baby outside lifted its chubby hand. Saul stood next to me and apologized, pre-emptively, for what was about to happen. As the baby's hand crashed into the side of the building, I recognized the bug clicking for what it was: they were laughing at us. I closed my eyes and just prepared for the inevitable.

I thought that giant hand was going to smash us into bits, but it didn't. I should have known better though since Saul had revealed that this was the halfway point of his nightmare. There was clearly more torture to go. When I opened my eyes, I discovered that Saul and I were in the giant baby's hand as it brought us up to its mouth. I looked around and saw that the bugs that had assaulted us on the roof had all run for cover. I didn't blame them.

The baby started shaking us like maracas and swinging us around. It felt like the wildest, most dangerous rollercoaster imaginable. My body felt like it was going to be reduced to jelly from the sheer speed. I screamed like I was on a death-defying thrill ride, but this was much worse because there were no seatbelts and everything in this world was designed to kill us.

Saul, who was right next to me in the palm of this creature's hand, was not screaming in the slightest. I could tell that he was being affected by the break-neck speeds too, but his only reaction was the tightening of his jaw. It made sense for him to be more stoic than me; he had experienced this many more times than I had. I reached for his hand, just like I would have if we were on an amusement park ride, and he held it tight. He wanted me to know he was there with me and that he would take care of me, but I couldn't imagine his powers could do anything against something so imposing.

Something in me just hoped that the baby would get tired or bored at some point and would release us. I doubted Saul's nightmares ever ended in such an anti-climatic way but there was always hope. After the baby swung us around so much that I thought my brains would come leaking out of my ears, it simply stopped and just held us at eye-level. It examined us like it didn't quite know what to make of us. Just when I was starting to catch my breath, the baby simply shrugged and tossed me and Saul straight up into the air as hard and as fast as its chubby little arms could manage.

And now we were airborne, rocketing through the clouds together. We were still holding hands, thankfully, because I didn't know what I would do if I was alone. I never had any fear of flying before, but it was a different experience without an airplane. I couldn't breathe up there and it was so, so cold. I have never been so cold in my entire life. I was more afraid of freezing to death than I was of hitting the ground.

I wished that I was able to talk to Saul, get some words of encouragement from him, but there was no way to hear him once we started falling back to Earth. The wind rushing past my ears was already so loud that I couldn't hear my own screaming. I could see the ground rushing up to meet us and I thought this had to be the end of the nightmare. No one ever hits the ground in their sleep; the shock of it was usually what made you wake up screaming in a cold sweat. That was all fine and good for Saul, but what about me? When Saul woke up from this nightmare, would I wake up too, or would I be splattered all over the ground?

I closed my eyes and said every prayer that my grandmother ever taught me. I even recited the prayer Saul had said to banish the demon from earlier. I just hoped that there was a god out there and it cared that I was in danger right now. After several prayers, I felt Saul squeeze my hand. I opened my eyes and I saw the giant baby beneath us. It opened its mouth and prepared itself to swallow us both whole and suddenly I was thinking that it would have been better to have just hit the ground and died. That would have been better than being swallowed by one of these monsters.

Saul pulled me into his arms and held me. He made me look into his eyes so that nothing else mattered anymore. We kissed for a moment before we fell into the giant baby's mouth and was swallowed. We were surrounded by complete darkness, much like the void we had encountered at Gracie Mansion, but it didn't feel like we were being crushed by gravity from all directions.

"Saul?" I called out.

I couldn't feel his arms around me anymore, like we got separated as soon as we entered the giant's mouth. I was floating in the dark and I felt extremely frightened. I felt alone, but at the same time, I felt like I was surrounded by millions of things in the dark.

"Saul!" I called out again, even more afraid than I was before. "Saul, are you there!?!"

He didn't respond and that just made me even more worried. I started to wonder what would happen if he got free from the Nightmare Box, but I didn't? What if I was trapped here all by myself? How could I possibly escape or even survive without him giving me intel on each individual monster hiding in the recesses of his brain? My mind was filled with all types of nightmare scenarios as I floated there in the dark. In a way, I was becoming him, filled with terrible anxiety that came close to paralyzing me.

I lost all track of time as I floated there in the abyss. I found myself getting disoriented since there were no dimensions there in the dark. I started to wonder if some of my own fears started to take form while I was here in the Nightmare Box. I had always been a little scared of the idea of sensory deprivation tanks; I don't know if it was the idea of being alone in the dark or being alone with my thoughts. The longer I stayed here in the void, the more I started to doubt my own sanity.

"What if I can't get out of here?" I asked myself. "What if I'm stuck here forever? I know Saul is trying to save me, save us all, but what if he can't find me? Or what if I was taken as bait, something to lure him right to the center of a trap he can't possibly escape? I don't want to be used to destroy him."

"Then maybe you should kill yourself, don't allow yourself to be used."

Whoa! Who was that? That voice wasn't mine. I would never think something like that. That voice might have sounded like me, but it definitely wasn't me. It was a pretty good impersonation, but it was definitely coming from outside my head and not inside. That voice was trying to communicate with me from somewhere in the darkness.

"No thanks," I replied cautiously against my better judgment. "I'm good."

"Are you really? You're trapped inside your boyfriend's diseased brain, being hunted by the creatures who keep him awake at night, and you honestly think you're good? I think you're *good* at deluding yourself, girl."

Under normal circumstances I would have recognized that this thing was trying to play mind games with me and would have laughed at the pathetic attempt, but I wasn't feeling as strong or confident as I usually did. There was something about the Nightmare Box that really wore you down. It stripped you of your self-worth, robbed you of your confidence, sapped your strength, and destroyed your will. It felt like the longer I was here, the more I was dying. Dying by imperceptible degrees with each passing moment. Now that I wasn't fighting terrifying monsters, I could finally feel what this place was doing to me.

"Just leave me alone," I replied weakly. "You don't know what you're talking about."

"You think I'm the one who does not know what they are talking about? That's rich! You're the one who is both literally and figuratively in the dark. How about I shed some light on your situation? I think you'll find it all very illuminating."

That's when the disembodied voice turned on the lights, like it adjusted the dimmer switch in the room. That's when I saw I was in no room at all. I was in the murky depths of the ocean, and I was surrounded by millions of corpses, all of them floating aimlessly but with their cold, empty stares all fixed on me! The closest corpse was none other than Special Agent Trevor Grimes! I almost vomited, but when my mouth opened sea water came rushing in, filling my mouth and my lungs. Apparently, keeping my mouth closed was the only thing keeping me from drowning in this sea of the dead.

I tried to swim out of there, maybe get to the surface, but there were too many dead bodies in the way. They seemed to be grabbing at me and trying to hold me in place, but that could have been my imagination playing tricks on me. It had to be. If there was anything that my life had taught me up to this point, it was that the living have nothing to fear from the dead. Unfortunately for me, there were more than just dead bodies floating all around me. With the lights turned up, I could see something behind all the corpses, something moving around and displacing the mass of bodies that were floating around.

There was something out there in the inky blackness, moving and shifting the dead bodies around, and it seemed to be getting closer to me. I wanted to scream out for help, but I knew if I did, I would come close to drowning again. My second instinct was to hide somewhere, but there was nowhere to hide. Even with all these dead bodies all around me, I knew that I was not at all hidden; in fact, I was probably more exposed here than I had ever been in my whole life. I desperately tried to swim to the surface, hoping that there was a surface to get to, and that I would know what to do once I got there.

Even though I wasn't technically in water, swimming still worked the same. I swam upwards past several anonymous corpses, none of whom looked familiar, but I was still keenly aware that there was something out there amongst the dead. I hoped that it was Saul and that the only reason why he wasn't calling out to me was because he didn't want to drown either. Even though that's what I was hoping, something told me that I was wrong. Something told me that whatever it was out there, I needed to avoid it at all costs. It was something so dangerous that it made every single hair on my body stand on end.

"I turned up all the lights and you're still in the dark."

It was my voice again, but not my voice. I had never heard my words dripping with so much cruelty before. I knew it wasn't me and all I wanted to do was keep on swimming to the surface. I had a goal and I couldn't let anything distract me from it.

"You're wasting your time. There is no surface to get to. There is only this one endless ocean. And even if there was a surface, how would you even know if you were swimming towards it? You could be swimming further down for all you know."

The voice was right. There was no way of telling if I was facing up. The place was so confusing and disorienting that I could very well have been going in the opposite direction of where I was hoping to go. It was also possible that it was lying all in an attempt to screw up my escape. I didn't know what was true, so I opted to stick with my original plan.

Whether I lived or died, it was going to hinge on my own choices, not anyone else's.

So, I swam upwards. I swam past strangers. I swam past old neighbors and classmates. I swam past old boyfriends. I gasped when I swam past my parents, almost drowning on a mouthful of seawater. I closed my mouth and went back to swimming and that's when I discovered what was hidden behind all the corpses: a huge shark about as big as the one Saul and I saw in Gracie Mansion before all Hell broke loose.

The damned thing was gliding through the...nothingness right where the corpses were their densest. It kept me from seeing it, despite the light that was now being provided, but I still knew that it was something to fear. Nothing in this place was designed to bring comfort.

I swam and swam until my arms and legs felt like they were on fire, afraid that if I stopped, I would sink back to where I started. I didn't want to start all over again, didn't want to see the faces of all my loved ones twisted into grotesque death masks. Right when I was about to give up because I didn't have an ounce of strength left, someone grabbed my hands and started to pull me up. My first instinct was to fight them off, thinking that the corpses had become zombies or something, but soon I was looking at Saul's smiling face. Apparently, he had been looking for me the whole time. I should have known that no matter what, he would find his way back to me.

We couldn't speak to each other, of course, but just together again was like a balm for the soul. We hugged and then he gave me a kiss on the forehead before pointing up to let me know that I had indeed been on my way to the surface the whole time. I had been here surrounded by the dead for what felt like weeks, but was at least several hours, and this was the first time that I felt even remotely safe. It didn't last.

The thing that was moving around in this lifeless sea emerged and ripped into Saul's torso with its rows and rows of sharp shark teeth. I gasped again, filling my lungs with more saltwater as I watched this monster devour my man. It looked at me with its black eyes and seemed to smile as it saw the terror on my face. It took several more frenzied bites before dragging Saul's mangled, bloody body back into the depths.

After the shark disappeared with him, all the other dead bodies turned to face me. I was going to gasp again, but I made sure not to. I knew what would happen if I did and I couldn't afford to let it happen. Each corpse, acting in complete tandem, pointed upwards and issued me a warning.

"Swim, Lita," they said. "Swim before it gets you too."

I didn't need to be told twice as I started swimming as fast and as hard as I could, ignoring the burning in my limbs. After seeing what had become of Saul, how could I not? My mind was focused on just escaping this nightmare in any way that I could. I ignored the chorus of the corpses as they all commanded me to swim. I already knew what I needed to do. At some point, I thought I could see the surface. I could see a fiery ball in the distance and I assumed it had to be the sun. I swam faster until I was mere feet away from it.

"Too late," the corpses sang out. "It's back."

The shark that had taken Saul burst through the mass of dead bodies, opened its huge mouth, and sank those razor-sharp teeth right into my left arm! I opened my mouth to scream and swallowed so much saltwater that it felt like I was filling like a balloon. The sharp combination of extreme pain mixed with a belly full of saltwater was enough for me to vomit right in the shark's eye, but that just made it gnaw on my arm even more. It even looked like it was taking a perverse pleasure in hurting me! That's when pain turned into rage and that rage turned into a desire to hurt this thing right back!

I found my knife, which was still at my side despite everything I had been through, gripped the handle and then plunged the blade right in the shark's eye. The same eye that I had just thrown up on. It opened its mouth like it was in pain and released my arm. I knew I couldn't swim away with my arm mangled like it was, so I knew flight wasn't an option. I knew I had to fight. I kept stabbing and stabbing and stabbing. I took out one eye and then the other, but I didn't let up for a moment. The shark's blood drained out of it while all the dead people just floated there and watched.

When I was done, the shark sank out of view. It didn't float there like the human bodies did for some reason. After the shark fell out of sight, I looked up to see how much further I had to go before I reached the surface. I started swimming again, but before I got too far, another shark appeared out of nowhere and bit into my mangled arm while a second shark went for my left leg. Before I could start stabbing them, a third shark came and bit into my right arm, making me drop my knife. A fourth came and began gnawing on my right leg. I was in the center of their feeding frenzy and it was more painful than imaginable.

"You're dying, Lita," the corpses began to sing out. "This is the end for you. You'll be joining your boyfriend soon."

I didn't want to die like that, agonizing in tremendous pain, so I opened my mouth and let the water into my lungs. I hoped to drown before I could be completely consumed. I started passing out and everything started going dark. In the end, I was pleased to just slip off into oblivion.

"You don't get to go yet," the corpses sang and then I returned to full consciousness. "Not yet."

The sharks released me and then swam behind me before biting into my arms and legs anew. They then began swimming at top speed, carrying me along with them. They carried me through the mass of dead bodies faster and faster, so fast that all I could do was scream. Before long, we got clear of all the corpses and I was able to see what was beyond. It was a giant octopus the same size of a fucking skyscraper...and they were bringing me right to it.

It was just one nightmare after another and I just didn't know what to do. I was in a perpetual state of dying, but these monsters wouldn't let me just go. They just wouldn't let me die...like they had done with Saul. They brought me to the octopus and it wrapped a tentacle around me and the sharks; it started squeezing us all to the point that it was like we were all in a big bear hug together. The pressure increased until the sharks all popped like water balloons and sprayed their insides all over me. With the sharks gone, the octopus only had me to squeeze.

"Goodbye Lita," the marine creature stated, perfectly imitating my voice.

It squeezed me until it broke every bone in my body. I blacked out after that, sure I was about to die. After everything went black, I immediately saw a brilliant flash of white light and heard the largest crack of thunder. I thought it must have been heaven...until I found myself lying on the ground, soaking wet, in front of a throne. Upon the throne, sat a foreboding hooded figure.

"It's about time you got here."

EIGHT
JOURNEY'S END

My name is Saul Copeland. I am a black man born in Brooklyn, New York. I've lived a fearful, unremarkable life. And then one day, because I was very, very careless, I destroyed the entire world. The thing that I regret the most is bringing Lita into all of this. Out of all the people I've ever met, she probably deserved pain the least.

She got trapped inside my Nightmare Box, the realm where my most terrible nightmares reside, and she lived every single bit of it. I eventually destroyed the box from the inside and we were released, but I know there's no way she could possibly be okay. How *could* she be? I saw her lying on the ground, soaking wet and shivering, and I knew that something had to be broken inside of her. She was now probably just as broken as me. She'd never forgive me for everything I had just put her through. I knew that as surely as I knew anything.

"Lita, are you okay?" I asked, rushing over to her and kneeling down.

I rolled her over to get a good look at her and I gasped in shock. All her long, black hair had turned white. Her eyes were wide, and she looked terrified, her teeth chattering in fear as though she were freezing. I took her into my arms and held her tight and she gripped me like she was afraid I would vanish.

"Is this real?" she cried. "Are you real? You're not a giant bug or a zombie or a shark?"

"I'm real, Lita," I said. "You're okay."

"Why would you lie to her, Saul? No one and nothing is okay and probably never will be again."

I recognized the voice immediately. It wasn't just the voice of the person who lured us to Nevada. It was also the voice I heard in my head whenever I was at my most pessimistic. I looked up and saw a robed, hooded figure sitting on an ornate throne made of human remains. We had reached our enemy. When the Nightmare Box exploded, it deposited us right at his feet.

"It's you," I said.

"It is," he laughed.

I looked around and saw that I was in a large chamber. We were in some sort of castle or fortress, his fortress. Lying a few feet away from me were Roxanne and Dr. Robinson; they were starting to stir. We were all here at the end of all things. At least I wasn't going to have to fight this thing alone.

"Where am I?" I asked. "What is this place?"

"This is my home," he replied, sitting on his throne with one leg thrown over the other, as though it were the most comfortable seat in the world. "Do you like it? I decorated it myself."

"I hate it," I answered truthfully, stalling to give Roxanne and Dr. Robinson a chance to rally. "Looks like you got interior design advice from Dahmer."

"You're...mouthier than I assumed you would be," he said, leaning forward as though trying to get a better look at me. "I was expecting a quiet, mousy coward who squeaked more than he spoke. I guess having me and my ilk curled up in your brain blocked your natural confidence and machismo. Aren't you glad we're free, so you get to be your natural self at last? That's why I had you come to Nevada instead of me coming to Haven; I wanted to give you time to really start enjoying the new you."

"Who are you?" I asked. "What's your name?"

"Oh, I thought you'd never ask," he laughed again before he removed his hood and revealed his face to me. "How about you call me Saul 2.0?"

He had my face. The leader of all these monstrous nightmares had my face. Ugh. It was so cliché; I almost threw up. I was the cause of all my troubles, so of course, my boogeyman looked precisely like me. It was so predictable that I wanted to gather my people and just walk right out of there. I knew it was only going to be a matter of time before Robinson hit us all with some perfectly plausible psycho-babble that explained why my worst enemy looked like me, but I really didn't want to hear it.

"Oh, look, you resemble me," I rolled my eyes. "What an unpredictable twist."

"Don't be a dick, Saul," he grumbled. "It's not a good look. And if you don't play nice, I'm not going to answer any of your questions. And you *do* want answers, don't you? You're dying to know how all this happened."

"You expect me to believe that you have answers?" I inquired as I spotted Roxanne get to her feet from the corner of my eye.

"I'm the *only* one with answers," he stated, his voice taking on a deadly serious tone, vastly different from the jovial tone from before. "I can tell you precisely what happened and it had nothing to do with some magic pills."

I really wanted to know how something like this had occurred and why it was all happening to me. What was so special about me? Since I wasn't ready for the big fight, I thought it couldn't hurt to listen to what he had to say. If nothing else, it would give Roxanne and the others a chance to get on their feet.

"So tell me your story, but I'm not calling you by that ridiculous name," I said.

"You think of yourself as an unfortunate young man who suffers from terrible anxiety, but you're wrong," he explained. "In truth, you're no more a man than I am. I look human, but I am decidedly more than that. A long time ago, your species would have called me...a dark god."

"A god, huh?" I smirked. "If gods were real, you would never have been allowed to exist, the damage you've caused would never have occurred. You're just a nightmare given flesh. And you know what, I don't really care where you came from. I came here to destroy you and put an end to this madness."

"You've read too many comic books," he said angrily as he got to his feet. "You think because your imaginary friend taught you a few tricks, you're a match for me? Do you even know where that power you're using comes from?"

I called forth my aforementioned powers and tried using them on him. I used the same strength that I used to disperse the tornado that he had sicced on us earlier. It picked him up and tossed him at his own throne. I felt like an anime character at that moment. A smile even came to my face. He looked hurt. I looked back and saw Roxanne shifting to her werewolf form.

"Detective Reynolds?" I asked.

No sooner than I called her name, she rushed past me and charged toward my evil twin. I stood there and watched as Roxanne delivered a flurry of furious claw strikes. She looked like she was going to reduce him to deli meat all by herself. All this time we were in fear of this thing and he was just a weak blowhard. I can't tell you how pleased I was right then. I even turned my back on the fight to go check on Lita.

"This is going to be over soon, babe," I told her, running my fingers through her silver hair. "Everything is going to be fine."

"No," she whispered, curled up in the fetal position. "Nothing is okay. Never okay. Nothing is okay. Never okay."

She kept repeating those phrases over and over again and it was breaking my heart. She had seen the worst things in the Nightmare Box and it looked like it had broken her. I didn't know if she would be okay again, but I was willing to spend my life with her and care for her until she was herself again. As I held her in my arms, Dr. Robinson crawled over to us and tapped me on the shoulder.

"What do you want?" I asked angrily.

"Bit of advice: never turn your back on your enemy," she replied.

"He's no threat, Robinson," I assured her. "Reynolds is making hamburger out of him right now."

"Saul!!!"

The voice calling my name bellowed so loud that it shook the entire fortress, maybe the entire planet. I immediately spun around to see my doppelganger standing next to his throne, looking bloodied and beaten, while holding Roxanne by the throat. His eyes were bloodshot and he was obviously furious as he looked in my direction.

"Is this your dog?" he asked. "You gotta keep it out of my yard, buddy."

And then he snapped Roxanne's neck right in front of me. He tossed her dead body at me with such force that it knocked me, Lita, and Robinson back several yards. We watched as she slowly turned back into a human before our very eyes. She was gone just like that and it served as a wake-up call on just how dangerous this guy was.

"You have the nerve to turn your back on a god?" he roared. "Is this my fault? Did I give you the impression that I was some sort of pushover? I am a hair's breadth away from destroying your entire pathetic planet. I am not to be fucked with, Saul."

I left Roxanne on the ground and gave Lita a solemn look before I turned my attention completely to my evil twin once more. He was right. I came here to finally put everything right and I needed to take it seriously right to the very last moment. I told Lita and Robinson to stay put and then I started walking towards the raging monster that was still standing by his throne.

"You're not a god!" I declared as I approached him.

"You're in my castle made out of the bones, hair, and skin of all the people I've killed, but you do not believe in my godhood," he smiled. "Fascinating. So tell me, what do you think I am? How do you think I accomplished all of this?"

"You're very powerful," I nodded. "However, I doubt you're a god. How could something so powerful and infinite be trapped inside my brain? How could something like that happen? No, you're something I dreamt up and somehow, some way, you got loose. You're nothing more than a child's monster drawn on loose leaf paper. And when I erase you, there will be nothing left of you."

"Wow, and people think I have delusions of grandeur," he laughed as I continued to walk towards him. "You think you created me and all the other creatures that have been ravaging your world? You didn't make *us*. We were banished to your brain by a humorless entity that didn't want to have to deal with us. So he cast us out of the dark and crammed us into your head."

"Seems to me that whoever banished you is the real god," I shrugged. "It also seems to me that my brain was chosen because I possess some power over you as well. I mean, why else would I have been selected to carry this tremendous burden?"

That comment seemed to anger him a great deal. He frowned and his eyes turned fiery red. I watched as his nails extended to the point where they looked like fangs. Yeah, he was mad all right. I didn't understand why at first, but it occurred to me eventually. I was facing down the monster that had destroyed my world and was kinda praising the creature that had locked him up in the first place. No one would be happy about something like that. He had to be feeling the same way Satan felt every time someone praised God.

"There's nothing special about you or your limited little brain, Saul," he hissed. "You're just another in a long line of mortals chosen to hold us captive. When one of you dies, tormented by a lifetime of nightmares, we all get transferred to the next cursed soul."

"So the god who imprisoned you trusted us to watch over you and keep you from escaping?" I asked.

"No, no, no, no, no!" he yelled, making the castle shake again. "You're not my warden, Saul Copeland! You're just my jail! And you've been a terrible one at that. You failed to hold me and my kind. Do you know how many times in the history of humanity, one of you flesh puppets have failed in your duty? Never! You're the first one in all of history to have failed at this! And all it took was you, what, wanting to be a decent boyfriend to a girl who *already* liked you? You're pathetic! You let your world fall to ruin for pussy!"

"Shut up!" I shouted. "My decision had nothing to do with...sex."

"Oh, come on!" he laughed and rolled his eyes at my comment.

"Every decision you humans make is about sex on some level or another. You want to believe you're not animals, but you have all the same hormones as any other beast crawling around on the surface of this world. Hell, you even manifested a giant *vagina* to hide from me at some point. I mean, could you be any more obvious? Speaking of..."

With that, he raised his left hand and it started glowing with energy, just like mine had done previously. I heard Lita scream out and I spun around to see that he had levitated her and Dr. Robinson. He used his powers to bring them all over to him and then started examining them with a discerning eye.

"So this is Lita," he said, his voice dripping with both charm and venom at the same time. "Perhaps I should be thanking *you* for my jailbreak, huh? He was so scared of losing you after his freak out in the photo gallery that he couldn't take those damn pills fast enough."

"I refuse to believe that the pills Dr. Robinson gave me did all this," I commented. "Unless she was your willing accomplice all along."

"Robinson is just a doctor," he sighed impatiently. "The pills weren't magic. It's more about what they represented. They represented your desire to let go of the burden you were carrying. You basically said you didn't want the responsibility anymore. And so...just like that...we weren't your problem anymore."

"I never meant to unleash you on the world," I said.

"Yeah, well, luckily for me, your *intentions* don't matter," he smiled. "All that matters is what you did. And now I'm free. Maybe we'll see how much you enjoy being locked up for a while."

"Why don't you tell him why you haven't killed him."

I looked back and saw Lex walking through the room towards us, as cool and calm as anyone you've ever seen. It didn't seem fazed by all the carnage we were surrounded by or the fact that an evil version of me was holding us all captive. I was surprised to see him; I had gotten the impression that he was afraid of the monster responsible for all this suffering, that he was hiding in my head specifically to avoid this devil.

"Oh, it's you," my doppelganger said in annoyance. "One big family reunion."

At this point, I was tired of all the doublespeak and tapdancing. I just wanted answers finally. I felt the power inside me bubble over and then explode outward. God-Saul's grip on us was disrupted, leaving us tumbling back to the ground. I got to my feet immediately and then faced my enemy angrily.

"If you and all the other monsters are just dark gods imprisoned in my head, then what is he?" I asked, pointing at Lex. "He's been nothing but helpful to me this entire time."

"You're the prison, he's the warden," my doppelganger revealed. "He's the voice in your head that's supposed to keep you living in fear, the voice that keeps you holding onto your demons instead of letting them out."

"So you were never there for me," I said, glancing over at Lex. "You were never doing what was in my best interests. You just did whatever was necessary to continue my viability as a prison for these creatures."

"I'm sorry, pal," he said, looking remorseful. "My responsibility was really to the world in large. But...I also knew that you'd never want this life for yourself, a life of knowing that you were the one who unleashed these monsters on the world."

"So you've all been using me all this time," I commented, as the realization of my status fully dawned on me in that dark castle. "The good guys *and* the bad guys. I've just been a pawn in some cosmic game this whole time. You people have made me miserable my entire life for a fucking game!"

In that moment, I was so full of rage. I couldn't contain it and I didn't want to. I wanted my doppelganger and would-be savior to feel the pain they had inflicted on me. I screamed and that scream brought the whole castle down. The building exploded outward and was immediately reduced to nothing but rubble. The only thing left intact was God-Saul's throne. Lex was staggered and my evil twin looked terrified. Obviously, neither expected that kind of outburst. As they all stood and watched me silently, I walked over to Lita and helped her to her feet.

"*Are* you okay, babe?" I asked, smoothing her silver hair with my hands.

She still looked terrified from everything that she had witnessed, but the smile she gave me let me know that it wasn't me she was afraid of. That made me feel better. It made me feel good to know that she still didn't blame me for everything that had happened. I hugged her tight and felt her warmth before I whispered in her ear.

"Don't worry," I said. "I'm going to end this right now."

"Make it quick," she said before she kissed me. "I wanna go home."

"Yes, ma'am," I smiled reassuringly before I turned to face my enemy. "So you're some dark god who has been loosed on the world, because of me, and now it's up to me to sort you out. That's fine. Let's get this over with."

"You sound really sure of yourself for a guy who didn't realize gods, dark or otherwise, existed until a few moments ago," my doppelganger stated as he sat upon his throne, the only thing left of his castle, once more. "How do you intend to *sort* me, Saul?"

"Like this, Luas," I replied, giving my dark mirror reflection a name suitable for him before raising a hand and throwing him from his throne and onto the dusty ground.

He looked shocked when he finally scrambled back to his feet. I might have been able to affect his castle and other structures he had created, but he didn't realize my powers had grown to the point where I could do things to him directly. I was kind of surprised too at this point, but I didn't let it show on my face. I just kept pushing him and pushing him and pushing him with my abilities until he started to get as angry as I had been. Once he had enough, he pushed back.

"Enough!" he shouted, waving his arm wildly and creating a burst of energy that pushed me back a few feet as well as kicked up a great deal of dust. "I will not be treated this way by some...mortal bag of flesh! I kept you alive out of curiosity, but your usefulness has reached its end."

That's when Luas lifted his left arm high into the air and created a purple spear seemingly out of nothing. He was intent on ending me before I had a chance to end him. His dark eyes narrowed in furious determination before he hurled his spear at me, right at my chest! I threw both hands out in front of me, trying to use my powers to stop the projectile or destroy it, but I failed to do that. Perhaps it was too powerful or maybe it was too fast, but I could not stop the spear that he hurled at me. Ultimately, it was Lex who ended up doing that...by stepping in front of me and letting the spear puncture his heart.

"Lex!" I yelled out as he fell to his knees with the spear in his chest. "What are you...? Why...?"

I couldn't finish any of my sentences because I didn't know what to say or think in the moment. Fortunately, Lex was the one who was going to end up doing all the talking. He shushed me so he could tell me some things that I needed to know.

"It's okay, Saul," he said as I kneeled and tried to tend to his injury. "It's all right. I'm not important anymore. What good is a warden once all the prisoners have escaped?"

"I'm sorry, Lex," I apologized. "I should have listened to you."

"Yeah, you really should have," he laughed a little as a trickle of blood escaped from the corner of his mouth, "but by the same token, we never should have been locking up dark gods inside of mortals and making them suffer for the good of all humanity. You can win this though, Saul. You are stronger than anyone I have ever known, and I have been around for a very long time."

"Who are you really?" I asked. "Honestly. Tell me the truth."

"Well, if you are Pandora's Box and your anxieties represent all the evils of the world, then that makes me..."

"Hope," I answered quickly, remembering all the mythology that I had been drawn to as a child.

"Yeah, but I'm starting to think it was stupid to put trust in creatures like me," he said as the light in his eyes began to dim. "I think instead of humans having faith in their gods, the gods should have had faith in you all along. You're humanity's hope now, Saul. Now go do what you must."

And just like that, he passed away while I held him in my arms. A few moments after he died, his body turned to dust and drifted off on the wind. I looked up at Luas after Lex died and saw that the dark god had a demented smirk on his face. He looked like he was happy over Lex's death and that just made me even angrier. I was way beyond wanting to wipe that smug look off his face; I wanted to wipe his face right off his body.

"I've had just about enough of you, Luas," I commented, my voice resembling a growl. "This has all gone on way too long. Let's finish this… for good."

"I couldn't agree more," he shrugged. "But I would be a real selfish prick if I kept you all to myself. We all want a piece of you."

Before I could ask what he meant, the ground began to tremble beneath my feet. Lita ran to my side while Robinson just stood there laughing hysterically. She had obviously lost her mind; there was no reason to have brought her along on this expedition at all. All it was going to do was get her killed in the long run. Lita held onto me as things started to rise out of the dirt. It didn't take long for me to realize what Luas had done. Every single nightmarish creature that had been ravaging the planet rose from the earth as I stood there.

"Shit," I grumbled as my fear began to overpower my anger. "This isn't good."

I felt my heart beating so fast and so hard, I thought it would rip right through my ribcage. If there was anything I knew, it was that my powers didn't work as well when I was afraid. They had their most significant boost when I was angry. I looked over at Reynolds, lying motionless several yards away, and it made me angry again. I thought I could perhaps use that.

"You don't need to be angry."

I heard the voice and thought it was inside my head at first. I recognized it immediately, the little boy in the library. The one who gave me the book that started unlocking my abilities. The guardian of my happy place. Well, the happy place in my mind…not the happy place I manifested in the real world. I thought he was in my head telling me that I didn't need to be angry…until he appeared before me.

"Who is that now?" Luas demanded when he saw the little boy appear. "How many of you am I going to have to kill before this is over?"

"You think that you need to be angry to use your abilities, but you don't," the little boy told me. "You are in complete control. You just need to believe you are."

"Is this you?" Lita asked, kneeling in front of the boy so that they would be closer to eye-level to one another. "Oh my god, it is you. You look adorable. You look...free."

"That's me, free of my anxiety," I stated. "He taught me about my powers."

"Then he probably knows what he's talking about," she said. "You should listen to him."

As I was considering what she said, Luas's creatures finished emerging from the ground and they were closing in on us. It was now or never, but I still couldn't push aside my fear, even now when it was going to be the death of me. And then it became easy.

"Kill the woman and the child first," Luas commanded. "I want to see him cry before I kill him."

That did it. That was all I needed to hear in that moment. Luas may have had control over these monsters, but I lived with them every single day of my entire life. I knew these monsters and I knew how to deal with them better than anyone else alive. It was time for me to show him, to show *everyone*, that I was not weak or a coward just because I suffered from anxiety.

The first things to approach me were about a dozen Possu. They were obviously looking to attach themselves to me like they had before. I raised a hand right as they were about to lunge at me and reduced them to nothing but a crimson mist full of fur and teeth. The second wave of attack took the form of werewolves and rats. I got fancy with this wave, belching up fire and burning them to ash. While I dispensed with Luas's forces, I made sure to keep an eye on him to see his reactions. He tried to remain stoic, but I could see him growing more and more upset with each lieutenant that I destroyed. And I destroyed these creatures as violently as possible because I needed him to understand that he was outmatched.

My doppelganger wasn't holding back though. He bombarded me with several overlapping waves of grotesque creatures. There were werewolves, bugs, rats, demons, giants, psychics, sharks that somehow existed outside of the ocean, zombies. They just kept coming. They were never going to stop because the plan was to drown me in my nightmares until I could no longer fight back. He wasn't going to get what he wanted. As I looked out over a sea of monsters, I knew precisely what I needed to do.

I shot a smile over at Luas, sitting on his throne and growing more furious, right before the ground started to quake. His fury quickly changed to concern because this time he was not responsible for the earth moving. It was all me. After a few moments, the kaiju penis erupted from the ground and towered over us all.

"It's time to come home, big guy!" I yelled out to the appendage and it obeyed my command.

Luas sat on his throne, gob-smacked, as the kaiju penis attached itself to my crotch. I ordered it to destroy everything in sight, all of the monsters standing between me and Luas. It roared (somehow) before it went about the task with brutal efficiency. It swept back and forth, up and down, crushing everything in my path. Every monster that I crushed got absorbed into the penis. Every single one disappeared, taken off the board in a way my doppelganger never saw coming. After his creatures were finally dispatched, my endowment shrank down and took refuge in my pants where it belonged.

"That...was the most disgusting thing I have ever seen," Luas yelled out across the battlefield. "I can't believe you did all that in front of the kid, Copeland."

"It's okay," Lita whispered into my ear. "I covered his eyes for all of it."

"It's your turn now," I called out. "Your monsters are gone and it's just you and me now. Don't drag this out."

"They're not gone," he smirked as he started to walk towards me, ever so slowly. "You absorbed them with that giant schlong. And since you made it apart of you, that means that all those creatures are entering you again, to be locked up all snug in your brain. You're a prison once more. Congratulations. But you've forgotten a few things."

"What's that?" I asked.

As he walked towards me, I started to feel really strange. I had felt so powerful before when I was thrashing those nightmare creatures, but as he walked towards me, I felt weak. I could feel the hairs on the back of my neck standing up and something inside of me kept telling me to run as far away as I could. Why was I feeling this way? Why was I so afraid?

"First off, absorbing all those creatures and locking them up again means that you're about to be a sniveling coward all over again," he laughed as he got closer and closer. "And we both know you weren't any use to anyone when you were in that state. And the other thing you've forgotten is that I'm the worst of the lot, and you barely stood a chance when you were fully powered. Now, you're just going to be the first corpse I step over when I ascend to rule this world."

I tried to push him back with my abilities and they didn't work on him. It barely ruffled his hair. His smile grew wider and wider as he got closer to me. Lita and the child got behind me as this devil continued his agonizingly slow walk to us. His approach meant doom. It meant death. We all knew that. I tried using my powers again and again, but they seemed to get weaker and weaker with each use. Before long, Luas and I were standing face-to-face and he was doing everything in his power to intimidate me; it wasn't that difficult because I was starting to feel like my old self, the way I was before I took that pill prescribed by Dr. Robinson.

"I still want to see you cry," he said. "How about it? Ready to watch the woman of your dreams die? Or should I kill the kid first? After all, why should you keep your innocence when no one else gets to?"

"Don't touch them, Luas," I said, mustering all my strength to keep my voice from shaking.

"Call me God," he said.

"Please," I said as I tried to kill my pride enough to call him a deity.

"Too late," he said.

He snapped his fingers and then I heard two loud cracks followed by two thumps. My blood turned to ice in my veins because I knew instinctively what had just happened. I took a few moments before I turned around and confirmed that Lita and the boy's necks had been broken and they were now lying on the ground dead.

"No, no, no," I cried, getting on my knees and pulling Lita into my arms. "What did you do?!?"

"And there's the waterworks I was looking for," he laughed. "Finally. You thought you were some big hero, but you're nothing but a loser. You couldn't even keep the person you cared most for alive in all this. I want you to ruminate on that for a while, sink as far into despair as possible. And then, only when you are at your lowest, will I crack your head open like an egg and let all the monsters out again."

It was over. Evil had won. I lost everything. Trevor, Roxanne, Lex, my inner child. Even Lita. Everyone was dead and gone, killed by the evil I failed to keep control of. They were all destroyed by a monster who wore my face and spoke with my voice. All I could think of, while Luas continued to laugh, was lying down with Lita and dying right next to her. I would have given anything to hear her voice one more time.

"This isn't the end."

I perked up when I heard that, thinking that she had come back to me somehow. But upon opening my eyes, I still saw her lifeless face in front of me. I looked up to see who had been speaking and saw Dr. Robinson standing over us.

"What do you want?" I asked.

"I'm your therapist, Mr. Copeland, and I think I owe you a session," she said in an uncharacteristically warm way.

"Oh, this is rich," Luas laughed. "The only ally you have left is the bitch who tried to kill you…multiple times. I cannot wait to hear what she has to say to you after all this. Come on, Robinson. Tell us what modern psychology has to offer to a man who has not only lost everything but is also responsible for ending all life as he knows it."

"This all had to happen, Mr. Copeland, because you still think strength is something that comes from outside," she stated. "It isn't. Never was. It's not about your powers or some happy place. It's not about the power of friendship, love of a good woman, or amazing sex. They're your demons, you've been fighting them your whole life, and you can stop them. Even the asshole who has been peacocking this whole time as though he isn't afraid of you."

"Why the hell would I be afraid of him?" Luas asked haughtily.

"You've been chipping away at him his entire life with literally every fear imaginable, every single day, and he has managed to keep you at bay," she replied. "Why the hell *wouldn't* you be afraid of him?"

I had every reason to not trust Robinson, but she was making a lot of sense. I gingerly laid Lita down on the ground next to my inner child and then I got to my feet. I turned to face Luas and he recoiled in fear. I don't know what he saw on my face that day (he was the only one with eyes at the time), but I could tell that it truly scared him. I took a deep breath, took Robinson's words to heart, and then I did what I had to do. I did what I was always going to have to do: save myself.

"One last time," I said. "Winner takes all."

"I should have killed you a long time ago," he said.

He raised his arm and created another spear, just like the one he used to kill Lex, and then he hurled it at Robinson. Clearly, he was upset about what she had shared with me. She didn't even flinch when it hurtled towards her, and I don't think it had to do with her blindness. I think it was because she knew there was no further need to fear Luas. And you know what, I wasn't afraid of him either.

"Not gonna happen," I said raising a hand and stopping the spear in mid-air. "This is all over."

With a simple nod of my head, the spear returned to its owner: right through his right thigh. He screamed out in pain before he dropped to his knees. Isn't that the way with bullies? They can dish it out, but they definitely can't take it. Well, he was going to take it today. I walked towards my doppelganger while he desperately tried to throw more spears at me, but none of them were able to connect because I stopped them all in the air and sent them all right back at him. By the time I reached Luas, he was practically pinned to the ground by his own weapons.

"So this is how self-proclaimed dark gods die, huh?" I asked as he struggled against the spears piercing his body. "Crying, bleeding, bested by a human.?"

"You've bested no one," he growled angrily. "You're nothing."

"You can't break me down anymore," I shook my head. "You've lost your hold over me. Your power is gone."

He tried to hurl more insults, but I was done with it. Before he could say another word, I grabbed his head and ripped it from his body. That's when the headache started. I dropped to my knees as I felt a pain so sharp and devastating that I wanted to die.

"What's happening to me?" I cried out.

"You won," said Robinson, walking up behind me and placing her hand gently on my shoulder. "You didn't think victory would come without pain, did you?"

I honestly did. The pain grew worse and worse until I heard a terrible sound, the sound of flesh ripping and shredding. I didn't know what it was until I saw Luas's remains float into the air, hover over me, and then start to lower itself. I discovered that the top of my had had split open, so I could reabsorb the dark god as well. It took all of five minutes, but it was so painful that it felt like five lifetimes. And then it was all over. It was just me and Dr. Robinson...and the corpses of allies, friends, and lovers.

"You just saved the world, Mr. Copeland," she said. "How does it feel?"

"Hollow," I answered honestly. "I beat them all and yet the people I care about most are no longer here."

"Victory can feel hollow sometimes, like it was all for nothing, but it doesn't have to be," she said. "Your mind was able to shape this world in truly horrific fashion. What makes you think you don't have the power to put everything back the way you found it?"

"I'm not a god, Dr. Robinson," I said.

"You're better than a god," she said. "You're the man who bested a god. Why don't you see what else you can do? Start small and take it from there."

She had been right about my having the strength to beat Luas, so maybe she was right about this too. I took a deep breath and then placed the tip of my right index finger on her forehead. In a flash, her eyes returned!

"Good to see you again, Mr. Copeland," she smiled ecstatically. "What else can you do?"

I brought back Lita next, not sure how much longer these powers were going to last. She was alive and we were both thrilled, hugging each other so tight that it hurt. She still had the silver hair though; I couldn't change that for some reason. I told her everything that happened after she had died, especially about how helpful Robinson had been. I don't know if that was enough for her to trust her, but it was a start; she didn't immediately start throttling the woman when she saw her, so baby steps.

In short order, I resurrected Roxanne, Lex, and my inner child. I soon came to realize my powers didn't need to be tactile; I didn't have to physically touch everyone to bring them back. I then let my powers spread out across the globe and resurrected everyone who died due to my demons running amok. They were all brought back safe and sound in their homes. I assured Reynolds she would be able to see Grimes again soon enough, but I still had some more work to do. It took a fair bit of concentration, but after bringing back all the people, I had to repair the planet itself. Once I put back everything, even the smallest blade of grass, I smiled and then fell asleep.

EPILOGUE

When I woke up, the world was back to normal. No more demons or super-intelligent rats or other monsters running rampant through the streets. Most people had been allowed to forget what happened, back to their workaday lives as though our entire world hadn't been plunged into a never-ending nightmare.

But I remembered everything. I remembered everything and so did Lita. We moved in together shortly after the world was repaired. We tried to go back to our old jobs, but that life seemed a little too small for us after everything that had happened. If I'm being completely honest, I think she couldn't stop seeing our coworkers with the bug heads. Luckily Major Stone and Special Agent Grimes remembered everything we had done for the planet and made sure to keep us on the payroll. I once asked if anyone cared about us getting paid when we were no longer working for the government and Stone admitted that most of Capitol Hill was getting paid for nothing, so why shouldn't we?

Detective Reynolds remembered our adventures together too, but she left the NYPD shortly thereafter to join the FBI right along with her beau, Grimes. He convinced her that she could do much more on a larger scale and she finally agreed with him on something. They all continued to check in on us from time to time. I wanted to believe it was because they loved our company, but some small part of me knew that they were looking for signs that this madness might start all over again.

It won't. I continued to see Dr. Robinson in weekly sessions, but I felt like I had a handle on everything better than ever before. Lita asked me, almost constantly, why I would choose Robinson as my therapist after everything she had done. Sure, she helped me save the world in the end, but she had been my enemy just as much as my ally on that quest. For one, Robinson remembered everything and therefore I didn't have to hold back in my conversations with her, but secondly, she needed me to stay well just as much as anyone. Our sessions never got too intense though. There's something about facing down your literal demons to reveal that you can handle anything thrown your way without much help. There was only one thing that worried me after everything we went through together.

Luas revealed that I was just a prison, a pandora box, where dark gods and other wicked things were imprisoned. He mentioned that other mortals had been prisons too. A long line of them before I was ever born. Now that I beat my doppelganger and saved the world, were they still up there in my head or had there been a prisoner transfer to someone else's mind? Was there someone else out there struggling with anxiety, doing their best to hold on, trying their best not to unleash their nightmares on an unsuspecting populace?

Perhaps, this was now someone else's plight. Maybe every single person with crippling anxiety is holding back a veritable damn of evil, saving us all from the things that keep them up at night. If so, I hoped that they find the strength to keep fighting, to keep that evil at bay. One day at a time. I hoped that they find their people and realize their strength and that they can see themselves for the powerful, unstoppable heroes that they truly are. I hold onto that hope for each and every one of them.

So now, with the sizeable paycheck I get from the federal government, I have returned to school to try to get my own degree in Psychology. I decided that I wanted to help other people just like me. When I am not taking classes or loving on Lita, my silver-haired goddess, I also run little therapy groups where people with anxiety get to see and talk and work on their issues. I share what I've been through (not the demons running wild bit) and hope that it helps as many people as possible. The therapy group is growing and that's good. But sometimes I wonder, just for a moment, if anyone in my sessions might be a pandora box as well.

The End

Made in the USA
Middletown, DE
13 October 2024

62022755R00172